PRAISE FOR
LINDA O. JOHNSTON'S
TIME-TRAVEL ROMANCE!

A GLIMPSE OF FOREVER

"A fast-paced blending of the Western and Time-travel romance genres! With more novels like this one, the O in Linda O. Johnston will stand for OUTSTANDING!"

—*Affaire de Coeur*

"A poignant and warm-hearted tale . . . very pleasurable reading."

—*Romantic Times*

"An impressive, steamy, romantic adventure!"

—*Rendezvous*

POINT IN TIME

"Action-packed [and] emotionally gripping!"

—*Romantic Times*

"I'm putting Linda O. Johnston on my list of 'you've got to read' authors!"

—*Rendezvous*

A HERO'S KISS

She wasn't sure if he had urged her onto her feet with his touch, or whether she had simply stood of her own volition, but suddenly she was facing him.

In his arms. His strong, heroic arms were tightly around her, and she felt right at home. She rested her cheek on his chest, feeling the coarseness of the hand-knit material of his shirt against her skin.

But not for long. His fingers lifted her chin.

She stood on tiptoe, for that was the only way she could reach him. But he bent down to her, too. He touched her lips with his—very, very gently.

His mouth was warmer than the fire, and it stoked some long-banked conflagration deep within her. When he began to pull away, she reached up and held his head down to her.

She ran her fingers through the silky inferno of his bright red hair. Her eyes were closed, the better to concentrate on her all-consuming sense of touch. She felt his hands at her back, kneading her skin—her skin! His hands were beneath her shirt, and the sensation of his flesh on hers made her even more crazy.

"Jack O'Dair," she whispered against his lips.

Other *Love Spell* books by Linda O. Johnston:
STRANGER ON THE MOUNTAIN
A GLIMPSE OF FOREVER
THE GLASS SLIPPER
POINT IN TIME

THE BALLAD OF JACK O'DAIR

LINDA O. JOHNSTON

LOVE SPELL BOOKS NEW YORK CITY

A LOVE SPELL BOOK®

October 2000

Published by

Dorchester Publishing Co., Inc.
276 Fifth Avenue
New York, NY 10001

ISBN 0-505-52404-X

The name "Love Spell" and its logo are trademarks of Dorchester Publishing Co., Inc.

Printed in the United States of America.

THE BALLAD OF JACK O'DAIR

Prologue

She had come at last! He had been waiting nearly all his very long life for her, for this day.

And now, there were matters that only he could set into motion.

He would need to be cautious. A lot depended on him, and how he dealt with her.

He had planned his approach forever.

He had followed Jessie Jerome's career over the last seven years, her mother's for much longer than that. He understood from news stories just how much of a mess Jessie's childhood had been. How hard-won her burgeoning career.

He knew from her publicity photographs exactly what she looked like. And now, at long last, Jessie Jerome had burst through the door of the Skagway South Saloon, her guitar case in her hand.

Her brown, wavy hair had been tossed by the Alaskan summer breeze outside. Her eyes searched the saloon.

She was looking for him.

He turned back to the bunch of local guys with whom he'd been sharing cold beers and tall tales. It wouldn't do to make it too easy for her.

He knew her public personality. But for now he could only guess at her private one.

He wasn't surprised, though, when she stopped a waitress, then approached his crowded table. His buddies stopped talking, and why not? She was a looker, and there was something about her that got a man's blood pumping fast. Even his, as old as he was.

Though he wasn't interested in Jessie that way. Oh, no.

He had other business with her.

She cleared her throat. When she spoke, her voice was a husky, provocative song.

"Excuse me," she said. He looked up slowly. Those flashing eyes, shining like the bluest skies Skagway ever saw, were trained right smack on him. "Are you by any chance Lizard Songthroat?"

Very slowly, very deliberately, he smiled.

Chapter One

This *had* to be the end of her quest, Jessie Jerome thought, standing uneasily among the Skagway South Saloon's surprisingly thick crowd of afternoon customers. She clenched her fist tighter around the handle of her guitar case.

The thin, bearded old man who was probably her quarry appeared as old as the glaciers, with a Santa Claus twinkle in his eyes as he assessed her with his gaze just as much as she studied him. Why was he smiling that way?

Jessie resisted the urge to glance down at herself. She figured her casual blue jeans and matching denim jacket fit the ambiance of this place just fine. She knew her waves of dark hair were unruly; they always escaped from the clip that held them off her face.

"Are you Lizard Songthroat?" she asked again, more forcefully this time. The least he could do was to answer her.

The man sat in a circle of straight-backed chairs filled with hefty men in T-shirts. Large mugs nearly empty of beer were in the hands of several of them. They'd been a rowdy group, catcalling and roaring with laughter when she had first noticed them.

Now, they all watched her. Quietly.

"Who wants to know?" the old man asked. His voice was pleasant enough, with a laugh in it that matched his smile. How old was he? Ninety? A hundred? Older?

"My name is Jessie Jerome," she replied. "I—"

"Yes, I'm Lizard Songthroat, Jessie Jerome." He spoke her name as though he had heard it before. And why not? They had something in common. He might actually be familiar with her work.

"I'm so glad I found you," she said impulsively, relaxing at last. "I've been looking for you for . . . well, years."

"And I've been looking for a woman like you all my life," slurred a voice in her ear. "You want a beer?"

Jessie glanced at the man seated on a chair at her other side. He was clearly inebriated, with his eyes half-closed, his head at a tilt and his hands clasped around a tall, nearly empty beer glass. She had dealt with plenty like him before, in other bars and saloons and clubs.

She glanced around in the duskiness of the Skagway South Saloon. It looked much as she figured it would have a hundred years ago, during the Klondike gold rush. The floor was wood. The walls were paneled. The huge bar that lined the far wall was an ornate, carved work of wooden art. A huge, traditional mirror with a gilt-colored frame rose above it. Maybe, since Skagway had been one of Alaska's primary gateways to the Yukon during the gold rush, it was real gold, though Jessie doubted it. The place smelled of spilled beer and the furniture polish that had probably been used over the past century to keep the ubiquitous woodwork gleaming.

This establishment was off the beaten path of tourists from the cruise ships that docked in the Taiya Inlet, but Skagway was small enough that the saloon still managed its share of afternoon customers.

And now, Jessie had to deal with one who'd obviously had too much to drink already. For now, she would humor him. She had long ago learned not to antagonize a potential fan.

"Thanks," she said with a pleasant smile. "I'd love a beer."

"Sure, baby," he said. It was all she could do not to grimace. He gestured toward a waitress whose lips were red and cheeks rouged beneath the plume in her upswept hair. Jessie figured the woman's red and black outfit was what dance hall girls must have worn in the days of the stampede to the Klondike that had been so vital to the history of this tiny town.

"Hey, Ed, it isn't enough just to order a beer," said Lizard. "Don't you know to give a lady a seat?"

That was as smooth as if Jessie had planned it herself. She smiled as Ed rose and found another chair— fortunately, at another table.

"Thanks," she said to the old man as she sat in the now-vacant chair at his side. She accepted the beer proffered by the waitress and took a long swig. It was cold and went down smoothly. She'd needed it, since her throat had gone dry.

She had found Lizard Songthroat. And he *had* to have the answers she sought. If so, she would go home a happy woman.

19

Up close, despite the saloon's dimness, she could see the grooves that fanned out from the old man's recessed brown eyes. They looked even more vigilant close up, and Jessie was glad for the place's dimness as his unblinking appraisal made her flush. He wasn't coming on to her, though she knew age was no deterrent to a man's lustful wishes. She felt confident his scrutiny was from an interest other than lechery.

She turned back to Lizard. "So tell me," he said, "why do you say you've been looking for me for years? You make it sound like a long time, but the years you've known are just a fraction of mine. How old are you—twenty-four?"

She smiled, not offended by the man's direct question. "Twenty-five. And it seems like I've been looking all my life for somebody who knows all the words to 'The Ballad of Jack O'Dair.' I've been told you're the one."

His sparse white brows raised into an amused arc. "What would a pretty young thing like you want with a song that has whiskers as long as mine?"

The white hair on top of his head was wispy, but his matching beard and mustache were full. His lips were pink and moist, and their edges had tipped up into a smile that revealed teeth too white and perfect to be his own.

Impulsively, Jessie grabbed his hands. They were cool and moist from his mug of beer, but she could also feel their leatheriness—reminiscent of the skin of his namesake. "Mr. Songthroat, like you, I'm a balladeer, a folk singer. My mother was Patsy Jerome—have you heard of her?"

"Who hasn't? She did great things in making people aware of folk songs. I liked that TV program she had for a while; never missed a show. But isn't she . . . ?"

"She died six years ago."

"I'd heard. I'm sorry." He looked genuinely sympathetic, and Jessie steeled herself against all the old, ambivalent memories that pressed against her soul.

"But not before she taught me her songs," she continued. "Though folk music isn't totally mainstream right now, I intend to help bring it back. I already sing at clubs in several major cities, telling stories and singing arrangements of the old standards that capture the attention of my generation, even teenagers. I know I have an uphill battle to fight, but I mean to go farther than my mother in popularizing folk songs." She leaned closer toward him. "Even before she died, I began hearing snatches of 'Jack O'Dair'—a verse here, another there. I know quite a few stanzas now, but they end in the avalanche, and I haven't been able to learn what happened after that." She had to find out. She simply had to, for that song, more than any other in her substantial repertory, had captured her imagination. Its melody ran through her head constantly, haunting her, intriguing her.

No, it was more than the song. It was the story. The man who was its subject . . .

Her voice more wistful than she had intended, she asked, "Can you help me, Mr. Songthroat?"

"Only if you call me Lizard." He grinned, then grew more somber. "The thing is, I can't sing you the whole thing."

"You don't know the ending?" Jessie felt as though he had drawn back his leathery fist and punched her. She hadn't anticipated this. She had felt so sure—

"Not exactly."

Jessie sighed. This was the answer she had gotten

21

before, from more singers and historians than she had cared to count. "But I'd heard . . . well, never mind. Maybe you know more of it than I do, Lizard, if you don't mind singing it for me."

"Nope, I don't mind. But though I'm still a born 'n bred showman, my old voice isn't what it used to be. You gotta help. And while we're at it, maybe we can entertain some of my friends here. I do that from time to time; the saloon's owner lets me have a beer in return, and everyone is happy."

Jessie forced a laugh. *She* wasn't happy. She had come a long way, possibly for a little, and probably for nothing. But she intended to make the best of the situation. "Sure," she agreed. "Let's do a show for the folks in the Skagway South Saloon." She extracted her fine, well-used guitar from its case on the floor beneath the table. She strummed a few chords, tilting her head over the instrument to tune out the conversation of the busy bar. She smiled. The guitar, as always, had a clear, true pitch. Then she nodded toward Lizard. "Go ahead."

He shook his head. "No, you start. But you've got to get everyone's attention first."

She nodded. She knew how to do this. She did it all the time.

Then why did she feel so nervous?

She was Jessie Jerome, she reminded herself. Entertainer extraordinaire. Folk singer fantastico!

But this was "Jack O'Dair". . . .

She stood beside Lizard's chair and began playing a rousing version of "Yankee Doodle" on the guitar. She nodded sharply on each beat, then stopped strumming to clap her hands until Lizard took up the rhythm as well. Soon others joined in the clapping until, finally, everyone in the saloon seemed to participate. Again she played "Yankee Doodle."

"Hi, everyone," she called out when she finished the song. She got a few tentative "hi's" in return, then hollered even louder, "Hi, everyone!" This time the response was more enthusiastic. "I'm Jessie Jerome, a folk singer from the lower forty-eight. I've just met my good friend Lizard Songthroat who's from these parts, and we're going to do a little show for you, if you'll let us."

As she had hoped, a few people began applauding. In a few moments, others joined in.

"Great!" She made sure her voice projected despite the lack of a microphone. "Now, I'm going to sing part of a song for you that comes from Dyea, a town that used to be near Skagway, or so I'm told. It's from the time of the Klondike gold rush, and it's about a genuine hero. It's called, 'The Ballad of Jack O'Dair.' "

She inhaled deeply, as she did every time she said the name of the song. Though she knew a lot of folk songs about a lot of outstanding heroes, none had captured her attention more than Jack O'Dair, who had reportedly done so much to help people at such a lawless time.

And none had left her feeling so frustrated, for she just *had* to learn the ending. Even if it wasn't here or now.

She played a few measures of introduction on the guitar, then began to sing to the haunting yet upbeat melody,

"He kept the peace without surcease,
Did mighty Jack O'Dair.
Through Dyea-town fights, and dread Klondike
    nights,
None other could compare."

She felt swept away by the tune, the words, the song—as she always did. But she was here with a purpose, and this time she had a collaborator as well. She turned to Lizard. "Next verse is yours," she said.

She wasn't certain whether the brittleness of Lizard's voice was a factor of age or of his style, but she enjoyed its melodious rasp nonetheless as he sang,

> "A brawny bear was Jack O'Dair,
> His voice deep, mellow brass,
> Bright red hair had Jack O'Dair
> And eyes green as Ireland grass."

Jessie loved the picture painted in her mind of this large Irishman. She was about to start on the next verse when Lizard touched her shoulder. "No," he said. "That didn't come out right. Let's start over."

"I thought it was fine," Jessie contradicted.

"Nope," he said stubbornly. "It has to be perfect."

She had to humor him; she had no choice. And so she started the first verse again.

Once more, Lizard picked up the second. This time, he even went on to the third:

> "Lawman Jack was bold in the Northland's cold.
> He struck the scoundrels down.
> With his wolf-dog Taku and his *ulu*, too,
> Jack tended Dyea-town."

But then, once more, he stopped. He shook his ancient head. "I just don't like it," he complained.

"Go on," cried someone in the crowd.

Jessie seconded it, but Lizard called plaintively, "It's just not good enough here. Maybe it's the acoustics. In the meantime, I need a potty break."

24

That was something Jessie couldn't argue with, no matter how exasperated she felt. The guy said he'd sung here before. What was wrong with the acoustics today?

"Okay," she said. "Take your break. I have a phone call to make anyway." She put down the guitar. The pay phone was in the same direction as the restrooms, so she followed the old man until he disappeared behind a door marked "Men."

She placed a call to her friend and back-up musician, Serena Sanchez. "How are things?" she asked, almost afraid to hear. She had left in a hurry after learning about Lizard Songthroat and how to find him, leaving instructions to cancel a couple of planned engagements.

"Oh, Jessie," Serena said. "I'm so glad you called. You've got to get back here. Your friend Curtis is doing his best to flush your career down the toilet."

"He isn't my friend," Jessie said coldly. "Curtis Fitzgerald is only my manager—my soon-to-be-ex-manager. And we talked about this; I expected he'd do something moronic to get revenge."

"It's more than moronic," Serena contradicted. "It's insidious. He went beyond canceling the couple of engagements you asked him to. He's calling all the clubs where he'd arranged bookings for the next six months and telling them you're canceling because you're in seclusion. He won't say why, but he doesn't deny questions about whether you're in a drug rehab program or hospitalized after a nervous breakdown. He mentions your mother. . . ."

Jessie hit the paneled wall with the flat of her hand, then tried to concentrate on the stinging feeling. "How could I ever have trusted such a snake?" Trusted him? Hell, she had come close to loving him.

25

She had made love with him. . . .

"I called him, Jess," Serena continued. "Told him I'd heard what he was doing. He pretended utter innocence but said if you're losing bookings, he's the man who can help save your career. He says he's the one who created it, after all."

Damn! She had been so careful in choosing Curtis Fitzgerald as her manager. She had seen what poor choices had done to her mother.

Darn it all, she had also known better than to let herself fall for her manager. She had seen that firsthand, too. Her mother had always fallen in love with whatever manager she'd had at the time.

Eventually, it had ruined her.

"Jessie?" Serena's voice blasted in her ear—just as Lizard erupted from the men's room door.

"I'll call you later," she told Serena.

"But your career. You'll have to do something right away, or—"

"I will. I promise." And she meant it. Her career meant everything to her. She was not about to let that slimeball Curtis ruin it just because she began suggesting the truth to his other clients, who were beginning to drop him now as if he had stolen from them.

Which, in a way, he had.

She would get out of Skagway and go home, find out what else Serena had learned. And then she would deal with her problems with Curtis—and her career.

But first, she was going to try to realize the goal she had had for so long. Or at least she would hear as much of "The Ballad of Jack O'Dair" as Lizard Songthroat knew.

After further reassurances to Serena, she hung up the phone and hurried into the bar, intent on getting Lizard to sing the rest that very night.

26

But the old man had become stubborn. Intractable. "Sorry," he told Jessie. "I just don't like the acoustics here."

"Can we go somewhere that you do like the acoustics?" She tried not to let her impatience show.

"Well . . . I don't know."

"There has to be somewhere, in the whole of Skagway, where you feel comfortable singing." Jessie hoped that she merely sounded coaxing and not insistent; she was certain that this odd old man wouldn't buckle under to demands.

Lizard Songthroat seemed to ponder it for a while. The wrinkles that turned his forehead into pleats grew deeper and multiplied. "I guess there is one place," he said slowly. "Though it's way out of town."

Uh-oh. Was this old man lecherous after all? "I don't—" Jessie began, but he interrupted her.

"You might really like to see it anyway," he said excitedly. "Especially if you're a fan of Jack O'Dair's."

"Why?" Jessie asked suspiciously.

"Because it's Jack's own cabin I'm talking about. It's the place where Jack O'Dair actually lived."

Chapter Two

Jessie stood on the sidewalk a few blocks from the Skagway South Saloon, her guitar case on the ground beside her. She scanned the narrow street, watching for Lizard Songthroat to drive by and pick her up.

All right. So she was intrigued. To the point of foolishness?

Maybe.

But she had come here to learn all she could about Jack O'Dair. She had found the one person in the entire world who seemed to know the most about him.

Who even knew where he'd lived.

Should she go with the old man, alone to an isolated cabin located heaven knew where? Probably not. But she had addressed her concerns outright—in front of everyone in the saloon.

"Not that I'm a prude," she'd said, "but I am prudent. Are you sure you know where Jack O'Dair's cabin is? And why should I believe myself safe going with you? Why don't you just tell me how to find it?"

It wasn't easy for a stranger to the area to find, Lizard had explained. And Ed and the others had laughed at the notion that old Lizard might be a hazard to a young lady's safety, let alone her virtue.

Should she have believed them? Maybe not. But if something happened to her, everyone at the saloon would know where she'd gone, and with whom. Lizard knew it, too.

Surely, he wouldn't be so foolish as to do something nasty.

He'd seemed so eager, though, for her to go with him. He'd tried to hide it, but his nonchalance when she wavered hadn't rung true.

It had made her a little uneasy, sure—but not uncomfortable enough to give up the opportunity.

Jack O'Dair's cabin!

And so, there she stood, waiting for Lizard, on the sidewalk of Skagway's main street, Broadway. The air was cool, and she inhaled deeply, exulting in the fresh crispness entering her lungs.

It was evening, but the gift shops lining the narrow road were still open, inviting tourists from visiting cruise ships to venture inside and shop. She heard a tune from a player piano in a bar across the street. She smiled wryly at the tinny sound.

Except for the cars on the street, and the stores selling souvenirs instead of mining supplies, Skagway appeared much the way it must have during the gold rush. During the days Jack O'Dair had walked here, for surely he had visited Skagway, even though he was neighboring Dyea's lawman.

An aged military Jeep pulled up, its canvas cover

closed. Lizard leaned from the driver's seat and shoved open the passenger door.

Jessie had been a little surprised to learn that someone who appeared as old as Lizard still drove. But he'd done nothing to indicate that any of his faculties were any less sharp than a well-honed *ulu*—the rounded knife used by Alaskan natives.

"Put your guitar in back and get in," Lizard said.

She complied, and he drove off—rather quickly, Jessie thought, for such a crowded street. He had donned a plaid flannel shirt buttoned at the sleeves and neck. Its shades of gray went well with his white beard. The car smelled vaguely of old fish.

"So where is it?" she asked.

"You'll see."

It wasn't the first time she had queried Lizard about the cabin's location. He'd been secretive. And he hadn't even promised to sing the rest of the ballad to her.

She would simply have to wait and see where they went. And to be persuasive once they got there. In the meantime, she tried to keep track of all the twists and turns, so she could find the cabin again herself.

Lizard drove through Skagway and beyond the town, along the foot of the mountains. "Dyea's over there," he said, pointing toward the distance. "Or what's left of it. It was as much of a town as Skagway once, but Skagway survived and it didn't."

He pulled the Jeep onto a gravel road that seemed little-used. Some time later, he parked the Jeep in front of a weathered wooden cabin with a dilapidated front porch.

"This is it?"

He nodded. "Get your guitar. We'll go inside."

The place was better maintained inside than out,

though not by much. Its walls were wood, and the whitewash had all but flaked off. A cast-iron stove with a vent through the wall sat at one end of the single room. The cabin was furnished with several wooden chairs, a lumpy-looking cot in the corner over which a fraying quilt had been arranged, and a small writing desk along the near wall. It wasn't the most luxurious of accommodations, especially for a hero. But Jack had lived there long ago.

The cabin smelled dank, with a hint of the fragrance of burned logs. The floor was a series of nailed planks with dirty braided rugs thrown here and there.

Lizard demonstrated how to light the kerosene lamps that were all around, even explained how to make a fire in the stove. Then he placed two straight-back chairs side by side near the iron stove. "Okay, Ms. Jessie Jerome, this is it—Jack O'Dair's place!" Lizard cackled gleefully. "Where else should we sing his ballad?"

"Where else, indeed?" A sense of jubilance and anticipation filled Jessie. Here she was, in the very place that Jack O'Dair had actually walked and slept and eaten.

He had fed his wolf-dog Taku here. Had he brought women here? His prowess with the dance hall ladies in town may have been legendary, but was there anyone he would have wanted to bring to his own home?

Why did the idea suddenly deflate Jessie?

She shucked off her momentary depression. This ugly, weather-beaten cabin exuded character because its former owner had. Jessie was thrilled to be here.

Except for one little question. "Since the place is in relatively good condition," she said, "who owns it?"

"I do."

31

Why wasn't she surprised?

"Let's get to it, Lizard Songthroat, shall we?" She pulled her guitar from its case. Her host grinned at her with those too-perfect teeth, and she laughed aloud.

Once more they took turns singing verses, while Jessie strummed chords on her guitar. The sounds reverberated through the tiny cabin so that it nearly seemed to hum in return.

They sang the first three stanzas again as they had at the saloon. "You do the next two," she told Lizard.

Lizard's melodic, raspy voice followed, his tone arch as he celebrated Jack's legendary prowess in matters of heart and hand:

"Jack bested the length of ten men's strength
Said the ladies in Sweet Helen's nest,
In noble fist fights, and through hard-drinking
    nights,
And Jack's kisses were clearly the best.
"What's more, it was said, that in ladies' beds
Jack O'Dair had no equal, 'twas true.
In card games most fair always played Jack
    O'Dair
And he won nearly all of them, too."

Lizard wiggled his thin eyebrows, and Jessie laughed. Together, they continued through the song, which described feats of heroism and Jack's attempts to assist the stampeders to the gold rush. And then they reached the last verse that Jessie knew: at the avalanche in Chilkoot Pass.

She stopped and looked at Lizard. "That's all I know," she said huskily, praying there were a few more verses he could sing. Even one would make her trip worthwhile. . . .

"Sorry, Jessie," he said. "I can't sing you any more of the ballad."

Can't or won't, she wondered angrily. "You care about Jack O'Dair's legend enough to own and maintain his cabin, but you don't know the end of his ballad?"

Lizard shrugged his bony shoulders beneath his flannel shirt. "I simply believe in paying debts."

"What do you mean?" He didn't answer, and she realized with resignation that it didn't matter. She couldn't force Lizard to reveal anything he didn't want to. "Well, thanks for bringing me here," she said wearily.

"Delighted," he replied with a big, happy grin. A sense of unease coiled through her; he seemed to really mean it.

She looked around again. Too bad she didn't believe in the supernatural. If such things were real, maybe the ballad's end would come to her here, in a dream or a flash of psychic insight.

Yeah, right. Just like the ghost of Jack O'Dair would somehow materialize in the place he had lived and sing it to her. She snorted aloud.

"Something funny?" Lizard asked.

"Not really."

"Okay, then. I need another potty break. I'll be right back." He stood. When he stepped off a braided rug, his footsteps thunked against the wooden floor of the cabin. He paused by the front door. "Lean back and close your eyes for a moment, Jessie Jerome. This is a place of memories, and you think highly of its former owner. Maybe what you want will come to you." He disappeared outside.

What a strange comment. What a strange man! Jes-

Linda O. Johnston

sie wondered what he had meant. And where he was going. Was there an outhouse here? There was a door to an unknown room that Jessie had assumed was a bathroom, but she hadn't looked.

And then she heard a car engine. The Jeep!

She reached the cabin door just in time to see its taillights disappear down the gravel road.

"Lizard, you son of a—! Damn it all, come back here!" But of course he couldn't hear.

And, with a sinking feeling, Jessie realized he wasn't returning.

The only illumination came from the kerosene lamps inside the cabin. It was dark out; not even the moon lit the sky.

No one at the saloon had believed that Lizard would hurt her, but had they foreseen that he would abandon her?

She would have to spend the night and try to find her way back to town tomorrow.

Unless . . . was this just a practical joke? Would Lizard return soon to pick her up?

Somehow, she didn't think so.

She turned back toward the worn wood of the cabin door. She would simply have to make the best of it.

Fortunately, there was no indication there'd be any rain that night. It rained here a lot in summer, and the roof undoubtedly leaked. Even with Lizard gone, Jessie doubted she would be completely alone, though her companions would likely be of the rodent or reptile persuasion. She shuddered. At least she'd seen no obvious mouse or snake holes in the walls.

Slowly, she sank down on the side of the cot. She recalled what Lizard had said: "This is a place of memories, and you think highly of its former owner. Maybe what you want will come to you."

34

Even if she didn't believe it, had he actually left her here thinking that the end of the ballad would suddenly and miraculously come to her in a dream?

And maybe Lizard also believed in ghosts, fairies, leprechauns and Santa Claus. After all, he did at least resemble the latter.

Well, even if the answer wouldn't come to Jessie here, she had no choice. She would remain for this one night that she would always remember. There would be time enough tomorrow to mourn the fact that her quest here had come to a dead end.

And to make sure she didn't have to mourn her career, too.

The cabin seemed larger when she was alone. She surveyed the place, wondering how it had looked when Jack lived there. The whitewash on the walls had probably been fresh. Did he have rag rugs on the floor? Were his bedclothes arranged neatly? Was anything neat, or had he lived in disorganized solitude, all of his belongings in disarray? Surely a man as heroic as he hadn't had time to keep things spotless.

Or was his heroism a myth?

Had he even really existed?

Jessie believed he had, for her research had yielded legend beyond the ballad: mentions in memoirs and books. No pictures, though, unfortunately. Plenty of photographs existed from the Klondike gold rush, but if Jack had been captured in any of them, his identity had been lost through the years.

"A brawny bear was Jack O'Dair," she sang softly to the tune that played so often in her head. Then, skipping a line, "And bright red hair had Jack O'Dair. . . ."

Though the old photos had all been black-and-white, surely a man as distinctive-looking as he would have stood out from the rest.

She explored the cabin. Sure enough, when she opened the door along the far wall, it led to a small bathroom. It appeared primitive, but at least it had running water.

In the main cabin, Jessie walked to the large, black stove. The furnishings probably had been replaced over the years. The stove, though, was most likely original.

She touched its cold side. Had heat from a fire inside this metal box kept Jack O'Dair and Taku warm on frigid nights in the brutal Alaskan winter?

She stared at her hand. Jack O'Dair might have touched the same spot a century ago. She felt a sense of connection. . . .

That she immediately discarded. "You're a fool, Jessie Jerome," she said aloud. "You're half in love with a legend, and you, of all people, should know better."

Assuming Jack had existed, he had still been a man. His sexual exploits were as legendary as his heroism. He'd have been no better than the men Jessie's mother had turned to for comfort and stability in an uncomfortable and unstable world.

He might have been no better than Curtis Fitzgerald, whose intentions with women involved love, all right—love of money. Love of his career.

But not, certainly, love of the women he seduced and sandbagged with his lies of being the perfect business manager.

Even Jessie, with all her wariness, had succumbed to the man's suave sophistication, his smooth seduction, his many, many lies.

She had learned she wasn't the only one.

And now that she was disclosing his treachery to the world, he intended to destroy her career.

"I'll be back in L.A. tomorrow evening, Curtis," she said angrily. "Then we'll see whose career is ruined. And unlike what you're trying to do to me, it'll be your own fault!"

She felt exhausted all of a sudden. It had been a long, ultimately disappointing day.

Here she was, stuck alone in a cabin in the middle of nowhere, thanks to that strange character Lizard Songthroat.

She still had not learned what had happened to Jack O'Dair after the last verse she knew. She had been singing parts of the ballad in her performances for some time, teasing her audience, tantalizing herself. But she had always been certain that some day she would discover the ending.

Now she realized she might never find out how the song ended. What had happened to Jack O'Dair after the avalanche struck?

Despite her frustration, her irritation with Lizard for leaving her here, she yawned. It felt way past bedtime. Her exhaustion did not stop her from feeling keyed up, though. With everything on her mind, she might not settle down to rest. She determined to sing herself to sleep.

Her mind played foolish games as she sat on the edge of the bed atop the ragged quilt, her guitar on her lap. She strummed a chord and sang aloud to the tune of the ballad, making up the words as she went along,

"It isn't fair, Jack O'Dair.
I've come so far and so long,
Only to learn, after twists and turns
That your fate is beyond my song."

37

She sighed and settled back, singing to herself "The Ballad of Jack O'Dair," starting with the very first verse. Before she had gotten far into it, she put down her guitar. She couldn't keep her eyes open. She let herself drop into a very . . . deep . . . sleep.

She didn't know how long she had slept when she awakened. She was shivering. The cabin had grown cold. *Extremely* cold.

And dark. She hadn't thought it got this dark even in the dead of night in Alaska at this time of year.

She heard a noise outside, like heavy footfalls on the rickety porch. A bark.

The door was suddenly flung open, and Jessie gasped.

"Who's there?" roared a deep voice. Jessie saw a huge dog bound into the room in the light of a lantern held in the hand of a man who filled the door frame.

If it wasn't just a reflection of the lantern's flame, the man had bright red hair.

Jessie clutched the quilt around her to protect her from the silvery, wolf-like dog beside the bed, snarling, teeth bared. She looked at the man who had invaded the cabin and gave her head an abrupt shake, trying desperately to clear it.

She was fully awake, wasn't she? If so—"Is this a joke?" she demanded. "Did Lizard Songthroat send you? You . . . you look just like Jack O'Dair!"

The man was silent, but only for a moment. His tone was darkly menacing when he finally responded, "I *am* Jack O'Dair, Miss. But who, exactly, are you?"

Chapter Three

"I'm Jessie Jerome," Jessie replied. "As if you didn't know. Now, call off . . . is this supposed to be Taku? You can tell Lizard he did a great job finding you both. But he didn't need to go to all that trouble for a joke. All I wanted was to learn the end of the ballad."

The dog's snarling and barking unnerved Jessie, so she remained where she was. But though the quilt was still tucked around her, she felt an icy wind blow in until the man playing Jack O'Dair had closed the door behind him.

Strange, that it should grow so cold so fast. But she'd never experienced an Alaskan summer before. Maybe the sudden temperature drop was normal. She shivered and drew the quilt more tightly around her, attempting to ignore the menacing dog. She had always gotten along fine with dogs before.

"Taku, rest," the man playing Jack finally said.

"Come." In moments, his dog sat at his side. Good thing an animal as ferocious as that was also obedient. "How was I supposed to know your name?" the man asked.

"You were hired to play a role," Jessie said, trying to keep the exasperation in her voice to a minimum. It quivered enough from the cold, and she made an effort to keep her teeth from chattering. "You're doing a fine job, too. But it's okay to break character and talk to me."

Jessie had to hand it to Lizard. He couldn't have chosen a more perfect actor for the role of Jack. He was dressed in a parka of thick, brown fur—it looked like a couple of seals had met their demise to keep him warm, darn him, though Jessie knew she shouldn't have expected otherwise in the rugged North. His pants appeared to be wool, and he wore heavy boots on his feet.

This "Jack O'Dair" was just as Jessie had pictured from the ballad: a grizzly bear of a man, tall and broad, with hair the brightest shade of copper. His brows were thick and stern, and beneath them shone the greenest eyes that Jessie had ever seen. There was something unnerving about his gaze on her. It appeared assessing, curious . . . Famished—and not for food.

Ignoring a hint of an answering hunger that tingled inside, she realized she had remained seated in bed and leapt up, still clutching the quilt. The dog darted forward at her abrupt movement.

"Taku!" the man warned. The dog immediately sat once more.

A thought niggled at the back of Jessie's mind. She had only met Lizard that day. How had he had time to set up this prank during the short time between when she left the saloon and when he picked her up on the corner? He must already have known about this actor who so resembled the description of Jack O'Dair. And then there was his dog. . . .

The man addressed Jessie. His wide jaw appeared as hard and flawless as if it had been chiseled by an artist from a block of ice—but it was shadowed by a hint of thick red beard. "If you were lost, miss, just admit it. I won't toss you out into the cold. I'm Jack O'Dair, the U.S. marshal in Dyea. I don't know why you claim I'm an actor, though I believe you might find actors among the stampeders. Some of the girls in Dyea and Skagway are entertainers, too. Tell me which town you want to go to, and I'll take you there in the morning. Meantime, I'll light a fire in the stove. You can put on my other jacket; it's hanging over there." He gestured with his large hand, covered in a worn leather glove, toward the wall at his side, where clothing hung along a series of pegs.

It wasn't just the cold that made Jessie keep shivering. The man sounded too sincere.

And there was more. Surely the wall to which he had just pointed had been as bare as the rest of the cabin when Jessie had lain down to sleep. There was a neat stack of wood beside the metal stove that she hadn't noticed before, either.

The bed looked much the same, but the small, rough-hewn table, with its single chair, was new. And hadn't there been a writing desk in the corner? A door, too, to the tiny bathroom—she didn't see one now.

She never slept that soundly; how could the place have been redecorated without her knowing it?

Something was wrong here.

Something was definitely wrong.

41

Her legs as limp as unstrung guitar strings, she sank back onto the bed.

Who the devil was this Jessie Jerome, Jack wondered. And why had she invaded his home?

Had someone in town put her up to it? His friends knew better. His enemies . . . oh, he had enemies, though few would admit to it, for he was the law. And they would surely have sent someone less skittish to make him lower his guard.

She claimed she thought he was an actor, only pretending to be Jack O'Dair. Why would he do that?

He had to ask in a way that would humor her, for her nerves already seemed jangled. Unless *she* was the actor. . . . Forcing himself to use a gentle tone, he questioned, "So, Miss Jerome, did you say you believe some lizard is playing a joke on you and that I'm part of it?"

"Not a lizard. A man *named* Lizard." He had noticed the smokiness of her voice before. Now it was even huskier. It suggested dark nights and slick bodies. . . .

The woman cleared her throat, wrapping his quilt around her once more. "Look, whoever you are. This is a great joke. Tell Lizard it worked fine, that I bit and thought you were real. But I don't want to wait until morning. Can't you drive me to town now? Skagway, of course, since Dyea—" She broke off.

"No," he replied, "It's not possible for me to drive you to town now, or even later." He didn't explain, but Dyea was not like San Francisco or Seattle, or even like a farm town in the United States far south of here.

And it was far, very far, from his home town of Atlanta.

He had no horse, and certainly no wagon. Not even a dog team and sled, though he borrowed one when he needed it. He could lend her snowshoes later, if necessary. He did not tell her that, though, for the woman named Jessie appeared even more upset.

"I don't believe for a moment that what I think may have happened actually happened," she said. "But if it did . . . look, whoever you are. Why don't you just admit this is a prank so we can both get on with our lives?" She rose and approached him, hands on her hips.

Taku stood once more and growled.

That didn't stop Jessie Jerome. "And call off your dog," she demanded, though she eyed Taku warily.

Jack considered allowing Taku to frighten this woman into fleeing the cabin. But she appeared more angry now than afraid despite Taku's wolf-savage snarl. Her words sounded crazy. Maybe she *was* crazy.

"Taku, rest," Jack finally said. "Come." In moments, his dog was once again sitting at his side, quivering as he watched the woman who did not belong here. If only this Jessie Jerome were as controllable as his canine companion.

But she was not, Jack felt certain. Not with the furious look in her flashing blue eyes. He shook his head as he stared at the strange-speaking woman whose hair was askew: lovely brown hair in wild waves from lying abed before he arrived. In *his* bed, where no woman had ever been invited; he spent nights in town when he felt the need.

His bed. He had wished no such violation of his privacy. He gave all that was required of him where he was needed and more, but his home was his own.

Still, if he were to permit any woman to invade his

43

home, he just might choose one as lovely as this one.

Annoyed at his own foolishness, he held himself tightly in check. Perhaps his uninvited guest, though clean-looking and with a face as fresh as the beckoning spring, was a madwoman. Not knowing if she was violent, he kept his voice calm. "This man named 'Lizard.' Why would he play a trick on you?"

"I don't know. But he must have." She took yet another step toward him, her small chin raised as though daring him to contradict her. She was a slender woman, clad much as some of the stampeders, in blue Levi's and a jacket of the same material. Why had she come here in such light clothing? She had not taken the heavier jacket he had offered, yet she still shivered.

And she remained staring at him as though enraged, expecting some reaction from him that he did not understand.

He might be unable to guess the reaction she wanted, but he could do something about her shaking. He approached the stove and placed wood into it from the neat pile he had left that morning. The woman was an intruder, but he would not want her to freeze to death here, in his cabin.

There were others in his past whose deaths had been his responsibility. . . .

He did not look at her as he said conversationally, "I have no idea, Miss Jerome, where you got the idea that I am for hire to play a joke, but since you seem so convinced of it—"

"Come off it!" She was on her feet now, stomping briskly toward him. "Of course it's a joke. It has to be, because if it's not . . ." Her voice trailed off, and then she whispered, "It isn't funny." Her blue eyes shone, as though they had filled with tears.

He stood abruptly from where he had knelt by the stove, then stared down at her. Her trousers were much tighter than those worn by any stampeder he had ever met. She was a little too thin, yet he nevertheless noticed how her pants embraced curves that were taut, yet all feminine.

She was not a large woman, and he took a step toward her. One step more, and they would be touching.

Touching. . . .

For an insane moment, he had an urge to sweep this Jessie Jerome—whoever she might be—into his arms. To wipe her eyes so that her unshed tears would never fall. To deposit her back into his bed, from where she had just come. To pull the jacket and Levi's and shirt from her slim body and find a much more pleasurable way than building a fire to heat his own chilled body—and hers.

He turned away so abruptly that Taku, sitting alertly at his feet, began once more to growl. Jack reached down and patted his dog's abundant fur. "Enough, Taku," he murmured.

The heat from the newly lit stove warmed the cabin, but it failed to lift the chill from Jessie's heart.

"Stay where you are," said the man who so resembled the description of Jack O'Dair that Jessie wanted to pinch him to see if he were real. "Morning won't arrive for a lot of hours yet. You sleep in the bed; I'll take the floor." Though his tone was friendly, there was an edge to his voice, as though he pretended a gallantry that he did not feel.

"Fine."

If he'd really been the heroic Jack O'Dair, he wouldn't have minded her taking his bed. But, then, if he had been Jack O'Dair, Jessie wouldn't have usurped his place; the bed, after all, would have been his.

This masquerader who refused to admit to the joke deserved all the discomfort he could get.

She hunkered back down beneath the quilt, watching him as he spread a large pelt from what looked like a moose onto the floor, then piled blankets on top of it. He had removed his fur jacket to reveal a suede shirt that, though loose-fitting, still managed to display his muscles as he spread and arranged the bedding.

Again, Jessie silently congratulated Lizard on finding an actor who looked the role so well. Bright red hair had this bear of a man who called himself Jack O'Dair. Of course, he could have dyed it.

But quickly enough for this prank? . . .

He settled down on the floor and pulled the blankets over him. His back was toward her. The dog who appeared to answer to the name Taku curled up beside his master.

"Good night, Jack O'Dair," Jessie called, unable to keep a hint of sarcasm from her voice.

"Good night, Miss Jerome," he replied, blowing out the candle. The only illumination in the room was a faint glow from the lit stove.

Jessie didn't sleep. She couldn't. Instead, she listened to the soft breathing of the man and dog.

If he truly were Jack O'Dair, he was a hero. Larger than life.

Sexy as hell.

And the man who shared the cabin with her certainly looked the part.

No wonder she couldn't sleep. Instead, she thought about what it would feel like to have him touch her. To fill the cabin with their cries of passion—

46

She put her hand to her mouth to keep from snorting aloud. That was what came of falling in love with a fictional character. She could dream all she wanted, fantasize about perfect, phenomenal love-making and never learn the difference.

Without making a sound, she mouthed some of the words from the ballad:

"What's more, it was said, that in ladies' beds
Jack O'Dair had no equal, 'twas true."

What about the man across the room? He was certainly good-looking—but he was an illusory Jack O'Dair. His sexuality was probably just as superficial. And no one real could be as dauntless as the hero of the ballad.

Goodnight, you fraud, her thoughts called to the man on the floor.

She would find out all about him in the morning.

The morning. She remembered that she had thought it didn't get so dark here at night in the summer. . . .

She would worry about that, too, when she awakened. Jessie closed her eyes.

A familiar discomfort awakened Jessie; she needed to use the bathroom. She blinked. Where was she . . . oh, yes. The supposed cabin of Jack O'Dair.

At least daylight had begun to break. A soft light washed through the cabin. The heavy breathing of the man on the floor indicated he was deeply asleep. Slowly, so as not to awaken him, she drew the quilt off and swung her legs toward the floor.

The room remained toasty warm. Was the fire in the stove still lit?

The dog curled up against the man lifted his head and stared at her with golden eyes. "Nice Taku," Jessie mouthed. "Stay."

Taku. The dog actually answered to that name. It couldn't really be . . . but around here, maybe everyone who had a dog resembling a wolf named it Taku. Her research into Jack O'Dair's ballad had taught Jessie a river in the Yukon was named Taku.

The wooden floor was cool beneath Jessie's feet. She padded softly toward the door to the bathroom—and stopped. She'd used the facilities last night, before this counterfeit Jack had appeared. When she'd awakened to find him here, she'd noticed the absence of the bathroom door.

Obscuring it must have been part of the joke. And yet . . . she let her hands range over what appeared to be a solid wall of mud-chinked logs that formed the inside of the cabin.

Icy slivers of fear scratched uncomfortably at her back. Had she been drugged, taken to another cabin? But how?

"What are you up to, Miss Jerome?" The deep voice, sexily shrouded in the huskiness of sleep, startled her. She turned to see him leaning on one elbow, staring at her.

"I . . . I just need to find the bathroom."

"Bath room?" He paused between the two words. "I usually bathe in the creek nearby when it's warm enough, but not till summer. This time of year, I bring water in, heat it and use it to clean up."

Jessie had a sudden image of this great, muscular bear of a man sponging himself clean in this very cabin. Undressed.

She cleared her throat. "You know very well what I'm asking for. I need to pee."

One thick, coppery brow lifted. "Well, Miss Jerome! Most women I know, even the roughest stampeders, are seldom so brazen in speech." His expression grew puzzled. "I know that the United States newspapers are full of stories about coming here to look for gold. You must have read that the amenities up here are limited."

"Come off it, will you?" Jessie's exasperation was too strong to hold back. "It's okay for you to break character, be yourself instead of Jack O'Dair. I won't let Lizard know. Just tell me where I can go."

"I've an outhouse out back," he replied. A wicked smile grew slowly on his face. "Or if it's too cold I use a bucket. I'll turn my back if you'd like."

"Darn you!" Jessie stamped her foot, but not too hard; her feet were bare, after all, and the wooden floor was hard. She glanced around the cabin, finding nothing helpful. In fact, there was only a single door. Canvas covered the windows.

"I'd suggest you put on some boots before you go outside. There's a pair near the door you can wear."

His boots. Without looking at him, she slid them on over her feet. They were huge, and she would have to be careful not to trip.

She pulled open the cabin's door . . . and froze. Almost literally. It was *cold* outside. Snow covered the ground. Ice hung from trees barren of leaves.

How could that be? When she had entered the cabin yesterday, it had been summer. Everything had been green.

She felt her breathing grow shallow, and a tiny moan escaped her throat. She'd had a fleeting thought, before falling asleep, that she had somehow slipped back into the time of the gold rush, but she'd shrugged it off. The joke was fine, but it was just that: a joke.

She had to keep believing that. Otherwise, she

would have to accept the utterly impossible alternative.

"Go on outside, Miss Jerome. Or come back in. Just shut the door so the cabin stays warm." The voice behind her was commanding—no hint of teasing now. It sounded the way she'd imagined the real Jack O'Dair's had . . . but he wasn't Jack O'Dair. He couldn't be.

She slipped back inside only long enough to grab from the peg on the wall the long jacket of reddish brown fur he'd pointed to last night and wrap it around herself. She didn't even want to consider that she was deriving her own comfort from the death of a real beast—let alone what species the poor creature had been.

She went outside, shutting the door behind her. She began to trudge slowly through snow up to her ankles.

Her shivering wasn't entirely from the cold wind that whistled about her.

She walked around the cabin. Hadn't it been bigger before? It would have been larger, had there been a bathroom attached.

Sure enough, there was an outhouse at the rear. A larger building, too, that resembled a shed. She hadn't gone behind the building the night before, so she couldn't be sure whether the other wooden structures had been there.

She went into the outhouse, appreciating even the meager shelter from the icy wind. She availed herself of the facility. At least it didn't smell as bad as most outhouses of her rare acquaintance, probably because it was so cold that everything odoriferous had frozen. Then, taking a deep breath, she plunged back outside.

When she had shut the door of the cabin firmly behind her again, Jack said, "I don't suppose you stopped in the shed to bring us anything for breakfast."

"Like what?" She whirled to face him, fear making her feel like lashing out. "Moose steaks? Rabbit? Sourdough bread? Isn't that what the stampeders ate?"

He stood near the stove, a small log in his hand. He had apparently been feeding more wood to the fire. His green eyes studied her, narrowed in apparent concern. "Miss Jerome, you seem very peevish. Is something the matter?"

"Yes!" she shouted. "Enough is enough. Really. Please, just stop the games and take me to town, will you? And when you see Lizard, you can tell him I don't think his joke was funny in the least."

To her chagrin, Jessie felt her eyes fill. She was deluding herself, she knew it. Maybe she was the subject of a trick gone crazy. Or maybe *she* had gone stark raving mad. But she was certain of only one thing: Something was astonishingly, terrifyingly wrong.

"I'll take you to Dyea," Jack said to Jessie as he shut the cabin door behind them. "It's the closest town— my town. It's where I'm marshal." He felt full after eating. He had fetched breakfast himself from the shed and cooked it over the fire: moose steak, just as she had suggested. She had hardly eaten a bite.

"Of course you are," mumbled the woman beside him. He looked down. Her pale blue eyes, the prettiest he had ever seen, appeared glazed as she surveyed the snow-covered scene.

Was she, in fact, mad? She seemed very frightened, but of what?

He had an urge to pull her into his arms, soothe

51

her, tell her all was well and would remain that way. But he had no inkling of the fears that tormented her. And he was the last person to soothe anybody.

Taku leapt off into the snow, chasing a white-pelted rabbit. He gave a sharp bark that sounded pleased to Jack; silver-colored Taku—part husky, part wolf—always appreciated a good hunt.

"It's a short walk to Dyea," he told Jessie. "If we do it briskly enough, we'll hardly feel the cold. While we go, you can tell me what's bothering you."

"You know what's bothering me," she said in a low voice that lacked conviction. She clutched a guitar case in one gloved hand. He took it from her to carry.

"Oh, yes. The mysterious joke. The man named Lizard. Why don't you tell me more about them?"

She glanced askance at him, as if to assess if he were merely humoring her . . . which he was. The jacket she wore was warm; it had once kept a grizzly comfortable in the Alaskan cold, before the bear had made the mistake of attacking Jack. Still, she shivered. He wanted to warm her . . . to take care of her, he corrected. He couldn't stand to see another human being in·pain, in peril. That was why he had made his way here, to this God-forsaken, frozen land. Why he stayed.

"I can't tell you more about Lizard than you already know," Jessie Jerome retorted. She kept up despite the brisk pace he set in the ankle-deep snow. He admired her pluckiness.

"Maybe," he said dubiously. "Is someone waiting for you in Dyea?" Perhaps she had come with her family, and they were now hunting their poor, slightly deranged daughter or sister or . . . wife. The latter idea made him stop for a moment.

She might belong to another man. Why did that

bother him? He had no interest in any woman, crazy or not.

Jessie's laugh sounded ironic to him. "No one's waiting for anyone in Dyea," she said.

Now, what was that supposed to mean?

They reached the outskirts of the town that, though growing rapidly as more and more stampeders arrived, still held more tents than wooden buildings.

Jessie's steps slowed. "Some ghost town this is," she whispered as they headed down the frozen center of the main street.

"There wasn't much here a few months ago," Jack said, "but it's hardly a ghost town."

They neared the teeming docks where hundreds of stampeders had just landed for their treks to the gold fields.

Jack scanned the crowd, assuring himself that all seemed calm. He allowed no one—no resident, no visitor to Dyea—to get unruly.

Anything might happen in nearby Skagway, where rowdies ran the town. But the Canadian Mounted Police, the U.S. Army—they were not needed here in Dyea. Not in *his* town.

"Oh, my," said Jessie, staring toward the busy dock. She nearly lost her balance, and Jack reached out to steady her. She grabbed his free arm and hung on. Her eyes were wide, her sweet lips parted as though she were terrified. He wanted to bend down to heat them with his own, to take away her fears . . . whatever they were.

But a kiss—that would be personal. That kind of aid he did not provide.

"It's really true, isn't it?" asked Jessie. "All of it. And that means . . . oh, my heavens!"

"What?" he demanded as she nearly crumpled to

the ground. He put her guitar case down in the snow and held her beneath her elbows.

"I . . . well . . ." She seemed to catch herself. She pulled away and stood straight, squaring her shoulders. "I never imagined . . . this can't be happening, but—" She stopped, then looked up at him with a lovely, unexpected smile. "I've always wanted to meet you. How do you do, Jack O'Dair?"

Chapter Four

Hills surrounding the inlet were covered with snow. In the midst of them, the tiny harbor of Dyea overflowed with stacks of supplies and hordes of people—mostly men dressed in the rugged garb of stampeders just like Jessie had seen in black-and-white photos of the gold rush. She could hardly believe her eyes.

No, she could hardly believe her *thoughts*. "You should have been called 'Wizard' instead of 'Lizard,' you old coot!" she muttered under her ice-cold breath. "How did you do this to me?"

"So, Miss Jessie Jerome, where would you like for me to take you?" She turned to face the huge man she now assumed actually was Jack O'Dair, who hadn't left her side. Of course he wouldn't. He was a gentleman, a hero, if the ballad were true. And his dog Taku hadn't left *his* side.

"I . . . I'm not sure where to go," she replied.

They stood on a makeshift walkway of long

wooden planks from which some of the deep snow had been brushed. The wooden shacks that stood in an uneven line along the walk could hardly be called shops, yet that was what they apparently were. The docks, rife with shouts and calls from the throng of stampeders, were now behind them, and the ramshackle town of Dyea lay ahead.

What was Jessie going to do here? She knew why she had come, thanks to Lizard: to learn the end of the ballad. Meeting its subject . . . well, that was a bonus.

Was this man really the subject of the song?

And how was she to learn the ending?

Once she did, would she go home? She had to, and in a hurry, if she wanted a career to go home to. She wasn't sure how she would manage it without convincing Lizard Songthroat to fix it for her. But she'd figure something out. Soon. For now, though, she would take advantage, learn all she could about the songs of this time—including that one, special ballad—now that she was here.

Here. In the Klondike gold rush, in . . . when? Was it 1897? 1898? Jessie laughed aloud. This couldn't be happening, but what other explanation was there?

She looked up at Jack, who regarded her with a bemusement that nearly made her giggle. "Is something funny?" he asked.

"Not really." Jessie paused. "I don't suppose you know anything about local folk ballads, do you?" In particular, one about you, she wanted to say. But she didn't. She had a feeling he would deny it, even if he had heard such a thing.

After all, the Jack O'Dair of the ballad was heroic without wanting recognition for it. *This* Jack O'Dair— well, although he had been kind to a woman who'd shown up uninvited in his house, he had hardly acted heroic.

He was, however, every bit as handsome as the man described in the song. And she hadn't been with him in any situation in which heroism had been called for—yet.

She would need to keep a close eye on him.

Jack's strong, coppery brow furrowed in puzzlement at her question. "Can't say that I know anything about songs, but you can try asking some of the performers in the saloons." He cleared his throat, appearing uncomfortable. "Not that I think a lady like you ought to go into such a place."

Jessie laughed again. "Thanks," she said, realizing it was a kind of compliment.

Jack shrugged his huge shoulders beneath his thick fur jacket. "This place is confusing for someone who's just arrived. Were you given instructions on what you'll need to take up into the Yukon?" He motioned toward the whitened mountains behind the town. "The Canadian Mounted Police at the top of the passes don't let stampeders through unless they've enough supplies to last a year. That's what the people looking for gold are called around here: stampeders. Most make several trips to the top of the pass to bring up enough supplies for their caches."

"I'm not here to look for gold," Jessie told him.

He regarded her skeptically. "Then why are you here?" His eyes ranged over her as though he were assessing her attributes for some of the other occupations that brought women to Alaska in the gold rush days.

"I'm a balladeer from California," she said huffily, pointing to the guitar case on the ground beside him. He had no reason to impugn her reputation, even by a look. And she might as well tell as much of the truth as she could. As long as Jack was only interested in *where* she was from, not *when* she was from . . . "I've heard there are new songs being sung up here about the gold rush. I want to learn them and take them back with me."

Why not? Some must have been lost over the intervening century. Maybe Jessie could preserve them.

In the meantime, she was bound to meet whoever it was who had first sung the tale of Jack O'Dair.

Maybe the song had already been written. Maybe its ending was already in place.

Had Jack already performed the heroic acts of the song? She hoped not. Since she was here, she wanted to see them occur.

"By the way—" Jessie looked up at Jack, who had turned to scan the thick crowd of people near the dock. He glanced at her. "I . . . I got a little confused on my way here. Could you tell me the date?"

He frowned slightly. "Best I can recall, it's March twenty-eighth."

"Is it 1898?" Jessie asked, feeling foolish. Even if someone lost track of the date, she should surely know the year.

Jack raised one of his thick copper brows as he nodded. "That's right, Miss Jerome." His tone sounded as though he wanted to laugh at her. Or humor her. Did he think she was a total flake?

What else could he think?

"Thanks," she said irritably, picking up her guitar. "Well, I'll see you around." She took a few steps, eager to put some distance between them. She might have been attracted to the heroic man of the song. She might even have been grateful for the real Jack O'Dair's kindness to her last night. But she didn't like to be patronized—even if she knew she sounded ridiculous.

"Hello, Jack," said a very female, very flirty voice behind her.

"Well, Jack, where have you been keeping yourself?" came another high-pitched utterance.

Jessie turned to see her former companion surrounded by a bevy of women, all dressed in warm clothes that didn't hide the fact that they were, in fact, women. Their faces were painted, and Jessie easily guessed what kind of women they were.

"Hi, Gilda," Jack replied. "Ellen. Sadie. Nadine."

The ballad's tune insinuated itself into Jessie's mind. Some of its words, too:

> "Jack bested the length of ten men's strength
> Said the ladies in Sweet Helen's nest . . ."

Not to mention:

> "What's more, it was said, that in ladies' beds
> Jack O'Dair had no equal, 'twas true."

The man undoubtedly attracted women like a magnet, no matter what their chosen careers. Fine. She might want to observe his heroism, but she needn't have anything to do with him otherwise.

Jessie tried to pivot to stalk off in the other direction. Mistake! As soon as she turned, she began to slide on the ice coating the wooden planks.

She drew in her breath as her legs began to fly out from under her. She heard a noise behind her as she struggled unsuccessfully to keep her balance, still clutching her guitar.

Two strong arms caught her from behind. "Careful, Miss Jerome," said the familiar, deep masculine voice. Jack sounded amused, damn him.

"Thanks," she said grumpily as he restored her to her feet. She didn't much care for his sense of humor; his occasional use of it seemed to be at her expense.

"Now, where was it you wanted me to take you?"

"Nowhere. I'll find my own way."

"Do you have someplace to stay?" he asked as if she hadn't spoken.

She sighed. "Not really."

"Come with me." He held her arm firmly as he walked along the planks with her. She intended to remain irritated with his high-handed behavior, but found she appreciated it, particularly when she nearly slipped a couple more times.

When they stopped, they were in front of a two-story wooden building that appeared less dilapidated than the rest. A sign in the front window proclaimed it was "Calvina's Boardinghouse."

"Calvina Sanders usually has room for a respectable woman to stay," Jack said. He eyed Jessie as though waiting to hear from her whether she was, in fact, respectable.

"Then she ought to have a place for me," Jessie retorted. "Unlike some of your friends."

Jack laughed so hard that she wanted to slug him right in the stomach. Not that he'd feel it through his thick winter clothes. "Probably," he agreed good-naturedly. She had the impression he had been teasing her all along. And he didn't even attempt to excuse the fact that he undoubtedly knew those women well.

And why should he? This man was apparently Jack O'Dair. Whether or not his heroic reputation had been warranted, his reputation with loose women might be. In any event, it wasn't her business.

A team of dogs hitched to a sled hurried by along

60

the icy street. Taku growled but did not leave his master's side.

"I'll go check on a room," Jessie said. "Thanks for all your help."

But Jack wasn't watching her. A couple of men were shouting at one another. They were in the crowd moving down the street from the docks. One stomped off. Jessie noticed Jack's frown.

"Not in my town," he muttered, then said to Jessie, "With so many new people arriving I need to make sure they know the law keeps an eye on things, so there's no trouble."

"Fine," she said. "Good luck."

She stood on the plank sidewalk, watching Jack approach the crowd. He melded in for a moment, then appeared right where the pair of men were arguing— standing a head taller than anyone else. A very *red* head taller.

She couldn't hear what he said over the roar of the rest of the throng. One of the angry men drew his arm back as though he were ready to hit someone: the other fellow, Jack . . . it didn't appear to matter to him.

Jack put up a hand that, at first, seemed placating. When the man didn't seem appeased, Jack moved. Quickly. So quickly that even Jessie, who had been anticipating his heroism, hardly saw him. The argument was over nearly before it had begun. Jack had the man's arms pinned behind his back and was marching him through the crowd.

The guy wasn't tiny. He was clearly still furious. But Jack handled him with ease.

Heroically.

Jessie sighed as she scanned the crowd. Was anyone jotting this down? Someone had written "The

Ballad of Jack O'Dair." She needed to learn who that someone was, sooner rather than later. Get that person to teach her the end of the ballad.

Only . . . "Oh, no!" she exclaimed. The end of the ballad couldn't have been written yet. If it was only March 28, 1898 the avalanche in Chilkoot Pass wouldn't occur for another week.

"Lizard, you son of a gun!" Jessie muttered aloud. "I can't stay that long. I have to get home." Otherwise, Curtis Fitzgerald would have had more than enough time to destroy her blossoming career without her being able to defend herself.

Maybe she could figure a way to have the ending of the ballad forwarded to her in the future, somehow.

But leave here she would—her absurd attraction to Jack O'Dair in the flesh, and not only in the legend, notwithstanding.

She had to go. Before it was too late.

But until she did, she'd have to find a way to survive in this strange world.

"I haven't got any money," Jessie told Calvina Sanders a short while later, "but I'd be glad to work in exchange for room and board. I suspect you need a little help."

Though Calvina Sanders' pale brown hair was caught up in a sophisticated bun at the back of her head, her smooth, pretty face said she was about twenty years old. She had met with Jessie in the small kitchen of her boardinghouse, where she was washing a huge basin-full of dishes. A fire burned in the stone fireplace along one wall, and a cauldron of a hearty-smelling stew bubbled within it. Calvina had dashed to stir the pot before hurrying back to her washing chore at the basin.

Calvina appeared harried. She appeared worn out. And she also appeared about nine months pregnant.

But despite her obvious exhaustion, her voice sparkled like her eyes as she said, "Who me? Need help?" She laughed. "Oh, yes, Miss Jerome, I could use some help. But like you, I haven't got any money. My husband takes all we've got for supplies. He's a stampeder, you know."

Jessie didn't know, but she wasn't surprised. She was perturbed, though, that the man wouldn't hang around to help his obviously needy wife. She didn't want to antagonize the woman with whom she was negotiating, though, so she simply said, "And will he be here when your baby is born?"

"I surely hope so. It took two of us to make this child, so he ought to be here to greet it." She laughed, then shrugged. "But I don't always know when he'll be back from taking a load up the Chilkoot Trail. He's made several trips already, so his cache at the top is nearly set to go."

And that meant the man intended to leave his wife for a year or more to venture into the Yukon looking for gold. Unless he intended to take her along once their infant had arrived.

But the boardinghouse looked as permanent as any structure in the shantytown of Dyea. Did Calvina intend to sell it and move on?

Bluntly, Jessie asked, "Will you travel with him after your baby comes?"

"No, ma'am," Calvina said firmly, wiping her hands on the sides of the long, white pinafore that bulged out in front of her loose shift. "The baby and I will wait here for Renny to return with all that gold he's going after." Her tone did not sound ironic, but Jessie heard in her voice a hint of the indulgence with which a parent regards a cute but wayward child.

Jessie would not, she hoped, be here for long. But she would do all she could to help this woman until she left. Maybe she would even be here when the baby was born, since Calvina appeared as though she could deliver any day.

"So, do you have a room I can use in exchange for helping out? A small one will do."

"I've one that just became available. Come on, I'll show it to you." Jessie followed Calvina from the kitchen, down a narrow hallway, and up a stairway with squeaky treads. Her hostess walked slowly with the extra weight she carried. She told Jessie, "A woman boarder finally convinced her husband to move up to the gold fields rather than sitting here deciding whether to go back home. He'd already gotten their cache together when he began to get cold feet." She laughed again. "No wonder his toes got cold way up there in the Yukon." Jessie laughed, too. Calvina finished, "They're both on their way to the gold fields."

"The woman wanted to go?" Jessie wasn't entirely surprised; she had read stories of the Yukon gold strike and the people who had tried to cash in on it. There had been quite a few motivated women.

But hardly anyone had actually struck it rich in the Klondike gold rush, particularly not the people who hadn't staked the first claims.

"Yes," Calvina replied. "Not every woman is as unadventurous as I am." She gave a wink.

"Or as wise." Jessie smiled at her hostess. She liked the woman's attitude, her sense of humor . . . even if she did seem a little too accepting of her husband's possibly capricious ways.

The room to which Calvina showed her was small

but clean. It had a bed, a small dresser holding a porcelain basin for water, and a wooden clothes rack—and nothing else.

Jessie needed nothing else. Not here. She wouldn't be here very long, if she had anything to say about it. And she did like the lacy knit curtains at the room's single window. They matched the spread on the bed. "Did you make those?" she asked Calvina.

She nodded. "We didn't have a lot of money for furnishing this place, so Renny made some of the furniture and I took care of the linens."

"That's wonderful!" Jessie said. Back home, in her time, she figured such pretty, antique hand-made goods would fetch a fortune. "I love this room. Now, just tell me the kinds of chores you'll need me for."

The work sounded time-consuming but not particularly onerous. When they returned to the kitchen, Jessie said, "Why don't you just sit for a while? I'll finish doing the dishes."

Not that she'd enjoy it. Jessie had refused to live anyplace in her own time that didn't have a good-sized, efficient dishwasher.

She watched as Calvina settled herself at the small kitchen table, then got to work on the dishes. "I'm a musician," she told her new employer. "I play the guitar—" She gestured with her head toward the case that was still tucked against the wall near the door, "—and sing. I'm hoping to learn songs being written here about the gold rush, particularly ballads about real people." And most especially one about a certain Dyea lawman. "Have you heard any?"

"Sure," Calvina said with no hesitation, making Jessie's heart leap. "Some are funny. Renny would be horrified to know, but I sometimes go to places decent women aren't supposed to visit, just for the show. I love music. Really love it."

"So do I," Jessie said warmly. She was beginning to truly like this woman. "Can you tell me the best places to go? And do you know any of the people the songs are written about?"

Calvina nodded. "I sure do. There are several fellows trying to get enough money for their caches by singing. They make up songs to get people's attention, then sing them at any saloon that will let them in. People sometimes pay to hear them sing, especially if the song is about them. Maybe you and I could go hear the singers together."

"I'd like that," Jessie said. She hesitated, then added, "I'm particularly interested in ballads about heroic feats. Have you heard any?"

Calvina's smooth, young brow furrowed. "Can't say that I have."

Oh, well. At least Jessie had a clue where to start.

And the more questions she asked, the more she might learn about "The Ballad of Jack O'Dair"—and its very masculine, very appealing, and very real, subject.

"Why, Jack O'Dair, how very nice to see you," Jessie heard Calvina say. "I trust, marshal, that there's no trouble that brought you."

Jessie, standing over a large pot of stew in the kitchen, felt her heart leap. He was here! Had he come to see her?

"No trouble. I sent a stranger to you a while earlier to see about a room. Her name is Jessie Jerome. Is she still here?"

"Sure she is," Calvina said. And then she yelled, "Jessie, come into the parlor. You have a visitor."

Jessie gave the pot a final stir and rested the wooden spoon on a metal holder on the hearth. The heat in the kitchen had moistened her forehead, and she wiped it with the back of her hand. She hoped she didn't appear too frazzled as she hurried into Calvina's small, neat parlor.

Jack stood near the door beside Calvina, his dark fur jacket unbuttoned to reveal a thick sweater over wool trousers. Taku sat quietly at his feet. When Jessie appeared, Calvina said, "I've just invited Jack to join us for supper."

"If it isn't too much trouble," Jack said, "I'd be pleased to stay." He looked Jessie in the eye. The flush that crept over her face had nothing to do with the warmth she had felt while cooking.

"Looks to me as if we've plenty of food," she said offhandedly.

"I'll go tend to supper," Calvina said. Despite the awkward waddle brought on by her pregnancy, she managed to leave the room quickly, but not before giving Jessie a speculative smile.

Jessie felt discomfited at her new employer's perceptiveness. She hadn't done or said anything to suggest she was interested in Jack O'Dair. All she cared about was his ballad. "What brings you here, Jack?"

"I wanted to check on how you're doing."

Why did that bother her? He was supposed to be gallant, after all. But she wasn't used to someone worrying about her—at least not someone who wasn't a business associate paid to worry.

She needn't have been concerned. Once he had ascertained she was okay, he treated her kindly but remotely, as though she were here as Calvina's helper.

Which she was, of course. But he didn't have to think of her that way.

Jessie helped Calvina finish cooking. At her hostess's direction, she went into the parlor, where Jack sat conversing with some of the other boarders, and got his help in moving the table to the center of the room. He handled the piece of heavy wooden furniture practically on his own, making it look easy. Jessie had no intention of being impressed by his strength—though in this, too, the ballad had apparently been right. She went back into the kitchen to help Calvina serve.

Calvina, as hostess, sat at one end of the table and directed that Jessie take the other end. Jack sat at Calvina's right. He had to call to Jessie to say anything at all to her during supper, and that consisted only of, "Please pass the stew, Miss Jerome." And, "Would you care for some more bread?"

He hardly looked at Jessie. She didn't care. Not at all.

It would have been nicer, though, if the only person in the room she knew besides her employer had been a little more friendly. Or at least had been seated a little closer to her.

She thought of throwing a piece of bread at him once to get his attention, but thought better of it. Instead, she said sweetly, "How are you enjoying supper tonight, Mr. O'Dair?"

"Very much, Miss Jerome—particularly the fine company."

She was certain he didn't mean her. How could he, from so far away? He asked Calvina lots of questions and conversed heartily with her hostess's other boarders—a noisy, friendly group with disparate backgrounds.

When they all had eaten, Jack pushed himself back

from the table set up in the parlor. "The meal was delicious, Calvina."

"It was," said Eldon Riggs, the most prosperous looking of Calvina's boarders. He was a portly man who had dressed in a suit for dinner. Jessie had gathered that he was one of the town bankers but had aspirations to be a stampeder like everyone else.

The others were quick to add their compliments.

"You can thank my newest helper, Jessie," said Calvina, who reigned from the head of the table.

"I didn't do anything," Jessie protested. "You had to direct me at every step, and—"

"And you did it all perfectly, even though you obviously weren't used to cooking for a large group. She's a musician," Calvina explained to the others, sounding proud.

Jessie couldn't help smiling at the recognition.

"What kind of musician?" demanded Tildy Emmet. She was a stocky-looking woman from Delaware who had come to Alaska with her fiancé. He had gone on to the Klondike, Tildy had informed Jessie, but Tildy had wisely realized she had no interest in the hardships ahead. She had remained in Dyea, supporting herself by taking in laundry. She was blunt-spoken and Jessie didn't care for her much.

"I'm a folk singer," Jessie said. "In fact, I'm here to collect songs about the gold rush. Calvina told me she knows of some people I should meet, but if the rest of you have any ideas I'd love to hear them."

"Come to Helen's place," said Whiskey Tom. He was a shaggy-haired, bewhiskered young man with a paunch that required suspenders to keep his trousers up. "That's where I tend bar. There's always a lot of people singing and having fun. I'll be going there in just a few minutes."

"You don't want to go to Helen's place," Jack contradicted. Jessie noticed the scowl he threw at Tom. "It's not right for a lady."

"Who says I'm a lady?" Jessie demanded, though she smiled to soften her irritation.

"You don't dress like one," Tildy agreed, eyeing her. Jessie was still wearing her shirt and blue jeans, although Calvina had offered to lend her some clothes. Jessie wanted to slug Tildy. She had seen other women in pants, but most wore warm and serviceable skirts, as well as blouses with high, uncomfortable-looking collars.

"You're new to these parts." Jack's gaze held a hint of humor, though his tone told her he wanted to keep the peace between the two women. "You don't know how to get around yet, and your reputation could suffer if you go to a place like Helen's."

"My reputation is my own business," Jessie said with a sweet smile. "And I'm not worried about it. No one from home even knows I'm here." An understatement, she thought wryly.

"Helen's was one of the places I thought I'd show Jessie," Calvina said mildly. "I've been there and agree it's a fine establishment for hearing local music. Maybe we can even go there this evening."

"I'd like that," Jessie said without a further glance at Jack. "Let's clean up, then go."

Jack had left soon after dinner, and the rest of the diners had dispersed quickly thereafter. But when it came time for them to leave, too, Calvina was too tired. "I'm sorry, Jessie," she said from the chair in the kitchen where she had collapsed while Jessie finished the supper dishes. "Maybe we can go tomorrow."

Disappointment surged through Jessie, but it wasn't the end of the world. Not even the end of the night. "Don't worry about it," she told Calvina. "You need your rest. I'll head there anyway."

"But—"

"But I would like to take you up on the offer of borrowing some of your clothes."

Jessie spent a while cajoling Calvina before she convinced her she would be all right at Helen's on her own. Dressing in Calvina's long woolen skirt and cotton blouse with a blessedly loose, though high, collar, took nearly no time. She declined a corset. Jessie donned borrowed boots and Jack's long fur jacket, this time hardly even uttering a mental apology to whatever poor reddish-brown creature had given its life to grant her warmth. Then, holding a lantern, she stepped out onto the slippery wooden walkway along the Dyea street.

She followed Calvina's directions until she reached three saloons in a row. The first was Helen's Last Chance Saloon.

"Helen's nest, that is," murmured Jessie, referring to the ballad.

The light from her small lantern was dwarfed by flickering illumination pouring from the nearby buildings. The roar of voices projected over tinny music from inside.

Jessie did not hesitate. She pushed open the door to Helen's and walked in.

The place was not so different from the saloon in her own time where she had located Lizard Songthroat: a huge, carved bar, gilt-framed mirror, scattered tables and chairs. Of course, the lighting in the future was electric and there'd been no smell of burning kerosene mingling with the aromas of liquor and beer. There was another scent, too—spicy and floral, like an overdose of perfume. The crush of men looked similar, although the warm outfits on these guys were even scruffier-looking than the ones Jessie had seen before.

Without meaning to, Jessie scanned the crowded tables for one familiar face: Jack's. His name had been tied with this place in the ballad. She knew he frequented it sometimes. Why not tonight?

He knew she was coming, after all—though he believed it would be with Calvina. But maybe he would consider her presence a reason to avoid the place. Jessie swallowed a sigh.

"Good evening, miss," said a woman who approached. She was attractive, despite the way her features were exaggerated by too much makeup. A skimpy outfit hugged her voluptuous body. The perfume aroma intensified as she came closer. "Are you here for some refreshment, or are you looking for your man?"

"I'm looking for someone," Jessie agreed, "and I'd imagine it might be a man, maybe more than one."

The woman lifted one dark brow skeptically. Her hair was upswept, held in place by a clip that was clearly gold. "And who might that be?"

Jessie quickly explained that she was a singer. "I want to learn all the songs I can about this era—I mean, this area." She coughed slightly, hoping the woman hadn't caught her misstatement. And why should she? No one sane would believe that someone she just met was a traveler from the future.

"Songs? Well, my girls sing and dance sometimes, in between the other entertainments they provide, if you know what I mean." She winked at Jessie. "And I do have a couple of good singers who come in between climbs up the Chilkoot. One of them, Arnett Kionski, will be here tonight." She held out her hand. "I'm Helen Sweet, proprietress of this saloon."

"Jessie Jerome."

Helen's grip was strong, as though she arm-wrestled with her male patrons. Jessie kept her own grip firm, as well. That brought a smile to Helen's full, red lips. "Well, Miss Jerome, suppose you come in and take a seat."

Chapter Five

Helen showed Jessie to a small, discreet corner table. Though she was in the mood for a smooth white California zinfandel, Jessie ordered whatever beer was available, not planning on drinking it anyway.

Whiskey Tom served it personally. "Welcome." He pushed a patron out of the way so he could squat near Jessie's chair. His hair and whiskers looked even more straggly, maybe because he had been drinking, too; Jessie smelled liquor on his breath. "I've told Arnett, our singer tonight, that you're here specially to see him perform. He's promised to play some of his best songs."

"Introduce us, Tom," cried a voice beyond the bartender. Jessie recalled her last sojourn in the bar where she had met Lizard. In her own time, she had to be kind to inebriates, as they were potential fans. Here, she would still have to be nice; everyone was a potential source of information.

Tom introduced Jessie to a dozen or so strangers, the majority of whom needed a bath and shave. The names of the men flew by her. She grinned weakly as each professed to be pleased to meet her and offered her a drink.

"Now, leave that poor little thing alone," commanded a shrill female voice with a fake-sounding Southern accent. A blond young woman in a bright red corset and high-heeled boots strutted through the crowd, which parted to let her pass. She stopped near Jessie with her hands on her hips, which made her bustline jut even more. Her scent matched Helen's. "Hi, honey. You come to join the girls here or just passing through?"

"Er—I'm a singer," Jessie said. "I'm here to—"

"To sing? That's great. I'm Gilda. They call me Gilda the Gold, right, men?"

A ragged chorus of "right" sounded behind her. A very masculine chorus. For the first time, Jessie noticed she was the only woman in the place except for those dressed like Helen and Gilda. Her discomfort made her take a deep, calming breath.

Gilda didn't seem to notice. "Someday I'm going up the Yukon like everyone and get me some gold. Sadie, too—right, Sadie?"

Another woman rose from a stout man's lap nearby. She had dark hair swept up into a pompadour. Her outfit was as skimpy as Gilda's and Helen's, though her bustline was even fuller, giving the effect that it might spill out at any moment. "I'm Skagway Sadie," she said. Her aroma, too, was similar to the other women's. Her voice, though, was quiet, and she didn't meet Jessie's eye. "Gilda's right. We're going for gold. But for now . . . well, I sing a little, too. What's your name?"

When Jessie told her, Gilda said, "Now you come right on up to the stage, Jessie Jerome. I'll get Arnett. Maybe you can both sing."

"I just intended to listen to Arnett tonight," Jessie said.

"The guys around here are always eager for new . . . talents," Sadie said softly, drawing guffaws from the men around them. Some leered at Jessie. She just smiled, calling on techniques of dealing with crowds she had learned at home. She was uncomfortable here, though, where she did not feel in control.

She noticed Gilda maneuvering through the thick crowd and went after her. Jessie scooted even faster as a few men squeezed her arms, caressed her back. Thank heavens she had put the heavy fur jacket she'd borrowed from Jack over her clothes.

In a moment, she reached the base of the slightly raised stage. On it, a man in a red wool shirt and baggy trousers with suspenders sat behind the piano.

"That's Arnett," Gilda said. "Arnett, this is Jessie."

"You're the one Helen said wanted to hear my songs?" The man was middle-aged, with ample gray in his hair, long whiskers and pouchy skin on his face.

"That's right," Jessie said.

"She's going to sing, too," called a man. Jessie looked down. The guy had been at the table beside hers when Gilda had invited her to sing.

"First, I want to hear Arnett," Jessie said. Feeling warm in the crowded saloon, she removed her jacket and folded it over a chair.

Arnett played a few chords on the tinny piano, then began a rousing song about an Alaskan who'd gone to the Yukon, slipped on the ice and been frozen till the summer thaw, then had gone right back to panning for gold. His voice was strong, and he could almost carry a tune.

Jessie, laughing at the tale, heard rumbling echoes of laughter from the bar's customers below the stage. She started clapping her hands in time to Arnett's music, and the rhythm was taken up by others until the bar rocked with the sound.

Jessie sang along with the chorus. Fortunately, she'd slipped a small slate and piece of chalk into a deep skirt pocket. Calvina had told her they'd been left by a previous boarder who'd come north with a child, only to turn right around for home. Jessie used them to jot down words and notes. If only she had a tape recorder!

Arnett sang a few more songs. A couple had familiar melodies; the tunes had been borrowed shamelessly from old standards from the United States. Each told a tale of courage or nonsense about stampeders and others who explored this part of Alaska.

"Where do the songs come from?" Jessie asked Arnett as he took a break.

"Can't always say. Sometimes I listen to new ones from guys in other bars and pick them up. Other times, if I hear a good story I set it to music myself. It's all part of the game." He broke into another song about a man meeting a polar bear.

Jessie couldn't help asking, after the final chords of one of Arnett's songs, "Do you know any songs about . . . well, the law up here? I've heard that this area of Alaska is wild, though the Canadian Mounted Police keep order over the border. Anyone who'd try to keep the peace here would make a good subject for a ballad."

"Can't say as I've heard any like that," Arnett said, scratching his thick gray hair.

"I just wondered," Jessie said hurriedly. If "The Ballad of Jack O'Dair" had been started by now, Arnett hadn't heard of it. But maybe this man would be the one to sing Jack's praises someday. After all, Arnett had said he sometimes made up songs to go with events.

"It's your turn to sing," Arnett said. "Do you play?" He nodded at the piano.

"I'm better with my guitar, but I left it where I'm staying."

"Then tell me what to play for you."

Jessie didn't want to say no. She was in the mood to sing.

Did she dare try out "Jack O'Dair" to see if Arnett would recognize it?

Not now. Instead, she put her slate on the chair with her jacket, then directed Arnett to start an old familiar tune: "She'll Be Comin' Round the Mountain." The lively song soon got the entire saloon jumping as stampeders clapped and sang along.

When the song was finished, Jessie thanked her audience, as always. Of course this group looked a lot different from her usual group of casually dressed, yet upscale, young adults of both sexes.

"More, Jessie," called a man just below the stage. It was the same guy who'd said she was going to sing, who had been at the table near hers earlier. He was young and serious-looking. He took a step forward and nearly tripped; he seemed oblivious, since he'd clearly had too much to drink.

"It's Arnett's turn," she said pleasantly.

"We want you." The man sounded belligerent, and he climbed up on stage. His dark hair was fuzzy on top, thicker at the sides, and his beard was trimmed. He wore a leather vest over his shirt and smelled as though he had spilled half his liquor on himself. "*I* want you, all to myself. You don't need to sing. We'll just go to one of Helen's rooms—"

Jessie sighed. She had dealt with drunk fans before. "Thanks for the compliment," she said, forcing a smile. "But I'm just a visitor here."

"Then visit with me in the back room."

That started a roar of laughter from the audience. The noise apparently encouraged the man.

"Tell you what, Jessie," he said. "I just brought back some gold from the Yukon. I like to share with my friends." He tried to make an expansive gesture toward his friends below and nearly fell off the stage.

Instinctively, Jessie made the mistake of reaching out to help him. Immediately, she was hugged so tightly in the man's arms that she could barely breathe.

"I'll go first," he said, "then we'll let my friends into our room, give them a turn, too. 'Kay, boys?"

"Okay!" yelled some men from below.

Jessie tried to break away but the man was too strong. She kept her voice pleasant but firm. "I told you I'm just a visitor, but I'll bet Helen can recommend someone—"

"I want *you!*" the man demanded, his tone suddenly angry. "You hear? I'll pay you good for me and for my friends."

"Come on now, Lester," said Helen, who had joined them on the stage. "Jessie isn't one of my girls. But we can fix things up for you. Do you like Sadie? Or how about Gilda?"

"I want Jessie." Lester moved quickly, yanking Jessie to the edge of the stage.

"Then you're going to have to leave," Helen said coldly. "I've already sent Tom for the law. This isn't the first time you've gotten out of control. I warned you before that next time you'd be thrown out, and you won't be welcome here again."

The law? Did that mean that Helen had sent for Jack O'Dair?

Jessie no longer felt afraid. She was going to be safe from this nasty character in just a few minutes.

She relaxed a little. Everything would be fine. In fact, she knew how to help it along.

Jack's blood seemed to have frozen in his veins, keeping him from reaching Helen's place as fast as he wanted. Or maybe the distance along the wooden walk from his jailhouse to Helen's place had somehow grown farther.

His pace just short of a run, he slid on the ice but caught himself before falling. He didn't slacken his speed.

"It's Lester Jones again?" he asked Whiskey Tom, who barely kept up. "I warned him last time that he had better shape up or I'd make him leave town."

"Looks like he forgot," Tom huffed behind him. "He was giving that Jessie Jerome a rough time. You sent her to Calvina's. She a friend of yours?"

"You could say that," Jack replied. An intruder, that was what she really was. She had intruded into his cabin. Worse, she was intruding into his thoughts—nearly every moment. Since he had taken her to Calvina's earlier that day, he had found himself wondering how she had gotten to his home. Why she had come. Where she was from.

What it would have felt like if he'd taken her into his bed.

"Here we are." Whiskey Tom threw open the door to Helen's. Jack reached for the large sheath on his

belt that held his *ulu*, then decided instead on the Colt
.45 double-action Lightning at his hip, ready to draw
it, if necessary, to restore calm.

Instead, an amazing sight greeted him.

Jessie Jerome, on a chair at the center of the stage,
was singing a sweet, sad song about blossoms cling-
ing to a vine, while Arnett played softly on the piano,
trying to pick out accompaniment to a song he apparently didn't know. Beside her, on the floor of the
stage, sat Lester Jones. He was crying like a baby.

Jack made his way through the dense crowd to
stand beside the stage. Many other big, bold stampeders were wiping their eyes with dirty handker-
chiefs.

"Okay, Lester," Jack growled. The man barely
looked at him with bleary eyes. "I warned you before—"

He became aware, suddenly, of the words Jessie
sang to the bittersweet melody she still crooned.

> "Thanks, Jack, for coming,
> But all now is well here.
> Poor Lester is sorry
> For all that he's done.
> I can forgive him,
> And so now does Helen,
> So please let go of
> Your gun."

His fury with the difficult Lester evaporated suddenly. As instructed, Jack moved his hand from the
gun at his hip. Someone shoved a chair at him, and
he sat in it.

Jessie returned to what must have been the actual
words to the song, although Jack had never heard it,

not from any of the troubadours who came to Alaska to entertain the stampeders. It was a song of a rambler who acknowledged the joy he was feeling that day. Even Jack felt a mistiness in his eyes, not because of the words of the song but because of the emotional way Jessie sang in her sweet, slightly husky voice.

When she had finished, the saloon remained silent for more than a minute. Jack doubted Helen's place had ever been so quiet during hours it was open. Then applause exploded everywhere. Jack joined in.

He kept his gaze on Jessie. She closed her eyes, as though the emotion of her song had affected her, too. When she opened them again, they were moist. As they met Jack's, they widened. She shot him an embarrassed smile, and then she stood.

"Thank you all," she said, "for letting me come up here and sing my songs for you."

"We love you, Jessie," called Otis Oetting, getting to his feet. Otis, about sixty years old and barely sixty inches tall, owned one of the supply stores in town. Though he had come to Dyea after gold like everyone else, he was instead making his fortune in his old age by selling caches to the stampeders.

"Get down, Otis," called someone from the audience. "Jessie wants nothing to do with the likes of you."

"I guess she's more interested in an ugly cuss like you?" Otis guffawed.

"I met her first." The other man vying for her attention was Eldon Riggs, from Calvina's boarding house.

But Jack had met her before any of them. Perhaps he should stake his claim, the way they did up the Yukon. . . .

What was he thinking? He still didn't know why

the woman had appeared, and at his home, with no explanation. She probably had an ulterior motive, though for now he couldn't imagine what.

In any event, he had done what he needed to do to uphold the peace in this, his adopted town. That was all he ever intended. Getting close to anyone . . . he would never make that mistake again.

"Thank you all," Jessie repeated. She smiled at her audience, the way she had learned always to do . . . no matter how much of a strain it felt.

And it certainly was a strain here.

Especially because Jack was there, watching, listening. . . .

Lester Jones had risen beside her. He regarded her with puppy-dog eyes. "Forgive me, Jessie," he pleaded. "You, too, Helen."

Helen remained on stage. She had stalked to Jessie's side as soon as her song was finished and laid into Lester, telling him to leave and never come back.

"I promise I'll be good." Tears still ran down Lester's pink cheeks, dampening his trimmed whiskers. "I just want to hear you sing again."

"That's kind of you, Lester," Jessie said. She actually did feel sorry for the young man, despite the way he had disrupted things. "But I won't be singing here again."

"Why not?" Helen asked. She took Jessie gently by the arm and led her to one side of the stage, her scent wafting around them. "Jessie, you're not the kind of girl who usually works for me. But the way you play a crowd—you'll draw men in like no one else. Will you come and sing nights? I'll pay you in gold."

"I promised to work for room and board at Calvina Sanders'," Jessie hedged. But the job might be perfect for accomplishing what she needed to do here. "I'll agree, though, if you get other singers in Dyea and Skagway to come in and teach me their songs. We can perform together, sing even longer that way."

"Done!" Helen stated. And then before Jessie could consider changing her mind, her new employer clapped her hands for attention. As the saloon's roar faded to a murmur once more, she announced, "Fellas, you'll all be pleased to hear that Miss Jessie Jerome will be performing here at my place regularly. Maybe every night. Be sure to stop in a lot to hear her sing, will you?"

The response was resoundingly positive. Jessie grinned despite herself. Though she had played to spirited crowds at home, they had never been as enthusiastic as this. Her manager Curtis would be—

Curtis! How had she ever forgotten him?

Here Jessie was, committing to sing in this saloon indefinitely, and at home, in her time, Curtis Fitzgerald was decimating her real career.

She couldn't stay. She had to find a way to leave, for she certainly had no intention of remaining in Alaska during the gold rush or otherwise.

She needed to find out who had written Jack's ballad—if it had even been written yet. To somehow leave a crumb trail so she could find the ending when she returned to the future. Then she had to leave. Quickly.

Somehow.

She glanced down from the stage at the object of the ballad that had brought her from so far away. Jack O'Dair regarded her with those famous green eyes, as though he attempted to read her thoughts.

The idea made her uncomfortable, and yet she allowed herself to smile uneasily at him.

She caught the back of her chair for support as she watched the lazy smile he gave her in return. It made her bones feel like they were ice in the summer sun, melting. Heated. Very warm.

When he was acting like a marshal, he was so damned serious. But when he wasn't, the guy liked to smile. And she, well, she really enjoyed those gorgeous, masculine, seductive smiles of his. Too much.

She took a step forward, as though drawn magnetically.

But she stopped abruptly as Jack was suddenly surrounded by three of Helen's girls: Gilda the Gold, Skagway Sadie and one whom Jessie had seen but hadn't yet met.

"Why, Jack O'Dair. We didn't see you at first in this mess of people," Jessie heard Gilda say. "It's so good to see you here again."

"Sure is," said Sadie. She put her reddened lips to Jack's ear and whispered something.

He smiled again. It wasn't the same smile as he'd sent toward Jessie, but one much merrier, and it was accompanied by a hearty laugh that, under other circumstances, would have made Jessie want to join in.

But not now. Especially not when the third girl rubbed Jack's chest and whispered into his other ear.

At least Jack was blatant in his interest in other women, not that it mattered to Jessie. Curtis Fitzgerald had been much more insidious, feigning a fidelity he didn't feel.

Not that Jessie cared. She had no interest in Jack other than as a subject of a much beloved song.

"Will you sing again now, Jessie?" asked Eldon Riggs.

"Sure." She replaced Arnett at the piano on stage and played a few chords, wishing she hadn't left her guitar at Calvina's. She would bring it next time she entertained here.

Looking straight at Jack, she began to belt out the song "Frankie and Johnny," all about a man who done a woman wrong.

Jessie hadn't wanted Jack to walk her back to Calvina's. But too many others had tried to insist on accompanying her, including Lester Jones and Otis Oetting. It would have been most logical for one of her fellow boarders to walk with her, but Eldon Riggs had gotten too tipsy and had left for home, and Whiskey Tom was tending bar until closing.

Jessie would rather have headed home by herself, but that wasn't an option with so many willing escorts. She therefore chose the least of all the evils—she hoped.

Now, aware of the large dog Taku trotting ahead, she walked as briskly as she could in her large boots beside the marshal of Dyea.

She was totally aware of Jack's height, size and strength as she tried hard not to slip on the ice. He again kept a firm grip on her arm, and she felt tucked against his side despite her own druthers.

She had to admit, though, that she only remained standing because of Jack's assistance. And she certainly felt warm despite the bite of the air. That was due to the heavy jacket she had borrowed, of course. It had nothing to do with his nearness.

"Thanks," she said grumpily as her left foot slipped and he righted her once more.

"You're very welcome, Miss Jerome," he said. His tone was amused, which infuriated her even more. He was on duty, after all, protecting her, despite her inclinations. He should be serious.

A shout caught her attention. It seemed to come from the dark alley beside a saloon they were just passing.

"Wait here, Miss Jerome," Jack ordered. "Taku, come."

"My name is Jessie," she yelled after man and dog. And she was darned if she was going to stay put when the shout was repeated. Someone was calling for help.

She followed Jack and Taku toward the alley, though gingerly so as not to fall. She stopped short, grabbing the log exterior of the saloon for balance, as she saw what was happening.

Eldon Riggs hadn't made it back to Calvina's. He was in the shadows, leaning against the outside wall of the saloon. The pale glow from the dim half-moon above revealed that the portly man's long woolen coat was open, his suit was rumpled, the tail of his white shirt pulled from his trousers. Jessie didn't see the fur hat he had been wearing before.

No fewer than six men surrounded him, though none appeared in particularly good shape, either. They swayed as though drunk. Five watched as one pummeled Eldon, demanding that he give up his gold.

"I don't have any yet," Eldon whimpered. "I'm a banker. I'm still working on getting my own cache together."

"You've got some gold," one said in a slurred voice. "You showed it off at Helen's. We saw you."

"I spent it there," Eldon responded dolefully. "It's all gone."

"Don't believe you," said another of the tipsy watchers. He took a step toward Eldon but looked as though he would crumple beside him in the snow.

"Not in my town," Jack said under his breath. He stepped between Eldon and two of the inebriated young men. Taku stood in front of him, baring his teeth and growling. "All right. You've had your fun. Eldon, go home. And next time you have a little gold, keep it in your pocket."

The six attackers seemed slightly sobered by Jack's appearance, or maybe by Taku's. Two took menacing steps toward them, but stopped when Taku snarled and snapped. The others drew themselves up to their full heights, hardly swaying at all. Jessie could barely make out their features in the dim light between the buildings, but she could see their sizes. And how many there were.

"It's time you all go back to where you stay and sleep this off," Jack said calmly. "You'll realize in the morning that it's not a good idea to steal other people's gold."

"It's a good idea for you to mind your own business," grumbled the largest of the group, who was also closest to Jack.

Though his size couldn't compare with Jack's bear-like stature, Jessie still was concerned. It was six against one—or two, if she counted Taku. In any event, the men were, all together, ominously advancing on Jack.

Chapter Six

Eldon slid to the ground moaning, utterly useless. Jessie had to step in and help, somehow. But what could she do?

She had never done anything heroic in her life. She loved to sing songs extolling others' bravery, but that would be of little help now.

She needed a weapon—that was it! She looked around, but saw nothing in the dark alley. She glanced toward the street. Could she tear up a plank from the sidewalk and use it as a club? She hurried in that direction. It was brighter here, where light spilled from the saloon's windows onto the street. With her leather gloves protecting her hands, she wiped away a layer of dirt and snow and tugged first at one board, then another. They were nailed solidly together.

"Damn," she muttered. She turned back toward the alley. Jack and Taku were surrounded. She took a step toward them, then stopped. She wasn't a Kung Fu expert like women on television. What could she do?

"You're going to wind up in jail," she heard Jack admonish cheerfully as one man swung at him. Taku was occupied with holding off two of the others.

Jessie drew in her breath in horror, but Jack agilely blocked the blow. He grabbed the man's wrist and shoved him so he fell into those of his compatriots who were arguing with Taku, effectively ceasing their advance—for all of three seconds.

Jack whipped his *ulu* from its case and brandished its sharp, curved blade menacingly. That again made the men falter, till they came at him from three sides.

Jessie determined to get help from the saloon. She was capable of that, at least.

"All right," Jack said. "I don't want to hurt you fellows, but I've had enough." He sheathed his *ulu* and ended the fight. As smoothly as if he knew self-defense techniques hyped in movies of Jessie's time, he used his arms and legs to best advantage, aggressively employing his fists and thick boots to disable his opponents, then blocking their attempts to assail him.

In moments, he had knocked out at least three of the young drunks, and shoved the others to their knees in the snow, leaving Taku to guard them. Only then did he draw his gun.

"Now, boys," he said calmly. "It isn't nice to attack a marshal. And especially not his dog. You'd better come along. You can sleep it off in jail."

The three who were conscious started to raise a ruckus. Jack didn't turn around but spoke to Jessie conversationally, as though he had no doubt she would be there. He hardly sounded winded. "Miss Jerome, Taku and I will stay here to keep an eye on these fellows so they don't run away. Would you be so kind as to go to the jail and get my assistant, Filby?"

"Of . . . of course." Her heart was still pounding, though Jack had taken the attack in stride, as if such things happened every day. Maybe they did here in Dyea. But, no, he wouldn't tolerate it in *his* town. She'd heard him say so twice already.

He explained which building housed the jail. It wasn't far from Calvina's. Jessie managed to get there after slipping only once and bruising her backside.

Filby turned out to be a kid with slicked-back hair, a swagger and a leer. But when Jessie explained what had happened he hurried past her, a gun in his hand.

Jessie hung around until the two lawmen had gotten the six inebriates to jail. Taku herded the bad guys and kept them moving, and Jack joked with Filby all the way. The perpetrators—did they use that word in this time?—slid on the ice, moaned and complained, but they obeyed Jack's every command. Jack, towering above them all and wearing a large fur cap, kept his footing as easily as Taku. Jessie followed, watching him. Shaking her head.

He had made it look so simple. He was every bit as heroic as his ballad said.

Some of the words drifted through Jessie's mind:

"On a Dyea night when the half-moon was
   bright,
A stampeder staggered to bed,
When a mob of wild urchins craving gold with
   no searching
Menaced the drunkard with lead.
" 'Help,' the man importuned, clutching his for-
   tune
And who was patrolling there?

The lawman extraordinaire with the bright red
   hair,
The dauntless Jack O'Dair.
"The fight was finished in minutes,
The stampeder's gold was saved.
And Jack O'Dair, with untousled red hair,
Set the wild young rogues on their ways."

This had been it—the incident from the song! It
wasn't exactly true. The only "lead" Jessie had seen,
assuming that meant bullets in a gun, had belonged
to Jack and Filby. And Jack didn't just send them on
their way; he took them off to jail. Plus, this verse
didn't even mention Taku's role.

And she couldn't tell if Jack's hair had been tou-
sled; it had been beneath his fur hat.

Still, the song had been awfully close. And although she knew that balladeers took poetic license,
there had been no exaggeration of Jack O'Dair's courage.

When the men were all behind bars, a couple already passed out on the stone floor, Jack thrust some
blankets in to them from beneath a cot in the main
room that served as Jack's office and Filby's bedroom. Then, he turned to Jessie. "Now I'll finish
walking you home, Miss Jerome."

"Jessie," she corrected. She wanted to tell him she
was perfectly capable of taking care of herself, but
the truth was that, after this little incident, she didn't
want to walk even the short distance to Calvina's
alone. The fight had unnerved her. The few minutes
it had taken her to hurry to the jail for Filby had
seemed like eons. She had peered into every dark cre-
vasse between buildings, just in case there were more
drunks waiting to leap out at her.

She managed just fine in her own time, but here . . . "That would be very nice, Mr. O'Dair," she said formally.

"Jack," he corrected with a broad smile that, in the light of the jail's flickering lanterns, nearly made her swoon.

Swoon? Jessie Jerome? She had been here too long already. Women in her time didn't swoon.

Not even when faced with a man as gorgeous and heroic as Jack O'Dair.

"Jack," she repeated firmly. She took his proffered arm again, thick and muscular and swathed in warm fur, as they braved the weather outside. Sometime between when they had brought in the drunks and now, which couldn't have been more than half an hour, a fierce wind had begun to blow. As cold as it had been before, now it was ten times worse. This was March. Hadn't she heard that the mean high temperature during that month was about eight degrees Fahrenheit? And this temperature was more than mean; it was downright vicious.

She didn't even want to think about the wind chill factor in this gale. "This is horrible!" she shouted into the wind.

"It isn't far to Calvina's," he informed her in a loud voice, although she already knew that. Taku managed to keep up with them, head down, at Jack's side.

"But you have a long way to go back to your cabin." The cabin in which she had spent the night with him . . . and nothing had happened, of course.

She wondered if she would look back with regret on that fact.

"I'm used to it." She was sure he was. And she doubted he would complain about something like a little bit of frigid weather.

Linda O. Johnston

She turned her head so that her face used Jack's massive upper arm as a shield. That helped her—a lot.

But it made her uncomfortable, too, to be clutching this man so tightly. To be relying on him.

The women in Sweet Helen's nest had clung to him, too.

That brought her up short. She slid a few inches before catching herself. No, Jack caught her, his strong, gloved hands beneath her arms. "Easy, Miss Jessie," he admonished, his words nearly swept away by the wind.

"It's not easy at all," she retorted loudly, though the sound of the rushing air made her feel as though she had whispered. "Nothing here is."

"It's worse up Chilkoot Pass," he called. "And once you reach the Yukon—"

"Good thing I'm not going there," she interrupted.

"Everyone here goes after gold." It wasn't just the attempted loudness of his voice that made him sound grim, and she looked into his face. He had his head down against the wind and didn't return her gaze.

"I told you that wasn't why I was here."

"You don't seem to want to be here at all," he shouted.

"That's true." She thought about her words for a moment. "Sort of."

"Then—"

They had reached Calvina's. Jessie lifted her hand to knock, but Jack simply opened the door.

Apparently here, despite the lawlessness, people didn't worry about home security systems.

Once they were inside, Jack closed the door behind the three of them, including Taku, who shook himself eagerly. Jessie stood in the front room, basking in the sudden enveloping heat. She breathed deeply, pleased to take in air instead of what had felt like ice.

"Thanks for walking me home, Jack," she said when she could talk again. She hated to send him out into the cold, but she felt uneasy, standing beside him in the room beyond the front door. The fire in the hearth had been banked and only a few embers glowed. They provided the only light in the room.

"You're welcome. I'll be right back." Leaving her there, he strode into the house as if he knew it well. What was he doing?

She sat in a chair facing the fire, right beside where Taku basked in the heat. She had removed her jacket and gloves, and she briskly rubbed her aching hands together.

In moments, Jack had returned. "Looks like everyone's in bed, including Eldon. I wanted to make sure he got home all right after that little difficulty."

Little difficulty. That was all the fight, the menace from six drunken men, had been to him.

And he was kind enough to check to make sure that Eldon had returned with no further problem.

Jessie shook her head slowly, as though hoping to clear it of years of brainwashing from hearing the ballad—to no avail.

Jack was everything she had imagined he would be.

"Are you all right, Jessie?" Jack had draped his heavy jacket over a hook on the wall, and he drew a chair toward her. His ecru sweater did nothing to hide the breadth of his shoulders, the expanse of his muscles.

"I'm fine," she said, though she knew the tremor in her voice belied her words. "Fine," she repeated more strongly. She glared at Jack as though daring

95

him to contradict her. If he did, she'd really get angry.

She had to.

She had never before met the hero of one of her pet ballads. She had half fallen in love with the idea of Jack O'Dair, even without knowing how his song ended. Now that she was faced with the reality of the man, her heart had not reached a sensible equilibrium. Of course she found him attractive. What woman wouldn't? But she was going home, as soon as she could—wasn't she? She didn't care for Jack, in any case, just the *idea* of him.

Then why, when she looked sidelong into his concerned face, did she want to kiss him?

"You don't look fine," he contradicted.

"I ... I'm just not used to all this cold. And excitement."

"I don't know about that." Jack pulled his chair a little closer to the fire—and a lot nearer to her. "You seemed to be right at home in all that excitement at Helen's. You had those stampeders bawling like babies at your song."

She had, hadn't she? She grinned. It wasn't every day that her ballads struck such emotional chords in her audience.

But then she realized that Jack's tone had not contained solely admiration; there had been another message—jealousy?

She nearly laughed aloud. He had no reason to be jealous. He hadn't any more interest in her than he had in one of Helen's girls, did he?

"Did you like my singing?"

She'd meant to ask if he minded that the other men had been so affected. She hadn't intended such a plaintive question.

But now that it had been asked ...

"I liked it, Jessie Jerome." He stood beside her chair. "I liked it a lot."

She wasn't sure if he had urged her to her feet with his touch, or whether she had simply stood of her own volition, but suddenly, she was facing him.

In his arms. His strong, heroic arms were tightly around her, and she felt right at home. She rested her cheek on his chest, feeling the coarseness of the hand-knit material of his shirt against her skin.

But not for long. His fingers lifted her chin.

She stood on tiptoe, for that was the only way she could reach him. But he bent down to her, too. He touched her lips with his—very, very gently.

His mouth was warmer than the fire, and it stoked some long-banked conflagration deep within her. When he began to pull away, she reached up and held his head down to her.

She ran her fingers through the silky inferno of his bright red hair. Her eyes were closed, the better to concentrate on her all-consuming sense of touch. She felt his hands at her back, kneading her skin. Her skin! His hands were beneath her shirt, and the sensation of his flesh on hers made her even more crazy.

"Jack O'Dair," she whispered against his lips. Her words resulted in his tasting her with his tongue. His kiss was not so gentle now. In fact, it was as strong and heroic as anything else she had seen about Jack since she had arrived here, in his time.

His time. Reality intruded abruptly. She was in the past, in the arms of a man who no longer existed in her world. Whose prowess in courage and in sexual exploits might be legendary, but it had long since disappeared.

And she was going home. Soon. She had to. She had a career to save. A reality to return to.

Still, as she pulled away, she did so reluctantly. Her breathing was heavy. So was his, she noted with grim pleasure. At least he seemed to have been affected by their kiss, as she had been.

"Well, thanks again for an interesting evening, Jack," she said as glibly as she was able. "See you around."

The sensual, hooded look in his bright green eyes disappeared, replaced first by incredulity, then remoteness. "Good night, Jessie Jerome," he said formally. "Taku—"

"Well, hello, there," boomed a voice from the door to the hallway. "I thought I heard voices. Jack O'Dair, what brings you to my parlor in the middle of the night? Hey, Taku."

A young man in a red nightshirt bent down to pat the dog. His light brown hair was mussed, as if he had been asleep. His nose was a little bent, as though it had been broken, which would not have been surprising since it was too large, in proportion to his face. His other features were soft, almost pretty.

"Hello, Renny," Jack said. "I didn't notice you before when I checked your house. I just saw your new boarder home. Miss Jessie Jerome, meet Renny Sanders, Calvina's husband."

"The stampeder?" Jessie blurted. She knew her face was nearly as red as Renny's shirt. How long had he been in the doorway? Had he seen her kiss Jack?

"None other," Renny said proudly. "I'm back for another load."

"I want to hear more about it," Jessie said, "in the morning. Right now, I'm tired. Good night."

She moved past Renny and Taku, fleeing from the room. But as she reached the door, she looked back. Jack O'Dair was watching her, a corner of his mouth quirked into a smile that might signify amusement or bemusement. She couldn't tell which.

Jack watched Jessie leave, half relieved and half perturbed. Even if Renny hadn't interrupted, he was certain that there would be little left to say between Jessie and him that night. Her host's arrival had at least ended the awkwardness between them.

Why had she so suddenly cooled during their kiss? He himself had been warm. Hot. Jessie Jerome had ignited a flame that had nothing to do with the kind of fire the stove contained. It was one that affected every part of his body—one part in particular, much more than others. That fire could not have been doused by simply walking outside, though right now the idea of a sudden dunking in an icy mountain stream almost sounded inviting.

With a final pat on Taku's head, Renny stood. He grinned, revealing his familiar missing tooth. "I haven't known you to walk home any other boarders," he said. "Though not many are as pretty as Miss Jerome."

"True." Jack made certain to keep his voice light. "Thing is, there was a little trouble outside The Yukon Saloon tonight. Miss Jerome was with me, saw me arrest a few boys who'd drunk too much and set upon poor Eldon. He'll feel it in the morning."

"I'll make sure Calvina treats him extra special. Miss Jerome, too." Renny cocked a look at Jack as though waiting for him to say more about Jessie.

He wasn't about to admit any interest in the woman, other than as another citizen he had to protect. He *had* no other interest in her—nor in anyone else. Never again.

"That's kind of you, Renny. She is a pretty lady,

isn't she? I haven't figured out why she's here. She claims she's not a stampeder, has no wish for gold, but why else would she venture so far from home?"

And where was her home? California, she'd said. Which town? San Francisco? She surely lived in a city, since she entertained. But she didn't seem a loose woman, as many women on stage often were.

Who was Jessie Jerome? And why did he care?

"Come into the kitchen," Renny said, "and I'll pour us both something to keep the cold outside."

Jack considered refusing, but for the moment he decided he wanted even less to be out slogging his way back home. This way, he would remain under the same roof as Jessie for a few minutes longer. Not that it mattered. "Good idea," he replied.

"So what reason does Miss Jerome give for coming here?" Renny asked as they sat at the small table in the corner, with a large tumbler of whiskey before each of them.

"She's a singer. That much I believe, since I heard her sing at Helen's." Her voice was as sweet as a flock of songbirds in an apple tree in summer. No wonder it had tamed so many of Helen's rowdy customers before Jack had even been able to get there. "She says she wants to learn songs about the gold rush."

"No better place than here to learn," Renny agreed.

Jack knew enough about the gold rush. He wanted to learn more about Jessie. He simply nodded, shifting on the hard stool at the bare wooden table.

"Has Horace spoken with you?" asked Renny, taking a long swig of his drink.

"Horace Martin? Far as I know, he's still not talking to me. Does he want to play another game of poker with me? Or is he ready to take up my challenge to fight with *ulus*?" Jack grinned, then reached for his own glass of whiskey and took a drink. It was strong, and he felt it burn on its way down. "After all, he did call me a cheater."

"Would you really fight him? It would be a massacre. Just because he has the biggest collection of knives for sale in town doesn't mean he knows how to use them."

"He has the biggest collection of everything for sale." Jack twisted the cool metal tumbler in his fingers.

"Not for long, though," Renny said. "Not at this rate."

"What do you mean?" Jack's full attention was captured.

"Rumor has it now that his supplies are disappearing like they'd grown feet and begun sneaking away in the night. I'd heard he was getting desperate enough to talk to the marshal about it."

"Maybe he's just begun charging fair prices so he's actually selling more."

"Horace, sell at fair prices?" Renny snorted. "I have to say, though, that his are no worse than any others in this God-forsaken outpost. In Skagway, either; I looked there, too."

"Well, if you talk to Horace, tell him you've convinced me not to hurt him. If he needs me to find him a thief, he only needs to ask."

"And you'll do it. Right quick, too, I'm sure."

"Of course." Jack took another drink to hide his grim smile. He was good at what he did. He lived to help people—people who deserved it. He gave no quarter to those who would take advantage of others. "I won't tolerate thieves in my town. No matter what, Horace deserves to sell his goods as he will. The stampeders who come here take their chances, and if they can't afford to go on, they don't belong in the Klondike after gold."

"That's part of the story of the gold rush," Renny agreed with a laugh. "I've heard tales of poor fools who die without finding a single nugget as well as tributes to those who do good here, save others' lives—like you. Maybe that Jessie Jerome ought to sing a song about you, Jack."

"Not on your life," Jack said with a scowl. "I do what I have to, that's all." He'd had no choice but to find a town like Dyea to protect, to attempt to make up for what had happened when he had failed those he had cared about. He didn't want anyone making a fuss about it. "You understand, Renny?" He tried to keep his voice even. "If you ever hear of anyone, including Jessie Jerome, wanting to build me a reputation I don't deserve, you tell me. I'll take care of it."

"Sure, Jack." Renny paused. "Looked like you were doing a good job of taking care of her when I walked in."

Jack felt his face redden. "She's not used to the weather here. I tried to help her get warm, that's all." He finished his whiskey in two gulps, ignoring the tears that flooded his eyes as the strong drink seared his gut.

"No one's used to the weather here," Renny said. "And there's no need to make excuses to me." Jack heard the laugh in his voice.

Nothing was funny. Not at all. "I don't know about you, Renny," Jack said, "but I'm tired. It's late. Come on, Taku. Time to go home."

"I'll tell Horace what you said," Renny called as Jack left the kitchen. "He can ask for your help, as long as he doesn't tell anyone what a good job you do."

"That's right." Jack stopped near the door long enough to close his jacket and put on his hat and gloves. Renny hitched his nightshirt around him as he followed.

"By the way, since you're so modest, there's a new boarder here you won't want to meet," Renny said.

"Who's that?" For a moment, Jack wondered if Renny meant Jessie, but that made no sense. He had already met her. And he had already begun to regret it nearly as much as he was pleased by it.

"He's a photographer," Renny said. "He's here to send pictures of the gold rush and the people here down to the United States. His name is Daugherty, and I'm sure he's going to want to meet you." Renny's laughter followed Jack and Taku into the night.

Chapter Seven

"You're a photographer?" Jessie asked the newest boarder at Calvina's, who regarded her with a much-too-intense stare over the breakfast table the next morning.

He nodded. "Dab Daugherty's the name, Miss Jerome." He'd have made an interesting subject for one of his own photos, with a face that would make people blink and take a second look. His nose was too flat, his lips too soft. But those scrutinizing gray eyes were definitely arresting.

"Mr. Daugherty came to town yesterday afternoon," Calvina told the others at the table.

"Did you arrive home yesterday as well, Mr. Sanders?" Tildy Emmet, the washer woman, asked Calvina's husband.

"Late last night."

Like Daugherty, he also stared at Jessie, and in his case she knew why. She flushed and looked down at her bowl as though her oatmeal had suddenly demanded attention. Renny Sanders's first impression of her had probably been that inappropriate—but so very stirring—kiss she had shared with Jack O'Dair.

"It's good to be home," Renny finished.

"It's wonderful to have you home," Calvina said softly. Jessie looked up to see husband and wife exchange fond looks. They were clearly in love, and Jessie felt a twinge of envy.

Not that she needed anyone to interfere in her life. Men had a habit of making women fall in love with them, then doing whatever they damned well pleased. She had seen that with her mother. That was her cursed manager Curtis Fitzgerald's chosen *modus operandi*, too. It was how he got so many female clients.

And hadn't Renny left his wife here, nearly ready to give birth, while he jaunted off to the top of Chilkoot Pass?

Well, maybe he was here now to stay, for Calvina was clearly due any minute.

"Are you going to the Yukon, Mr. Daugherty?" asked Tildy Emmet. Her reddened hands reached over the table for the sugar bowl, which she nearly emptied into her oatmeal.

Jessie rose immediately and took the bowl to the kitchen to refill it. She kept her ears open for Dab's response.

"That I am," he agreed. "Though so's everyone else here, I'd wager." As Jessie returned with the sugar bowl, Dab looked around the table. At least Jessie wasn't the only one he seemed to study. In fact, he appeared to size everyone up to see how photogenic they were. "The difference is that I intend to make my fortune off all of you."

"What do you mean?" demanded Eldon Riggs. He

looked a lot less confident this morning than he had at the supper table the night before. His set-to with the young men who'd tried to rob him had left him with a black eye and a suspicious scowl that he trained on Dab Daugherty.

Dab laughed. "I'm not after anything of yours or anyone else's, Mr. Riggs, except perhaps your likeness. I'm going to sell the true story of the gold rush, in pictures, to anyone who'll pay the price. This is history in the making, you know."

Jessie knew that better than anyone. "I agree, Mr. Daugherty." She took her seat once more. Since he would probably be poking around everywhere, speaking with people she might never meet, she said, "I'm here for a similar reason. I'm a musician, and I'm collecting songs about the gold rush. If you hear any interesting ones, particularly about heroic figures, will you let me know?"

"Glad to, Miss Jerome. In fact, maybe we could work together."

"Maybe," she said noncommittally.

"Jack O'Dair was here last night just after I arrived," Renny said. He was looking at his wife. Nevertheless, Jessie surmised the comment was intended to remind *her* that Jack existed.

As if she would forget that quickly. If ever.

It also assured her that Renny had seen the kiss. He must think he was protecting Jack's interests by his gentle admonition. A woman whose affections were otherwise engaged in this era probably didn't plan research expeditions with other men.

Just in case that was Renny's thinking, Jessie determined to set him straight. "Mr. O'Dair was kind enough to walk me home last night," she said. "There was a little problem that Mr. Riggs can tell you about,

106

if he wishes." She stole a glance at Eldon, who did not look pleased at the attention. "Afterward, it was late, and Mr. O'Dair apparently thought I needed an escort back here."

"Good thing he came along," Renny said. "A nice woman shouldn't walk these streets alone at night, even when there's no trouble. And since the marshal was here, I told him about the missing supplies at Horace Martin's warehouse."

"Aren't Horace and Jack feuding?" Calvina asked.

Renny smiled. "Horace is. Jack's a good sport, considering the fact that Horace as good as called him a cheater at cards."

"But O'Dair is as straight-shooting at poker as he is with everything else," said Whiskey Tom with a yawn. He had obviously worked late at Helen's. He was so quiet, with eyes so bloodshot from lack of sleep, that Jessie wondered why he had even appeared at breakfast. "The marshal is good enough at cards he doesn't need to cheat."

Of course he would be. In fact, Jessie knew it. Some lyrics from the ballad ran through her mind:

"In card games most fair always played Jack
  O'Dair
And he won nearly all of them, too."

She was finding a lot of "The Ballad of Jack O'Dair" to be true. And as much as the fictional hero had appealed to her, the real man seemed even more fascinating.

Which was why she had to fulfill her mission and leave, if she could, before she became as enamored of the real person as she was of his legend . . . before she was hurt, when she inevitably realized that no one could live up to Jack's reputation—not even Jack. *But how was she supposed to leave?*

What if she had to stay here? Would that be so bad? She didn't even know if, let alone how, she could go back to her own time. Lizard Songthroat wasn't here to help her. Perhaps spending another night in Jack's cabin . . . She swallowed hard at the suggestive thoughts that brought to mind.

Since everyone professed to be full, Jessie stood quickly and began clearing the plates. Calvina and Tildy also helped to clean the table. The others—all men, of course—remained seated. Jessie forbore from any caustic comments to that effect. After all, this was long before even most women recognized women's rights.

"Since you're a full-fledged stampeder, Mr. Sanders," Dab Daugherty said, "would you mind if I followed you around, took a few pictures?"

"I'm not doing anything all that interesting," Calvina's husband demurred, though a smile of pleasure lit his face. "This morning, I'm going to Horace Martin's warehouse to arrange for my next load of goods to take up the Chilkoot."

"Aren't you planning to wait till the baby's born?" Jessie hadn't intended to blurt the question. Horrified, she glanced around. Calvina was in the kitchen scraping plates. Jessie doubted she'd heard, thank heavens.

"Calvina feels sure it won't be for another week. I can be up to the summit with one more load, then back in plenty of time."

But the fact that he still intended to trek up the Chilkoot with supplies for his cache indicated he planned to head into the Yukon for gold soon. He might be around to see the baby born, but then he would be gone again.

Even though Renny Sanders seemed to love his wife, that was not enough to keep him here for her—not even when their child arrived. That only gave further credence to Jessie's belief that no man could be trusted to stay when a woman let herself care.

"But I do intend to hurry. In fact, I'm going to Horace's warehouse first thing this morning to buy my next supplies. I wish now I'd bought my gear in Seattle like the stampeders just coming up from the States; Horace and the others charge too much. But now I have no choice. You want to come, Daugherty?"

"Sure do!" The young man leapt to his feet. "I'll get my equipment."

"You might want to come along, too, Miss Jerome," Renny said with an arch smile. "I'm going to see that Jack talks to Horace while I'm around, so Horace's grudge won't get in the way of his telling the marshal all he knows."

"I have plenty of work here to help Calvina," Jessie told him, half to chide him for his own inattention to his wife.

"I'll be fine, Jessie." Calvina stood in the doorway to the kitchen. "You've done so much already. Run along."

"I don't want to go just to—"

"If you're looking for songs," Renny said, "Horace's and the other stores are good places to be. Sometimes fellows who've given up on trips into the Klondike hang around and recite their hard-luck stories in poems. Even sing their tales, if they're musically inclined—and that includes some too bashful to sing 'em in the saloons."

"Really?" Jessie wasn't sure whether to believe Renny. On the other hand, she didn't want to miss an opportunity.

"Sure. It keeps us all entertained while we pick out our supplies. We even pay a few coins to the guys who've given up already. It makes the rest of us more determined to succeed."

Renny laughed, but Jessie failed to see the humor. She considered his words, though. If Jack happened to be at the warehouse . . . so what if she saw him again? She needn't avoid him. That kiss hadn't meant a thing.

Horace Martin's warehouse was huge. It was actually an amalgamation of two buildings joined by canvas tents strung together and braced with wood. It appeared to be the largest structure in Dyea.

Above it towered the snow-covered mountains that nearly surrounded the town. Was that an eagle Jessie saw soaring up by the closest peak?

A crowd milled outside the warehouse. "What's going on?" Renny asked a man in a heavy parka at the end of the line.

"Shortages," the man grumbled. "Someone said Horace is out of condensed milk, evaporated potatoes, rolled oats and soap. Maybe more."

"I can do without soap," Renny said, "but the Mounties at the top are strict about making sure stampeders carry enough food for a year."

Jessie regretted that he sounded so cavalier about the soap. Though the air remained so cold that her breath seemed to freeze before her eyes, she could still smell the unpleasant odor of too many active people crammed together in too little space. She kept her breathing shallow. "Can't you take what Horace has now for this trip and pick up something else the next time?" she asked.

"Sure, but I can't be certain he'll have later what he lacks now."

Eldon Riggs stood off to one side talking with two of the girls from Helen's place, Skagway Sadie and Golden Gilda. Jessie heard an angry shout from the front of the crowd. It was followed by another. She made out the words, "You low-down thief." Before she realized what was happening, the horde erupted into a wave of yells and shoves and punches that spread from the warehouse outward.

"Step back," Renny hollered, taking her arm. But he was pushed away so suddenly that Jessie stumbled as his grip loosened. She looked around to see Dab Daugherty fight his way to the fringe of the crowd and start to set up his camera, only to see him tackled. She thought she saw him grab the fragile box before his tripod and he tumbled to the ground.

Something hard struck Jessie's side, and she found herself on her knees in the snow. She was wearing a skirt borrowed from Calvina, and it hiked up so that her legs were exposed above her boots. She gasped. Not that she had any false modesty here, even though women in this day didn't show bare skin beyond their faces and arms, but it was unbelievably cold.

She tried to rise, but the mass of people around her, fighting and screaming and shoving, made it impossible. She couldn't stay on the ground. She would be hurt if any of them fell on her.

"Let me up," she hollered but knew no one heard her over the roar of the riot. A man who had been punched stumbled and trod on her hand. She screamed in agony, "Get off me!" Her heart pounded in fear. She had to get out of this. "Help!" she cried.

A bark sounded in her ear. She looked around through tears of pain and frustration, and there was the welcome, wolf-like form of Taku. He snarled and snapped at the men around her until they began stumbling away. In a moment, Jessie was hiked to her feet, then swung over a strong, hefty shoulder like a sack of laundry. "Hey!" she cried, twisting around to look up at the back of Jack O'Dair's head. His bright, coppery hair left no doubt of his identity.

"You shouldn't be here, Miss Jerome," he said. In no time, they were at the opposite side of the dirt street. He gently set her on her feet. "Go back to Calvina's," he ordered. And then he stalked off toward the melee.

Instead of obeying his order, Jessie looked around to see if she could help. She had no weapon. She wouldn't find a fire hydrant and hose to turn a stream of water on the mob. She hadn't even a bullhorn to make noise to get their attention.

Her thoughts were interrupted by two gunshots. She jerked her head, only then noticing that Jack had climbed onto a pole supporting the canvas at the center of Horace's warehouse. He pointed a gun into the air. Though the crowd did not become silent, the noise was less intense.

"I'll sic Taku on the next man to throw a punch!" yelled Jack. His voice carried over what was left of the riot.

"Oh, yeah?" came a voice from the crowd. Jessie saw a hefty young man toward the front strike someone standing near him.

In a moment, Jack's gun was trained on him. "Taku, attack!" No shot sounded, but the dog leapt onto the man, snarling and nipping at his throat.

The man hollered, "Get him off me!"

"Taku, quit," Jack called. The dog stopped worrying at the man's throat but remained standing on his chest. "Does anyone else want to continue the fight?"

Apparently no one did. The crowd dispersed so

rapidly that in five minutes few people were left. Jessie would have thought she had imagined the entire episode except that Jack stood beside Filby and two other men, one of whom was the large young fellow whom Jack had ordered Taku to grab. He watched the dog warily. Taku sat at his master's side, panting with evident pleasure, looking like an overgrown wolf puppy.

"That dog could'a killed me, Jack," the young man whined.

"Only if I told him to." Jack regarded him sternly. "I don't allow riots in my town. Next time, maybe you'll help me stop the crowd instead of becoming part of it, right, Vanning?"

"Well, sure." He didn't sound certain, but he shrugged and walked away.

With the riot over, Jessie saw Renny appear from an alley between stores, dusting off his pants as if he had remained in the thick of the fray. Dab Daugherty was behind him. She hadn't seen Dab since he'd fallen, but he appeared to be all right. Tildy Emmet had joined up with them.

"What caused them to get so riled, Horace?" Renny asked the man who still stood with Jack and Filby outside the warehouse.

The establishment's owner was tall and thin, and his sad eyes looked all the more lugubrious thanks to the complementary droop of his mustache. "I didn't have everything they wanted," Horace replied. "And not because I didn't plan ahead." He turned to Jack. "Marshal, someone has been robbing me. Every morning, when I come in, more supplies are missing. I've hired men with guns to stay overnight and keep an eye on things. I've even stayed here myself to make sure it wasn't the guards doing the looting. But whoever it is sneaks in somehow, and nothing prevents it." Jessie saw his prominent Adam's apple bob up and down, as though he had a hard time spitting out what he wanted to say. "Look, Jack," he began, "I know you and I haven't always gotten along over our card games—"

"It's hard to get along well with someone who calls you a cheater," Filby cut in.

Jack's bushy red eyebrows raised in apparent amusement as Horace glared at the deputy.

"Maybe I was a little hasty," Horace allowed. "But, marshal, can we put all that behind us? I need help."

A lesser man than the Jack O'Dair celebrated in the ballad might have exacted revenge for the insult by turning his back on the plea for help. Jessie held her breath, wondering if the real Jack O'Dair would live up to his legend.

But the real Jack O'Dair had already proven himself of similar mettle. He had attacked the young inebriates in the alley who were bothering Eldon. He had waded into the mob and extracted Jessie from danger.

She wasn't surprised, then, when Jack said, "Let's go inside, Horace, and see how we can save your supplies."

Chapter Eight

If there had been any singers at Horace's warehouse that day, the riot had scared them off, for Jessie came across none.

Standing inside the door beside Renny and Tildy Emmet, she supposed she should not have been surprised at the inside of Horace's warehouse. Supplies in huge piles, taller even than Jack, lay everywhere: canvas sacks labeled "rice" and "dried fruit" and "sugar." Crates of blankets, nails, axes, shovels, socks and rope. Stacks of pans—some, with handles, to be used for cooking over fires, and plain round ones for dipping into streams for gold. Jessie could see a resemblance to the warehouse discount stores of her time.

A hand-painted sign on the wall proclaimed, without modesty, that this was "The Greatest Outfitter in Dyea, Horace Martin, Proprietor." The area smelled of coffee and spices and something sharp that Jessie identified as gunpowder.

The place brimmed full of goods, yet Jessie saw empty spaces among the stacks. Were these the areas of pilferage?

Horace confirmed it, pointing them out to Jack. "See these?" he demanded. "The 'Seattle Steamer' came through two days ago, brought me a lot of goods. I put it all away yesterday, nice and neat and organized like always. When I came in this morning, things were gone. Wouldn't you know they were the very supplies that the stampeders who came in today were demanding?"

"Make me a list of what's missing," Jack said. "And I need to talk to your useless guards, too." He was solemn, on the job—no humor at all in his flashing green eyes. He was drawn up to his full height, broad shoulders so stiff that she could have stuck one of the shovel handles through his white shirt and he might not have noticed. There was something about his rigid stance that moved Jessie. He was a real, breathing human being, yet he looked every bit as heroic as the subject of her ballad.

Handsome, too. A warmth oozed deep inside Jessie, and she recognized it immediately for what it was: a stirring of sexual awareness. Odd place, odd time, but definitely there.

Oh, yes, Jack O'Dair was an appealing hero, in many more ways than one.

But could he solve the crime?

Sure, if the ballad had been accurate. And so far, Jessie had found nothing in it to be untrue. If the crooks knew how determined he looked, they would be shuddering in their snowshoes.

But just maybe he needed a little help.

Jessie had heard the marshal tell his deputy Filby to stay outside and patrol around the warehouse, to let him know if there was any trouble outside. She watched Jack's large, limber form as he walked among the many stacks, kneeling now and then to pick up something from the dirt floor. She wondered what kinds of clues he was looking for.

"Do you see any footprints in the dirt?" She stooped beside him. "I suppose it's tamped down pretty hard, plus it would be hard to distinguish a thief's from anyone else's."

He turned to look at her, his expression as blank as though she had begun speaking in the language of the Chilkats, a local Indian tribe. "What do you mean, Miss Jerome?"

This was after the time Sherlock Holmes was written, wasn't it? Didn't detectives know about footprints? How about fingerprints? Even if they knew about them, though, they wouldn't have computerized files to check against. If hairs were found, a policeman might compare its color with a suspect's, but DNA would not be discovered for decades.

"Er . . . where I come from, I've heard police talk about the clues they look for to solve crimes. I can't tell you much, but if there's anything I can do to help—"

"Hi, Horace," sang a lusty feminine voice from behind Jessie. She rose in relief and turned to see Skagway Sadie and Golden Gilda, along with Whiskey Tom and Eldon Riggs. "What happened here?" It was Gilda who spoke, and she edged her way to Horace's side.

The thin man flushed, then stammered, "Some damned thieves took a lot of goods last night. The

117

lack of some supplies caused the stampeders to riot. Did you see it?"

"Sure did." Sadie sounded scared. Her vehement nod rippled her body enough that her ample bosom threatened to spill out of her low-cut gown. Jessie looked from one man's face to another's to see how many pairs of eyes widened in anticipation. Eldon's and Tom's certainly did. Even Renny's, despite his being an apparently happily married man. But to Jack's credit, he didn't seem to notice. Maybe it was because he was still crouched near the floor, searching for clues.

He stood and approached the group. "Tom, did you see anything around here on your way back to Calvina's last night?"

The bartender shook his head. "Can't say I did. I usually don't walk near Horace's; it's not the most direct way."

"Gilda? Sadie? I'd imagine you were awake late as usual. Did you see or hear anything suspicious?"

"Oh, I was awake," Sadie said in a come-hither sensual voice that hinted of why she'd not been asleep. "But I didn't leave Helen's last night. When I was done entertaining, I was tired." She edged closer to Jack, keeping her eyes downcast. "I can't relax while I'm relaxing customers."

Gilda laughed uproariously at that, but Sadie's smile seemed shy.

A lazy grin spread over Jack's masculine features. "I might see how relaxed you can make a man one of these days, Sadie."

"Oh, try me, too, Jack," Gilda purred.

"Wouldn't miss it," he replied, glancing sidelong with his bright green eyes.

Spare me, Jessie thought. His sense of humor had

returned, even though he was on duty. Or maybe he wasn't attempting humor at all. She muttered beneath her breath,

> "What's more, it was said, that in ladies' beds
> Jack O'Dair had no equal, 'twas true."

He looked at her sharply. "What was that, Miss Jerome?"

"I'm just trying to remember a song I learned long ago, Mr. O'Dair," she said sweetly, approaching the nearest pile of goods, a selection of hand-made *ulus*. She picked one up by the curved handle and examined it. Its blade appeared sharp. There were things she could use an *ulu* for, right about now—like lopping off one of Lizard Songthroat's most treasured extremities, if she ever got hold of him again. He was the one who'd sent her here, after all. But why? To hear the end of the ballad? So far, she'd not even heard an inkling of even its beginning—except for verses she repeated to herself. And the avalanche hadn't occurred yet. Would she stay until she knew it all? Even if she learned it, she would still need to find a way home. If not—

"Will you sing it for us tonight at Helen's?" asked Whiskey Tom.

Jessie startled. "What's that?"

"The song you were just remembering. Everyone enjoyed your singing last night, Miss Jessie. I heard lots of compliments."

"Really? Well, thank you, Tom." She smiled her pleasure at him. She was appreciated here by some people, at least. She'd have some friends and fans, if she were forced to stay.

She glared at Jack, who was immersed in further conversation with the women from Sweet Helen's nest. She didn't know whether the information he was trying to elicit by asking them questions was personal or professional, but she had no doubt he was enjoying it.

And he clearly didn't want her assistance.

She wouldn't sing the song about him tonight or any other night. Not without knowing whether it had been written yet. She merely wanted to know its ending.

Sexy Jack O'Dair might appeal to Helen's ladies. He might be a hero, with plenty of successful exploits to come. But to Jessie, whether she stayed here or went home, he was an unattainable figment of someone's imagination—even if it was her own.

Jack was aware of Jessie Jerome's gaze on him as he discussed the theft with Sadie and Gilda.

They probably hadn't seen much, but he had learned through experience that women in their business had excellent hearing—as well as other talents. And thieves, as well as other crooks, tended to brag about their exploits. More than once, he had caught a robber thanks to an indiscreet comment to a cooperative lady of the night.

"You'll let me know, then, if you hear anything?" he asked Sadie. The poor woman had told him her story, how she had been forced into this kind of life by necessity. He tried to be kind to her, though he'd never sampled her wares. She seemed a little uncomfortable batting her eyelashes at him, and puffing out her bosom beneath her low neckline. At least she had Gilda as a friend—a bubbly, sexy, man-pleasing friend who took control and helped Sadie through.

Jessie's body was much more slender than either Sadie's or Gilda's. He wondered how her small breasts would feel in his hands. Strange thought, he told himself, while he was surrounded by so much willing flesh.

"I'll let you know anything I can," Sadie replied earnestly.

"Come by and see what else I can do for you," Gilda chimed in, licking her full, red lips suggestively.

Jack laughed, knowing he had to play along to secure their cooperation. And because he liked the women. What red-blooded man wouldn't?

Jessie didn't paint her lips, but they were still pink and lush-looking. Kissable.

Jack had already discovered that. . . .

"Thanks," he said abruptly. "I'll stop by Helen's later."

He turned to see Jessie Jerome talking with Whiskey Tom. The bartender grinned at her.

She wore a heavy skirt today of Mackinaw wool, probably borrowed from Calvina. She had on his large grizzly jacket, too, yet none of her heavy clothes hid her appealing curves. Jack was certain that Tom was well aware of Jessie's slim form beneath her warm outfit. He had an urge to interrupt their conversation, to tell Jessie to go back to Calvina's—to return to her home, wherever it might be. She was disrupting his life much too much.

She was even telling him how to do his job.

Footprints? Had she believed he was such a backwoods fool in this remote town that he would not have thought of that?

But inside Horace's, where there was no mud or snow, the thieves were hardly likely to have left footprints—unless they tracked some in. And he had already looked by the time Jessie had made her suggestion. He had found none.

Two sheepish looking men with guns at their hips sidled over to him. They were Horace's guards. Of course, they weren't the thieves themselves; they swore it. But the looks they shared as they also swore they'd been awake and present all night, told Jack the real reason the pilferers had prevailed.

Nor had he found any other clues. Not yet. But judging by what was still there, a lot of goods had been removed. Maybe there was significance in what had been stolen.

He would find the thief, oh, yes! No one would get away with this in his town.

Horace had begun letting customers back into the warehouse. The areas between his piles of goods were becoming crowded. If there had been evidence that could lead to the thieves, it would all be obliterated quickly. Jack could have stopped Horace, but to what avail? He had already seen all he had needed to, and had found nothing.

Jessie came up to him. "Jack, Tom told me this was not the first looting of goods for sale to stampeders. Is that true?"

Jack nodded warily. Where was she going with this? Another interference in how he did his job?

Of course. "Does there seem to be any pattern?" she asked. At his irritated stare, she seemed to flush. "I mean, the police where I'm from sometimes study similar incidents. Crooks often give themselves away by doing the same thing over and over. Maybe you could set a trap, if you can figure out when and where they'll strike next."

That was, in fact, a good idea. One that Jack had

already thought of. "I haven't been able to figure out a pattern, Miss Jerome," he said pleasantly, though his teeth were gritted. "Maybe I should turn all the information I have over to you and we could discuss where to go from here."

Her lovely blue eyes widened in apparent pleasure. "Well, sure. I'd be happy to help. When do you think we should talk?"

"Tonight. Over supper." Now, where had that come from? Jack hadn't asked a woman to join him for a meal since, well, he couldn't remember when.

"That would be very nice," Jessie said softly.

Jack wanted to call back his words, but it was too late. He would seem ungentlemanly if he retracted his invitation. He would have to go through with it, that was all.

But instead of aching to kick himself in his own butt for his foolishness, he found he wanted to pat himself on the back.

Jessie was glad when Jack came for her at Calvina's early that evening, as she'd requested. "I'm going to Helen's tonight to sing," she had warned before they left Horace's. "I won't be able to spend much time talking about your investigation."

His expression had turned dour, as though he hadn't really wanted to speak with her about his investigation. But why else would he have asked her to supper?

When he arrived at Calvina's, he wore his fur coat, but the hood was pushed back and his Texas-style hat seemed more stylish than warm. His trousers, though wool, were of a much dressier cut than usual.

Jessie had dressed up, too, thanks to Calvina's open-closet policy—a blue flannel skirt and white

123

blouse with a high, lacy collar. She had even swept her hair on top of her head in a close proximation to a style that seemed popular—a pouffy bun.

"You look nice, Miss Jerome." The look of appreciation in Jack's green eyes said even more than his gruff words.

"Thanks. So do you, Mr. O'Dair."

They said little on the stroll down the wide muddy strip that was Dyea's main street. The weather had warmed just a little, and some of the snow had melted into a slushy mess.

Jack led her to a large building with a high, peaked roof. A sign on its top proclaimed it the "Washington House," and another stated that it had meals available at all hours.

Jessie didn't expect much, but she was pleasantly surprised to be led to a small dining area within the hotel. The scattering of small tables was arrayed with linen tablecloths and brass candlesticks. Nearly every table was filled. A merry fire blazed in a large stone fireplace along one wall.

The aroma of warm bread filled the place, and Jessie salivated. "This place smells good," she exclaimed.

"Yes," Jack agreed. But he was standing close to her, helping her off with her jacket, and he seemed to inhale her fragrance rather than the restaurant's.

Jessie felt herself redden as she sank onto a hard wooden chair. She noticed, when Jack removed his own jacket, that he wore a suit coat. It was cut in a way that seemed old-fashioned to her, of course, but he looked wonderful in it, with its high, narrow lapels, buttoned jacket and the tie outside his white shirt collar.

A woman in an apron approached them. Her smile

contrasted with the forbidding style into which her iron-gray hair was arranged. "Hi, Jack. Miss—"

"This is Jessie Jerome, Abigail," Jack said. "Abigail is the proprietress of the Washington House and the best cook in town, though I'll deny saying that if you tell Calvina."

Jessie laughed.

"We're serving salmon or hash tonight, folks," Abigail said. Both Jack and Jessie ordered salmon.

After their hostess had brought them wine, Jessie said, "I hope I didn't give you any wrong ideas. I don't really know a lot about criminal investigations— just what I've read and seen on TV—er, what I've heard about, I mean." Without even saying anything, this man flustered Jessie so that she blundered. She could just see herself trying to explain to him that she had come from the future to find out if he was killed in an avalanche as described at the end of a ballad about him. And that she loved to watch cop shows on television, which brought the world right into a person's house via a small box. She laughed at the idea of even mentioning it.

"You're pretty when you laugh, Jessie Jerome." Jack's voice was just as gruff as when he'd complimented her earlier. But there was an appreciation in his eyes that made her feel suddenly shy.

"Thank you," she said softly.

"What were you laughing about?"

She lifted her eyebrows as she tried to decide on a response. "I'm just happy to be here," she said. And she was. For as long as she had been intrigued by "The Ballad of Jack O'Dair," she had never, in her most fanciful moments, imagined she would be having dinner with the devastatingly handsome, impossibly intrepid hero of the song.

She would remember this night forever, after she returned home.

If she ever returned home.

"Suddenly you don't look very happy." Jack's soft comment interrupted her thoughts. "Is something wrong?"

"I was just thinking of home," she said truthfully. "I don't really belong here, you know. I'll be going back soon." *Maybe*.

A shadow passed over Jack's face, stiffening his craggy features. Was she imagining it, or did he appear to care that she would be leaving?

His expression grew impassive quickly. "Just where is home, Miss Jerome? California, wasn't it? But which town?"

"Jessie," she said. "Please call me Jessie. And as a musician, I can't say that I have just one home. I travel a lot, entertaining." Again, she was able to tell the truth. "It's my life that I have to get back home to. I have a singing career that will evaporate on me if I'm gone so long that my fans start to forget about me."

"I see." He didn't sound happy about it.

She didn't want to talk about herself. That road was fraught with peril, since there were so many pitfalls in what she could say. She asked, "And what about you, Jack? Where are you from?" The ballad, for all its celebration of his life here in Alaska, didn't even give a hint of his background.

"Georgia," he said brusquely. "But that's not my home any longer. Dyea is."

"Did you grow up—"

He interrupted, "I feel as if I was born here, Jessie. Let's leave it at that."

He apparently didn't want to talk about his childhood. Intrigued and curious, Jessie wondered why.

But she felt certain she wouldn't learn the answer tonight.

Abigail served their salmon. "This is incredible!" Jessie said after taking a bite. "It never tastes like this at home—er, in any of the places I entertain." She had caught the raise of Jack's shaggy coppery brows again. Actually, she did have a home, a house in Los Angeles. But she didn't want to have to explain her stucco cottage in the San Fernando Valley. In this time, the area where her house was located was probably in the middle of an orange grove.

"How did you get to be an entertainer, Jessie?" Jack asked. "Did your family approve?"

She understood the unspoken question behind the spoken ones. Most women entertainers at this time were thought to be only a cut above the "career women" who worked at Helen's place. "My mother was a singer, too," she said truthfully. "I never knew my father." Oops. Though in her era the idea of a single woman raising a child held little stigma, at this time, Jessie knew, that not only her mother but she would be branded by all sorts of nasty epithets. Would Jack think less of her?

The idea made her heart sink clear to the toes of her heavy boots.

"I mean—" she began.

"I assume your father died when you were young." Jack's tone was soft and firm. He was a hero even in this, Jessie thought. He didn't want her to feel embarrassed.

Embarrassment was not the emotion that warmed her even more than the fire that blazed in the restaurant fireplace. It was affection for the man who had invited her here, then tried to make her feel comfortable despite what could have been the ultimate social gaffe.

"Thank you, Jack." She slid her hand across the table, and he took it. His skin was heated and rough as he squeezed her fingers in his. His touch felt as if he had struck a match and ignited some inner fire within her, for she felt sensual stirrings inside that seemed wholly inappropriate for a public restaurant in nineteenth-century Alaska.

"Thanks for what?" His green eyes held hers as though engaging her in a deep, unspoken conversation. They conveyed compassion and understanding. They conveyed appreciation—and they spoke of an answering fire within him.

Her voice was a husky whisper as she managed to say, "Everything."

"Everything?" His timbre deepened even further, and Jessie wondered how Abigail's other customers would react if she led him from the dining room and into the hotel and—

A horrible choking noise sounded beside her. Jessie turned, aghast to see a man in a well-cut suit at the table next to theirs clutching at his throat.

Another gagging sound erupted from him. His supper companion, a woman who might be his wife, screamed, "Hank! What's wrong? Someone help him, please!"

In a moment, Jack O'Dair had risen from his seat and was at the man's side. He loosened his collar. He pounded the man's back.

The man's color turned blue. As he slipped to the floor, his eyes rolled up in his head.

Chapter Nine

"Use the Heimlich maneuver!" Jessie screamed to Jack as she stood beside them.

"What?" Jack stared at her.

"Lift him up."

Jack did so.

"Now, get behind him, hold your hands together under his rib cage and hug him—hard!"

Watching Jessie, who demonstrated the hand clasp and motion in the air, Jack complied. The man still looked limp in his arms.

"Again," Jessie commanded. "Keep doing it until he can breathe."

Jack looked a little disgruntled about taking orders from her. Or maybe he just thought her nuts. But she had to hand it to him—he didn't question her; he just obeyed.

On the third squeeze, something popped out of the man's mouth, and he groaned and began once more to breathe. Jack gently lowered him back to the floor.

"Oh, thank you, Marshal O'Dair," sobbed the man's female companion as he attempted to sit up.

"You're welcome, Mrs. Nanager," Jack replied. He hadn't taken his eyes off Jessie. "But I think you have Miss Jerome to thank—"

"Not at all," Jessie broke in. "It was Mr. O'Dair all the way. I didn't do anything." Except tell him how to use a technique that won't be developed for a hundred years.

Jack held out Jessie's chair without another word, and she lowered herself into it. She was glad she had nearly finished her salmon and the excellent bread that Abigail had served with it, for her appetite had fled.

Jack O'Dair had gotten up immediately when an emergency had arisen. With no hesitation, he had thrown himself into action to help someone in need.

Once again, he had shown himself to be as heroic as the legendary man of the ballad.

The sexy, legendary man with whom Jessie had, she admitted to herself, fallen in love. At least on some level.

The sexy, legendary man who was, in fact, real.

She didn't love the actual Jack O'Dair. It was folly.

It was fate.

But she could only be hurt.

When Jack was seated across from her once more, he said in a low voice, so no one else could hear, "What did you call that little move—the high-something maneuver?"

"Never mind. I . . . I just said whatever came into my head." But something else came into her head just then—another piece of the ballad. She had assumed it was just an absurd part of the story, something of legendary proportions that could not really have happened. She certainly hadn't equated it with something as mundane as a person choking in a restaurant who was saved by the Heimlich maneuver:

"Upon the floor lying was a man who was dying
Jack was moved by the tears of his wife.
Jack stood, 'twas a fact, and then our Jack
Squeezed the dying man back to life."

Tonight, when she was by herself, she would sing all of the ballad that she knew. A lot of its verses had already come true. She would have to keep an eye on Jack to see if the rest did, too.

Then there was that damned avalanche. The one in Chilkoot Pass occurred in early April of 1898. This was the end of March.

She wanted to go home—to save her career, she told herself.

To save herself from further heartache, she realized. Just in case.

She had no doubt that Jack would behave heroically, faced with the natural disaster. But now that she had met him, how could she bear it if he didn't survive?

Jack received congratulations and back-slaps from nearly every patron in the room. He tried to make it clear, however, that he was not due the credit for saving Mr. Nanager. But each time he tried to explain Jessie's role, she shook her head and laughed with that sweet, husky voice, "Oh, he's just being modest. We all know how much of a hero Jack is."

He expected, at least, to hear a mocking tone at

those words, but could detect none. Did she actually consider him a hero?

Not that it was true, but the idea that she might deem him so made him want to stand and roar aloud in pride and pleasure.

Soon, though he felt eyes on him from everywhere in the crowded restaurant, the other patrons returned to their meals, leaving him alone again with Jessie.

"Is your salmon tasty enough?" he asked as she took a small morsel of fish and cut it with her fork until it was so tiny it nearly disappeared. "I could ask Abigail to heat it again for you."

"It's fine. Really." With what appeared to be an effort, Jessie raised the bite to her lips.

Her lips: They were full and lush and tantalizing, and she had apparently shut them against him to avoid blurting more secrets. What had she demanded that he do to save Mr. Nanager? Some kind of high maneuver?

"So, Miss Jerome—Jessie—do you know any more maneuvers like that 'high' one?" he asked conversationally. He broke off a piece of bread and began chewing the deliciously crusty mouthful.

"I think you mistook what I said," she replied. "I only wanted you to think about hieing off somewhere for help . . . er . . ." She stumbled a bit over her words. "I mean—"

"I don't believe I mistook anything," Jack said after swallowing. "I don't suppose you know how to squeeze life back into a gunshot victim—no, not after too much blood had escaped or some vital part inside was sundered. How about, do you know any maneuver that might bring the breath back to a drowned man?"

"It's called CPR," she shot back, then rolled her

lovely blue eyes toward the ceiling. "I mean, no, I don't know any such maneuver."

"C-P-R." Jack repeated the letters. "What do they stand for?"

"Curiosity promotes revenge," she hissed through her perfect, white teeth. And then she shook her head as though chastising herself. She had caught her lovely brown hair up in a knot at the top of her head, but the motion loosed some of its wayward waves. He wanted to reach over and smooth them back. No, actually, what he wished was to pull the pins from her hair, let it shimmer over her slender shoulders. . . .

He took a large swallow of wine from the glass that Abigail had refilled. And then he took another one . . . and met Jessie's eyes. There was a twinkle in their blue depths. "Am I driving you to drink, Mr. O'Dair? I could certainly say the same about you." She also reached over for her glass and took a much daintier sip than he had done. Her eyes never left his, and he felt a heat rise through him as though his blood had mixed with his wine and had begun to simmer.

"You may drive me to drink any day, Jessie," he responded from deep in his throat.

She looked quickly away. "What's your next step in investigating the theft at Horace's?" Her tone was all business. He knew she was interested—much too interested—in his work, but he also realized that she was trying to find a new topic of conversation.

"I'll work on it after we are done eating," he replied, "once I have walked you to Helen's for your performance this evening."

"Then you won't stay for awhile to listen?" Was that a touch of disappointment he heard in her voice? The thought lifted his spirits.

"I'm sorry. Filby managed to take a couple of those

who misbehaved at Horace's into custody today when they became inebriated at one of the town's saloons. They made threats that they would visit any outfitter in town to take whatever supplies they pleased. I have to go back to the jail to question them."

"Do you think they helped themselves to things at Horace's?"

"Maybe, but I am more likely to believe that they are simply talking big. They were still not themselves when I left to call on you, but perhaps by now they can coherently answer a question or two."

"I have a few I'd like to ask them, too. I've some ideas to help you get the truth from them."

"No."

Her small chin raised in defiance. "Why not?"

"It's my job, and you have something else to do. If I can, I'll come to Helen's later." Jack in fact hoped he would be able to do so; he wished more than anything to listen to this sweet, exotic, mystifying songbird enchant him for awhile with her melodies. But he could only do so if he had first had an opportunity to perform his own obligations. Alone.

He might have known, however, that when Jessie argued no further while they finished their meal, she had something on her mind.

Not that she didn't argue with him as they ate. She tried to insist that they each pay for their own meal at Abigail's—Dutch, she called it. He finally convinced her it was his responsibility since he had invited her to supper, and he also agreed that some day she could pay for them both. Over his dead body, of course, but he would deal with that situation later.

Then he walked Jessie to Helen's door—and she promptly began following him back down the icy street, hugging his fur coat around her.

"Where are you going?" he demanded.

"With you. I want to hear what your prisoners have to say. I can sing whenever I want; that's my deal with Helen."

"Stay here, Jessie."

Her stubborn refusal was written all over her lovely face. He sighed. Short of tying her up or shooting her, he could not prevent her from coming.

He would simply have to find something for her to do while he did his job—something to protect her.

"What do you mean you want me to stay out here and write out a report on the guys under arrest?" Jessie could hardly believe her ears. Did Jack O'Dair think she was some simpering little scribe? She had come here to help—really help.

She sat behind the small, rickety table that served as the marshal's desk in the slapdash wooden building that constituted his office and the . . . jail. It was just off Dyea's main street, near the docks. The acoustics weren't great; Jessie could hear snores of at least two men from beyond the closed wooden door that hid the cells.

"It would be a great favor," he said in a voice that oozed more vexation than plea. His nonchalant stance as he lounged against the door frame did not fool her; the flashing of his green eyes underscored his true, perturbed state of mind. "It's a vital report. I must send it to my superiors in Anchorage, but I have not been able to complete it with all that has gone on here."

"Delegate to Filby, then."

"He has been busy as well. Right now, he is not even here; he has gone off to get his supper."

"Tell you what," she said sweetly. "I'll be glad to

help. Let's question your inmates first, though. I'm curious about what they have to say about the thefts at Horace's and other outfitters. Then we'll both work on your report together; two people should be able to do it twice as fast as one."

Jack scowled, drawing those thick, coppery brows so close together that they nearly met. "It's *my* job to question the prisoners. What they say is not—"

"My business? Maybe not, but neither is your darned report!"

He drew his mouth into a tight line. "I could take you to Helen's right now."

"Try it." She crossed her arms and settled more into the chair.

"I enjoyed our evening, Jessie."

She stared at the soft caress of his voice.

"And I fully intend to listen to you sing at Helen's later." He took a step toward her, his large hands flexed at his sides.

"Really?" Pleasure washed through Jessie.

"But I have a job to do," he continued, "and I intend to do it to the best of my capability. I will not interfere in your performing or your work at Calvina's, and you must not intrude on my responsibilities."

"I won't intrude. I just have some . . . well, knowledge, that might be of use to you." She could hardly explain that the mysteries she loved to read, and the movies and television she enjoyed watching in her own time, had given her a tiny bit of insight into investigative techniques yet to be invented.

An emotion that Jessie did not understand passed over his strong features. His voice, when he spoke again, was so low she could hardly hear it. "People who get involved in matters that do not concern them can be hurt."

She glared at him. "Was that a threat, Mr. O'Dair?"

"No." The single syllable seemed fraught with pain, and he strode past her. He stopped beside his makeshift desk, his broad shoulders hunched. His handsome features were etched into a mask of sorrow.

What was going on?

"Jack?" She took several steps toward him, then reached out to touch his arm. "What is it?"

He took a deep breath as though bracing himself, but then he grinned, as arch a grin as she had ever seen on him. And she had already seen him smile many a roguish time.

"Never you mind, Jessie. Despite your stubbornness, I most definitely should not have allowed you to come to the jail tonight, when there are prisoners here. I knew far better. Now, either you hurry yourself along to Helen's, or I'll use some kind of high maneuver of my own to carry you there."

"No way," she said, folding her arms stubbornly.

He took a step toward her, then another. His coppery brows were raised in challenge. Jessie blinked, half in dismay . . . and half in anticipation.

She wanted to find out what he would do.

No, she didn't. "Stop, Jack," she demanded.

"Then go. It's early enough that there'll be plenty of people still on the streets. You can get to Helen's in just a couple of minutes."

"But I want to help you here. I'm *going* to help you." But she poised herself for flight as he got within arm's distance. Too late. She was going to find out what he intended to do to force her to leave, whether she wanted to or not.

"Now, how does that high maneuver go? Or is it 'C.P.R.'—convince a pretty renegade?"

She opened her mouth to respond, but he gripped her arms tightly. And then he shut her up with a firm kiss.

She moaned against his lips as his tongue encouraged her mouth to open. He tasted warm and even more intoxicating then the wine from dinner. A thread of something heady, damp and hot wriggled through her, and she drew herself closer to him. She murmured aloud as she felt how hard his chest muscles were against her breasts, and how much harder his masculine contours down below pressed into her.

"Jack," she whispered, her muscle tone suddenly the consistency of heated gelatin. What was it he was trying to convince her of? To leave? Hah! This was hardly the way to get rid of her. She clung to him, feeling him sway as well, wondering if, together, they would sink to the floor of the . . . jail. They were in the jailhouse in the gold rush town of Dyea. Beyond the door were some men who might still be sleeping it off—but if their snores had been so audible to Jessie, her sounds of lovemaking mixed with Jack's would clearly be audible to the drunkards and thieves who were locked up.

"Mmmm," Jack muttered against her mouth. "Convinced, pretty renegade?" His lips moved downward, causing shudders of desire to course through her as he nipped gently at her neck.

"No," she whispered as her mouth was set free.

He didn't stop, but his tongue began to stroke her collarbone with moist abandon. How had he managed to undo the top buttons of her blouse without her knowing it?

"Jack, no," she repeated more firmly. She tried to

push him away, but her will hadn't caught up with her traitorously aroused body. Instead, she continued to cling to him as his languorous, exquisite assault on her senses continued. "This is insane," she muttered. Taking a deep breath, she managed to step back.

She watched the glaze of passion in his slitted eyes segue to awareness. He cocked his head in amusement as a tiny smile lifted one corner of the incredibly sexy mouth that had been all over her a moment earlier.

No not all over her. If it had been, she might never have mustered the strength to pull away.

"Seduction isn't going to keep me from helping you," Jessie said conversationally, although her breathing had not settled down to anything near normal.

"Just who was seducing whom?" Jack asked, irony painting laughter into his deep voice.

"It doesn't matter. Look, let me stay for now. If you want, I'll feed you questions rather than ask them myself. But I may be of assistance. Really."

All trace of amusement vanished from Jack's face. "You're not going to get involved—"

"I am." Jessie glared at him, her hands on her hips. She noticed his gaze travel from her eyes downward, and change from hard determination to interest. Quickly, she redid the buttons of her blouse.

"Tell you what," she said. "Just leave the door to the cell room open. I don't have to go inside. I'll listen from here. We'll devise a signal. When you hear it, you can come out and I'll give you my suggestions. They won't even know I'm here."

"They'd have to be pretty thick-headed not to know what's going on."

Jessie took heart; at least this time Jack didn't say

no. "You'd still be protecting me," she argued. "They may know someone's here, but they won't know who. Okay?"

Jack shook his head, but apparently more in exasperation than denial, for he strode toward the door and pulled it open.

The argument with Jessie had been for naught, Jack realized as he went over Filby's notes to prepare for interrogating the prisoners.

He could have been more insistent. He could have thrown her out bodily so he could get his work done. But, to be honest with himself, he had begun to wonder what questions she would want to ask the prisoners.

She seemed highly intelligent. Her insight in saving Mr. Nanager and otherwise had been impressive.

And her idea of keeping behind the door: she was right; it should be sufficient to protect her identity.

So he regretted—a little—having argued with her over this, a relatively small matter.

He suspected there would be matters of far greater significance in which he would not wish to concede.

And that kiss? . . . *That* he did not regret. Not in the least.

"I've jotted down a few preliminary questions," she said, interrupting his thoughts. He looked up at her. She stood beside the desk with a piece of paper. The expression in her lovely blue eyes seemed anxious, as if she were eager to please him.

That, clearly, was an act. Jessie Jerome would do as she wished, without worrying about pleasing anyone.

Still, the idea that she cared about his opinion sent a surge of pleasure through him.

He glanced at her notes. She had come up with a list of questions that, taken in the order she suggested, might subtly elicit a full confession from the thieves. Amazing! She started with some apparently innocuous queries, such as whether they were stampeders, what kinds of supplies had they been told would be needed in the Yukon, what supplies had they brought with them, and how had they intended to pay for more. She suggested asking where they resided while in Dyea and where their caches had been stored. Were there any others who were their traveling companions? All were logical, non-threatening questions.

But then her suggestions meandered into more incisive questions about what supplies the prisoners now had, whether they had more than enough for themselves—and how they had obtained the extra supplies.

A good approach, he had to admit. Well, perhaps he needn't admit it. . . .

"Preliminary questions?" he asked, referring to her comment. "These appear to be an entire interrogation."

"Maybe so," she admitted. Her eyes scanned his as though trying to determine his opinion. "But it should work, don't you think?"

He shrugged casually. "Perhaps. But don't you think I should be more forceful, demand that they confess?"

Her expression turned scornful. "Do you intend to use thumbscrews? Threaten their mothers or their privates?" He raised his eyebrows in amusement, but she shook her head so that her lovely waves of hair swept her shoulders. "I've never seen a crook yet who just caves under the pressure of a lawman who just requested a confession. Not without something more."

"And have you seen a crook cave under the pressure of thumbscrews or threats to his privates?" Though teasing, he was interested in her response. He suspected there was more to Jessie Jerome than a mere beautiful balladeer or pretty renegade. She still had not explained how she had come to his house that night. Or why. Had his superiors in the U.S. marshal's office sent her to spy on how he was faring as the law in Dyea?

They would have better things to do with their time and resources. For one thing, things were going on in neighboring Skagway that were scandalous. A blackguard named Soapy Smith had all but taken over the town. Fortunately, he had not attempted to spread his nefarious influence to Dyea—yet. And if he ever did, Jack was fully prepared to take action.

Nothing like that would be allowed in *his* town.

"I . . . I haven't seen such things in person." Jessie appeared mightily discomfited. Jack wondered why.

"Then where have you seen them?" he asked.

"I've . . . just heard about them."

He knew she was lying. He just did not know why. But before he could question her further, she said, "Why don't you just go ahead and start questioning your prisoners, as we discussed. If anything else comes to mind, I'll let you know."

"I am certain you will," Jack said wryly. But rather than argue with her anymore, he walked toward the door behind which his prisoners lay.

Chapter Ten

Jessie practically kept her ear pressed against the door, Taku panting at her side. Jack had left his dog at the jail during dinner to help Filby guard the prisoners, he had told her. Taku had seemed glad to see him on his return. Jessie, too. She'd befriended the dog with frequent praises and pats.

Jessie thought she heard most of what went on inside the cell. She felt proud that Jack seemed to follow her script, though he added nuances of his own—clever ones that elicited spontaneous, incriminating comments.

Maybe she hadn't needed to help him after all.

But she had seen so many different kinds of witness-interrogation techniques on "Law and Order," and "NYPD Blue," not to mention reruns of "Columbo." Surely her efforts had been helpful.

The prisoners' answers, however, were not—at least not entirely. As Jessie had anticipated, no one broke down, fell to his knees and confessed all. Instead, they seemed disgruntled that the marshal had delayed them by a day in their next trek to the top of Chilkoot Pass.

"Let us go, marshal," muttered one whom Jessie had nicknamed to herself "Dismal" for his constant complaints. "We won't drink any more in town."

"What about those supplies that disappeared?" Jack asked. "What do you know about them?"

"Not a thing, I swear."

"Well, then, have you seen anything unusual in your treks to the top of the pass? Maybe run into someone who has enough extra to sell goods?"

"Like I told you before," Dismal sniveled, "I don't keep track of nobody's business but my own."

"And if I go to where you're boarding, I won't find anything in your room but your own business?" Jack's voice had gradually turned cold. "No extra supplies?"

"How would I know?" Dismal grumbled. "I ain't been there since this morning."

"Since you didn't deny it, I'm going to suppose there is extra stuff there. How did you get it?"

There was a pause, as though Dismal were considering his reply. "I didn't do nothing wrong," he finally whined. "Someone gave me—"

"Shut up!" hollered the other prisoner, whom Jessie had nicknamed "Foghorn" since his voice was low but still carried over everyone else's.

"Maybe you have something else to say?" Jack asked.

"Not me," Foghorn said. "I ain't saying nothing."

"Then let your friend talk."

But Dismal had gotten the message and shut up.

"Tell me about the extra things in your room," Jack demanded anyway.

"Ain't none," Dismal grumped.

"I can find that out easily enough," Jack said.

That caused Jessie to thump on the wall—the signal Jack and she had devised. In a moment, he joined her behind the door. He had removed his suit jacket, loosened his tie and unbuttoned the top button of his white shirt.

He looked unhappy. "I think I've gotten as much from them as I'm going to for now," he said.

Jessie grinned. "Tell them that the person who just banged on the wall was Filby, who's come from Dismal's room."

"Dismal?"

Jessie shrugged. "Your more talkative prisoner. Tell them that Horace was there with Filby, too, and identified some goods stolen from him. You're about to file charges to keep Dismal in jail for the rest of his life, which won't be too long; stealing from caches can be a capital offense, can't it?"

Jack nodded. "That's what the vigilance committee at the top of the pass wants, though most thieves are just flogged. But the stuff in Horace's warehouse hasn't made it to a cache yet."

"Dismal won't know the difference. You can tell him anything."

Jack grinned and nodded. "You're right."

In another minute, Dismal was singing like a light-addicted canary whose cover was snatched from his cage. He did have stolen goods in his possession. He hadn't stolen them, though. Nor could he tell them who had.

But he did admit one very important thing that would help Jack, Jessie was glad to hear: He and Foghorn, whose real name was Madden, hadn't acted alone. There was a gang of thieves. The thefts from Horace's had been connected with those at other outfitters' stores.

And Horace's theft would not be the last.

"So admit it," Jessie said lightheartedly as they walked through a blustery night wind toward Helen's. The evening had grown much colder. Jessie's lips worked slowly in the frigid air. "I done good."

"What do you mean?" Jack's hands were stuck in his pockets. Jessie turned sideways to peer at him around the hood that she had turned up to shield her head. She could see in the dim lights from candles in windows that Jack's face was scrunched up against the cold beneath the hood he, too, had pulled up over his ears; he had left his western-style hat at the jail. Taku trotted at his feet; for now, Filby had been left alone to guard the prisoners after Jack had checked the lock on the cell door.

"I done good," she repeated. "I came up with a system of interrogation that helped you get some helpful stuff on those guys."

They passed before a hotel, where the lights were a little brighter. The look Jack shot at her was quizzical. "Where did you say you were from, Jessie Jerome? I understand all your words, but sometimes you sound as if you're speaking another language."

"Oh, it's English, all right." But Jessie realized she had better try to restrain herself from the slang of her time—as long as she could distinguish it from the language of the day. "Anyway, admit it, O'Dair. I helped you."

"Okay, you helped me. But you didn't need to—"

"Stow it," she said good naturedly. "Admit defeat gracefully, Jack."

She could feel his glare without turning to see him. And then she laughed aloud. "Have I got a ballad to sing to you tonight," she said. At her feet, Taku let out a bark as though agreeing with her, and she laughed again.

When they reached Helen's, a lot of stampeders and other patrons recognized Jessie. They shouted greetings to her. "What you gonna sing for us tonight?" a man she'd met previously called to her. "I wanna hear something mighty sweet, Jessie."

"Did your trip to the Yukon go sour, Efraim?" she joked. The audience laughed.

She got her guitar from the back room at Helen's where she had left it the night before. Whiskey Tom put a chair on the stage, and she sat down, crossing one leg over the other beneath her long blue skirt.

She noted some familiar faces in the audience, including Lester, the guy who had caused all the fuss the previous day, portly Eldon Riggs and one of the town's outfitters, Otis Oetting—all the men who had been so complimentary of her singing the night before.

Good, Jessie thought; a friendly crowd.

Helen informed her that Arnett would not be there that evening, so Jessie would supply all the night's entertainment.

She watched Jack settle down at a table with some people he apparently knew, Taku lying at his feet. Then Jessie began the song she had vowed earlier to sing to Jack. It was one no one here had ever heard, for it was a popular ballad from a time between now and her own. It was sung to the old tune of "Mighty Joe Magerac," and it was the story of a bull-headed man who was a lone lumberjack—until a beautiful woman from a nearby town outsmarted him. A sweet songbird sang in the tree he had targeted to ax. The woman suggested a bet to save both tree and bird, and the over-confident man agreed. He lost to the clever woman, but at the same time won as they together worked out a compromise. He came to appreciate the birds, and she came to realize the worth of building new homes with the wood he chopped.

Since Jessie hadn't sung this song for a while, she had to pay more attention to fingering her guitar than her audience's reaction. She glanced up now and then but couldn't find Jack in the crowd.

Strange. With his bright red hair, he should stand out. He had promised to be there, to listen to her. She didn't think him the kind of man to break promises— was he?

When she finished her song, there was a silence in the saloon filled with nearly all men. And then Sweet Helen shouted, "That's the way, Jessie!" Her applause was taken up first by Gilda the Gold, Skagway Sadie, and the rest of the girls. The male patrons seemed more reluctant to cheer but soon joined in enthusiastically.

Jessie looked around again. Jack was there after all, in a corner, partly hidden behind the end of the bar. He had stayed!

As well he should have. She had intended a gentle message to him through the song: that a big, strong man could have a sensible, sensitive side and take a woman's suggestions gracefully. Jack's hands were raised as he clapped, but his eyes seemed not to be on her but on Eldon Riggs and Otis Oetting, who both sat at his table. Damn. Had he paid any attention at all to her song?

She sang a few more ballads—well-known folk-tunes of the past plus a couple of her more obscure favorites: a sea chanty and a lively Appalachian reel. They were all received with more spontaneous enthusiasm than her song with a message—not that she was surprised. Since the tunes she played now were second-nature to her, she hardly had to glance at her fingering. Instead, as she belted out rip-roaring adventure songs, as she crooned emotional tunes of woe, she watched Jack—as he watched her. Whether or not he had paid attention to her during the first song she would never know, but for now he didn't take his big, beautiful, intense green eyes off her.

She sang to him. For him.

And as she ended "Oh, Susanna," her fingers unconsciously slid into the introductory chords of, "The Ballad of Jack O'Dair."

As she realized what she had done, she immediately segued into a rousing rendition of "Clementine."

What would Jack have done if she had continued? If she'd begun to sung the paean to his heroism right here, in front of this crowd?

He wouldn't have liked it. She felt certain of that.

When she had finished the last chorus of "Clementine," Jessie called, "I need a break, folks. Thanks for being such a great audience."

"Don't stop, Jessie," yelled a plaintive male voice.

"We love you, Jessie," cried another—who sounded like Lester. At least he wasn't drunk beyond control.

Smiling, she blew a general kiss toward them all. Then, she joined Jack.

He was not alone at the table, but his human companions were strangers to Jessie. She glanced around but did not see Eldon or Otis. In fact, the only others she knew in the saloon besides Jack were Whiskey Tom and Sweet Helen. She recalled how Otis had praised her singing previously. Obviously he had not become her biggest fan, after all.

"So," she said, settling onto on a hard wooden chair, "what did you think of my first song?"

"Which was that?"

"The lumberjack one," said another man at the table sourly. "Who would want to save a stupid bird anyway?"

Jessie drew herself up straighter. "Anyone who cares about nature," she responded stiffly. "This place may still be a wilderness, but someday there will be so many people in the Lower Forty-Eight—er, I mean, the United States—that a lot of people will come to consider every natural resource, every bird and animal, to be precious."

"Where are all them people gonna come from?" asked a grizzled older man, eyeing her suspiciously.

Jessie laughed, trying to hide her discomfort. "Oh, I don't know," she said. "I'm just being silly."

She dared a glance at Jack. He was staring at her as oddly as the rest of the men at the table. She grinned and shrugged. "Looks as though it's time for me to sing some more. What's your favorite?" she asked the man who had been plying her with questions.

He had been a Union soldier in the Civil War, he told her. He chose, "Battle Hymn of the Republic."

It was a song that Jessie loved. Back on stage with her guitar on her lap, her eyes closed, she started it softly, gradually increasing the volume, and emotion, in her voice. When she had finished there was utter silence for a long minute, as there had been after her first offering of the evening.

She opened her eyes and looked around in alarm. Had they all hated this one, too? Maybe all but the old man would have preferred "Dixie." She could sing it, too, if they wanted. . . .

And then the entire place swelled with the loud staccato of thunderous applause. Relieved, Jessie felt herself smile as men whistled, rose to their feet, called her name.

She dared a glance at Jack. He stood near his table, clapping more enthusiastically than anyone. Jessie glowed proudly inside. He had liked her song, too.

The evening passed quickly as Jessie took requests. Many of them were for songs reminiscent of the customers' homes—"Dixie," "My Old Kentucky Home" and "Deep in the Heart of Texas." Even a few of Helen's girls whom Jessie had not met before shouted out names of songs they liked.

Jessie had just started "Danny Boy" for a man who'd come from Ireland when the door to the saloon burst open.

"Marshal O'Dair, you in here?" Horace Martin rushed in, looking highly upset.

Jack stood. "Right here."

"You have to come. I got another shipment today—and my place has been robbed again."

"Not in *my* town, damn it!" muttered Jack.

Jack wished Horace had not announced the burglary so publicly. Nearly everyone at Helen's trooped down the dark, cold street after them, toward Horace's.

Among them was Jessie Jerome. "Maybe I can help," she had whispered before he had left.

"You can help most by staying here," he had replied without even looking at her. "Keep everyone amused and out of my way."

151

"Including me," she had fumed in his ear. And then he had known he would not be able to stop her from coming unless he used some "high" maneuver and locked her in jail.

Which would not have been a bad idea. But just then, he hadn't time.

Horace had lit torches that blazed inside his large store, the flickering glow visible in the distance from the windows and inside the canvas between the buildings as they approached.

When Jack held back a flap to let Taku go in, Jessie, at his side, asked, "Hadn't you better tell everyone to wait out here? You don't want them contaminating any evidence."

He glared at her. He had intended to stand in the doorway, surveying all he could from there—and blocking anyone else's entry. "What a fine idea." He smiled through gritted teeth. "I never would have thought of it."

"No need to be nasty. I was only trying to help."

"I told you before how you could help," he replied. But this time his tone was kinder.

"You'll be glad I'm here," she said. "Wait and see."

He didn't respond, though somehow, deep inside, he *was* glad she was here. He did not know how she knew anything about law enforcement, but the questions she had suggested he ask the pair in jail had, in fact, been useful. Maybe she would have something to offer here, as well.

And somehow he just liked having her around. Where he could keep an eye on her, of course . . . keep her out of trouble.

"Anyway," Jessie continued, "obviously the thieves

this time aren't Foghorn and Dismal—unless Filby's let them out of jail."

"He'll be there instead if he allowed them to escape," Jack said grimly. He faced the crowd. "All right," he called. "I don't want any of you inside until I say so. I need to look around without anyone 'contaminating the evidence.' " He shot a wry glance at Jessie, who smiled broadly.

It was all he could do not to smile back.

He followed Horace into the warehouse. "Where are your guards?" Jack asked.

"Fired 'em, after last time," Horace replied. "I've an agent in Seattle who's sending up a couple more, but they haven't come yet."

Jack forbore from mentioning that it might have been prudent to keep on the former guards, for show at least, till the new ones arrived. Maybe not. They'd been of little assistance before.

Taku was already inside, sniffing around and whining. Several piles of goods that Jack had noted earlier were much smaller, though he didn't know whether that was due to Horace's activities or that of the thieves. The place was filled with a pleasant aroma, as though containers of smoked beef had been opened.

"I closed up, like always, about six o'clock," Horace told him as they strode farther inside. "I'd already put aside goods for some of my customers to add to their caches. That's one reason that stack of flour and that other of dried potatoes are so low. But look here." He pointed to an area in a corner that seemed scrambled. "This is where I had everything sorted. Now it's nearly all gone."

"Did you do an inventory?" asked a feminine voice from behind Jack.

He whirled. "Didn't I do just as you said and tell everyone to stay outside? That meant you, too."

"Oh." Was that a touch of embarrassment on her lovely face? If so, she hid it quickly. "I assumed you meant everyone else, since I told you I could help."

"It included you. The best help you can be is to keep out of the way." A thought struck him. "Maybe you can make sure everyone else stays out. Yes, that's what you can do."

"But—"

"Goodbye, Miss Jerome." Jack turned his back on her and waited a moment to make certain she had time to leave. He listened for receding footsteps behind him before he asked Horace, "Now, *did* you take an inventory?"

The older man smiled thinly. "Miss Jerome had the right idea, didn't she? Yes, I took an inventory, but that was before I brought the new shipment inside. And then I began stacking things into caches. Plus, some stampeders came just before I closed and took their supplies. The inventory won't help now."

Jack wandered around looking for evidence, Taku at his side. At one point, the dog got excited and barked, but he only had found a piece of the smoked meat—perhaps dropped by the thief, but not something to help identify him.

Jack wanted to slam something. Horace had been robbed again, practically under Jack's nose, and there was nothing he could do about it.

"Jack," called Jessie. She had not left the store after all. Instead, she stood near the door watching him. "Have you found any clues?"

"Stay out, Jessie," he grumbled.

"I assume that means no. Look, I won't get in the way of your investigating, I promise. But may I make

154

some suggestions to Horace to help him catch the thieves if they come back?"

"You think they'll come back *again*?" Horace sounded stricken.

Jessie was beside them both in a second, as though Horace had invited her. Maybe he had.

"I've just seen . . . er, read of a few techniques that'll make it easier to identify crooks if they do come back. You can follow them, then let it be known you've taken steps to make the thieves give themselves away if they dare to return. That way, they'll be more inclined to rob someone else, someone whose establishment will be less trouble for them to hit."

"Great idea," Horace said.

It wasn't a bad idea, Jack thought—not for Horace. But for him . . . "What good will it do if they simply steal from someplace else?" he demanded.

Jessie shrugged. "If you advise the other outfitters about the techniques, it may make it impossible for thieves to steal from anyone here without being detected. Maybe you'll catch them. At worst, maybe they'll move on and steal from people in some other town."

"What are these wonderful techniques?" Jack asked. He intended not to sound the least bit interested—but he was.

"Well, you can set bait," she began. And then she described ways to hide pepper in boxes that, if grabbed wrong, could shoot the stinging material into thieves' eyes. Then there was the idea of putting coal dust along areas of the floor. "If the weather stays like this, it won't help much," she said. "But once it starts snowing, footprints will show up like anything. You'll need to sweep it all up each morning, though,

155

or you'll only catch a bunch of the next day's customers. And," she said, catching Jack's eye. "I have one idea that's the best of all—a guard dog."

She glanced quizzically toward Taku and back. Jack assumed she was asking if he would be willing to lend his dog to the cause.

He wasn't. He needed Taku to be able to do his work most effectively. And Taku was *his* dog, his companion. "I have a friend in Skagway who's brought a bunch of sled dogs there recently," Jack said. "I'll help you train one for protection, if you want, Horace."

The old man's sad eyes brightened. "That might do the trick. Especially if we can find us a dog that doesn't much like strangers and isn't afraid to bite a thief."

Jack nodded. He turned back to Jessie. "You have some fine ideas, Miss Jerome. Sometime we'll have to discuss where you heard of them."

Her smile was a little mysterious, and, if he knew human nature, a lot uneasy.

This was something he would pursue with her. Later.

For now, he still had work to do. He was about to address Jessie again when the tent flap opened and people started streaming in.

"We've waited out there long enough," said Eldon Riggs. "We want to know what's going on."

"That's right," Otis Oetting agreed. "Do you have any information yet about what happened? I sent a couple of my employees over to my store to make sure no one robbed me, too."

Jack noted that Skagway Sadie hung onto Eldon's arm, and Gilda the Gold stood right beside Otis. He'd been aware of the four of them talking after Eldon excused himself from Jack's table. The way the women had pressed themselves against the men . . . well, it was no surprise Jack hadn't noticed any of them later in the crowd at Helen's. They had obviously paired up in rooms upstairs. He only wondered why they were done so quickly. But as he well knew, there were plenty of other interested men to take over with Sadie and Gilda when Eldon and Otis were finished. If he didn't have a job to do, maybe even he . . .

Who was he trying to fool? He had no interest in these women. In fact, if they offered their wares to him for free this evening, he would turn them down.

His mind was on Jessie.

He wished his body were, too.

She stood near him, but not near enough. "You can help with this," he said to her. "I don't want the whole town here now. Tell them you're going with them back to Helen's, then continue your show. I'll come by for you there to walk you home later, after I'm done here." He paused and looked at her steadily, knowing full well that issuing her orders, no matter how sensible, would do no good. "Please, Jessie," he said softly. "I don't know of anyone else here who can get this crowd back where it belongs besides you."

Surprise widened those large blue eyes of hers. Was that pleasure he saw there, too?

He liked that look. Liked it a lot.

He would have to see if he could put it there again.

But only in a crowd, as now. For that expression created an urge in him to kiss Jessie—and he knew how foolish that was.

"Sure, Jack," she told him softly. "I'll take care of the crowd for you." She walked away from him, and he observed the soft sway of her hips beneath the long, heavy jacket she wore. His jacket. It kept her warm, caressed her curves . . . just as he wanted to do.

"Come on, everyone," she called, fortunately breaking his foolish train of thought. "We're in the way here. But there are a lot more songs coming up at Helen's. Follow me!"

The crowd parted to let her through as though she had drawn a heated knife through soft butter. They all turned to pursue her. Of course they would. They were mostly men. What man wouldn't follow Jessie?

Only then did she turn back in Jack's direction. She lifted her hands and began clapping a rhythm that everyone took up as a thunking of thick glove on glove rather than flesh on flesh. Jessie smiled at her followers as she began singing "Sweet Betsy From Pike."

But then she gave a long, slow, seductive wink, and Jack felt it had been directed just at him.

At least Jack had listened to her sing earlier, Jessie thought a long while later as she sat in a corner at Helen's nursing a drink of sarsaparilla. She had just sung her heart out again, and her throat and fingers now needed a rest.

She figured Sweet Helen's nest, still teeming with customers, wouldn't close till the sky was nearly light—late morning. But she could not sing that long.

Jack had said he would come back to walk her to Calvina's, but he clearly had gotten caught up at Horace's.

She didn't need to wait for him.

She took her glass back up to the bar, which was surrounded by men with drinks in their hands. "Sing something else, Jessie," slurred one of the men who had been there all evening.

"Tomorrow," she said, pinching the man's cool, loose cheek. The customers around them laughed.

"See you back at Calvina's," Jessie said to Whiskey Tom, who was pouring a whiskey into a large glass.

"You leaving?" he asked.

Jessie nodded. "Helen wants me back to sing again tomorrow—er, tonight. I'll need some sleep."

Tom grinned. "Right."

When Jessie stepped out of Helen's, she noticed right away that the night was even colder now than when she had followed Jack and Horace only a couple of hours earlier. The wind howled between Dyea's buildings. She pulled her coat tightly around her and hugged the fur hood about her head.

Maybe she should have borrowed a bed that night at Helen's. On the other hand, she had seen Helen's girls appear and disappear all evening onto the second floor. If she had been correct, Eldon had gone with Sadie and Otis had been with Gilda. At least they had shown up paired that way at Horace's.

In any event, upstairs at Helen's was not a place Jessie aspired to. In any way.

It wasn't far to Calvina's, she told herself. The dirt street was hard, its mud frozen to brown ice.

Jessie stepped out to cross a small alley between two buildings and thought she heard a sound.

And then something heavy was thrown over her head.

Chapter Eleven

"When did she leave?" Jack tried not to take out his irritation on Whiskey Tom. The bartender had no control over Jessie Jerome's comings and goings. No one did—especially not Jack.

He hadn't intended to take so long finishing up at Horace's. But he'd had to be thorough.

He had appreciated Jessie's unexpected crime prevention techniques, but they were not enough. Jack was going to catch the thieves—quickly. And that meant making certain he missed no clues.

But, curse the sly cunning of the crooks, he had found nothing helpful. And Jessie had left for Calvina's without him.

Tom shrugged. "She left maybe half an hour ago."

"Thanks." Jack buttoned his jacket again, called to Taku and left Helen's, his re-lit lantern in his hand. He should head home, he figured. Filby had things at the jail under control. Jessie was probably safe in bed at Calvina's.

But he had promised to walk her home. That had made her his responsibility, damn it! Not that he wanted any more responsibilities. But he wouldn't be able to sleep without assuring himself that the stubborn woman was all right, even though he had no reason to believe otherwise.

A light was on in the front parlor at Calvina's. Jack knocked softly.

Renny opened the door. "Jack, my friend." He ushered Jack and Taku inside and closed the door against the cold. "What brings you here again in the middle of our long night?"

"Same as last time," Jack grumbled, unbuttoning the top buttons of his jacket in the cozy room warmed by a blazing fire. Taku immediately settled down in front of the stone hearth. "Miss Jerome. This time, I didn't walk her home, though I'd intended to. Is she still awake?"

A frown creased the young man's otherwise unlined brow, exaggerating the prominence of his bent nose. "I would assume so. She hasn't come in yet."

"What?" But Jack knew he should not have sounded so surprised. Somewhere, deep in his gut, he had feared that she had not gone home. That something had happened to her.

Foolish. That's what he was. The woman was clearly not of the inclination to become one of Helen's girls, but neither was she shy and retiring. Maybe she had gone home with one of the stampeders who had come to hear her sing that night. She flirted with everyone, after all. Shamelessly. So seductively it got him right where it hurt: his gut, and below.

161

But now Jack's heart was pounding, and the harsh rhythm was knocking all sense out of his mind.

"Is there some reason to worry about her? I'll help you search for her." Renny went to the clothes rack near the door and took down his own heavy fur jacket.

"Don't bother. I'm sure she's fine." Jack spouted his theory about a tryst with one of Helen's customers.

"Do you think that's so?" Renny sounded as dubious as Jack felt. "You know her better than I do."

But Jack didn't know her—not well enough.

Still, he did not want to look ridiculous by raising an alarm and embarrassing both Jessie and himself when he located her, quite willing and contented, in some man's room.

He wanted to slam something at the thought—even though he couldn't believe it, not with all indications, and his instincts, to the contrary. But where was she?

"I'm sure she's fine," Jack lied. "I'm going to head home myself. Come on, Taku."

Outside in the cold, a scarf wound about his face, Jack walked briskly while he pondered what to do. Beside him, Taku whined. His dog always sensed when Jack felt uneasy. He bent and patted the dog with a thick leather glove. "What do you think, boy? Should we go look for her?"

But where? She wasn't at Helen's. Dyea, though not huge, was growing every day. Was he to awaken every stampeder in town looking for Jessie—just in case?

No. He would do exactly what he had told Renny: go home. In the morning, he would check Calvina's and Helen's again, and if no one had seen or heard from Jessie, then he would have reason for concern. Not now.

Then why did his skin prickle as much as if he had pulled off all of his outer garments in the frigid Dyea night?

Just in case, he retraced the most direct route between Calvina's and Helen's, his glance darting from one end of the street to the other. He used his lantern to peer into alleys between the wooden buildings.

He found a drunk he awakened and sent on his way. Good thing, too; the fool probably would have frozen to death by morning. The temperature might stay above zero degrees; then again, it might not. He had at least fulfilled part of his responsibility as marshal that evening: saving a life.

He did not find Jessie.

He peered into the window at Helen's but did not see Jessie there. He was beginning to feel awfully cold, and Taku whined a lot. Still, Jack made one more trip between Helen's and Calvina's. He peered in the window in Calvina's lighted parlor. Renny was asleep in a chair. If Jessie had come in, they would still be conversing . . . wouldn't they?

Jack shook his head. It would do no one any good if he froze while on a wild goose chase for a female who would resent the pursuit, if ever she learned of it. It was time to go home.

Keeping his lantern high enough to light his path, he headed out of town.

As he reached the last couple of buildings at the edge of Dyea, Taku barked and began running. "What is it, boy?" Jack called. His dog barked again from the alley.

And then he heard a groan.

Quickly, he followed the direction in which Taku

had gone. In moments, he fell to his knees on the frozen ground.

Jessie lay there. Taku was nudging her side. She moaned again, but did not awaken.

Jack touched her face. It was as cold as the ice on the Chilkoot steps. "No," he muttered. "You'll be all right, you understand me, Jessie?"

With no hesitation, he lifted her into his arms and hurried to the nearest place of shelter he could think of on this side of the growing town: his cabin.

She was cold. So cold. Jessie was aware there were blankets over her, and still she shivered.

She slitted one eye open, then let it drop closed again.

"Oh, no," said a familiar male voice. "Wake up. You've been out long enough."

Jessie tried to shake her head, but it was too much of an effort.

"Come on, Jessie." She felt herself being pulled to a sitting position.

"Leave me alone," she tried to mumble, but she couldn't quite say the words; her teeth were chattering.

"What was that? Talk to me."

She felt her body slump like a rag doll's, only to be propped upright again.

"Sit up," the voice demanded.

"Too cold," she protested.

"Here." In a moment, she felt her arms being massaged by the rough wool of the blanket. It scratched her. Her skin suddenly felt as though it was on fire.

"Stop," she shouted, opening her eyes.

She was in familiar surroundings: Jack's cabin. Clothes hung on the pegs along the wall. A fire

Thrill to the most sensual, adventure-filled Romances on the market today...

FROM  LOVE SPELL BOOKS

As a home subscriber to the Love Spell Romance Book Club, you'll enjoy the best in today's BRAND-NEW Time Travel, Futuristic, Legendary Lovers, Perfect Heroes and other genre romance fiction. For five years, Love Spell has brought you the award-winning, high-quality authors you know and love to read. Each Love Spell romance will sweep you away to a world of high adventure...and intimate romance. Discover for yourself all the passion and excitement millions of readers thrill to each and every month.

Save $5.00 Each Time You Buy!

Every other month, the Love Spell Romance Book Club brings you four brand-new titles from Love Spell Books. EACH PACKAGE WILL SAVE YOU AT LEAST $5.00 FROM THE BOOKSTORE PRICE! And you'll never miss a new title with our convenient home delivery service.

Here's how we do it: Each package will carry a FREE 10-DAY EXAMINATION privilege. At the end of that time, if you decide to keep your books, simply pay the low invoice price of $17.96, no shipping or handling charges added. HOME DELIVERY IS ALWAYS FREE. With today's top romance novels selling for $5.99 and higher, our price SAVES YOU AT LEAST $5.00 with each shipment.

AND YOUR FIRST TWO-BOOK SHIP-MENT IS TOTALLY FREE!

IT'S A BARGAIN YOU CAN'T BEAT! A SUPER $11.48 Value!

Love Spell ✦ A Division of Dorchester Publishing Co., Inc.

Get Two Books Totally
FREE—
An $11.48 Value!

PLEASE RUSH
MY TWO FREE
BOOKS TO ME
RIGHT AWAY!

Love Spell Romance Book Club
P.O. Box 6613
Edison, NJ 08818-6613

AFFIX
STAMP
HERE

danced in the stove at one end of the room, the brightness of the flames creating dancing reflections on the canvas at the windows. One of the stove's black metal doors was open, and Jessie could feel heat radiate into the room.

Why was she still so cold?

She must have asked the question aloud. "Because you were unconscious in an alley a little while ago. Your jacket was unbuttoned and your boots were off."

"Why?" And then it came to her. "Someone attacked me!"

Dazed, she looked at Jack. He sat beside her on the bed. He had stopped massaging her, and now he just stared. His expression was unreadable. There was something in his eyes, though. Not pain . . . was it? Concern? Anger?

Fear?

Not Jack O'Dair. He wasn't afraid of anything.

"Do you remember now what happened?" His voice was even, not reflecting any emotion at all.

"No," she said quickly. Then she amended, "A little. I was just walking, and . . . and someone threw something over me, I think. And then—"

"Then?" he prompted.

Her shoulders went limp. "He hit me on the head. Here." She raised her hand from beneath the blanket to touch her right temple. At even her own soft touch, she winced. "I don't recall anything after that."

Her fingers were followed by Jack's. She gasped at the fierce pain as he felt around the sore area.

"You have a big bump there. I found it earlier, when I checked you over for broken bones."

He had checked her over? Only then did she realize. . . . "I'm naked under here!" She pulled the blanket away and glanced down at herself. "And you

165

examined me?" Indignation nearly made her leap out of bed. At the same time, a warmth trickled through her that had nothing to do with the fire burning in the room, everything to do with a heat radiating from deep inside her.

Jack O'Dair had undressed her. And, darn it all, she hadn't been conscious to react.

She shook her head to rid herself of the absurdly inappropriate thought.

"Your clothes were wet—clear through," Jack said. "There wasn't a lot of snow on the ground. I think whoever attacked you wet you down, left you to die of exposure." He paused. "It might have looked like an accident, especially if it snowed tonight."

"Oh." Jessie felt like curling into a little ball. She knew her horror was reflected on her face.

Jack touched her cheek gently. "Do you know who did it?"

She shook her head, and grimaced again at the pain. "Why would anyone in your town want to kill me?" She had begun shivering anew, but it had little to do with the cold. Her teeth clicked like percussion instruments, and she thrust her tongue out just far enough to stop the sound.

"I was going to ask you the same question."

"I haven't been here long enough to make any enemies." She didn't really have many enemies anywhere. Curtis Fitzgerald, perhaps. But her insidious business manager had faded from being the most important person in her life to near-nothingness.

Just as her career must be doing, thanks to him.

"I need to go home," she muttered. She took the blanket and wrapped it about herself more securely.

"Good idea," Jack said. "California, isn't it? I'll ask around, get you on the next ship heading south."

Jessie felt her heart plummet at his eagerness to be rid of her. Well, what did she expect? She'd been the one to mention leaving. He had made it clear he didn't want her around.

Her laugh was bitter. "It's not quite that simple, Jack."

"What do you mean?"

She sighed. "My home isn't exactly California. It's a long way away. You wouldn't believe me if I told you where. Suffice it to say that no ship can get me there."

She lifted one eyebrow wryly at the questions in Jack's green eyes. She didn't want them to reach his mouth, since her mind wasn't clear enough to spar with him right now. Instead, she asked, "So how did you find me?"

"You didn't stay at Helen's, like I told you."

"You were late. I wanted to go back to Calvina's."

"You'd have had a better chance of getting there safely if you had waited for an escort."

"I didn't know that at the time. How did you find me?" she repeated.

"After checking at Helen's, I went to Calvina's," Jack's voice was casual, but again there was something in the intensity of his gaze that said he was not expressing what he felt. "Renny said you weren't there. I assumed you were having an evening of pleasure with a stampeder, but as I walked home Taku spotted you."

"You thought I was taking the place of one of Helen's girls?" She didn't even try to keep the outrage from her voice. "It isn't any of your business what I do." She clutched the blanket in her fingers as tightly as if she had Jack around his substantial neck. "But

167

for your information, I have no intention of being a lady of the night. Or day, for that matter."

He didn't reply, but she saw a muscle working in the side of his cheek. Didn't he believe her?

What was this man thinking?

"And you didn't have to tell me all that anyway," she finished in a huff. "You could simply have answered that Taku found me."

"Okay," he said agreeably. "Taku found you."

All the fight left Jessie suddenly. "And I was nearly dead," she whispered. "I would have died if you hadn't . . ." She couldn't finish. She swallowed hard, studying the logs of the wall beside her as avidly as if they suddenly had all the famous ballads of the world written on them. She would not let this man see her cry. She wouldn't.

But she felt the straw mattress on the bed dip beside her. An arm touched her shoulder. And she felt lost. A sob escaped her, and she buried her face in her hands.

"Jessie," Jack said softly. "It's all right. I won't let anything happen to you. Not again."

She was in his arms suddenly. She wasn't certain if she had bolted into them, or if he had wrapped them about her. Maybe both. In any event, her face was pressed into the warmth of his cotton shirt, and she no longer could stop herself from crying.

She noticed that he smelled of masculine strength and burning wood. She noticed how good his arms felt pressing her close. How gentle were his murmurs of comfort, even though she could not make out the words.

Her sobs subsided. She took the clean handkerchief he proffered and dried her eyes.

She couldn't look at him. He was a brave man. A hero.

He must think she was a wimp, crying out of fear like that.

But his fingers took her chin and moved her face so the only way she could avoid his glance was to close her eyes. She refused to show weakness any more, and so she kept them open.

For an instant, he looked perturbed, but then his expression shuttered.

"I'm sorry," she said stiffly, trying to wriggle away from him on the bed. She recalled she was bare beneath the blanket that separated them, and she pulled it even tighter around herself. "I didn't mean to break down like that. I know it's too late for me to go back to town tonight, but if you'll just let me stay here on the floor—"

"Don't apologize to the likes of me." Jack's tone was as conversational as if he were asking if she wanted a drink of water. "I nearly failed you tonight. There are others I failed, and it killed them. They wanted to help me, too. But it won't happen again. I won't fail you, Jessie."

His voice might be calm, but his eyes were not. They again burned, this time with a ferocity that she had never before seen in them. But the fury in them was directed inward.

He was angry with himself.

"What's wrong, Jack?" she asked softly. "Who did you fail? I can't believe—"

"Believe it," he said with a half smile that was more a grimace. "I failed those most dear to me: my parents. My fiancée."

His fiancée? Why did the idea that he was engaged pierce Jessie as poignantly as if he had stuck her with a knife?

"What happened to them?" She tried to keep her

tone as conversational as his but failed miserably.

"They died." Jack knelt once more by the stove, stoking the fire. Near him, Taku stirred, then rolled over onto his other side.

Jack had given the answer she had expected to hear. "How?"

"It doesn't matter now. It was a long time ago."

Jessie rose, clutching the blanket around herself. She knelt on the floor beside him. Taku glanced up at her and moved away.

"Of course it matters," she insisted. "It obviously matters a lot. But it might help to talk about it. I'm sure that whatever happened, you didn't fail anyone. You must have—"

Jack pivoted so quickly toward her that she nearly stumbled. He grabbed her arms to steady her. "You talk too much, Jessie. And about things you don't understand."

She opened her mouth again to reply, but he didn't let her.

His kiss was far from gentle. In fact, it was almost brutal. Harsh. And the most erotic thing Jessie had ever experienced.

His tongue thrust into her mouth, and she met it with her own. Jack O'Dair's taste was unique. There was a sweetness to him, with just a hint of liquor and honey.

But she hardly had time to focus on his flavor, for her other senses were reeling. He pulled the blanket, her only covering, from her and let it drop to the floor.

The cabin was warmed from the fire—or was it the blaze burning inside that made her shudder not from cold, but from desire?

Her skin tingled everywhere his hands touched. His caresses were as firm as his mouth, and they assaulted her almost everywhere . . . except where she really wanted him.

Oh, she loved the way his fingers massaged her scalp beneath her hair, her shoulders, her back, even her rump. But why did he not move forward? Her breasts ached with carnal need. And down below— oh, down below—that was where she truly yearned for him to touch her.

"Please," she begged. Was that really her?

"Tell me to stop," he demanded. But as he did so, he finally reached around and cupped her right breast, rubbing a thumb over the nipple. She gasped. "Tell me to stop," he repeated. "Right now. Or I won't."

"Don't," she said, practically crying at the erotic sensation as he continued to explore her with his hands. She wanted to feel him bare against her, but he was still fully dressed. She reached for the buttons on his shirt.

With no further warning, he did stop. He pulled away from her, his chest heaving. He looked beyond her, toward the wall. "You're in my cabin for protection, not this. This isn't right."

"It's very right," she contradicted shakily, wanting to reach out to stroke the granite-hard set to his jaw. "I need you to chase away the demons. I want you to be with me. Please, make love to me, Jack."

He turned back to her. His breathing remained ragged. His green eyes searched hers. "You're my responsibility," he insisted harshly.

"I'm my own responsibility. And I take full responsibility for this." She realized her own voice had grown hard. More softly, she repeated, "Please, Jack." She had never pleaded with anyone to make love with her before.

But, then, she had never wanted to make love with anyone the way she needed to with him.

He didn't take his eyes from hers as he first unbuttoned his shirt sleeves and pushed them up, just a little. She glanced down. There was nothing sexier than a man's bared forearms—unless it was his biceps, which she noticed next as Jack pulled off his shirt. No—the amazing contours of his massive chest—that had to be the sexiest part of this incredibly sensual man.

But then he reached for the buttons on his wool pants, and Jessie knew she had been mistaken. In a moment, he was bare—as was the most erotic part of him. Most definitely. Her knees went weak, but she did not have to worry about sinking to the floor. In moments, she was in his arms, and he deposited her gently onto the bed.

"It's too late now, Jessie," he told her. This time, when he touched her with his rough, sensual fingers, he followed them with his lips until she writhed beneath the welcomed onslaught. She moaned, but she refused to allow him to have complete control over their lovemaking. Her hands were not idle, either. She felt his rock-hard biceps, the angled contours of his magnificent chest, his flat belly—and below. He gasped when she wrapped her fingers around the thickness of his erection and began gently to move them in the rhythm of love.

She did not need to encourage him any further. In moments, he had rolled on top of her, urging her legs to open. "Tell me to stop now," he demanded again. His teeth were gritted against her answer as though he fought for control, but she trusted him. She knew that if she told him to, he would stop.

But she did not want him to stop. "Go on, please, Jack. Now."

He did, and Jessie gasped as he entered her. In moments, their rhythm united into an eternal, peerless song. Her eyes were closed at first, but when she slitted them open, she found him watching her, his eyes dark with immeasurable passion. She smiled as her breathing quickened even further—and in moments she gasped as her entire being shattered in incredible fulfillment.

Jessie opened one eye. She wasn't certain how long she had been asleep, but it hadn't been long enough. Her muscles had turned to mush. So had her mind.

But parts of her felt wonderful. . . .

Jack lay beside her in his bed. He wasn't sleeping, either.

"So," she said, "I think I have a few more demons for you to chase away, Jack O'Dair. You ready yet?"

He laughed. "We can find out."

She loved the sound of that laugh. She loved even more when he reached for her and began stroking her.

"Seems to me like you're good and ready," she murmured, then gasped as he touched one of her more sensitive spots.

"So are you."

The second time was every bit as incredible as the first.

And as the night grew even later, Jessie discovered the third time.

A shred of daylight had begun to penetrate the canvas over the cabin's windows when Jessie finally awakened. She reached across the bed—but Jack wasn't there.

She sat up, clutching the blanket to her. Jack wasn't in the cabin. Neither was Taku.

Maybe they were both out for a morning constitutional. Still, after last night, Jessie felt suddenly alone. She missed Jack.

She wondered what a fourth time might be like. . . .

She looked around. Her clothes were hanging on a rope he had stretched across one end of the room, not far from the black metal stove. They looked dry.

She realized, as she got dressed, that she was still here, in the past. She had wondered before if spending the night at Jack's cabin was the key to going back and forth in time. Of course, this time she hadn't sung Jack's ballad first. She was beginning to like it—*really* like it, in the past, but if she ever got to the point of desperation to return to her real life, she would try to recreate all she had done, right here in Jack's cabin, the night she had come to this time.

As she finished dressing, the cabin door opened. Taku entered first, followed by Jack.

She smiled at him, but his strong, handsome features—the face that she had caressed and kissed the night before—remained impassive. She felt her own expression begin to droop as a chill that had nothing to do with the open door pervaded her. "Good morning," she said brightly nevertheless. "Is it cold outside?"

She wanted, instead, to thank him for an unforgettable night. Maybe even to tempt him into an even more unforgettable day. . . .

"Good morning, Jessie," he said with good humor. "It snowed, but not a lot." He removed his gloves and rubbed his hands together in front of the warm stove. "Glad you're dressed. I'll walk you back to town."

Nothing. No acknowledgment of all they had shared last night.

Had he only made love to her to warm her up after her brush with an icy death?

174

That would only have made sense the first time.

"No need to go with me. It's daylight. I'll be fine." She refused to allow him to see how hurt she was.

But he must have known it anyway. He crouched on the floor beside Taku and ran his fingers through the wolf-dog's thick hair. "I'm sorry, Jessie," he said. He did manage to look up at her, at least, though his face remained expressionless. "I told you last night that what we did wasn't right. Don't get me wrong; it was wonderful."

Then why didn't he stand up and take her back into his arms and kiss her? Make love to her again?

All she said, though, was, "But . . . ?"

"But I'm here because I have a job to do—a job I take seriously. I will take care of you; you can be certain of that. I won't let anyone hurt you again, though you have to listen to me to stay safe."

"Then you just made love to me as part of your job?" Jessie didn't even attempt to keep the outrage from her voice.

"I didn't say that. But I've a lot of people to protect. I can't spend too much time taking care of any single one."

What was going on here? They'd shared such tenderness, such passion last night. It all seemed a dream this morning.

She met his eyes. Did she see a flash of regret in their green depths? If so, it vanished in a second, replaced by emerald hardness. He was shutting her out.

She got it then. He had opened up to her too much last night. Or not enough. He had told about what had hurt him.

He clearly had no intention of being hurt again.

"You're a coward, Jack O'Dair," she said conversationally. "I thought you were a hero, but heroes care

175

about the people they save. Cowards just take advantage of them."

She saw his mouth open in protest, then close again. "I left some biscuits for you on the table," was all he said.

She forced the tears that welled in her eyes back down again. After all, they were liable to freeze there once she went outside. She put on her boots without looking at Jack, then took her fur jacket from the peg on the wall.

She knelt to hug Taku and rub her cheek against the dog's warm, soft fur. She ignored Jack as he got himself bundled once more for the cold.

And she continued to ignore him as he followed her brisk walk back to Dyea.

Chapter Twelve

Later that day, Jessie went through the motions at Calvina's of helping to cook and serve lunch.

The regulars were there, including Eldon Riggs, wearing a suit, and Tildy Emmet, in a worn dress with a wrinkled pinafore that she often donned before washing clothes for the stampeders.

Whiskey Tom slouched at the table, his hair more unkempt than usual, as though he had not even run his fingers through it upon awakening. His eyes were half closed. He noticed Jessie, though. "Did Jack find you last night?" he asked.

"Yes," Jessie replied, a shade curtly. She didn't want Tom to ask any more questions about where, or how. She didn't even want to think about last night. How terribly it had started and ended . . . and how wonderful it had been in between.

Tom murmured something that Jessie didn't hear. "Excuse me?" she asked.

"There's another singer starting at Helen's this afternoon," he said a little more slowly and a lot louder.

"Really? So, am I out of a job?" Jessie tried to sound glib but was horrified when she realized how fatalistic and sad the words sounded. She forced a grin. "If I've lost my night job, maybe Tildy will hire me to help her at times Calvina doesn't need me." She winked at the homely young woman, whose eyes saucered in surprise.

"Don't think so," Tom replied. "Arnett's gone on to the Yukon, and the new fellow's just come back from there."

He wasn't likely to know the ballad, then, unless . . . "Has he been here before?"

Tom shook his head. "Nope. He's been in Skagway, I heard, but this is his first trip to Dyea. Maybe he'll have some other songs to teach you."

Songs that she could bring home, even if she never learned the end of Jack's ballad. For if she continued to feel this miserable, she *would* find a way back home.

"Helen told me that this guy likes to make up his own songs," Tom continued. "Mostly about people he meets, that kind of thing. Especially people who do interesting things. Helen told him about our marshal."

"Jack O'Dair?" Jessie perked up. Maybe she was about to meet the person who would write the ballad. If so, when?

As soon as she was done helping Calvina clean up, she hurried to Helen's. The new singer was there, sitting at the piano and playing tinny arpeggios. She introduced herself, and he stopped long enough to hold out one bony hand. "Newlin Herlihy," he said, planting a kiss on the hand that Jessie proffered in return. Her skin crawled at the contact, for Newlin Herlihy reminded her of Curtis Fitzgerald.

Oh, his hair wasn't as impeccably styled as Curtis's, but it was just as black. He wasn't as tall as Curtis and appeared much thinner. Jessie was certain that Newlin Herlihy didn't belong to a gym to keep himself trim and buff. But there was a shrewdness in his gray eyes that suggested that he wanted to get far beneath her skin.

She forced a smile. "I'm Jessie Jerome," she said. "I sing here, too. I understand that you write ballads."

"That I do." His smile was unctuous, and she wanted to find the nearest stream, no matter how cold, to wash herself off.

Panic surged through her, even as she reminded herself that he was not Curtis. She needn't compare the two. After all, right now Curtis was at home, in her present—playing around with the rest of his female clients and destroying *her* career.

Drat it all! What was she doing here? She should be finding a way home to salvage whatever she could of her life.

Would this man write Jack's ballad? If so, he was talented, even if he made her want to throw up. But if she never learned the ending to Jack's ballad, so what? Maybe it was better that way. She didn't want to know now if Jack died in the avalanche, did she? She had made love with him, after all. Even if he didn't love her . . . even if she didn't love him—the real him—it would hurt more now to find out how heroically he had acted, as usual, how he had saved a lot of people . . . and died. For such things were often celebrated in ballads.

One-night stands weren't, though. And that was all she had been to Jack.

"I'll look forward to working with you tonight," she lied to Newlin. Hurriedly, she grabbed her guitar from behind the bar where she always left it.

"Don't you want to rehearse with me?" He made the innocent words sound like the lewdest of propositions.

"Maybe later," she said. She took a deep breath when she reached the plank walk outside and her throat nearly iced up. She made certain her fur coat was fully buttoned, her hood up, her gloves on securely, and walked calmly to the jail.

Jack O'Dair was in the office. Taku, at his feet, padded over to Jessie for a pat as she walked in the door.

Jack looked up. At first, she thought she read pleasure in his eyes, but if so it disappeared immediately. "Is everything all right? I didn't think you'd be in danger during daylight, with so many people in town. A beautiful woman like you need only shout and every man around will come to your rescue."

"Right." She glared. Was that supposed to be a compliment? She couldn't read his expression, but he seemed occupied with a ledger that he had picked up from his desk.

"I'll have Filby watch over you, if you'd like," he continued.

"No need."

"Fine. I'll be at Calvina's at eight to walk you to Helen's."

"Don't bother."

"It will be dark then." His smile as he met her gaze was as cool as his voice. "I'm going to protect you, Jessie, whether you like it or not."

"I don't like it. And I don't need it. I'll take care of myself." She hustled away, feeling his eyes boring

180

into her. But she had learned what she had needed.

He wasn't at his cabin.

And after last night, after today, she had made up her mind.

Her guitar case still clutched in her hand, she hurried as much as she could through the mud on the crowded streets of Dyea. Jack was right; there were a lot of people around. Even if whoever tried to kill her last night were around, he—or she—would hardly try it again with the entire town as witnesses.

It made sense for her to stay where the crowds were.

But she had another agenda.

She passed Horace Martin's warehouse and Otis Oetting's outfitter's store. A bunch of stampeders milled outside both establishments, but they seemed to be peacefully waiting in line.

There was a singer on the street, entertaining the waiting shoppers. Renny had told her that sometimes happened. She listened to the blond-bearded tenor for a minute. His voice was clear and melodic as he sang a hymn. Jessie wanted to ask him about his repertory, but she didn't want to interrupt him. And she was in a hurry.

She continued on, wending her way through noisy crowds, passing Calvina's boarding house and Helen's nest. No one paid attention to one lone woman walking as briskly as she could in the swarm of people. No one at all cared where she went—except her.

She looked around nervously as she reached the less crowded outskirts of town, but no one seemed interested in her. Surely she was safe to do what she had to. Sweeping her skirt above her ankles to allow more ease in walking, she hurried along the narrow lane into the woods.

It didn't take long to reach Jack's cabin. It was, of course, unlocked. She went inside, then bolted the door.

Maybe she shouldn't do that, she thought. If what she hoped would happen did, Jack wouldn't have an easy time getting back inside.

So what? He was strong. He was resourceful. It would be his problem, not hers.

The single room was cold; the fire in the stove had gone out. So what? She wouldn't be here long.

Sitting on top of the quilt, she stared down at Jack's bed. Was it only hours ago when she had shared it with him? When they had made love over and over—passionate, memorable, extraordinarily wonderful love.

And then he had pretended it had been meaningless. Maybe it had been, to him.

With a deep sigh, she pulled her guitar from its case. She strummed a few familiar chords.

This song had brought her here. Right now, she needed it to take her home. She had only idly considered the possibility this morning. Now, she needed this to work. She began to sing.

> "He kept the peace without surcease,
> Did mighty Jack O'Dair.
> Through Dyea-town fights, and dread Klondike
>   nights,
> None other could compare."

Tears rose to her eyes. Not all in the ballad she knew had occurred, and yet, in many ways, Jack was every bit as heroic as the protagonist of the song.

She had come to care a lot for the real Jack, but he had made it clear that all he wanted from her was

182

to protect her, as he did with everyone in the town where he was the law. No more.

She needed her career back. She needed her life back.

Even if her dreams were forever shattered.

She sang the rest of the ballad, all she knew. A lot of the heroic acts it celebrated had already occurred: Jack's saving Eldon from the drunks; squeezing life back into the man on the floor by the "high" maneuver, as Jack called it; even catching some of the people who pilfered from stampeders, though Jessie knew that not all the thieves had been caught.

He hadn't solved the crime of the man left bleeding in the snow, though—at least not that Jessie had heard. And she would have heard if it had happened since her arrival.

And then there was the avalanche yet to come, and its still-unknown result.

Singing the ballad here, in this cabin, that night with Lizard Songthroat had to have been the catalyst that brought her here. Singing it again here had to be what would send her home.

She was ready. Though she had not fulfilled her goal, it was time to leave.

But when she had finished singing, nothing happened.

Of course not, she told herself. The conditions were not identical. She had been asleep when she had traveled here.

She lay down in the bed. She thought she smelled the musky masculine aroma of Jack, their own mingled scents while they had made love. She recalled every sensuous moment of last night.

Damn! How would she ever sleep? She closed her eyes nevertheless . . . and drifted off.

*   *   *

She didn't know how long she slept. Her eyes flew open. "Am I back?" she asked aloud.

It was still daylight. That was a good sign, since she had left her own time in the middle of an Alaskan summer, when there were few dark hours. She sat up and blinked.

But the rack of clothes along the wall hadn't changed. There was no door signifying a bathroom. The furnishings were those from Jack O'Dair's time, not Lizard Songthroat's.

She had failed.

"Lizard, you wretch!" she cried aloud. "I can't stay here. It's too hard, damn it!" But as tears rolled down her cheeks, she realized she was not getting away from here so easily. Maybe learning the end of the ballad was the key, since Lizard seemed to have sent her here to find it.

Maybe there was no key. No way home—

The door to the cabin rattled. Jessie started, remembering her attack the previous night. She'd tried to make sure no one followed her—but had her assailant done so anyway?

"Jessie, are you in there?" The voice was Jack's, and he did not sound happy.

She was nevertheless relieved. He might be angry with her, but she knew she had nothing to fear from Jack. Unless it was losing her heart. . . .

Irritated with the way her thoughts were heading, she yelled, "What do you want?" She wiped her cheeks dry with the back of her hand. She didn't want Jack to know she'd had a moment of weakness.

"Filby told me he saw you heading in this direction. I told you I'd come for you at Calvina's to walk you to the saloon, not here. Now, let me in."

184

Jessie checked herself over. She still wore one of Calvina's borrowed outfits. She tugged the long skirt straight as she stood and sauntered slowly to the door. She might be about to obey him, but she didn't need to act eager about it.

She unbolted the lock and pulled the door open, letting a gust of arctic air blow inside, along with Taku. Jack's frame dwarfed the entryway. His scowl looked furious enough to have blasted down the door if she had made him wait any longer.

Without saying a word, Jessie turned, letting him follow her in. She knew he had entered and closed the door when the cold from outside stopped intruding into the cabin. Taku sat beside her, and she bent to pat the dog's cool fur.

To her surprise, Jack didn't say anything either. She felt his presence, though, the same as if he had stood on a crate and yelled chastisements.

No. The atmosphere was highly charged, but not with anger.

Slowly, she turned to face him.

His green eyes were luminescent fire. A muscle at the edge of his mouth moved, and she noted that his fists were clenched at his sides. He hadn't removed his jacket, as though he wore it as a shield.

She could see the passion raging within him. It was evident in his yearning stare.

Her own traitorous body began to respond in a molten rush.

"What time is it?" she asked. Her voice was hoarse. "I fell asleep. Is it time for me to go to Helen's?"

"Not for a while." There was a huskiness in his tone, too. He hesitated. "Why are you here, Jessie? You couldn't have known I would follow—did you?"

She shook her head, ever so slowly. She felt mesmerized by his hungry gaze. She had to set him straight. Quickly.

"My coming here had nothing to do with you." He would see through her lie. It had everything to do with him . . . just not in the way he would assume.

His laugh was brief and ironic, accompanied by a reproachful shake of his head. "You have a perfectly nice place to stay in town, Jessie. It would have been safer for you to remain where it's crowded. But here you are, right after you came to see me at the jail. I had considered that, maybe, it was because you believed I would follow. We did spend a very pleasant night last night. I hoped . . . that you came here to wait for me." He lifted one coppery brow optimistically.

Jessie swallowed hard. "I thought, after this morning, that you had no more interest in me that way. In any case, that's not why I came."

The ardor in his expression cooled as fast as if he had strode back outside. Suddenly alarmed, Jessie stepped farther away from him.

"Oh, I'm interested. But why are you here?" He paused, but not long enough to allow her to formulate an answer. Instead, he leapt to his own incorrect conclusion. "Damn it, Jessie, did you want to be here while I wasn't? Did you come here to steal from me? Or maybe you're hiding some of the goods here. Are you one of Horace's thieves? No one would ever think to search the marshal's home." His eyes darted from one end of the spartan cabin to the other. There were hardly any hiding places in it.

He thought her a thief? "Try your shed," she spat. "Better yet, you can dig right down in the muck of your outhouse."

"Then you're not denying it?" Where was his usual

endearing friendliness? He had obviously hidden it behind his marshal's badge, and Jessie felt herself tremble. She'd have leapt into the outhouse muck herself before letting him see it, though.

Taku, sitting near the cool stove, whined, obviously uneasy with the tension between the humans in the room.

Jessie nearly stamped her foot on the floor before she realized she was in stocking feet, without her boots. "I don't need to deny a thing," she raged. "You have no right to accuse me of stealing just because I won't fall back under the covers with irresistible you." She spotted her boots where she had left them by the door and edged by him—getting close, much too close, to his substantial body. She could feel his heat.

She wanted to feel much more. . . .

No, she didn't. It was the hero of the song she had fallen for, she reminded herself. The real man had too many flaws. Not the least of which was that he was a big, bruising egotist. How dare he imagine his love-making had drawn her back here!

She had recalled every moment of it once she was here. But that was beside the point.

It also wasn't fair that he had lashed out at her, accusing her this way, just because she hadn't succumbed to his charms once more.

Not that she wasn't sorely tempted . . .

She had to get out of here.

"Pardon me," she said through gritted teeth.

She carried her boots back to the bed, where she sat down to put them on.

"Jessie?" Jack's voice had lost its edge. She glanced up at him. He sat on a chair near his small table, watching her.

"What?"

"If you didn't come to see me or to avoid me, why did you come?" His head was cocked sideways, and his gaze was curious. He looked like a winsome child. A very mature, very handsome child. . . .

She smiled wryly. She decided to tell him the truth—sort of. "I was hoping to find some answers, Jack, about why I came here, and how I can get home."

"I thought you told me you came here to learn songs about the gold rush. And as for getting home, I told you I'd put you on the next ship."

He still sounded darned eager to get rid of her. And that hurt. She snapped at him, "And I told you—never mind." She sighed. "Will you walk me to town now?"

He nodded.

The woman was as confusing as a gold strike rumor, Jack thought as he followed Jessie Jerome back along the path toward Dyea. And just as unreliable.

Even though it was still daylight, the air was cooler, and frozen mud beneath their feet crunched as they walked beneath the bare-limbed trees. He could even hear Taku's footsteps as he pattered off into the shadowy woods and back, never straying too far from Jack's side.

Why had Jessie gone to his cabin? Her claim of learning why she was here and how to go home made about as much sense as heading for the Klondike without any boots or snowshoes.

She had done that, hadn't she?

"So why did you come to Dyea, Jessie, if it wasn't to learn songs?" The question spilled from his mouth before he had a chance to consider the consequences.

She had been tramping ahead of him, as though

she couldn't stand to be in his presence. That didn't bother him. He didn't care, after all.

She slowed, then turned to look at him. "I didn't make much sense back in your cabin, did I?" she said with a sigh. She waited for him to catch up with her, then walked at his side as she continued, "Not much around here makes sense to me, either. But I did come to learn songs. Really. One in particular, in fact. I've felt very frustrated that no one seems to know it."

"You've mostly talked to the singers at Helen's. One night when you're not working, I'll take you to some of the other saloons, introduce you to their entertainers. Maybe you'll find your answers there." Now, why had he offered that? The more time he spent with her, the more perplexed he felt.

He wanted her. No doubt about that. Even now, he wanted to take her back to his cabin, undress her beneath the light from a warm fire, and make love to her over and over throughout the long, dark night.

He could slake his need with any of the saloon girls in town, of course. But there was more to his need of Jessie. There was more to Jessie.

And that unnerved him.

It was all the more reason to put her on a ship out of Dyea—for her safety, and for his peace of mind.

"Tell me about the song you're wanting to hear," he told her, just to make conversation. To him, the entertainment in the saloons hadn't meant much before except as a diversion to keep drunken customers from fighting with one another. To make his job of keeping the peace just a little easier.

That had changed, though, when he had heard Jessie sing. Her voice was husky, so mellow and sweet that he could listen to her forever. . . .

What was he thinking? He balled his gloved hands

into fists. He was here for penance. To help people. Many people.

From a distance.

"I . . . I can't really tell you a lot about the song," Jessie said. She sounded flustered.

Song? Oh, yes. He had asked her about the damned song that was a reason she was here. Maybe he could help her find something out about it so she'd leave. Quickly.

"It's . . . it's something I've only heard pieces of for a very long time." Her voice was strangely hesitant.

He looked down at her, suddenly very conscious of her apparent discomfort. She was still walking beside him, her head down. Why was she acting so reluctant to talk about a song?

Unsure why, he had a sense that it was important that he find out.

"Why don't you sing me what you know of it?" he said casually, curious what her response would be. "Maybe I've heard part of it, too, and can help you out."

They had reached the edge of the woods. The buildings of Dyea came into view.

"Thanks," Jessie said, "but I don't think so." She speeded up again as though trying to get away from him as they passed the cluster of tents and wooden buildings and maneuvered along muddy streets that grew more crowded the farther they got into town. He easily matched her pace, but wondered why she was racing.

"Is something wrong, Jessie?"

"Wrong? Of course not." But she walked even faster—or at least tried to, given the press of people.

"It's too early for me to go to Helen's," Jessie said

as they neared Calvina's. She was a little out of breath. "You don't need to wait. I can get there myself later."

"I told you before," Jack said slowly, intending to make his point yet again to this exasperating woman. "I will walk you to Helen's tonight. After what happened—"

He didn't finish his sentence, for just as Jessie opened Calvina's door Tildy Emmet rushed out to greet her. "Calvina's having her baby!" she cried. "It's been coming for hours already."

"Really?" Jessie turned toward Jack, a fearful look in her eyes. "There isn't a hospital here, is there?"

He shook his head in wonderment as much as in response. This was the wilderness, not a big United States city.

She turned back to Tildy. "Well, has someone at least called Calvina's obstetrician?"

"Ob—what?" Tildy looked bewildered.

"Her doctor," Jessie said slowly, as though speaking to a backward child. "Has anyone called her doctor?"

"I heard a doctor came through here two weeks ago," Tildy said, "but didn't he say he was going to try to make his way up Yellow Pass instead of Chilkoot?" She looked questioningly at Jack.

"Do you mean," Jessie said through gritted teeth, "that this God-forsaken, poor excuse for a settlement doesn't even have a doctor?"

"Only when they pass through," Tildy answered.

"Then who's going to help Calvina have her baby?" Her blue eyes were huge and pleading as she looked at Jack.

Oh, no, he thought. He had come here to help peo-

191

ple, but dealing with women having babies—he drew the line there.

"She's a strong woman," he said, trying hard to keep the desperation out of his tone. "I'm sure she'll be just fine."

"Herself? You expect her to have a baby without any help? Some hero you are, Jack O'Dair."

Jessie stomped into the house, grabbing Tildy's arm as she went.

Jack stared helplessly after them.

Chapter Thirteen

Calvina was doing fine—or at least as fine as she could be under the circumstances. Jessie went to her bedroom to make sure, then hurried to the kitchen to start water boiling. That was what people did in these days, wasn't it? If for no other reason, boiled water should be good for sterilizing things that would come in contact with the mother and new baby.

Some gentleman Jack was. Jessie believed that, in her time, most lawmen were taught first aid and basic life-saving techniques—even assisting with labor. But if Jack had taken such training, which was doubtful, he obviously had no intention of putting it to use now. As far as she knew, he hadn't even come inside the house. She had not seen him since she had turned her back on him at the front door.

How did that verse of the ballad go? It ran through Jessie's mind as she put more fuel on the fire beneath the kettle.

"Jack was rough and Jack was tough
But the gentlest of gentlemen, too.
From saving the ladies to birthing babies,
There was naught our Jack couldn't do."

"He did save *this* lady from dying of exposure, I'll grant him that," Jessie mumbled aloud, referring to herself. "But he sure didn't dig right in to help birth Calvina's baby."

"What was that?" asked Tildy Emmet. She just come into the kitchen carrying a stack of clean towels.

"I said, it's time for us to dig right in to help birth this baby," Jessie said brightly. "All of us." She paused. "Have you ever assisted before?"

"Who, me?" The stocky young woman looked incredulous. "My daddy's a minister in Dover. He wouldn't have allowed me anywhere near a lady having a baby."

"But he allowed you to come all the way to Alaska?" Jessie was half teasing, but she was curious about how Tildy had wound up in Dyea. She knew that it had something to do with a man who'd already gone up to the Klondike.

Tildy snorted. "I ran away with Samuel. Biggest mistake I ever made. I thought it would be a fine adventure, that we'd be back at Daddy's doorstep in a couple of months with all the gold we'd ever want, and plenty to give to Daddy's poor parishioners besides. I wound up on Calvina's doorstep instead. Samuel's somewhere in the Yukon still, I suppose. I haven't seen him in months. Nor have I seen an ounce of gold, except for the occasional nugget some of the stampeders who return like to show off now and then."

"Don't you want to go home?"

194

Tildy shook her head so vehemently that a few strands of her dark hair escaped from the pins that held it off her face. She swept it back with one thick hand. "I like it here. I can do as I please. I don't mind washing laundry; it's a chore that gives me lots of time to think. It's respectable, too, and the stampeders pay well for it."

Jessie heard a moan from down the hall. "We'll be right there, Calvina," she called. To Tildy, she said, "Are there any midwives here or others who know what they're doing around someone giving birth?"

"Abigail of the Washington House had two babies of her own, but she isn't willing to help; she had to leave her children with her mother back home, and she misses them too fiercely to be around any here. I suspect some of the saloon girls have had babies, too, but none of them would be too keen on helping, I don't think. And—"

"I get the picture," Jessie said. "Well, I've watched The Learning Channel and even a few soap operas. Shall we go?"

She ignored the confusion on Tildy's plain face and marched past her down the hall to Calvina's room. Her room and Renny's. It was small and neat, with a hand-crafted wooden dresser and matching chair, and dominated by a lumpy-looking bed with a snow-white down comforter on top. And on it lay Calvina.

"How close together are your contractions?" Jessie asked. She wasn't sure what would be significant, though she knew that the more frequent they were, the more imminent the birth.

"I don't—" Calvina didn't finish. Her pretty face contorted with pain, and she gasped. "It hurts," she managed.

"I'm sure it does," Jessie soothed. Oh, heavens. Could she do this?

What choice was there? Tildy stood in the doorway, shock and fear turning her face to stone.

Jessie lifted the blanket that draped Calvina's legs and performed the best examination she could. She didn't think she saw anything resembling the top of the baby's head, but she wasn't sure what it would look like.

"Here," Jessie said to Calvina, returning to her side. "You hold onto my hand the next time you have a contraction. And then I want you to watch my face. Breathe just the way I do, okay?"

Puzzlement joined the pain in Calvina's eyes, but she said quickly, "All right." Her light brown hair was loose around her face, dampened with sweat, and lines of concern and pain were etched into a forehead that before had held the smoothness of youth.

She would be fine, Jessie told herself. So would the baby.

They had to be.

During the next contraction, Jessie raised her voice a little to be heard over Calvina's cries. "Inhale, then breathe out like this," she said, demonstrating the blowing technique she remembered seeing in films.

Her eyes wide, Calvina attempted to comply, until she cried out. "It hurts!" she exclaimed.

As she settled back to normal after the contraction, Jessie gave her a quick lesson in breathing and panting, the best she could recall from what she'd seen on television.

"Where did you learn that?" Tildy asked in amazement.

"Here and there," Jessie replied vaguely.

The next contraction came quickly. Jessie encouraged Calvina to breathe as instructed. Calvina's labor continued for a long while. Jessie checked often to see whether the baby's head was visible. It wasn't, not for hours, until . . .

Yes! At least . . .

"Oh, no," she whispered before she could catch herself. At least she spoke softly enough that she hoped Calvina, engrossed in panting in rhythm, didn't hear her. But Tildy did. She looked at Jessie with a kind of quizzical horror on her face.

"We're going to get some more clean towels," Jessie told Calvina. "We'll be right back."

"What's wrong?" Tildy hissed as soon as they were away from the room.

"I think the baby's head is in the wrong position. I may be wrong. I *hope* I'm wrong. Babies' heads do get distorted in the birth canal, after all. But if I'm right, it's not good."

"What's not good?" inquired a familiar masculine voice.

"Jack!" Jessie said in amazement. "What are you doing here?"

"I went to see if I could find Renny, but neither Horace nor Otis have seen him today; they think he's already on his way back up the Chilkoot."

"But you came back."

He nodded. "I don't know if I'll be any help, but I assisted during foalings at farms near where I grew up. I doubt it's the same, but—"

"Oh, thank heavens." Jessie quickly explained what she thought was the problem. "Have you ever helped where the position wasn't quite right?"

"Sure, with horses." Still, after Jessie explained her concerns, Jack washed his hands, then stepped into the room. "Hi, Calvina. I've been around babies being

197

born." Jessie noticed he didn't mention their species. "And these young ladies haven't so they've asked me to help you. Okay?"

"Sure, Jack," Calvina gasped. "Do you know if Renny—?" She couldn't finish, as another contraction set in.

"Renny's going to get here as soon as he can," Jack assured her. "I've put the word out, and it'll be all through the Chilkoot as fast as a lightning bolt. You'll see."

Jessie knelt beside Calvina and took her hand, trying not to wince as the young woman squeezed through her pain. "Breathe, Calvina," Jessie told her and began panting to show her how.

Meantime, Jack had set to work beneath the blanket. "I see someone who wants out," he said, his tone light and soothing. "Now, I'm going to need to give a little push here, then a pull, but then it'll be fine."

Jessie hoped he knew what he was doing. But whatever he knew, it was more than she knew, so she simply closed her eyes, held Calvina's hand and prayed.

Calvina cried out once, then again. A look of concentration drew Jack's heavy brows into a single coppery line. She knew he must be working with the baby's position. Calvina moaned. Time seemed to drag. The contractions came closer and closer together. It was hard to get Calvina to concentrate on the breathing, but Jessie figured it was important to try—so she wouldn't be thinking as much about what was going on below.

And then, Calvina screamed. Tildy gasped. Jack laughed aloud. And in a moment, a baby wailed angrily.

And Jessie began to cry.

*   *   *

They had put the boiled water to good use, cleaning the baby and Calvina. Jessie had wrapped the baby in one of Tildy's towels, and they had proudly handed the infant to Calvina, who smiled through her exhaustion.

"What are you going to name him?" Jessie asked.

"I'll wait till Renny gets back," Calvina said. "We talked of several names, but I want him to make the final decision."

"Aren't you going to name him 'Jack'?" Tildy asked in apparent amazement. "I mean, Jack O'Dair was the one who—"

"I just happened to be here, that's all," he interrupted from the doorway. He had left the room as soon as the baby was out after muttering something about "women's work" and "Calvina's modesty."

Jessie had a feeling he'd been embarrassed, both by having had to assist another man's wife with such an intimate process and by having played such an important role in it.

He *had* been a gentleman. And he had certainly helped to get this baby born. Score another point for the ballad, Jessie thought.

There wasn't a lot left in it that hadn't yet happened. Maybe she would get bored here, with Jack having few further heroic feats to accomplish till the avalanche.

Oh . . . but there was still one incident left that she knew of, about a stampeder left bleeding in the snow. . . .

"Thank you, Jack," Calvina said in a heartfelt voice, thankfully interrupting Jessie's colorful but disturbing train of thought. "And thank you, Jessie and Tildy." Jessie began to disclaim her role much as Jack had done. So did Tildy. And Calvina smiled through her obvious exhaustion. "I guess this was a one-woman job," she said. "One woman, one baby, and some mighty special, mighty modest friends."

The baby began to fuss. "I'd better try feeding him again," Calvina said. The others left the room.

"I've got to get to work," Tildy said when they were in the hall. "I've promised a lot of laundry to stampeders. I didn't know Calvina's baby would choose today to be born."

"Run along," Jessie agreed. "I'll stay with Calvina, at least till this evening. And I don't think anyone but the baby knew he'd choose to be born today."

"Calvina and Renny certainly didn't," Jack said.

After Tildy left, Jessie said to Jack, with a big grin on her face, "This time *you* done good, Jack." He walked down the narrow hallway of the first floor with her, toward the kitchen. Their shoulders nearly touched. Rather, because of the difference in their height, Jessie's shoulder nearly touched Jack's biceps, which bulged beneath his plaid wool shirt.

"Yes," he said, "I did. But I'd like to know what all that huffing and puffing was about. How was it supposed to help what was happening at a woman's other end?"

"It's . . . well, it's a pain management technique, for one thing. And I've heard it helps a mother control when to push."

"You're a musician, Jessie. And an unmarried one?" He looked at her questioningly.

"Of course I'm not married," she fumed. "I have no intention of marrying, not while I'm still working hard on my career." If I still have a career, came the unbidden thought. She swallowed a sigh. She'd tried to go home, and she'd failed. She was convinced now that she would be here at least until the avalanche occurred and she learned how the ballad ended. Maybe even beyond. Maybe forever.

She was stuck here, with Jack O'Dair, who had performed another heroic act from that dratted ballad.

Yet another reason she would have to fight her overwhelming attraction to this exasperating, intrepid man.

"And, no," she continued with irritation, "before you ask, I've never had a baby." They had reached the kitchen, and Jessie pivoted to face him, her hands on her hips. She had wished more than once that she'd had on her jeans and t-shirt while helping Calvina; they would have been more comfortable than her borrowed frilly blouse and flannel skirt.

His green eyes widened as though she had slapped him. "I didn't mean to malign your reputation, Jessie. I only—"

She laughed at his obvious discomfort. "You only wanted to know where I learned breathing techniques for childbirth."

He nodded, obviously relieved she understood. One corner of his mouth quirked wryly. "It doesn't seem the kind of skill a balladeer of excellent reputation would need to know."

"You'd be surprised what a balladeer of excellent reputation needs to know," she teased. "Let's just say I've been around, learned a lot of stuff in songs and otherwise that comes in handy now and then. I haven't heard anyone sing about those breathing techniques yet, but you never know."

"You're right," he said. "You never know."

But Jack wished he *did* know—a lot more about Jessie.

Many women here in the North, gold-seekers as much as the men they followed, were individualists. Some smoked and drank as hard as their men. A lot wore pants, as Jessie had done when he had first met her.

But there was something extraordinary about Jessie.

"Are you still performing tonight at Helen's?" he asked. He stood with his hand poised on the knob of Calvina's kitchen door, looking down at Jessie, who had followed him.

"I intend to, even as late as it is. I won't leave until some of the boarders are here to keep Calvina company."

"Then wait till I get back here to walk you there."

"You let me walk to Helen's the other day all by myself without giving me a hard time."

"It was early enough that there were plenty of people out on the streets, so it was safer. And," he said ominously, "it was before someone attacked you."

He expected further argument from her. He always got an argument from her.

He was therefore astonished when she said meekly, "Okay."

"Okay?"

"Okay." She nodded decisively, though her full lower lip jutted out in a pout. She obviously didn't enjoy giving in so easily, even when he was right. Maybe especially when he was right.

He had an urge to bend down and decisively kiss the pout away. Instead, he tilted her chin upward, then lowered his head just enough to barely meet her mouth with his.

Oh, lord. The small contact was just enough to whet his very hearty appetite. If it hadn't been Calvina's kitchen, right in the middle of the day....

But it was. And he had made it clear, after their night of love-making, that he had considered it a mistake. So had Jessie.

A delightful mistake, but one that could not be repeated. He had enough on his mind, enough duties, without adding further responsibility for Jessie to his list.

And if he took her to bed again and again, the way he wanted.... He heard the wail of Calvina's baby from the bedroom—a reminder of exactly what kind of responsibilities could result.

"I need to go, Jessie," he said gruffly.

She blinked up at him, her eyes still unfocused, as though that small kiss had affected her the same way it had him.

"See you later." He gave her a quick, harder kiss, then hurried out the door.

Tildy had been delayed with all the laundry she had to complete that day. Eldon Riggs, that stuffy wannabe stampeder, had made it clear he would not babysit for anyone, not even his charming hostess along with her adorable newborn—Jessie's words, not his.

Whiskey Tom was bartending, as usual, at Helen's that night.

And so, Jessie had prevailed on the newest border, the footloose photographer Dab Daugherty, to keep an eye on Calvina and the baby. Dab was definitely a nice guy, willing to help out when needed.

But there was a limit to his kindness. He had a big, important poker game scheduled late that night, and he simply wouldn't miss it. "If I win," he'd told Jessie, "I'll have the rest of the money I need for my cache."

"But I thought you weren't going after gold," she'd said in dismay.

"Like I said, the gold I'm going for is the documentation of this historic event. But the Mounties at the top of the pass don't care why I'm there. As far as they're concerned, if I've ventured into their territory, I'm a stampeder. I'll be treated the same as everyone else. That means I bring in a cache. And that means I need more money."

And his situation that night meant that Jessie had to perform early at Helen's.

That was why she put on one of her prettiest borrowed outfits, dressed warmly, and stood indecisively by the kitchen door.

She had last stood there earlier, with Jack. She had promised to wait for him right here, so he could walk her to Helen's.

But that was before she knew she had to get there soon. If she walked to the jail to tell him so, she might as well walk to Helen's.

On the other hand, a promise was a promise. She would go tell him first. If he had time to walk with her from the jail, then he would. If not, she would at least have kept her word, sort of. She would have allowed him to accompany her to Helen's. It wouldn't be her fault if he couldn't do it so early.

She buttoned up her fur coat, pulled up the hood, and took a deep breath to brace herself against the usual evening cold. Then she pulled on her gloves and swung open the door.

"Brrr," she grumbled. She ducked her head and headed in the direction of Jack's office.

There weren't a lot of stampeders out, even though it was still early evening. Not when it was this dark, and this cold.

Still, there were a few. And Jessie hurried toward them, still unsure why she had been attacked the other night but certain that whoever had done it would be reluctant to try it again with an audience.

Of the half-dozen men walking down the street, no one appeared particularly interested in her. In fact, none paid attention to her at all.

And not one of them headed down the side streets toward Jack's jail. It would be safer if she stayed with the group. She could explain her rationale to him later.

She followed the crowd down one main street, then the next, which was crowded with outfitters' stores. Horace Martin's warehouse was at one end. Otis Oetting's smaller but more substantial structure was near its beginning.

As Jessie passed Otis's shop, she glanced toward it . . . and stopped. There was a light inside.

No bright illumination, though, that would signify that Otis was there selling goods or stacking inventory. It appeared there was a single lantern bobbing around in the store.

When the group of men she had latched onto for safety continued down the street, Jessie didn't join them. She stood on the plank sidewalk, looking in the window at Otis's.

At first, she couldn't see anything except the light behind some tall stacks of boxes.

"Hmmm," Jessie said to herself. She walked quietly, glad she was wearing soft leather boots that made no noise on the wooden walk. She hurried around to one side of the two-story wooden structure, into an alley formed by Otis's and his neighbor's store, about five feet away. There was another window there, and Jessie lifted her gloved hand to shield her eyes from the glare of lights from a saloon across the street. She looked inside again.

And saw Otis. The short, older man had put down his lantern, and was hefting a crate onto the top of a pile. It looked as if he did not find the feat easy.

Why was he doing this now?

Jessie couldn't tell much in the dim lantern light, but the boxes Otis was moving looked about the same size as the crates of dried potatoes stolen from Horace.

But all containers of similar goods looked alike. And Otis was successful. He had no need to steal from his competitors. Jessie had no reason to be suspicious of him.

Except that he was doing this practically in the dark. Without help. Surreptitiously.

It looked to Jessie as though she was, after all, going to visit Jack at his office tonight before she went to Helen's.

But as she turned to go, she was grabbed from behind.

Chapter Fourteen

Jessie tried to scream, but the hand over her mouth didn't let her. She tried to bite, but that hand was encased in a heavy leather glove. She wriggled fiercely, then let her body go slack. Her assailant was taken unawares and let her go—almost. They both wound up on the wooden sidewalk. Jessie thumped down hard on her backside. Fortunately, her jacket was thick and long, and it padded her fall on the ice-covered dirt.

At the same time that she heard an uneasy canine whine, a whisper sounded in her ear. "Damn it, Jessie, keep still."

Jack? Jessie obeyed the command and stopped moving, all except her head. She turned to try to confirm, in the near blackness of the alleyway, just who her attacker was.

She heard a whine again, then a wet dog tongue slurped along Jessie's cheek. "I'm fine, Taku," she whispered, hugging the wriggling dog. "No thanks to your master."

She wanted to slug Jack for scaring her that way.

At the same time she wanted to hug him . . . in relief, she told herself, since it had been he who'd grabbed her, not whoever had previously attacked her and left her for dead.

Not because she was glad to see him for any other reason.

She felt herself being pulled roughly to her feet. Without looking at Jack, she brushed off the ice that stuck to her clothes. Despite wanting to yell at him for scaring her that way, she kept her voice low. "I've something to tell you, but we need to get out of here before we're seen." She began hurrying down the alley.

He grabbed her arm before she reached the main street, turning her to face him. His voice was soft, too, as he bent toward her, but its tone was ominous. "What the hell were you doing here? You might have ruined—"

The front door to Otis's shop was thrown open abruptly. "Show yourself!" shouted an angry voice. Startled, Jessie stared toward the man who stood there. He was short, filling the doorway better sideways than up and down. Lights streaming from the window of the saloon across the street were enough to show that Otis Oetting held a shotgun. It was aimed at Jessie and Jack.

"Put that away, Otis," Jack demanded. He thrust Jessie behind him. "We have some talking to do, and you'll only make it worse if you aim that gun at a U.S. marshal." His angry words were punctuated by a snarl and series of barks from Taku.

"Jack? I thought you were one of the thieves." Otis

immediately lowered the barrel. He smiled, and his voice softened. "And Miss Jessie, how nice to see you. I was planning on stopping at Helen's later to find out if you were singing tonight. I didn't want to miss one of your fine performances."

"Thanks, Otis," Jessie said sweetly, then added, "We want to know what you were doing in the dark with all those crates."

Jack hissed in her ear, "Miss Jerome, you are over-stepping—"

"I'm still assisting in your investigation, Mr. O'Dair." She put an *ulu*-like edge into her voice, hoping she was conveying her unspoken words just as sharply: *Whether you like it or not.*

"I was doing nothing wrong." All the former friendliness had disappeared from Otis's voice.

"Then why were you shifting boxes in the dark?" Jessie asked. "Did they happen to be borrowed from—"

"Stop interfering, Jessie," Jack interrupted. He sounded so angry that Taku growled as if in sympathy. "Otis, I'm going to walk Jessie to Helen's now. I'll be back in a while, and then we'll have us a little discussion."

"About what? I have nothing to say. I was working in my own store with my own supplies. If I choose to do it in the dark, or even to set a torch to it, it's my business, no one else's. Now, go ahead and take Miss Jessie to Helen's, Jack, but don't bother coming back. I won't talk to you." He walked back into the store and slammed the door behind him.

"What did I tell you, Jessie?" Jack had drawn himself to his full height to loom over her. The redness in his cheeks clashed with the copper of the late-day shadow of his beard. His nostrils flared as though he were about to breathe fire. "You have destroyed my investigation."

"What investigation? I was just—"

"You were just interfering." He took Jessie by the arm and began to lead her down the street.

Though Taku loped easily at his side, Jessie had to hurry to keep up. How could he always be so sure-footed on streets this uneven and icy? She wore boots, too, but they never seemed to help.

"Didn't you promise to stay at Calvina's tonight until I came to walk you to Helen's? Not only did you break that promise, but you let someone I suspected know he was under observation."

"Then you already considered Otis a suspect?" Jessie was taken aback. She'd thought she had made a startling discovery: that the small, seemingly innocuous man who made goo-goo eyes at her as she sang might be a sneak thief, one of the gang that had robbed Horace's warehouse.

It made sense, in a warped kind of way. Horace appeared more successful than Otis. Why not injure the competition while enriching himself?

Jack and she were back on the main street, and there were other people around. Some walked as fast as they did to hurry out of the cold, a few plodded on horseback. No one spared them a glance. Jack could be abducting her, and no one would be concerned.

On the other hand, she wasn't screaming, either, no matter how frustrated she felt with this man. He was angry with her, and all she had been trying to do was help. He could have told her he was investigating Otis.

"Otis has been acting strange lately," Jack finally said in response to her question. He apparently had been mulling whether to reply at all as to whether he considered Otis a suspect.

"Strange how?" Jessie asked quickly. She wasn't about to let him toss out a statement like that without explanation.

Jack shook his head in exasperation as he looked down at her, but he didn't slacken his place. "He's been spending a lot of time at Helen's, for one thing. He kept to himself before."

"He likes my singing," Jessie said proudly. A lot of people seemed to, even if Jack came to Helen's because it was part of his job, rather than to listen to her.

"Yeah, he does." Jack didn't sound happy about it. They were on a stretch of street bereft of saloons. Jessie felt the corner of her lips curl up in a nasty little smile. She quickly straightened them before Jack noticed in the dim light. He wasn't jealous, of course, but still. . . .

"I think he likes me," she continued mercilessly. "If it turns out he's not a crook and I wind up staying here, maybe I should plan to get to know him better."

"Another thing he's been doing strange," Jack said with a snideness in his voice, "is to spend a lot of time with some of the saloon girls. Like I said, he used to keep to himself a lot more, so that isn't normal for him. I wouldn't feel too pleased, if I were you, if he spends a lot of time talking to you under those circumstances."

"He's not equating me with one of Helen's girls." Jessie felt affronted. "He treats me respectfully."

"He treats the others respectfully, too, but that doesn't stop him from paying for their attention."

They had once again reached an area where saloons were plentiful. Jessie heard music emanating from the

211

first one. A handpainted sign over the door proclaimed it was The Fortymile Saloon. "Thanks for accompanying me. I'm going in here."

She wanted him to leave. She'd had about enough of the company—and criticism—of Jack O'Dair for one night. But he walked in beside her.

"Haven't you learned yet that nice ladies don't go into strange saloons all by themselves?" he demanded.

"I work in a saloon," she shot back. "And haven't you learned that, though I'm nice, I have no intention of living up to your idea of a 'lady'?" Without letting him reply, she continued, "I'm here to listen to music. I heard music coming from this saloon. It called to me, so I'm answering."

Without another word, she hurried inside. She looked around—and wished she weren't there. At least Helen's was clean. Her clientele might be scruffy, but the place and people weren't too rough.

Jessie couldn't say the same about this place. She saw no women at all, not even saloon girls. A few men had passed out at the tables; others played cards as though they meant it. The place smelled of liquor and regurgitation. She couldn't see well because there were so few lanterns lit along the walls, but she was sure she wasn't missing anything.

Men stood along the bar, which seemed to be nothing but a long series of planks nailed together on sawhorse legs. Some laughed raucously; others belted down their booze.

But beside the bar, that was what Jessie had come in for. A man sat on a bench before a piano, and he was singing.

Ignoring the leers of the men as she passed, Jessie walked toward the troubadour. She didn't stop to find out if Jack followed, but she was certain that he did, for none of the staring men came over to her.

She watched the musician's hands on the keyboard until he finished his song, one she hadn't heard before, about a miner and a polar bear. Jack edged over until he stood at her side, Taku right beside him.

The singer turned his head to look up at her. His eyes were bloodshot and he badly needed a shave.

"Hello," Jessie said. "I'm Jessie Jerome, and I liked your song." She held out her hand. The man blinked at it as though uncertain what it was for. Then he reached over and grasped it for a moment in his own. His was hot and sweaty, and it shook. He looked up over her shoulder toward Jack and let her hand go nearly immediately.

"I'm Brownie Howard," the man said. He didn't look directly at her but kept staring nervously at Jack.

"He won't hurt you," Jessie assured Brownie. "He just thinks he's protecting me. I'm here collecting songs of the gold rush." She suddenly felt a little desperate. How long had she been here? A week? The avalanche hadn't occurred, but someone might already have started singing of the exploits of Jack O'Dair. Was she frequenting the wrong saloons? Asking the wrong people, and just missing the one person she wanted to meet?

It wasn't easy to ask Brownie Howard if he was the one with Jack staring over her shoulder, but she leaned toward the musician. She said in as low a voice as she could, considering that she had to be heard over the growls and curses of the men surrounding her, "I'm especially interested in songs about real people of this area. Maybe even people who live in Dyea. Do you know of any songs like that?"

He blinked blearily and shook his head. "Can't say

that I do. I've a friend over in Skagway who's a journalist. He's sending stories to his newspaper back in Baltimore about that evil fellow Soapy Smith who runs the town, but I haven't heard of a song even about him."

"Do you mind if I listen to you? I'll stay here for a while, so I can send my babysitter home." She glanced at Jack, who scowled.

"Stay as long as you want," said Brownie.

"One question first, though. I want to know if you can identify this tune." He scooted to the edge of the long piano bench, and Jessie sat beside him. She glanced up at Jack. He was glowering at her.

Brownie, on the other hand, appeared as pleased as punch. Instead of sitting as far from her as possible, he had moved his rump over so that it touched hers.

She sighed. She had put up with such nonsense before as an entertainer and was certain that she would again. Giving a half-hearted smile to her fellow singer, she played one verse of the melody of "The Ballad of Jack O'Dair."

He seemed terribly regretful when he shook his head in the negative. "Sorry, Jessie. It's a new one to me."

To everyone here, too, she was beginning to think. Was the entire song not written until the avalanche? If she were here that long, she might learn how it *should* end, but never hear the actual ending. What if whoever wrote it didn't do so till years afterward, based on whatever legend of Jack may have been passed down?

But the episodes so far had been very accurate. Memories weren't perfect. It would be hard for someone to get events right from sometime in the future.

"Are you ready to go now, Jessie?" asked the hero of that very song.

"No," she grumbled, unwilling to have him boss her around.

She leaned on the piano while Brownie sang an off-key rendition of "Turkey in the Straw" and a bawdy song of the Yukon that she hadn't heard before. She acknowledged the overt winks and grins he shot her way with a long-suffering smile of her own.

She ignored Jack's glower.

Finally, she'd had enough, too. "I'm ready to leave," she told Jack sweetly.

"Fine."

She said good-bye to Brownie, who promised to look her up at Calvina's or Helen's if he learned any new songs about people in Dyea. He spoke loudly enough that Jack heard. He glanced curiously at Jessie, who covered by saying, "I promised Helen I'd find out if anyone was singing about her place or her girls."

He looked dubious but didn't say anything.

They bundled up and went back outside. Jessie was surprised when Jack, taking her arm, led her in the opposite direction from Helen's. Taku darted off to explore between buildings.

"It's later than I expected to accompany you there. Right now, I have to go back to the jail."

"To relieve Filby in looking after the prisoners?"

Jack shook his head beneath his thick fur hat. "No. They're gone."

Jessie halted in surprise. "Gone where? They surely haven't been put on trial yet, have they? Or did they escape?"

She felt Jack's irritated glare, even though they were again in an area of little light. "No, they didn't escape. There's no judge close by, so we sometimes take matters into our own hands and set bail. We don't know where these fellows got the money, but they posted it."

Jessie stared. "You don't really think they'll be here for trial, do you?"

Jack's laugh was a hearty rumble. "Hardly. But they won't be back at all, if they know what's good for them. They've gone on to Skagway or up into the Klondike. They know if I see them again, they'll be shipped over to Juneau or somewhere else where they will be tried." He paused. "They won't be back."

"Frontier justice," Jessie murmured. He was probably right. The only problem with his logic was that, if they were guilty, they would be off robbing people in other towns.

But that wouldn't be Jack's problem.

And they didn't, after all, seem particularly dangerous. Or smart. They'd probably wind up in someone else's jail, at least for a while, till that lawman set bail.

Jessie found herself laughing, too.

They reached the jailhouse. Filby was in the office. "Everything's quiet here, Jack." He patted Taku. "I'll go grab supper, if that's all right." He looked questioningly at Jessie.

"Fine," Jack said. "I'll accompany Miss Jerome where she's going as soon as you get back."

Jessie's ire rose again. "But I don't need—"

"I could have been anyone when I grabbed you outside Otis's. I could have meant you harm."

"That was different. You sneaked up on me." She was perturbed to see him take off his fur jacket and hang it on a hook near the door.

"So did the person who hit you the other night. Jessie, it isn't a sin to need protection."

"I don't need protection. I need my freedom."

She didn't like Jack's sly grin. Or maybe she did like it. A lot. He was a handsome man even when he didn't smile. But when he smiled like that, he was a killer. So to speak.

"Why are you grinning?" she demanded.

"Because I know how to get you to listen to me."

Intrigued, Jessie barely noticed Filby slip out the door. "Just how do you intend to do that?"

"I'll tell you exactly why I was at Otis's before."

With a smile of her own, Jessie took off her jacket. She settled down in a wooden chair in front of Jack's desk.

He had planted one foot on top of his own chair and leaned toward her. His jacket was off, and the sideways strips of the plaid of his wool shirt emphasized the breadth of his shoulders and chest.

He certainly was a heck of a good-looking man.

"Okay," she said. "Tell me."

Jack smiled at Jessie's eagerness. He took the opportunity to sit in the chair behind his desk, settle himself comfortably, go through some wanted posters that had arrived that day on a ship from Seattle.

He could feel Jessie stew as she sat facing him, glaring.

As a U.S. marshal, Jack was reluctant to discuss a case with someone who wasn't a superior or deputy. But with Jessie, he had already alluded to his reasons for sneaking around Otis's in the dark.

And as much as he hated to admit it to himself, Jessie had been helpful so far in his quest for the thieves who had robbed Horace Martin's warehouse, and in making suggestions to prevent further thefts.

He had another reason for telling her more, too: He wanted her to hang around until Filby's return so he could accompany her then, safely, to Helen's.

He didn't need to maintain someone in charge at the marshal's office at all hours, particularly when there were no prisoners to guard. But early evening, after darkness had fallen but before stampeders were settled down for the night, was a time particularly susceptible to altercations, arguments and outright brawls.

Jack had learned the hard way that either Filby or he needed to be in a location where they could be easily found in case of trouble, for there was often trouble. And the easiest place to be found was right here, in the office.

He put down the wanted posters and began straightening his desk.

Jack heard a growl and looked at Taku, who lay before the hearth at the wall across from Jack's desk. Near him was the bed where Filby slept. A stack of clean blankets lay on the floor beneath the foot of the bed.

But the growl had not come from Taku; it had come from Jessie. "Okay, Jack, tell me." Her husky, sweet voice was a little sharp. "What were you really doing at Otis's tonight?"

He looked up and feigned surprise at her irritation. "I was getting to it." He leaned back in his chair and met her gaze. "Someone told me Otis was our thief. I decided to keep a close eye on him."

Jessie's pretty blue eyes narrowed. "He did look suspicious, but who ratted on him?"

"Ratted?" This was another example of the strange

turns of phrase used by the lovely woman who had dropped into his life so mysteriously.

"Squealed. Informed. Accused."

"Oh." Jack allowed his amusement to show, but only for a moment. "I can't tell you that."

Jessie drew in her breath in obvious indignation. "Why not?"

"The person asked me to keep that confidential."

"But I'm trying to help you. If I know the source—"

"Your knowing who made the accusation won't help us determine whether it's correct. Now, since we have a little time here, tell me exactly what you saw when you spied on Otis."

He suspected that Jessie would not be distracted by his sudden modification of the subject. "He was moving things from one pile to another," she began in response to his request. "He was almost in total darkness, acting stealthy. That seems suspicious to me." And then, as he anticipated, she returned to her own inquiry. "But it might make a difference in interpreting his actions if I knew who said to check up on him. You see—"

"What I see is a very pretty but very inquisitive woman who wants to interfere even further into my investigation. Jessie, don't you realize that our little conversation with Otis earlier has put him on guard? Not only won't he talk to me more about what he was doing; if he actually was hiding supplies he stole from Horace, you can be sure they won't be identifiable if I try to get in his store to look for them."

"We could go tonight, before he can hide them or change their labels or whatever. You got a list from Horace, didn't you?" Jessie leaned forward eagerly in her seat. Her long, slender hands were clasped together in her lap, and she smiled in anticipation. Though she had tried to tame her wild brown curls by keeping them pulled back with a ribbon, they had a habit of escaping their confinement and framing her smooth and lovely face.

Damn, she was a sexy woman! She was sitting still, in the middle of his office, and his body was responding just to seeing her, as if they were back in his cabin trying to keep warm. Very warm. With their clothes off—

"How do you get a search warrant way out here in the middle of the night?" Jessie demanded. "Or do you need to worry about such things yet?"

There she was again, talking oddly. He shook his head. Though his seductive thoughts of her hadn't gone away, they were dissipated by his having to think and respond. "The best way for me to stop the thieves is to catch them in the act."

"You could set a trap," Jessie said. She stood and began pacing. Her boots kicked up the edges of her long skirt.

Why was it that Jack had the feeling that she wasn't completely at home in the clothing she wore here?

Surely, wherever she was from, she didn't customarily wear the Levi's in which he had first seen her. Such garb was common in Dyea, for women on the way to the Klondike. But down in the United States, ladies seldom wore pants, except for those frilly bloomers he had occasionally seen.

When he didn't respond, she turned to look at him. "You're not listening to me."

He rose and approached her. This woman seemed full of boundless energy, more full of ideas to assist him, even when he didn't want assistance. "I'm definitely listening to you, Jessie Jerome," he said. "A man would have to be crazy not to listen to such a sweet songstress."

He nearly smiled at the look of pleasure that washed over her face. But it immediately disappeared into a suspicious scowl. "You do like my singing, then?" she asked dubiously.

"I'd have to be made of stone not to. The way you strum that guitar of yours and your voice follows, then leads—it's a near miracle to the ears, Jessie."

He was standing right in front of her now, so close he could touch her. But he didn't. He merely looked down at her. He inhaled her fragile, feminine aroma with each breath.

He'd started out to distract her, to tease her, but he found he was telling the truth. Her singing was more than special; it was an experience that took his breath away. And he had seen from others' faces that he wasn't alone in such a reaction.

"I'm glad you think so, Jack." She was staring up at him with an intensity that he didn't understand. Her hands were clenched at her sides. He wanted to reach down and take them into his own grasp and ease them open. To stroke her soft palms. To feel the calluses on her fingers from the guitar strings. "It really means a lot that you, of all people, like my singing."

A warm surge of something proud rushed through him. What was it about this woman that kept him so off balance? One moment he was trying to outwit her; the next he was trying not to grab her and kiss her and . . .

Their eyes met. And held.

And his resolve not to kiss her? It disappeared in an instant as her arms went around his neck and he felt her fingers buried in his hair, pulling his face down toward hers.

Chapter Fifteen

She had to be crazy. Had the cold addled her brain? Maybe it was the entire experience—traveling in time, indeed!

But Jessie could no more have stopped herself from kissing Jack O'Dair than she could have stopped a Yukon storm from blowing.

Jack's lips didn't just cover hers; they explored them with the fervor of a stampeder searching for gold. They were hot and firm and creative, stirring up feelings within her in areas far, far away from her own eager mouth. They tasted the corners of her lips, her ears, her temples. She had never considered any of them erogenous zones, but had she ever been wrong.

And then there was his tongue. It teased hers, just the way this man always seemed to torment her, frustratingly. Deliciously.

Oh, lord, could this man kiss! She had known it

already, of course. No matter whether she went home, no matter what happened during the rest of her life, here or in her own time, she would never forget what it had been like to make love with Jack, in his cabin outside Dyea, with the Alaskan cold whipping the world outside—and Jack's body filling hers.

But here. She was in his office, in the small building that was the Dyea jail. Someone could walk in at any moment.

And she didn't care.

"Oh, Jack," she murmured. He was inspiring her to be just as creative. She tasted his flesh, let the shadow of his red beard rasp along her own tongue, nipped at his Adam's apple and down along his neck.

Oops . . . their clothes were disappearing . . . her boots. Then his. "No," she tried to whisper, but it came out as an eager moan.

Hardly ceasing his kisses, his caresses, he stretched to lock the building's entrance, pulled down the canvas that covered the building's sole window. Then he danced her body past Taku, who barely looked up, toward Filby's bed. Breathing heavily, she glanced down at the bare mattress.

Jack let go of her. She stood alone, feeling as though she would cry for wanting his touch again. But he stayed away only long enough to arrange clean blankets over the mattress. Then, he placed his own and Jessie's fur jackets over the tops.

He took her into his arms once more. This time, their clothes did disappear. She had taken to wearing an undershirt, since she had only the bra she had arrived in and since it was so cold here that the extra layer felt good. Jack fumbled a little as he removed her blouse, then undershirt. She surmised it wasn't lack of experience, but the trembling of his hands.

223

He laid her back on the bed he had made for them. The soft, warm fur tickled her, cradled her. Welcomed her.

Jack lay down beside her. The desire that she saw in his deep green eyes nearly made her cry out, and then she closed her own eyes as he kissed her once more.

Jack apparently needed her as much as she did him. Oh, yes. For as her hands eagerly explored his brawny body, they moved from his sculpted chest downward, downward, where the pole of his desire strained for her touch. "Ah," he gasped as she gripped him. "Jessie."

He explored her as well, and she writhed beneath his touch even as she caused him, too, to buck and moan. She buried her face against his flesh, inhaling his gloriously musky masculine odor.

And then he rolled over, on top of her, and entered her. She muffled her scream against his shoulder, nipping at his salty flesh as he moved inside her. And Jessie sang, in her head, in her heart, as the tempo rose and intensified, until she shattered even as Jack cried aloud.

And as she lay back in his arms, her quick, uneven breathing melding with his, the melody from Jack's ballad pulsed soothingly in her mind.

"We'd better get dressed," Jessie murmured a short while later, burrowing her face into Jack's warm shoulder. "Filby will be returning."

"Yes, he will." Jack planted a soft kiss on her forehead, then rose. He held out his hands to help her to her feet.

She noticed his appreciative gaze as his eyes scanned her still-nude body. She smiled, in turn taking in the magnificent sight of the genuine Jack O'Dair, in the buff.

What a shame to cover up such an imposing work of art, she thought regretfully as he began to dress, his glorious muscles rippling as he moved. Still, she hadn't thought to see him that way again. Not after the last time. They shouldn't have made love then. They shouldn't have now.

But she didn't regret it. She had simply chalked up another memory to take home with her. An incredibly wonderful memory.

She dressed quickly, too. Who knew when Filby would get back?

Jack was quiet as they picked up the furs and folded the blankets.

Jessie took the chair facing Jack's desk. As their eyes met, she began to smile warmly at him.

His return gaze was intense, searching, as though he were demanding the answer to a question that she should know without his asking.

Did he want to know if she loved him? *Yes*! she shouted inside.

For all that he was a celebrated hero of song, he was a modest man. Maybe he was too shy to profess his own feelings. Should she say something first?

But he spoke before she did. "Oh, Jessie," he said softly.

"Yes?" She leaned forward in her seat, wondering if she could make it easier for him if she approached, touched his strong shoulder, sat in his lap or—

"I came here to do a job," he continued. "That was the only responsibility I intended to assume ever again. But things are different now. This shouldn't have happened once, let alone twice, but it did. And now I will take responsibility for you, too—"

225

"Like hell you will!" So that was it. He thought she would believe he owed her something. Or that he had to preserve her reputation, such as it was. But that was a bunch of malarkey that was outmoded even in this time, here in the rugged North. "Don't kid yourself, Jack," she practically spat. "Didn't you get it the last time we made love? Just because we're good together in the sack doesn't mean I expect you to become my Prince Charming and sweep me away to your castle, take care of me forevermore. Women who think that are only deluding themselves." Like her own poor mother. "I knew what I was doing, and so did you. It was enjoyable, and now it's over. Unless we both choose to do it again sometime for the fun of it—which I doubt. I don't want to give you the wrong idea, either. I'm here for a purpose, but whether or not I fulfill it, I don't belong here. If I'm given the chance, I'll go home as soon as I can. So don't sweat it, Jack. I'm not your responsibility. Ever."

He regarded her with bemusement on his face. After a long moment, he said, "Chance? There are plenty of boats that travel south. I'll be sorry to see you go, though, Jessie, even if it's for the best. I will certainly miss your strange way of speaking. Maybe before you go you can explain—"

He was interrupted by the door opening, and Filby walked in. "It's cold out there," he said, rubbing his red face. "Anything interesting happen while I was gone?"

Jessie glanced at Jack. His green eyes were regarding her with their usual amusement. She hurriedly looked back at Filby. "Nothing interesting at all," she replied sweetly.

* * *

Jack walked down the Dyea street beside Jessie. He had insisted on accompanying her to Helen's that night, though she had made it clear she would have preferred anyone else's company—Taku's. Filby's. Even a non-violent prisoner, if there had been one handy.

Jack had left his lantern at the jail; the nearly full moon lit their way.

Now, he listened to their footsteps crunch on the ice, for that was the only sound either one of them made. He felt the frozen bite of the bitter wind and realized it was no colder than Jessie's attitude toward him.

He should have felt relieved. She had made it clear that she did not want him to feel responsible for her. Very clear.

Clear also that she had only engaged in sex with him both times for the momentary enjoyment, not for a lifelong commitment. All the more reason he should feel relieved she expected nothing from him like marriage, for wasn't that the ultimate responsibility he had been fearing?

He had always failed those he had cared about, to whom he had owed a duty to be reliable. That was why he no longer allowed himself to care about anyone.

And right now, he was failing Jessie.

Jessie glanced toward him. "Are you all right?" Her tone was remote, as though they were mere acquaintances. As though their bodies had not melded so delightfully such a short time ago.

"I'm fine." He didn't mean to sound so gruff, but what did it matter?

He saw the bright lights ahead cast out onto the street by the three saloons in a row, heard the cacophony of music and shouts that competed among them.

"I'm close enough," Jessie said. "You don't have to walk any further with me." Her tone suggested that she didn't want to walk any further with him.

"Filby is on duty now," he replied with a shrug. "I think I'll have a drink before returning to work."

"Suit yourself."

This time, Jessie did not go straight to Helen's. Someone was singing off-key in the Gold Grubstake Saloon, the farthest one, and the loud sound apparently acted as a magnet to Jessie. She walked into the Gold Grubstake as if she belonged there, too.

When the singer had finished, Jessie went up to him and chatted for a while, much too familiarly. But that was Jessie's way. If she was aware that Jack had followed her inside, she didn't show it. But she seemed very aware of the attention of the slew of men who patronized the saloon. They made her aware of their presence, crowding around, leering at her. Some even called her by name. She laughed and joked until they roared with laughter, and she along with them.

Jack saw no reason to laugh. No reason to smile. Didn't she know what these men wanted from her?

And then he did smile—a small, sad, ironic smile. These men wanted from Jessie Jerome exactly what *he* had gotten from her: pleasure. A gratifying experience, with nothing else.

Nothing else. . . .

She looked up then and caught his eye. Her soft brown brows lifted slightly. She couldn't know what he was thinking, could she?

A short while later, she was by his side again, putting on her fur jacket and pulling up her hood over her loose brown waves. "That singer has a fair repertory, but he didn't know the ballad I'm looking for, either. We made arrangements to exchange songs at Helen's later."

She popped her head in at the saloon next door, Binns's. She talked to the singers there, too—all scantily clad saloon girls—and teased their audience. The men would all show up at Helen's, Jack was sure, to see more of Jessie.

His hand began to cramp, so he unclasped his fist.

On Jessie's way out again, she passed Jack as he stood in the doorway. He followed.

"You could have been in Helen's already, having your drink," she told him while she strode down the sidewalk, her arms clutched around her to block out the bitter, windy cold. He stayed by her side. "Or you could have stayed at the Gold Grubstake or Binns's. You didn't have to hang around me."

"Yes, I did." Jack didn't like the sharp edge to his own voice, nor the startled glance it brought from Jessie. "You might be in danger," he said more reasonably. "Someone has already hurt you."

"Yes," she agreed without looking at him. "Someone has."

They reached the door to Helen's. "Jessie," Jack said gently. "Please believe that I didn't intend to hurt you."

This time, Jessie met his gaze with a smile that seemed genuine. "Do I look hurt? No strings, Jack. I understood that. And, by the way, the ladies in sweet Helen's nest were absolutely correct. Your kisses *are* the best." With that, she turned her back on him and sashayed through the door into Helen's, leaving Jack wondering what she was talking about. Who at Helen's had said his kisses were the best?

And whoever it might have been, no matter how

exaggerated it was, he couldn't help feeling mighty pleased that Jessie acknowledged it was true.

He *hadn't* hurt her, Jessie told herself as she retrieved her guitar from beneath the bar. He could only hurt her if she let him, and that she would not do.

She sat on her usual seat on the stage. To her surprise, Taku jumped up onto the stage, too, and sat beside her. He nuzzled her arm, and she patted him. He stared at her face with his large golden eyes and whined as though he sensed her own inner disquiet. "It's all right, boy," she lied.

She wasn't all right. But she couldn't think about that.

She wondered why Jack had such a fear of responsibility—he, who was responsible for the safety of the entire town of Dyea. He had alluded to letting people down.

Well, it didn't matter. He couldn't let her down.

Not any more than he already had.

"It does hurt," she sang softly to Taku as she strummed a chord. His long pink tongue emerged from his mouth, and he panted a little, looking as though he wanted to sing along.

"Louder!" shouted a member of the audience.

"What do you want me to sing?" Jessie called in response. She gave Taku a gentle squeeze, then looked down at the people seated around the saloon.

She was on stage. Her show was about to begin. She donned her performer persona just as she did the big, borrowed fur jacket she wore outside in the cold Alaskan air.

"Clementine," someone called, and Jessie complied. She sang it sweetly and full of feeling.

And her eyes were not still, as she caught the gaze of first one stampeder, then another.

She knew just where Jack was sitting, watching her. And she purposely avoided looking toward him.

But she made certain everyone in the place knew she was having one heck of a good time up here on stage, entertaining them all.

Sweet Helen brought her a glass of water that she set beside Jessie's chair. Jessie could see some of Helen's girls swinging through the saloon, serving the men and sitting on their laps.

She thanked heavens for her good voice; singing, and not their kind of entertaining, was the career she wanted.

What would she do if she got home but Curtis had managed to decimate her real career so it could not be salvaged?

Of *course* she could salvage it, somehow. But did she really want to go back?

Would she even have the choice when she learned the end of the ballad?

Why wait?

"Calling Lizard Songthroat," she belted out incongruously in the middle of one of her songs. "I'm ready to go home. The only future I want to see is my own."

The audience was clapping in time to her music but the beat was thrown off by her strange lyrics.

"What's that, Jessie?" called one of her fans.

"Something I just made up," she replied. "It's the story of a stampeder who's ready to give up and go home and follow his real future."

She was met by boos and catcalls, and she laughed and began singing a song Arnett had taught her about a successful stampeder who'd gone home with a ship-

231

load of gold. That brought cheers and kisses and a shower of coins up on stage.

Jessie laughed . . . and looked down at Jack. He leaned against the bar staring at her. She couldn't read his expression.

She didn't want to. She just kept on singing.

During her second chorus of "Erie Canal," she heard a disturbance in the audience and looked down just as Taku leapt off the stage.

"Jack O'Dair, are you here?" cried Horace Martin. Filby was with him.

Jessie stopped singing as Jack stepped forward. "What's wrong?" He addressed his question to his deputy.

"There's been another theft," cried Horace Martin. "And this time, it wasn't just my place."

"That's not all, marshal," Filby added. "There's someone dead."

No one would have paid any attention to her singing anymore that night, Jessie rationalized. She had told Helen she had to leave, then had put her guitar away and followed the crowd as it hurried after Jack, Horace and Filby.

Everyone was talking quickly, repeating what they had heard. Jessie was sure that, by the time she learned anything new, it had been magnified and distorted.

The story she heard, though, made some gruesome sense.

"The body's still lying there," one stampeder confided in her. "Filby wanted his boss to see it before it's moved."

"He said it's a bloody mess," said another stampeder.

The surge of people in the small town of Dyea quickly reached the side street where many outfitters' shops were located. The body did, in fact, remain right where it had been discovered—in a snow-crusted alley between Horace's and Frank Dungel's shops. Frank was the other outfitter who had been robbed, Horace had said. Filby and Horace had left him to keep an eye on the street and the body, and to alert three other nearby outfitters so they could check on their own wares, too. Lights streamed from lanterns from all five shops, and the owners and their employees swarmed around like a nest of ants.

Jessie sighed. If Jack had had any hopes of finding evidence as to who had committed the murder and thefts, whatever clues might have been there probably were obliterated by now.

Jack apparently shared the frustration. She saw him take Filby aside, and though she couldn't make out what he said to his deputy, she did hear his severe tone.

Jack used long rope to cordon off the alley where the body lay. He deputized a couple of stampeders to make certain no one violated the dividing line.

Jessie nevertheless managed to get close enough to see the corpse lying in the snow. However the man had died, it had been violent. Blood stained the snow.

Was this another episode from Jack's ballad? If so, she could think of only one more thing that was supposed to happen before the avalanche occurred. This could certainly be it:

"On a windswept night, the moon again bright,
The snow was crimson with blood.
A man lay dead, a deep wound in his head.

Dyea's citizens quaked—as they should.
" 'Where's our Jack?' they did shout from every
    house.
'Who else can protect us from dying?'
Brilliant Jack O'Dair, with his dog Taku's flair
Readily solved the crime."

Readily solved the crime? How? Without the possibility of finding clues, he would need to find the
smoking gun, assuming the fatal injury was caused
by a bullet, of course.

But maybe Jessie could help.

She made her way through the crowd. It contained
a lot of familiar faces, many who had been at Helen's
earlier: Helen herself. Eldon Riggs. Several of
Helen's girls, including Nadine, Gilda and Sadie.
Stampeders who had been clapping to her music and
singing along, and who now appeared sobered and
sorrowful. Jessie wasn't certain where Dab Daugherty
had been before, but he was busy now, setting up his
camera stand and taking pictures both of the crowd
and the body.

There was more she knew about from the future
that might help here. She had to talk to Jack, no matter what he thought of her after their earlier episode.

No matter what she thought of him. Damn! This
was no time to get maudlin and sentimental. Someone
had been killed—in Jack's town. He undoubtedly was
furious.

After words with the stampeder on guard—one of
her fans at Helen's, it turned out—Jessie ducked beneath the rope and hurried into the alley.

Jack was kneeling beside the bloody body. Jessie
sucked in her breath. It was not a pretty sight, with

the red contrasting so brutally with the whiteness of the snow.

Jack looked up, then rose hurriedly to his feet. "What are you doing here, Jessie?" He glared at the man who was supposed to be guarding the alley. "I left strict instructions not to allow anyone—"

"Don't get angry with him," she insisted. "I just thought I might be able to help you."

He stared at her, then quirked one of his coppery brows up in challenge. "All right," he said. "What's your idea? How can you help?"

"How did he . . ." Jessie nodded jerkily toward the corpse without looking down again, "die?"

"Gunshot wound to the head."

She nodded. "I thought so. Now, I'm not sure whether you're aware of it, but each bullet is affected by the gun that shoots it." She was rather fuzzy on ballistics, but in case he didn't know anything about it, she could give him a fair rundown on what to look for to determine which was the murderer's gun.

He nodded.

She continued with her explanation, including angles of bullet entry to determine the killer's height, how gunpowder residue would remain on hands—or gloves, assuming that the perpetrator used gloves to keep his hands from freezing out here—and everything else she could think of that she had learned from mystery novels and televisions shows.

When she was through, Jack said, "That's all very interesting Jessie. Very helpful. And now, let me tell you how helpful. The killer is about five-foot four. He's a male, and he shot this guy with a Marlin repeating rifle, .38 caliber, twenty-six-inch round barrel. He was wearing yellow leather gloves with a slight rip between the thumb and forefinger of the left hand."

Jessie stared at him. "You could figure out all that?" Boy, detection techniques today were a lot more sophisticated than she had given them credit for.

Jack grinned. "Sure could. You see, the guy on the ground was one of the thieves—one of the fellows we had over at the jail a couple of days ago. He was caught in the act by Frank Dungel, who shot him in self-defense."

Chapter Sixteen

"Oh," Jessie said, feeling deflated. Jack didn't need her for this, either.

All he needed her for was an occasional roll in the hay, or, rather, in the jailhouse blankets.

So what? She had used him the same way. Only . . .

Only her initial interest in him had been sparked by hero worship. The spark had ignited, carrying her much farther than she had contemplated a ballad ever could.

But that didn't matter. Jack didn't need her.

"So," she said brightly, "I guess you've solved this one."

"Mm-hmm." Jack nodded distractedly. He turned the body over. Jessie didn't look down. She couldn't, not with all that red, red blood in the white snow.

Beside Jack, Taku whined, echoing Jessie's inner disquiet. "Good boy," Jack said. "Stay there."

Linda O. Johnston

But Jessie wasn't about to just slink away in the dark. She still wanted to offer assistance. "So from what you've said, this thief was caught in the act by Frank, who shot him. Isn't that still a homicide? Maybe manslaughter, but—"

"It was self-defense. Madden had a gun. He pointed it at Frank and Frank shot first."

"Madden?"

"The dead man. You knew him. He's the prisoner you called 'Foghorn.' "

Oh, yes. Jessie recalled the stentorous voice demanding that his cohort keep quiet. "Any sign of Dismal?" she asked.

Jack rose to his feet and shook his head. "Maybe he was smart enough just to leave my town and not come back."

"Maybe." Jessie wondered, though. Foghorn—she couldn't think of him as Madden—had seemed to dominate Dismal, even if he couldn't get him to shut up. If Foghorn had returned, maybe Dismal was around someplace, too.

Filby arrived with a blanket, and Jack arranged it over the body, stirring up a little snow in the process. "Get a couple of the men and take him to the barbershop," he told Filby, then looked down at Jessie. "Our barber is also the undertaker."

She had heard that barbers on the frontier had often acted as dentists and even doctors, too. Alaska was certainly the frontier in these days. And why shouldn't a barber be an undertaker as well?

"You look tired, Jessie. It's been a long day."

She darted her glance up at his face. Was he referring just to the killing or to what they had been doing earlier? There was was a glimmer in his eyes. He was remembering, too. Jessie flushed, and not entirely

238

from embarrassment. Darn it all, just a look from this man and she felt desire course through her as though it had settled permanently into her bloodstream. "Yes, it's been very eventful," she agreed. "I think I'll go on to Calvina's and get to sleep so I can forget all about it." She emphasized the "all" as she stared defiantly up into his face.

"It's better that way," he agreed. He motioned to Dab Daugherty, who had just picked up his camera stand. "Will you walk Miss Jerome back to Calvina's?" he asked. "I have to hang around here to talk to some more people tonight."

"I'd be proud to." Dab darted a flirtatious smile at her.

Jessie couldn't help returning it; she had conditioned herself to respond in a friendly manner to an audience. She darted a sidelong glance at Jack. He looked less than friendly. A lot less.

Why should he care whether she flirted? He'd made it plain how limited his interest was in her. "Good night, Jack," she said airily. "I'll probably stop by the jail to talk to you tomorrow." This time, she emphasized the word "talk." She didn't want him getting the wrong idea. "I'll be interested in hearing if anyone besides Horace and Frank had their shops looted. Maybe I can help."

"You can help best, Miss Jerome," Jack said in an ominous grumble, "if you keep out of the way."

"I'm getting some wonderful photographs," enthused Dab Daugherty as they tromped through the deep snow toward Calvina's.

Jessie hardly heard him.

On top of everything else, Jack thought she was just in the way.

239

Well, he didn't know how much in the way she could be. Not yet. But she would show him, if that was what it took for her to learn the ballad's end and go home.

"Do you know today's date?" she asked Dab. She swung the lantern that lit their way. They had gone past the busy area where light from saloon windows illuminated the night. Now, they were in a dark and quiet part of the mushrooming town where shadows of houses loomed on both sides of the snow-covered streets. This late, few had lights burning inside.

Dab looked at her in confusion. The flatness of his nose seemed emphasized by the tall fur hat he wore. "It's March something. The thirty-first, I think."

Good. The time was drawing closer. The avalanche had occurred on Palm Sunday, April 3, up in Chilkoot Pass.

"Have you taken many pictures in the Pass?" Jessie blurted.

"Not as many as I intend to," Dab replied. His flabby lips quivered a bit in the cold. She noticed that his strides were not as determined as Jack's. His legs weren't as long. Plus, as usual, he carried his large camera stand that was much bulkier and probably much heavier than the sleek tripods of her time. And then there was the unwieldy camera itself.

"How about Jack O'Dair?" Jessie found herself asking. "Have you taken the marshal's picture?"

If so, none had survived to her time. Or at least none that she had found.

"Sure have. The man's about the bravest, smartest fellow I've ever seen. He's going to be a big part of the story I plan to tell about the gold rush—he and others who helped keep the peace here in this god-forsaken country."

He admired Jack, even sang his praises, so to speak. Just to be sure he wasn't the person she was looking for, Jessie asked, "Have you ever written a ballad?"

He nearly stopped dead beside her. "Who, me?" He laughed. "My only talent is taking pictures. Besides, no one would want to hear me sing." He began walking again, his pace in time to a rendition of "Ol' Dan Tucker." Or at least Jessie thought that's what it was. The words sounded familiar, but the sounds emanating from Dab's throat were a cross between a wolf's howl and a tuneless throb from a kettle drum.

With a broad smile, Jessie took up the song, and together they warbled on their way to Calvina's the story of how poor Dan Tucker was too late for supper.

"Is the baby all right?"

If Jessie's nerves had suffered at Dab's caterwauling, now they were standing on end as tiny screams penetrated every corner of the boarding house from the parlor where Jessie and Calvina stood.

"Just a little colic, I think," Calvina said. Her tone was calm, but the panicked look in her eyes showed that her nerves, too, were suffering. A tear rolled down her cheek. "I feel so helpless that he isn't feeling well. Tildy came down a little while ago to see if there was anything she could do, but he just wouldn't quiet. And it didn't help at all when Eldon came into the parlor and just stared, as though that would somehow convince the little one to settle down."

Men were useless in such situations, Jessie thought. When she had arrived with Dab, he had taken one look at the scene, mumbled some excuse and hurried off to his room.

Linda O. Johnston

She wondered what heroic thing Jack O'Dair might do to soothe this suffering infant. Or would he just flee, the same as Dab?

One thing she had learned was that Jack, though courageous and intrepid, was far from perfect.

Calvina held the baby to her shoulder and danced around the room. The little, nearly bald head bobbed gently. The infant's face was bright red and his mouth remained open as he shrieked.

Jessie's mind raced ahead for a sure-fire cure for colic from her time and came up with none. She sighed and sank onto one of the wooden chairs. The dining table had been pushed against the wall. The stiff chairs were arranged in front of it and around the braided rug for the residents to gather and chat in the cozy room. A fire blazed in the fireplace, and the pleasant aroma of burning wood inundated the air. The scene filled her senses, including, unfortunately, her ears. She had pinned her hair up for comfort but considered letting it down for the small barrier it would make between the shrill cries and her eardrums.

"I'd imagine you've already checked his diaper," Jessie suggested hopefully, her voice raised to be heard.

"I changed it no more than five minutes ago," Calvina replied without stopping her movement around the room. Her long skirt billowed, and as she neared the fire the air she fanned up caused it to sputter slightly.

"Have you decided on a name yet?" Jessie thought it inappropriate to keep referring to the little one as "the baby" or "the infant," or just "him."

Calvina shook her head vehemently. "Not till Renny comes home."

242

Whenever that might be, Jessie thought.

Calvina began humming. Jessie could barely hear it over the baby's cries and did not recognize the tune. In fact, maybe there was no tune, just a soft attempt to soothe the baby and stop his screaming.

It began to work. The baby's cries became less intense. The more quiet the infant became, the more Jessie could hear of the song. It was a repetitious melody in a minor key, sweet and compelling. Jessie was certain she had never heard it before.

She was about to ask Calvina what it was when Calvina began to sing words to it:

> "Hush, my son, hush,
> Go to sleep.
> Daddy is far away.
> He's gone to the gold fields
> To find you some nuggets
> He'll be home one of these days.
> "Hush, my son, hush,
> Go to sleep.
> It's cold out but warm inside.
> Mama loves you, and
> Mama loves Papa,
> And together we'll always abide."

Calvina sang the lullaby twice through, and by the time she was done the baby had quieted. "I'll go put him in his bed now," she whispered to Jessie.

While she was gone, Jessie sang the song quietly to herself, wishing she had her guitar here instead of at Helen's. She nevertheless put chords to the song in her mind. Then she used a pencil with a tip that had been sharpened with a knife to jot down notes and

243

words onto some paper she had found to replace the slate she had used earlier.

She loved the song, was thrilled to have learned this new Alaskan gold rush lullaby. That was what she would call it, unless she happened upon it elsewhere with a different title.

She had pulled her chair over to face the fire and was staring into it, singing the lullaby again when Calvina returned. She didn't interrupt Jessie, but pulled another chair close by. When Jessie was done, Calvina said, "You have such a lovely singing voice, but that's such a silly song." She sounded wistful. When Jessie glanced at her, she noticed again how exhaustion seemed to be aging this pretty young mother. Lines strained the corners of her eyes, and her shoulders were rounded.

"It's not silly at all," Jessie contradicted. "It's beautiful. So poignant, especially the melody. Do you know who wrote it?" She would want to give credit where it was due, of course. Even pay to sing it in public, if necessary. If she brought it back to her own time, though, no copyright was likely to still be in effect, even if there was one now.

Calvina gestured dismissively in the air. "Oh, I know who wrote it, all right. It was me."

"You?"

"Well, sure. I simply started singing to calm the little one, and that's what came out."

"Right now? Just like that?"

"Just like that," Calvina confirmed. Her eyes twinkled almost mischievously.

Jessie smiled in amazement. She had sometimes made songs up extemporaneously like that, but she was a trained singer. That was what she did. Calvina, on the other hand, was a boardinghouse owner. "That was wonderful!" she said. "Would you mind if I sang it in public sometime? If I get paid to sing it, I'll give you a portion of what I earn."

"Really? That silly thing?" She waved her hand again. "I know, you don't think it's silly. But . . . but I could actually make money for something like that?"

"It's how I earn my living back home," Jessie confirmed. "And some spending money here as well." A sudden thought struck her. "You haven't sung a song about . . . about anyone you know around here, have you?"

Calvina looked down at her hands, which were resting on her lap. They were rough and reddened from work, and she wore a plain gold band on the ring finger of her left hand.

That, Jessie feared, would be the closest this family would ever get to a gold strike here, from all she had heard of successes in the Klondike gold rush. But she didn't say so to Calvina. Instead, she waited breathlessly for her answer. Her hesitation told Jessie that she had, indeed, made up a song—or songs—about people she knew.

Had Calvina Sanders, of all people, written "The Ballad of Jack O'Dair?"

What a coincidence that would be! Here she was, staying in the woman's home.

Or maybe it wasn't a coincidence. Lizard Songthroat had somehow sent her back here to learn the end of the ballad. Maybe he had orchestrated this, as well.

But Jessie's hopes were immediately dashed as Calvina spoke. "I have made up just one other song," she said quietly, "and it's about someone I know: Renny."

"Oh. Well, as I've told you, I'm collecting songs here. I'd love to hear it."

"But I thought you were only after songs sung in the saloons, ones other people had heard."

"I'm after any and all songs that I like," Jessie replied. "Please sing it for me."

She was just being polite, but it wouldn't hurt her to listen. After all, Calvina had already demonstrated that she had a pretty, if untrained voice, and a talent for making up songs.

"If you really want me to." Calvina rose and straightened the pinafore over her long skirt. She was still wearing clothes she had worn during her pregnancy.

"Sure," Jessie urged.

This time, the melody was sweet and mellow. Calvina smiled fondly as she sang about her husband—and Jessie nearly cried. Unlike the lullaby, this was a silly song, full of nonsequiturs and contradictions, but clearly filled with feeling.

> "Sweet as sugar, tough as sand
> And as fast as a flying dove,
> That's my Renny Sanders
> The man I'll always love.
> "He treats me fair and wants the best
> For me and for us two
> He'll find us gold one day I'm sure
> So we'll have a life that's new.
> "He loves to dream and his dreams are big
> As big as the sky above.
> That's my Renny Sanders,
> The man I'll always love.
> "And when someday we both look back
> To this time of dreaming bold,

Even if the Yukon yields nothing,
Our love is more treasure than gold."

Jessie said nothing as Calvina finished. She couldn't. This woman obviously loved her husband, despite all his possible failings. She recognized him as a quixotic, hopeful man who wanted riches and might find nothing, but she let him follow his dream. She seemed untroubled that he hadn't even been there to witness his baby's birth.

Jessie wondered what it would be like to love a man that way.

And what if the man was as strong, heroic and down-to-earth as Jack O'Dair?

She shook her head so fiercely that her hair tumbled down from its pins and about her cheeks.

"Is something wrong? Did you hate the song? I'm sorry." Calvina, standing near the fireplace, looked distressed.

"I loved the song," Jessie managed hoarsely. "But how do you . . . I mean, people aren't perfect. Sometimes they do wonderful things, but sometimes they do things that are not wonderful, maybe even hurtful. If you fall in love with someone, how can you—"

"See past their imperfections and love them anyway?" Calvina sat down again beside Jessie and touched her cheek with her warm, callused fingers. "Oh, Jessie, I don't know about anyone else, but with Renny, I love him for all the good *and* the bad. Maybe it's because the good is so very good. He has a kind heart. And even if he is a dreamer, he wants the best for me and now, I'm sure, for our son. The best part is that he loves me. He loves us. That's the most important thing of all."

To be loved. That was what Jessie's mother had

craved all those years ago, but she had never found it.

And Jessie? She had fallen for a fictional hero, and when she had met him in the flesh he'd had a lot of heroic qualities, but he wasn't perfect. Calvina said that didn't really matter.

But Jack O'Dair had made it clear that, though he might attempt to assume responsibility for her, he didn't, he wouldn't love Jessie.

And that, if nothing else, was a fatal flaw.

She felt tears fill her eyes, and she quickly stanched them. She didn't need him. She didn't need love. She had made that decision years ago, when she had seen what searching for it had done to her mother.

"Even though that's a wonderful song," she told Calvina, "not every woman needs a man in her life."

"Maybe," Calvina said, but she looked at Jessie shrewdly. "But those women who don't must be very lonely. And I don't think you, Jessie Jerome, are destined to be one of them."

She was, however, destined to stay here for the time being. And to do that, she had to be able to live with herself.

That was why, the next morning, Jessie headed straight for the street where most of the outfitters were. She intended to help stubborn Jack O'Dair, whether or not he acknowledged he needed her assistance.

The temperature was a little warmer today than it had been since she'd arrived, and the dirt road had turned into a sea of mushy mud. Jessie kept her fur jacket unbuttoned, and it flapped open to expose her muslin blouse.

She was glad Calvina had lent her a sturdy pair of

boots, though the going was slow; she had to drag each foot out of the mire with every step, for the way she was going was not lined with wooden walkways. She only wished she had put on her blue jeans instead of the long skirt that she had to keep holding up to keep from trailing in the muck.

Poor horses, she thought, staring at the few animals pulling wagons along the Dyea streets. Their owners hollered at them, as if that would help them progress more quickly. Would dog sleds work better in this mess? She didn't know, but saw no mushers trying it.

The streets were filled with people, mostly men with solemn, determined faces, who appeared to have destinations in mind. The air smelled dirty and thick, and Jessie could almost taste the mud in her mouth.

She didn't much enjoy fighting every step of the way, for her energy was already sapped; she hadn't slept well the night before. Calvina's songs had kept running through her mind.

Calvina's love for Renny, no matter what, enthralled her.

No, it disturbed her. No self-respecting woman should subordinate her own needs to a man's that way.

But Calvina seemed content. More than content: happy.

And what could be better than that?

The street where Horace's store lay seemed busiest of all. Stampeders seemed to occupy every inch. Jessie had to wriggle her way through the crowd, saying "Excuse me," over and over.

There was a line at Horace's, but she maneuvered her way to the front. "I'm not buying anything," she said apologetically to the grim-faced men in worn jackets and muddy legs who had clearly waited in line for hours.

As she went inside, she was met by Taku, who licked her hands as soon as she removed her gloves.

If the wolf-dog was here, his master had to be close by.

Sure enough, she was met by a less-than-enthusiastic greeting a moment later: "Jessie, what are you doing here?"

How could that voice, especially in that unwelcoming tone, still manage to send sensuous shivers up and down her spine? Foolish, foolish woman, she admonished herself as she turned toward Jack, pasting a bland expression on her face. "I just wanted to see if there was anything I could do to help. And, yes, I know, you think the best help I can be is to stay far away." She looked way up that spectacular broad body of his. He was clad today in a loose ecru shirt and leather vest over woolen trousers. He looked all man, especially since he had apparently neglected to shave that morning, and his red beard shadowed his already craggy features.

She had a sudden urge to scratch the sensitive skin of her fingers along his stubble. She didn't act on it, though. She had no intention of ever touching Jack O'Dair again.

Her gaze met his green eyes, expecting his expression to be stern and forbidding. After all, she had ignored his admonishments to stay away from his investigation.

Instead, there was a humorous glint in them. "When have you ever paid attention to what anyone else says?" he asked lightly.

She grinned. "You're beginning to know me, Jack O'Dair," she said.

"I'd like to know you even better," he murmured.

Startled, she looked up at him, but he had started to move away among the shoppers at Horace's. Had she heard him correctly?

Hardly. He had made it clear that he had gotten to know her more than he'd intended to, and that he was backing far away. And that was fine with her.

Jack had headed toward Horace, who was standing nearby. He began examining a pile of stores that apparently already had been sorted for a stampeder, for it contained all sorts of goods.

Jessie turned her back toward Jack in case he again got upset about her meddling. She said to Horace in a low voice, "I know you're busy, but I'd really like to know what was taken this time. Also, were other outfitters robbed yesterday?"

She was thinking of Otis Oetting, whose store was a block away. If things had been stolen from him as well as the others, then that might show he wasn't the perpetrator of the thefts, but perhaps another victim.

But Horace replied, "My next-door neighbor Frank Dungel was the only other one robbed that I know of so far. I've told others on the street to check their supplies, too, just in case, but no one has reported anything else."

"Which store is Frank's?" Jessie asked.

Horace nodded his thin face toward one side of his tent warehouse. "He's on my east side." Of course, Jessie thought. She had seen Madden's body the night before in the small alleyway between Horace's large store and Frank's smaller wooden building.

Taku was pacing uneasily in the crowd of stampeders, and Jessie said to him, "Do you want to go outside with me, boy?" When the silvery dog stayed at her side, she called to Jack, "Taku is coming with me. I'll bring him back in a minute."

Jack didn't look overly pleased, but neither did he object.

Next door, Jessie met Frank Dungel's wife, Emmie, a small, worried-looking woman in a loose black dress. Jessie fibbed a little when she introduced herself but figured Taku's presence with her would bolster her credibility. "I'm an unofficial deputy marshal," she told the troubled woman. "Jack O'Dair and Filby are busy, so I'm asking questions to help determine what happened around here last night. My name is Jessie Jerome."

Emmie's face was pale, as if she hadn't seen sunlight in a long time, but it was rutted from advancing age. She did not look particularly friendly—especially because her dark eyes were small and suspicious. "Aren't you the woman I've heard about, the one who sings at Helen's?"

Jessie nodded, smiling broadly as though she didn't realize this woman didn't think much of her. "You've heard of me? Great! I'm here mostly to learn local music, but I've had an unofficial law enforcement background, too." Very unofficial, she thought: observing fictional detectives in unreal situations and in exaggerated-reality TV shows. But she didn't need to tell anyone here that.

"Really?" The woman's trust had clearly not been won with Jessie's words.

"That's right," Jessie said, becoming all business. "Now, I'd like to get a statement from you. Were you here when the theft at your store was discovered?"

"Was I ever!" stated Emmie Dungel. "I was in the back room while it was going on."

Chapter Seventeen

Jack knew that Jessie wasn't just playing a social call on Emmie Dungel. Excusing himself from Horace, he went next door to see how Frank was faring after having shot a thief. He also needed to follow up on his investigation of last night's theft and shooting. And to check on his dog.

The fact that he would see Jessie . . . well, that did not matter. Not in the least.

He was not surprised when she confronted him. "I need to talk to you." She took his arm. Taku whined and followed them.

Much as Jack didn't want to, he liked the feel of Jessie holding onto him. It reminded him of what it had felt like to be with her skin-to-skin, to touch every inch of her, to feel her beneath him. Around him.

Oh, lord, the woman could affect him even without saying a word.

But then she did speak. "I talked to Emmie," she

whispered urgently as she tugged him into the empty alley between Horace's and Frank's and released his arm. Coming back to reality, he automatically glanced down at the area where Madden had lain last night, but patches of snow had melted, even here in the cool alley between the two buildings, where shadows prevented the late winter sun from penetrating. Though there was a dark stain in the mud that was probably the dead thief's blood, it did not form the same stark contrast that it had with last night's new fallen snow.

Taku sniffed the area and moved away with his nose toward the ground, as though following a scent. Jessie seemed distracted as she watched him. "Do you think Taku can tell who was with Madden? He wasn't alone last night. That's what Emmie told me."

"Is that so?" Jack knew he sounded skeptical, but Jessie had to learn that *he* was in charge of the investigation. He had questioned Frank. He had looked around for clues. He'd put together all the information available on the theft at Frank's.

He knew all there was to know about what had happened last night. Didn't he?

"Emmie was hidden in a back room," Jessie said, nodding vigorously. "She heard voices. More than two."

Jack scowled. "Why didn't she tell me before?"

"Frank told her not to. He was afraid the others would hear that she knew something, come back after her."

"But she just happened to tell you?"

Jessie nodded solemnly but said nothing more. An innocence in her expression, though, told him there was something she hadn't revealed.

"Just why was that?" he pressed.

"Women in your town stick together." She smiled complacently.

He grasped his hands behind his back so as not to throttle her. "And?" he prompted. "Emmie Dungel isn't the kind of woman to confide in a stranger, especially when her husband told her not to talk to anyone."

"Not all women obey every command of their menfolk." He was perturbing Jessie. Did it ever feel good! Besides, he was more likely to get a straight answer from her if she spit it out instead of playing angel.

Angel. She looked like a wayward angel, with her brown hair spilling in waves about her face. It was warm enough out that she wore neither hat nor hood. She was still clad in the grizzly fur jacket he had lent to her, but she hadn't buttoned it, even though the alley was chillier than the sunswept but mountain-shadowed street. He could just make out the angry rise and fall of her breasts as she breathed hard in irritation with him.

He enjoyed the view. He would have to irritate her more often, especially indoors, where she wore no jacket at all.

Meantime, he had to keep her anger stoked. "I don't know about wherever it is that you're from, Jessie, but around here, in *my* town, it's a rough world. Women who accompany men to the Klondike need discipline. They're taught to obey their men."

"Hogwash!" She had hesitated for a split second before exclaiming, and he had a sense she had been about to use a more colorful expression. Oh, how he enjoyed seeing those blue eyes blaze, those full lips pout as she stewed.

He wanted to kiss those lips. Instead, he said, "All right. Let's assume Emmie Dungel chose to disobey

Frank for a good reason. Suppose you tell me exactly why she told *you*."

"She trusted me."

"Why?"

Jessie met his gaze full on, then glanced away, murmuring something.

"What was that?"

She rounded on him, hands on her hips. "I told her I was sort of a deputy of yours. That I have an unofficial law-enforcement background."

"I see. I've wondered about how you seem to know so much about my job. I don't know of any women in law enforcement, but up here I can believe anything. Tell me more about that 'unofficial' background of yours."

Maybe her father was a policeman. Or her brother. She had to have gotten her information somewhere. And now it was time for her to tell him. He wanted to solve the mystery of who Jessie Jerome was. How she had shown up in his home. Where she really was from.

But once again she equivocated. "It's a long story that you wouldn't believe. Maybe some day I'll tell you—as long as you promise not to put me in a loony bin." She laughed and started walking down the alley, away from him.

Taku was waiting on the street. He greeted Jessie at the mouth of the alley, leaping on her happily and barking.

He was muddy, but she didn't seem to mind. She laughed even more and embraced the dog.

Most women he knew would have been disgusted to have been dirtied that way.

Most women he knew weren't Jessie Jerome.

He followed her back into Horace's. The crowd on

the street had thinned. So had Horace's line of customers.

Horace came over to Jack. "I can't afford to have any more supplies looted. And I can't be here all the time. It was just dumb luck that Frank happened to be around when his place was robbed. Good thing he got one of the thieves, but I don't guess there was only the one."

"No," Jack said, recalling what Jessie had told him. He would need to go question Emmie Dungel himself, to get her full story. "I understand there were several."

"You gonna let our grudge get in the way, or you gonna hang around here to protect the place?" Horace was tall, but a lot thinner than Jack. His eyes seemed to pierce instead of droop, as usual, like his mustache. "You're bound to do better than the no-good guards I tried."

"I have no grudge against you, Horace," Jack replied. "You're the one who seemed . . . unhappy that I beat you at cards. I would never let that get in the way of doing my job. But I can't spend all my time protecting one citizen's belongings."

"It isn't just me; it's the other outfitters on this street, too, like Frank. If you can't do it, have Filby watch. I've been robbed three times now, Frank once. And the thieves haven't been caught, not all of them."

Jack noticed that Jessie stood behind Horace, listening. "I can't spare Filby's time, either," Jack said. "He's usually on duty when I'm off." Not that he would allow her to do anything dangerous, but he had an idea to call Jessie's bluff; he didn't believe she had a real law-enforcement background. "There is one more person in town who claims to know a lot about police work. Maybe that person could hang around this street during the cold nights, in the dark stores, all alone, unprotected. She could keep an eye out for the thieves." He looked over Horace's shoulder and grinned at Jessie. "Of course, she already has two jobs, one during the day and one at night. Maybe she'd like three, the more dangerous the better."

"In your dreams, Jack O'Dair," she retorted, as he had hoped she would.

But what if she hadn't, you darned fool? he asked himself angrily. What would he have done if she had called *his* bluff and agreed? That had not been the smartest thing he had ever done. When Jessie Jerome got an idea, no matter how crazy, he had already learned it was impossible to change her mind.

Thank heavens she hadn't agreed to his half-witted suggestion.

But he wasn't getting off that easy. Oh, no, not with Jessie. He could see the contemplative look on her face, and he nearly cringed. What was she thinking?

She didn't keep him in suspense for long. "There is someone who could be assigned to keep an eye on things," she said slowly. "He could slip in and out of the buildings without attracting attention and might even be able to round up the thieves, if they come again. He would know right away if they were here, and in which store."

Jack couldn't help himself. He snorted in disbelief. "And exactly who is this paragon of protection, Miss Jerome?"

Just then, Taku came up and nuzzled her side. She stooped down to pet him, then grinned up at Jack.

"Oh, no," Jack replied in dismay. "Not my dog."

* * *

A while later, Jessie helped to hang wet laundry on ropes strung throughout the small boardinghouse kitchen.

The baby was asleep down the hall, and Calvina had told Jessie she was taking advantage of the quiet to get some work done. Though Calvina hired Tildy Emmet to do heavy washing, she now laundered diapers daily, with Jessie's help. Fortunately, Jessie only got involved at the end of the process, when the diapers were clean and just needed to be hung to dry.

"Didn't Jack have misgivings?" Calvina asked. Jessie had explained the events of earlier that day. "That dog's closer to him than any six people."

Certainly closer to him than she was, Jessie thought ruefully. He'd been quick to suggest that *she* hang around to keep an eye on the outfitters' stores, even if he had been joking. But he hadn't wanted to even consider leaving Taku. Not at first, at least.

"His misgivings were at least a mile wide and a skyscraper tall," Jessie acknowledged absently as she stretched to hang a diaper over a rope, then stopped. Would Calvina know the word "skyscraper?" If so, the buildings to which the term referred in this day would be shrimpy, compared with those in the future.

Calvina, hands on her hips, she grinned at Jessie and shook her head. Some of her light brown hair had come loose from the bun at the back of her head, and it was damp from perspiration. But her reaction wasn't to the word. "You convinced him anyway," she said, her tone amused. "And Jack O'Dair's as stubborn as they come. You're amazing, Jessie."

"Just persuasive."

Jack certainly hadn't been thrilled with her suggestion. But she had worn him down with her brilliant arguments. And common sense. Taku could hear better than any person, so he could guard more than one store at a time. Plus, a thief who happened to see him would think twice about tangling with an angry dog. Might even be scared off without stealing anything.

Jessie wondered, in retrospect, if she were pleased at her success. Taku was a dear. What if something happened to him?

She bent and picked up another clean diaper, wringing it out over a basin as if it were a thief's neck. Nothing would happen to Taku. It couldn't.

Calvina kept supper simple that night: bread, bacon and dried fruit, a meal fit for a stampeder. That suited Jessie. It also meant that supper was over quickly, and the boarders dispersed. Both Whiskey Tom and Eldon Riggs said they were going right to Helen's. Jessie and Calvina finished the supper dishes quickly, and Jessie went to her room to dress.

She had only been there a short while when she heard a scream. Calvina! Fortunately, Jessie had everything on but her boots. In borrowed stockings, she tore down the stairs toward the kitchen, trying not to slide on the slippery wood floor.

When she reached the kitchen, she was embarrassed to see her hostess locked in her husband's arms, their lips pressed tightly together as Renny whirled her around the room.

"Excuse me," Jessie mumbled, turning to leave. Tildy Emmet was behind her; she must have heard the scream, too. "Everything's all right," she assured the other boarder. "They're having a reunion."

"They should have it more quietly," Tildy grumbled and left the room.

Not for the first time, Jessie envied Calvina her

happiness in her marriage, even if Jessie wouldn't have wanted a husband who was usually off following a foolish dream.

Jack O'Dair had his feet planted firmly on the ground. Maybe too firmly. Would it be any easier to love a selfless man who put others' needs in front of his own? Or maybe his only needs were physical. Maybe he wasn't capable of caring for one woman.

And that might be even more difficult than loving a man who adored his woman but was seldom around to show it.

Jessie sighed. Unfortunately, whether she liked it or not, she was learning how it felt to care for the real Jack O'Dair.

"Sorry, Jessie," Renny said, putting his wife back down on the floor. "Didn't mean to make you feel uncomfortable."

"Don't worry about me," Jessie said. "I'm glad you're back, Renny—and I'm obviously not the only one."

"Come with us, Jessie, while I introduce Renny to his son." Calvina glowed as she grabbed her husband's hand.

"Don't you want this to be private?" Jessie asked, though she did want to see the look in Renny's eyes when he was presented with his child.

"We'll have time for privacy later." A huge smile bisected Renny's youthful, almost pretty face—revealing the gap where one tooth was missing. "Right now, I want everyone to share our happiness."

Jessie didn't need another invitation. She followed them down the hall toward the rear of the first floor. Calvina invited Tildy, who had gone into the parlor, to join them. Stolid Tildy seemed pleased to come

261

along on this mission of love. Who could have figured, Jessie wondered.

The timing was perfect, as the baby was just beginning to fuss. Calvina picked him up and cuddled him, then handed her son to his father.

Renny beamed. "He's perfect. You're perfect." He bent forward to kiss his wife again.

Calvina's smile could not have been happier. "Now," she said, "It's time to give our son a name. He has been without one for a day already."

"We talked of a name before I left." Renny sounded troubled. "Did you change your mind?"

Calvina shook her head. "I wanted to make sure you didn't."

"Then," Renny said, "it's settled." He turned the now fussy baby around to face Jessie and Tildy, who stood near the door. "Ladies, we would like to introduce you to Lazarus Sanders. He's named for Calvina's grandfather."

"Thank you." Calvina stretched up to give her husband a fond kiss on the cheek.

"No," said Renny. "Thank *you*, my darling." And the kiss he gave his wife was much more than fond.

Jessie glanced at Tildy. The woman actually seemed misty-eyed as she said, "Beautiful, isn't it?"

Jessie nodded. Before she could say anything else, she heard a knock at the front door. "I'll get it," she said. Since Tildy had also left, she closed the Sanders' bedroom door behind her and went to the front door.

It was Jack O'Dair. "Have you come to see Renny?" Jessie asked. "He's back."

"I've come to see you," he replied. "Are you singing at Helen's tonight?"

Jessie nodded.

"I'll accompany you there."

She didn't need an escort; it was early enough that the streets would still be crowded. But just for tonight, Jessie wouldn't argue with him.

"I'll go get my—your—jacket," she told him with a smile that he returned.

The weather had turned cold again, though there had been no more precipitation, so the boardwalk along the street was dry. Nevertheless, Jessie was pleased when Jack tucked her hand into the crook of his arm. She drew close to him, easily matching her strides to his as he walked slowly, holding a lantern in his other hand. Their footsteps created a pleasant, slow rhythm on the boards. A mild breeze caressed Jessie's cheeks, and she inhaled the fresh Alaskan air.

"Have you checked on Taku?" she asked anxiously. "I might have been out of line. If so, I'm sorry."

"No, it was a fine idea," he said, though he sounded a little stiff. "And, yes, I've checked on him. Everything seems quiet around the outfitters'." He paused for a moment, then asked, "Was having a dog work for the law one of the things you learned in your 'unofficial' capacity in policing?"

Jessie felt a redness climb her cheeks and was glad that Jack held the light away from her. "Not exactly. There were just a lot of guard dogs where I come from."

"Where exactly is that, Jessie Jerome?"

She suddenly wished she could tell him, could unburden herself from the incredible secret she had been hiding. But for tonight, she didn't want to argue with him, or even be teased by him. And so she couldn't even hint at the absurd truth.

"Though I spend a lot of time in Southern California, I was originally from the East: New York." That, at least, was true.

"Why was that so hard to admit?" Jack's tone was light, but she knew he was interested in her answer.

"I may be an entertainer, but inside I'm a private person." It was as good an answer as any, and somewhat true.

"I'd like to get to know you better, Jessie." He had stopped walking and swung around to face her. She looked up into his eyes. The light from the lantern in his hand glittered in their greenness. She had never seen them look more intense.

"I . . . I'd like to get to know you better, too." But she knew her tone was not as candid as his. "But, Jack, I'm not sure whether I can stay even if I want to."

"Why is that?" He sounded gruff but did not look away.

She shrugged beneath the fur jacket. "I came here . . . on a whim, and someday soon I may just . . . simply leave. My real life will call me home." Or so she imagined. As soon as the avalanche occurred, at least, and she knew how the ballad would end.

Of course, would Lizard show up then?

And now, now that she had met the real Jack O'Dair, had made love with him, nothing in her life at home seemed quite so inviting.

Except for her career, she reminded herself. She had carved out a brilliant niche for herself. She needed to get back to it.

Jack apparently sensed her sudden change in mood. "There's nothing I can say, then, to convince you to stay . . . longer?"

He had hesitated before inserting the word

"longer." Had he wanted to ask her just to stay? Forever?

Oh, how wonderful that sounded.

Your career, she reminded herself sternly.

But a career wasn't everything.

Still, they couldn't have a real relationship. A relationship was built on trust, and there were things she couldn't tell him.

But there were things she could ask him.

"Is there a saloon more quiet than Helen's?" she asked.

"We can go to the Washington House Hotel and have a drink in the dining room," he told her. "Would you like that?"

Jessie nodded.

They were only a block from the Washington House. Abigail greeted them both as if they were old friends. "It's good to see you both back here," she said. "My customers can't stop talking about how you squeezed life back into poor Mr. Nanager, Jack."

An exasperated look marred his handsome features. "It wasn't—"

Jessie bumped into him. "It was a wonderful thing he did, wasn't it? Very heroic."

And some day, she thought, people would even sing about it.

"Very heroic indeed," Abigail agreed, then hurried off to greet some other customers.

"It wasn't heroic at all," Jack grumbled. "And if anyone's a hero, it's you; you told me what to do."

"And you did it perfectly," Jessie said with a smile.

Shaking his head, Jack helped her off with her jacket, then removed his own. He wore a leather vest over his shirt, and his wide shoulders bulged far beyond the vest's edges.

He asked for a whiskey, Jessie a brandy. And then he said, "Tell me, Jessie. I really want to know all about you: how you knew that 'high maneuver' that helped me save Mr. Nanager, why you claim to have a law enforcement background, how you came to be a singer, why your career is so important to you . . . and why you must leave soon. Everything." He held her gaze, his broad chin raised as though he were in a battle of wills with her that he had no intention of losing.

She sighed, then tried to figure out which of his questions she could respond to without brushing him off—and without sounding ridiculous. "I . . . I've been able to watch some people who were police. I became a singer because it's in my blood, and it's important to me because it's who I am, and how I earn my living."

"Have you no father or brother, or other man in your life, to take care of you?"

Grrrr! she thought. Why was it that a man always assumed that a woman wasn't whole unless she had another to fulfill her needs? Curtis Fitzgerald had made it quite clear that he believed himself necessary to her existence in more ways than simply managing her career. And not just because they occasionally had sex. Didn't a mere woman need guidance in handling her money?

Her money. She'd earned it. She didn't need Curtis. She didn't need any man.

"No!" she snapped at Jack. "I was an only child. I never knew my father. And the only man with whom I'd a relationship recently was my business manager, that mangy son of a b—er, witch." Her anger wound down as she saw Jack's expression: an odd combination of sympathy, amusement and shock. She didn't need to get upset with him. After all, this was more than a hundred years before her time. Men's viewpoints were, by definition, archaic here. "Sorry," she finished. "The simple answer is, no, but I believe a woman is perfectly capable of taking care of herself. At least *this* woman is."

"I've no doubt of that," Jack said. Jessie figured that was a fib; Jack O'Dair, hero though he might be, was a male chauvinist of the highest degree. Maybe all the more so because he was an all-masculine hero. "Then your mother raised you herself? No grandfather either?"

He just didn't get it. Jessie sighed. "My mother was an entertainer, too. She thought a bit like you. Though she did a great job of earning money to keep us both comfortable, she was always looking for a man to take care of her. It inevitably led her into disaster." Jessie took a deep breath and drank a quick gulp of brandy. Feeling it sting on the way down, she looked up at Jack. "It eventually killed her. Rather, she killed herself when she realized that yet another man had let her down. She taught me that men might be interesting companions, but a woman needs to rely only on herself."

"I see." He sounded much too sympathetic—so much so that Jessie unwillingly felt tears rise to her eyes. It didn't help when he reached across the table and took her hand. "Some men care for their women, Jessie."

She was feeling much too maudlin suddenly. She had to change the subject. "Is that the way you were raised, Jack? Tell me about your family."

His expression shuttered. Jessie thought she could almost see the warmth in his eyes fade into blankness. "Not much to say," he said stonily.

But there was. She knew it. He had alluded before to having shirked some responsibility. Did it have something to do with his family?

"I told you a little about my mother," Jessie said. "Now it's your turn to tell me a little about yours."

He didn't say anything for a long minute. One of Abigail's other diners appeared to have captured his attention, but when Jessie turned to look, he was staring at an empty table.

Jessie was about to make a joke about it when Jack said quietly, "My mother was a kind, generous woman. And she was cared for by my father, in all ways. They loved each other till the day they died."

Oh, heavens. If she survived this night without bawling aloud, it would be a miracle, Jessie thought. "What happened to them?" she asked softly.

His handsome features contorted then into a mask of sheer agony. This time Jessie didn't even try to stop the tears from running down her face in sympathy for a pain she did not understand.

When he spoke, his voice was husky but level. "I killed them," he said simply. "I killed my parents, and along with them, my fiancée."

Chapter Eighteen

"Tell me what you mean, Jack," Jessie demanded, though she kept her voice low. No other diners were seated close by, but this was not something anyone else needed to hear.

"I said what I meant." Jack's laugh was as brittle as old glass. "My father owned a general store in the small town where we lived, near Atlanta. He was proud when I chose to join its law enforcement agency. Curious, too. Though it was frowned on, I sometimes invited him along to assist in arrests. There was a gang of thieves who were attacking travelers. My fellows and I rounded them up one day, but one got away. He knew my family. He waited until one evening when my parents were both at the general store, my fiancée as well, then set it afire. He did not allow them to escape." Jack's voice broke.

"Oh, Jack," Jessie whispered. This time it was she who reached across the table. He had been grabbing for his drink again, but she took his hand. It was cold, and it shook. She held it firmly.

Jack hadn't finished. "He did not stop there. He shot three more innocent people until I killed him."

"It's not your fault," Jessie said fiercely. "You did all you could. More people could have been hurt or killed if you didn't round up the gang. You couldn't have known what that horrible person would do."

"No, but I failed in my most elementary charge as an officer of the peace. I did not fulfill my responsibility of protecting citizens in my charge. And those who were killed included people I cared most about."

"I'm so sorry, Jack," Jessie whispered.

"It was long ago," he said in a tone of cold steel. "I went west afterward. For a while, I wandered, taking on jobs as deputy to sheriffs trying to bring order to their towns, but I kept moving till I heard of the Klondike gold strike. I figured a lawman would be needed here, so I came. I was right. Dyea is my town now. I've put the past behind me."

"But it's why you—"

"It's time now for me to walk you to Helen's." Jack rose like an automaton and assisted her with her jacket. He put his own on, then settled up with Abigail.

"Come back soon," their hostess chirped. Neither of them looked at her.

Outside, an icy wind blew, but it was only a fraction as cold as the chill projected from Jack. Jessie wondered that his very presence didn't douse the kerosene lantern he carried.

"I didn't mean to dredge up old horrors," she told him. "But, Jack, I meant what I said. You didn't do anything wrong."

"Tell that to my family," he said curtly.

This time, she had a difficult time keeping up with his brisk pace. His eyes were focused straight ahead, and his mouth was set in a grimness she had never seen there before.

They would be at Helen's in a moment. How could she keep them from parting like this? She couldn't allow him to dwell on his past for the rest of the night—or longer. Not when he had somehow put it behind him, but she had dragged it to the forefront of his mind.

In desperation, she grabbed his arm hard enough to get his attention. He stopped, but barely glanced down at her.

"Would you really like to know why I'm here, Jack?" Jessie demanded. "I'm here to study ballads; that part is true. But do you know what ballad brought me here? It brought me a very long way, in fact—from a place you couldn't even imagine."

That seemed to capture his attention, at least a little. "Where is that?" he asked in a monotone.

"Oh, it really is Southern California and elsewhere in the Lower Forty-Eight. That's what they call the contiguous United States in my time, since Alaska's a state, and so is Hawaii."

He bent his head, his coppery brows lowered in confusion. "What on earth are you talking about?"

Jessie forced a laugh. "Pretend I'm spinning a tall tale, like one glorified in the songs I sing. But, Jack, I'm here because of a ballad that intrigued me for years. I had to learn the ending; that's why I came. It's the story of a very brave, selfless hero, who kept the peace and helped a lot of people."

"Why did you say, 'in my time?' "

Drat. He was fixed on that instead of the ballad.

"Never mind," Jessie said. "Aren't you the tiniest

bit curious about who the hero of my ballad is, Jack?"

"Should I be?" He stared down at her as if she had suddenly sprouted moose antlers. "What are you trying to tell me, Jessie? Do you think that by making up some kind of strange story that you'll make me feel better about all the harm I did?"

"You didn't do harm," Jessie practically shouted in exasperation. "And whether or not you believe it, I'm not making this up. I'm from the future, Jack. I came here to learn the end of a very special ballad—a ballad about *you*."

The woman was incredible—in the truest sense of the word.

Jack found himself suddenly howling in laughter. "You're amazing, Jessie. You turn a man's senses upside down with your craziness. What you said doesn't change what I did, nor the guilt I live with every day of my life. But I thank you for changing the subject in a manner that would make my heart lighter, if anything could."

"It's not crazy." Darned if the remarkable Jessie didn't sound as if he had hurt her feelings.

"I suppose you're going to insist it's true."

"I am." Then she did the most astounding thing of all. She pulled him over in front of the nearest building, a pharmacist's. Though they had reached the street with three saloons in a row, and music and laughter from all of them spilled outside, Jessie's voice overshadowed the noise when she began to sing in that clear, throaty voice that never failed to drive him crazy.

Crazy? What she sang was definitely crazy:

"He kept the peace without surcease,
Did mighty Jack O'Dair.

272

Through Dyea-town fights, and dread Klondike
    nights,
None other could compare."

"That's quite a song," Jack growled. The quivering
of his body had nothing to do with the temperature,
everything to do with the tension with which he held
himself. "But why did you—"

"I'm not through," Jessie interrupted. "We're not
far from Helen's. I won't sing it all now, but here's
another verse:"

"Lawman Jack was bold in the Northland's
    cold.
Jack struck the scoundrels down.
With his wolf-dog Taku and his *ulu*, too,
Jack tended Dyea town."

"But—" Jack tried to interrupt, but she didn't let him.

"One more for good measure," she insisted, then
sang,

"What's more, it was said, that in ladies' beds
Jack O'Dair had no equal, 'twas true.
And in card games most fair always played Jack
    O'Dair
And he won nearly all of them, too."

"This is insane, Jessie!" Jack nearly yelled but he
lowered his voice as a couple of stampeders walked
by, eyeing them curiously as they stood in the doorway. "You are making me out to be some kind of
extraordinary person, a man with 'no equal.'"

"I don't know about your card-playing skills, but if
anyone asked I'd vouch that you had 'no equal' in bed."

"Jessie—" Jack couldn't help his low, menacing tone, but it didn't do him any good.

"There's more," she said tauntingly. "I'll sing it all to you one day, at least what I know. I haven't found the end yet."

"Found it? Written it, you mean." Despite his anger, Jack couldn't help feeling just a little flattered that Jessie had made up a song about him, one that made him out to be a hero.

Even though it wasn't true.

She shook her head. "No, I learned it in my own time. I was hoping to find exactly who did write it. That way, I might be able to learn the ending early, though I doubt it. The avalanche hasn't occurred yet."

"What avalanche?" Jack was beginning to feel as though his brain had been frostbitten. Nothing Jessie said made sense. Her time? An avalanche?

"The historically famous one that will occur in Chilkoot Pass on Palm Sunday. That's April third, a couple days away."

"You must be thinking of the flood in September, last year," Jack said, "when a glacier on Mount Cleveland let loose."

Jessie shook her head. "I hadn't heard about that. Trust me, there'll be a big avalanche soon. That's the reason I wound up traveling back to this time from my own, I think. I'm from more than a hundred years in the future, Jack. I just need to know . . . Never mind. But what *you* need to know is that you'll be in Chilkoot Pass during the avalanche."

That was the final straw that elicited deep laughter from him. "Your imagination is wild, Jessie. Or is this a joke? Today is April first—April Fool's Day. Only

I'm not a fool. Traveling through time . . . I almost thought you crazy enough to believe it. But me up the Chilkoot Pass? I climbed it once when I arrived a year ago to see what it was like, a couple of other times as part of my job, but I certainly never wanted to go after gold. The idea that I'll suddenly climb it for no reason in two days' time. . . . Do you imagine I'll just go up now in case there's an avalanche, because you've said so?"

Jessie had been trying to interrupt, but when he finally ended his outburst with another laugh, she said stiffly, "Thank you for walking me to Helen's. I'm sure I can make it the rest of the way myself."

She maneuvered past him toward the street, and he followed.

Her tone had made it clear that she had no doubt she could have made it the entire way on her own. Maybe she could have. But he had wanted her company.

What a walk this had been, though. She had brought racing back to his mind all the misery of the past he had intended never to think of again. And then she had tried to push it all away by her ridiculous, flattering song about him.

She had to have written it, even if she wouldn't own up to it.

And the rest of her tale. Utter nonsense! What a strange sense of humor the woman had.

Though her pace was swift, he was faster. He remained at her side, despite her pretending to ignore him. In a minute, they were at Helen's. He pulled open the door. They were assailed by the warmth from within, the loud laughter, the usual mingled smell of whiskey, burned wood, perfume, and men seeking wild women. Jessie hurried inside, to the calls of greetings from a dozen drunk men. As usual, Jack wanted to throttle them all, especially when Jessie, taking their adulation in stride, gave each of them individual friendly greetings.

Didn't she know they all wanted to undress her, to treat her like Helen's girls?

And didn't she know that the idea of other men wanting to do to her what he had done made him crazy?

He sighed, watching her say hello to Helen as if they were close friends. Even some of Helen's girls seemed glad to see Jessie. Gilda the Gold, Nadine, Skagway Sadie and other scantily-dressed women approached her, and they shared a laugh.

As Jessie got her guitar from behind the bar, Whiskey Tom grinned at her; though he worked at Helen's, he had the same lewd thoughts about Jessie that every other man here did.

She's mine! he wanted to shout. But she wasn't. She was simply another of his responsibilities in this, his adopted town. No more, and no less, although he might need to take special care of her if she truly were crazy and believed her ridiculous tale. Unlikely, though. If she made it up just to cheer him, she had succeeded. In any event, he would not go up the Chilkoot. He wouldn't fail Jessie, either—nor would he get any closer to her.

He knew too well what it meant to care for someone, and then fail to take care of her.

"Sing for us, Jessie!" It was Lester Jones, one of her biggest fans. Jack had to concede that, after that night when Lester had drunk too much and harassed Jessie, he had sobered up and calmed down—the result, he readily admitted, of not wanting to be forbidden to hear Jessie sing again.

"What do you want to hear, boys?" she called from her customary chair on stage.

" 'She'll Be Comin' Round the Mountain,' " shouted Dab Daugherty. He sat at a front row table with Eldon Riggs and Otis Oetting.

Jessie complied. As she finished her first song, men shouted the names of others, and she sang them all, from "Home, Sweet Home," which brought tears to the eyes of more than one stampeder, to a rousing rendition of "John Brown's Body," and even "Old Dan Tucker" and "On Top of Old Smoky."

She didn't sing the song about him, though more than once she caught his eye and grinned, as though telling him she was considering it. He'd have been furious. He did not want anyone to laud him for simply doing his job. It was bad enough that she had made up that ballad, but if she dared to try to share it with others he would take her over his shoulder and throw her in the nearest icy creek.

She had been singing for perhaps an hour when Jack noticed Horace Martin enter Helen's. Right behind him was Frank Dungel.

What were they doing here? Was Taku all right? He had intended to check on his dog when he left here but had stayed much longer than he'd meant to, entranced by Jessie's voice.

He rose from the bar and approached the two outfitters. "Everything all right?"

"Everything's fine," Horace said with a smile that brightened his usually somber face.

Evidently Jessie noticed their entrance, too. She finished a song, then called, "Time for me to take a break, boys." Despite the friendly grumbling, she took

277

no more requests. "Later," she assured her audience. She made her way through the crowd to where Jack stood with Horace and Frank.

She, too, asked if everything was under control at their stores. "Couldn't be better, thanks to you, Jessie," Frank Dungel said loudly.

As several nearby stampeders asked what was going on, Horace explained that it had been Jessie's idea to have the outfitters' street guarded by Taku. "So far, he's just been patrolling and eating some dried meat we left out for him," Horace finished with a laugh.

Jessie appeared relieved. "Don't make him sick," she warned.

"Not us." Frank guffawed.

In a while, Jessie went back to the stage. Jack had to go relieve Filby, after checking on Taku.

But first, he approached the table where Dab, Eldon and Otis sat. He asked the two who were Calvina's boarders, "Are you both hanging around till closing?"

They were.

"Then see Jessie back to Calvina's, will you? But don't tell her I said so, or she'll want to go on her own."

"We'll make sure she gets home just fine," Dab said, and Eldon agreed.

Jessie felt exhausted that night when she finished at Helen's. She hadn't planned on staying quite so late, but her audience had been enthusiastic.

And she had been half hoping that Jack would return to walk her back to Calvina's.

Not that she needed accompaniment. Sure, someone had attacked her once, but that didn't mean she was more in danger than any other woman here. It had probably been a mistake.

Still, she wasn't stupid. When Dab Daugherty and Eldon Riggs offered to walk her to the boardinghouse, she had agreed.

"Thanks, gentlemen," she told them when they stood inside Calvina's parlor. Renny was there, holding little Lazarus.

"Was the baby fussing?" Jessie smiled at the small bundle Renny held in a warm blanket. Lazarus was awake and stared at Jessie with brown eyes that appeared interested, which was crazy, Jessie knew, for newborns couldn't even focus for weeks. Still, it made her grin all the more.

"My son lives by his own rules already," Renny said proudly. "He's an Alaskan through and through. He likes to be active when it's dark outside."

"He'll grow out of it," grumbled Eldon Riggs. The banker headed immediately toward his bedroom.

"I'd like to take some photographs of little Lazarus soon," said Dab Daugherty. "He's a special part of the Yukon gold rush, brand new, with his entire lifetime ahead of him."

"I'd be pleased," Renny agreed.

Jessie excused herself and went to bed. She was so tired that she anticipated dropping off right away.

But she didn't. Too much was on her mind.

She thought of Jack O'Dair, how he believed he had let his family down, how they had died, and how he blamed himself.

"It wasn't your fault," she insisted aloud in the solitude of her bedroom, just as she had told him as they'd walked through Dyea. But he hadn't heard her then any more than he did now.

In response, she had told him much more than she'd ever intended about her own background. He had thought her nuts, and no wonder. And then she had been foolish enough to sing him part of the ballad.

He had hated it. Had hated the very idea that his heroism would be recognized at all, let alone memorialized for posterity.

He had mistakenly thought she had written the song.

That gave him two reasons to dislike her, for she had also put his beloved dog Taku in possible jeopardy. If the thieves returned, they probably wouldn't even think twice about hurting a person, let alone a dog.

"Damn!" she said aloud. At least it was April. There was a lot more daylight now than in the middle of the Alaskan winter.

She was still awake when the earliest glow of dawn hovered beyond her window.

This wasn't her idea of spring. It was still cold out, especially early in the morning. She bundled up and hurried from the boardinghouse, toward the street where Horace Martin's warehouse sat in a row beside Frank Dungel's and others'.

She saw few people at that hour. In this boom town of four thousand stampeders, didn't anyone else rise at dawn? Maybe they all stayed out late at the many saloons. Or maybe she was simply on the wrong streets. Perhaps all the early risers already had started on their latest treks up the Chilkoot.

Once she reached the street where the stores were, she stomped on the hard-packed earth to alert Taku to her presence.

She didn't see him.

"Taku, where are you?" she called.

Still no Taku. Had he fallen asleep inside one of the stores? But he was an alert animal. Surely a strange noise, like her footfalls, would awaken him. And if they didn't, her call would.

"Taku?" she whispered, suddenly afraid for him. Was he all right?

He had to be. She was just being silly. Maybe Jack had decided this was a bad idea and come for his pet last night. In any event, there was no need for her to worry.

But telling herself that didn't stop her.

She reached the Dungels' store first. She peered in the window and gasped.

The place was a mess. Supplies were scattered everywhere.

She ran to the door and pulled it open. It wasn't locked, though she thought she had remembered Emmie saying Frank was going to use a chain and padlock to keep things secure.

The store was full of shadows. The sparse daylight from outside barely penetrated through the few windows. Still, Jessie could see barrels of flour had been split open, thanks to the use of the hatchets from crates also open on the floor.

But why? She had thought the thieves were stealing things for their own use, not simply vandalizing the outfitters' stores.

She wandered for just a few more moments . . . until she gasped again in alarm. There were dog footprints in the flour.

"Taku?" Jessie called. "Are you here?"

A faint noise seemed to come from a stack of boxes of dried potatoes. Quickly, she headed in that direction.

She fell to her knees. She had found Taku. Blood stained the sides of his wolf-gray fur. But he was alive. He lifted his head and whined. His tail thumped on the floor.

"Oh, Taku, I'm so sorry!" Jessie tried to gather the large animal in her arms. She couldn't leave him. "We'll find Jack."

But then she heard a footstep behind her. She tried to turn and rise at the same time.

Before she could, something hit her on the back of the neck. Pain rocketed through her and the world went black.

Chapter Nineteen

A loud snarl followed by a yelp of pain made every hair at the nape of Jack's neck stand on end. "Taku!" he cried.

He was at the end of the street where Horace Martin and Frank Dungel's stores loomed in the early morning light. He ran in the direction of the sound.

"Taku!" he called again, but heard nothing. He made himself stop to listen, swallowing his own fleet, irregular breaths. Where was his dog?

Day had just broken. Should he have come earlier? He'd been awake. He hadn't slept well. He had missed Taku's company.

It hadn't helped that his thoughts had twisted and twined around his strange conversations with Jessie the previous evening. How had she drawn his deepest secrets from him? They were things he had not spoken of for many years, not since he had left Atlanta.

How had her imagination carried her into such

strange realms? She claimed she came not only from a distant place, but a distant time, as well. Nonsense!

And was she using madness as an excuse for writing a song that falsely lauded him for—

He heard another sound. "Taku!" This time, he was rewarded with a whine. It seemed to come from inside Dungel's.

Jack drew his Colt .45 Lightning and made certain it was loaded. Then, he edged up to the store's main door. He waited. He listened.

Nothing.

He reached over and slowly turned the doorknob. Again, he stood still and then slammed the door open and leapt inside, immediately crouching, with his gun ready to fire. He hustled toward a crate and ducked behind it.

Nothing happened. No one appeared.

Not until his dog crept toward him along the dusty wood floor, between boxes and sacks scattered haphazardly. Had the place been robbed again?

"Taku, you're hurt!" Jack saw the matted blood on the dog's side, the way he edged so slowly. Jack reached toward him, and Taku whined. "Let me see—"

But Taku moved away—sluggishly, clearly in pain—toward an upended pile of crates off to one side. He stopped only long enough to turn to look at Jack, then continued his obviously excruciating journey.

Jack caught up with him. When Taku edged around several fallen boxes, Jack followed, then halted when he saw a crumpled, bloody heap of fur and clothing.

"Jessie!" Jack cried. His heart beating frantically, he knelt beside her.

*　　*　　*

"I'm fine. Really." That wasn't the first time Jessie had insisted that her injuries were minor. But it was the first time she could make her voice loud enough to be heard.

"You're certain?" Jack stood beside her bed at Calvina's. Jessie wasn't sure how she had gotten there, her boots off, a blanket tucked beneath her chin. The last she remembered was finding poor Taku bleeding.

And then . . . She propped herself up, then reached slowly to touch the back of her head, and winced. "Ouch."

"You're not fine," Jack said angrily. "Let me see your head."

"I *am* fine," Jessie insisted. "Or I will be once I've rested a little."

Jack snorted in disbelief.

Jessie was getting irritated with his attitude. She was conscious. Her head might hurt like the devil, but she had survived.

Thanks to her hero, Jack O'Dair.

She knew full well that whoever had hurt Taku and her wouldn't have left either alive if Jack hadn't come along.

She wanted to throw herself into his arms and thank him.

But she didn't move. Especially not with the way he was acting.

"All right," he said. His tone was milder, as though he finally heard her. But then he demanded, "Tell me what the hell you were doing in Frank's store in the middle of the night?"

Jessie started at his latest sharp tone. The movement caused her head to throb. "I was checking on your dog." She winced at the sound of her own raised voice. "I was worried about him."

"Why? You were the one to suggest that he guard the street."

Jessie felt tears rush to her eyes, but she refused to give him the satisfaction of seeing them fall. "I love your dog. That's why I had to make sure he was all right."

"But he wasn't."

"No." Jessie bent her aching head; those damned tears rolled down her cheeks despite her best efforts to hold them back. "Did he . . . I mean, was he—?"

"He's doing better than you," Jack said gruffly. "In fact, I think he saved your life. He growled at your assailant, maybe even attacked him. I heard him. . . ." Jack tapered off.

"You heard him growl?"

He nodded. "And yelp. I think the dirty bas—the coward kicked him. When I called out, the guy ran off."

"Oh, poor Taku! Where is he?"

Jack smiled for the first time. "With Calvina in the kitchen, warming up in front of her fire. She's babying him just like Lazarus. His wounds weren't deep. He should be fine. Right now he's enjoying treats Calvina keeps tossing him."

Jessie laughed. "I want to see him."

"Soon." He hesitated. "Jessie, when I saw you lying there I—" He cleared his throat. When he spoke again, his tone was all business. "Did you see who hurt you?"

She started to shake her head but stopped as the motion sent a new wave of pain through her. "No, damn it. I wish I had, but—"

She stopped. There was something, some fleeting memory she needed to capture before it disappeared completely.

"What?"

She waved her hand gently to silence him while she thought. And then, "The smell!" she exclaimed. She smiled broadly. "That's it. I remember the smell."

"What smell?" Jack's coppery brows furrowed.

"As I went toward Taku, just before I was struck, I inhaled an aroma—a familiar one. One I experience every night."

"What are you talking about?"

"It's Helen's signature perfume! She imported it from Paris and insists that all her girls wear it to identify them as coming from her saloon."

"You think one of Helen's girls attacked you?" Jack sounded skeptical. Of course he assumed all bad guys were *guys*.

"It could have been a woman," Jessie replied testily. "Or a man who was with one of Helen's girls last night. In any event, I think we've narrowed the list of who's stealing from the outfitters."

Jack couldn't believe his eyes. It was eight o'clock that night. He had just walked into Helen's, and Jessie was there.

He almost smiled in pleasure at seeing her, then caught himself.

He had given her strict orders to stay at Calvina's and rest. He had given Calvina strict orders to keep her there.

But here she was. And he knew he couldn't blame Calvina.

Jack maneuvered around tables toward the bar where Jessie stood. Beside him, Taku growled. That stopped Jack. He had seemed better this afternoon, so Jack had brought him along. He might be able to point out who had harmed him and Jessie.

But though the dog's hackles were raised and his eyes bulged in his agitation, he didn't rush at anyone. Instead, he seemed alert, upset, and angry without directing his ferociousness toward a single person.

Jack knelt. "It's okay, boy. And it'll be especially okay if you happen to attack whoever you're mad at."

Holding the loose skin at the back of Taku's neck, Jack continued toward the bar, using the pressure of his hand to direct the dog to remain at his side.

In a minute, they stood beside Jessie. "What are you doing here?" Jack demanded.

"I work here."

Jack closed his eyes to calm his temper. Taku growled and pulled away. As Jack turned, his dog snapped at Lester Jones, one of the many men who continually flirted with Jessie.

"Your dog almost bit me," Lester cried in alarm. He stared at the hand Taku had nearly nipped, then ran it through his fuzzy hair.

Had Taku identified the attacker? "Where were you last night?" Jack demanded, holding the dog back.

"Up in the Pass," Lester replied. "I just got back this afternoon after dropping off the latest goods for my cache."

"Were you with anyone?"

"Sure. I walked this trip alongside Brownie Howard. He'll be here tomorrow or the next day to sing. You can ask him."

The two stampeders could have conspired to provide alibis for one another. But Jack would follow up on this man whom Taku had assailed. He turned back to Jessie, who bent to give Taku a hug. Jack felt a twinge of jealousy.

Of his dog? What was wrong with him?

When she rose, she whispered so no one else could

hear, "I'll see if I can get more out of Lester. We're definitely going to catch whoever hurt Taku. You'll see."

"He hurt you, too," Jack reminded her.

"As if I could forget." She looked around. "I started asking questions when I got here, but Helen hasn't come in yet. I'll get her alone in her office."

"To get her accounting of which stampeders were with her girls last night?"

"Right," Jessie said. "I also intend to question both the girls and their johns."

" 'Johns?' "

"Oops. That's a term from my time, but I forgot. You don't believe I'm not from around here." She gave him a sidelong glance as though assessing how he dealt with her teasing.

He wasn't in the mood for levity. "I believe you're from far away. And that you'd be better off back where you belong."

"That's for sure." There was a hint of hurt in her voice.

"Jessie, I didn't mean—"

"Jack! I didn't know you were here." Skagway Sadie hurried down the stairs and to Jack's side. She smiled at him shyly, getting between Jessie and him and taking his arm.

Taku began to snarl and bark. Jack moved to take control of his dog, but Jessie had already grabbed him. "What's wrong, boy?" She glared at Sadie speculatively, then back toward Jack.

Was it suspicion that caused Jessie's obvious dislike of Sadie—or jealousy? Jack felt his lips twitch as he considered the latter.

Still, Taku had accused Sadie. But then he'd lunged at Gilda, too, who had followed Sadie. Jessie seemed barely able to hold him, especially when Whiskey Tom hurried around the bar and Taku nearly attacked him as well.

Jessie remained on her knees, hugging the dog. She scowled up at Jack. "Poor Taku's upset. He's shaking."

"I'd better take him out of here," he said.

"Don't go yet." Sadie sounded disappointed. "Jessie seems to have everything under control."

"Maybe." Jack still wanted answers, without Jessie getting more involved. Since Helen wasn't available, the way to get information was to speak directly to the girls. He inhaled deeply and recognized the perfume Jessie had mentioned. He had noticed it before at Helen's but had chosen to ignore it. It was reminiscent of the magnolias and other warm-weather flowers back in Georgia. His home. The place he wanted to forget.

He shook off his memories; he had to concentrate on the present. On making sure that Dyea, his home now, became safe once more. For the moment, Taku seemed quiet, so Jack began, "Sadie, there was another theft last night at one of the outfitters. Someone was hurt."

"Oh?" Sadie said. "Who?"

"It doesn't matter." With Jessie's apparent antipathy toward Sadie that day, he didn't think it prudent to mention that she'd been the one injured. He saw movement from the floor. Jessie was listening. He might have hurt her feelings.

But more than that had been hurt before. He needed information any way he could get it. "I have reason to believe the attacker was a stampeder who was here last night, probably someone who went upstairs with you or one of the other girls. I'll need names from each of you."

Sadie's big brown eyes looked sad. She sighed. "Sorry, Jack. I'd be glad to help, but I didn't have gentlemen callers last night. I was under the weather. Female thing." She looked away, apparently as embarrassed as he felt. "I went to bed early and slept late. How about you, Gilda?"

Gilda's grin was one of the most lascivious Jack had ever seen. "Oh, I had three gentlemen upstairs with me last night, one right after the other. I'll tell them all you want to talk to them, Jack. Maybe you'll like what you hear well enough to come visit me, too."

Sadie shifted beside Jack, and he could tell she was displeased. Sadie had been trying to get Jack to visit her for a long time.

He couldn't help glancing toward Jessie, who was standing now. Taku's left side was against her skirt, and she patted his right side to keep him beside her. He could practically feel the daggers she glared, sharpened as keenly as his *ulu*.

He grinned at her. Let her believe what she wanted.

He turned back toward Sadie, who still frowned at Gilda. "I'd appreciate it if you'd tell the other girls I'd like information from them, too."

"Sure," Sadie said.

Jack noticed that Jessie had started a conversation with Whiskey Tom. As Eldon Riggs joined them, Taku growled and lunged once more. Jessie grabbed him, and Eldon took off toward the poker tables.

Two stampeders gestured, and Gilda and Sadie walked away.

With Taku beside her, Jessie returned to Jack's side. There was a tension around her eyes that told

291

him her head still ached. He was about to say something sympathetic when Jessie spoke. "That looked cozy. A *ménage à trois* in the making?"

Jack had learned drawing room French as a child. Though the phrase she used belonged more in the gutter than the drawing room, he understood it. But she didn't give him a chance to respond.

"Did Sadie and Gilda tell you who they turned tricks with last night?"

" 'Turned tricks?' "

"With 'johns,' " Jessie told him, her forehead raised in a sly expression that did little to hide her pain. She sounded disgruntled, though. Could she actually be jealous?

He allowed himself the merest of smiles to annoy her and kept his voice low. "Oh, yes. Another term from your time in the future." He shook his head. "Jessie, you should put that tale into one of your songs."

"Never mind the sarcasm. Did you learn anything helpful?"

"No." His mind turned to business once more. "It's my job to find out who attacked you, Jessie, and I'll do it. But you need to stay out of it. You'll only be in more danger."

"So I should be a good little girl and obey you?"

He pretended not to notice her sarcasm. "You understand, then. That's fine."

"It's not fine."

"Jessie?"

"Yes?"

He swallowed his irritation with her and said merely, "Don't leave tonight without me. I'll walk you home."

She stuck out her tongue briefly as she turned. But

as she walked away, he heard her say, "I wouldn't think of leaving without you, Marshal O'Dair. After all, someone has to hang around to protect you from Helen's girls."

When Helen approached, Taku nearly attacked the saloon keeper. Jessie was relieved that Jack finally decided it was time to take his dog home. Poor Taku. Jessie had never seen him like this.

But, then, he had never been attacked by someone who smelled like so many people here at Helen's: Helen herself, her bartender, her girls, and the girls' customers.

Before Jack left, he assured Jessie he'd be back soon. "And don't ask questions," he admonished. "You'll only rile people."

She enjoyed riling Jack. It was good for him to have his male ego knocked down a peg.

Especially when Helen's girls seemed intent on building it up to astronomical heights. Not that Jessie cared.

Riling other people seemed a good way to get answers.

She began with Helen. "Can I speak with you alone?" Jessie asked.

Helen looked worried but motioned for Jessie to follow. Jessie watched the sashay of the buxom woman's hips beneath her tight red dress as she preceded Jessie through the crowd. Every man's eyes seemed to be on that curving, swaying behind. Jessie felt a sardonic smile coming on, then stopped herself. It wasn't funny when men considered a woman nothing but a sex object, even if the woman brought it on herself.

Nor did it make her happy when Jack O'Dair

treated her as less than competent, just because she was a woman. She would show him. She would find out who her attacker was.

They entered a small room behind the bar, and Helen shut the door. "What is it, Jessie?" There was a catch in her breathy voice, as though she were concerned. Did she know something about the attack last night? The thefts?

Jessie told about her visit to Taku the previous night, finding the dog injured, the attack upon her. She watched Helen's face closely.

There was a lot of kohl around Helen's small brown eyes. They widened as Jessie spoke. Either the saloon keeper was innocent and clueless, or she was a good actress.

"That's terrible," Helen exclaimed when Jessie had finished. "Do you know who did it?"

"That's what I needed to speak with you about." Jessie was surprised as Helen visibly relaxed, sinking into a wooden chair behind her plain wooden desk.

"I was afraid you were going to quit," Helen said, sounding relieved. Her eyes narrowed. "You're not, are you?"

Jessie shook her head. "Not yet, at least." She still didn't know, though, how long she would be here.

"Good," Helen said. "So what can I do?"

"We . . . I have reason to believe that whoever hurt me last night has a connection to your place."

Helen bolted out of her chair. Her eyes suddenly radiated fury. "What gives you that idea?"

"His smell." Quickly, Jessie explained her recollection of the lingering aroma around her attacker. "I think that was why Taku acted so crazy today, too. So many people around here pick up the scent you have your girls use."

"I see." Helen stroked the loose skin beneath her chin contemplatively. Jessie was surprised to note how short the woman's nails were. They weren't polished, either, and her hands appeared dry and callused. It appeared that Helen worked for a living in more ways than one.

Did her hands get rough from carrying crates of goods from the outfitters?

"So how can I help?" Helen asked. "I certainly don't want some crazy thief hanging around my place, either."

Pretending she didn't suspect the woman, Jessie asked which girls had worked the previous night, and which stampeders they had been with. Helen kept a log, obviously to keep track of the income her girls were pulling in. She copied names of women and men on a piece of paper and handed it to Jessie.

It contained no surprises: the usual girls had been working. Jessie recognized most, but not all, of the men's names.

She couldn't tell from the list who had attacked Taku and her. Not even the times written meticulously beside names told her, though they might give some of them alibis.

Jessie had more digging to do.

Chapter Twenty

"That's a good idea," Jessie told Otis, meaning it. She leaned across the table near the bar, her chin on her hand. "I'll have to think about it, though."

She already *had* thought about Otis Oetting's suggestion that she go up Chilkoot Pass herself and see what it was like to be a stampeder, and had decided in favor of it.

But not for the reason he'd believed. He had been trying to convince her to join him and go after gold.

But what Jessie really wanted was to find out who'd been robbing the outfitters here, and who had hurt her. And Taku. And Otis's suggestion just might help.

At the top, she could nonchalantly question people about what they'd seen of others' caches, preferably those belonging to Helen's patrons. Had some caches grown too quickly? Had purportedly penniless stampeders somehow rounded out their supplies? Had there been rumors about who'd been robbing the outfitters down in Dyea?

Otis himself might still be guilty.

And Jessie hadn't any better ideas. For the past few hours, since her conversation with Helen, she had alternated between singing and interrogating stampeders who'd been upstairs as customers the previous night, as well as the girls who had been with them. She hadn't gotten a single new clue. She had hardly been able to rule anyone out as a suspect, let alone thrust others to the top of her list.

She needed a different approach.

She had looked toward the door numerous times to make sure Jack hadn't returned. That handsome, stubborn, overbearing marshal wouldn't have liked her asking so many questions. Not that it mattered.

She was getting impatient to find the culprit. A hike up the Chilkoot would at least be a positive action.

Besides, after all she'd heard about the trek, the old photographs she had viewed, she was curious. If she didn't go now, she might never see the Pass, for the avalanche was due in a couple of days, and it might be the impetus to send her back to her time.

Then there was the fact that, if she went up there now, she might drop hints about the avalanche, maybe save some lives, since Jack O'Dair had made it clear he had no intention of going up Chilkoot Pass on what he considered her crazy notion. So much for his heroism up there, hinted at by the ballad. Maybe that was why she'd never found the ending: He wasn't even there.

"I'm leaving first thing tomorrow," Otis said. "I'll take my time, rest at camps on the way, then head up to the top before coming back for more supplies. It'll be a good trip for a woman to come along." It also sounded as though he'd take his time reaching the Scales, so he would not be in the area when the avalanche hit. She probably didn't have to warn him.

Jessie was surprised, though, that the short, plump outfitter, who'd seemed to be doing well selling supplies, had decided to go forward with his original dream of finding Yukon gold. Maybe it wasn't greed that motivated him, but the spirit of adventure.

And maybe not. "Why do you want gold?" Jessie asked him. "I thought you were making lots of money as an outfitter."

"Horace is doing a lot better than me," Otis grumbled. "Frank Dungel and the others, too. I need more money than they do because . . . because I just do."

Whatever his reason, had it led him to steal from the other outfitters? He had never provided a good explanation for his surreptitiousness the night Jack and Jessie had caught him sneaking around his own store.

"Come with me, Jessie," Otis begged. Not likely, she thought. He had been flirting with her from her very first night in town. Had hinted over and over, like Lester Jones, that she become one of Helen's girls. She knew better than to take him up on his offer to accompany him up the Pass. But that didn't mean she was stuck.

"Sorry, but I'll have to wait, at least until next time." Jessie tried to insert a barrel-full of regret into her voice. "I've responsibilities here at Helen's, and at Calvina's. Plus, I'd need to get my own supplies ready."

Looking disappointed, Otis said, "All right. Next time."

Jessie knew that Renny Sanders also was planning another trip up the Chilkoot starting tomorrow. Despite what Jessie thought of his leaving his wife and new baby again so quickly, it wasn't her business. And if she could take advantage of Renny's presence, slow him down at first so he wouldn't be near the avalanche, then hurry him along so he would return to Calvina more quickly, all the better.

She herself would feel bad about leaving Calvina. Her landlady seemed to thrive on motherhood; she had recovered a lot of energy over the last couple of days. Still, Jessie wasn't sure she could handle all the housekeeping chores herself.

Well, Jessie wouldn't be gone long—nor would Renny, if she had anything to say about it.

She was on stage when Jack finally walked in. Her heart sped up at the sight of him, but she didn't miss a note. He looked harried, though that didn't detract in the least from his good looks. Taku wasn't with him.

To the tune of "Old Dog Tray," Jessie sang:

> "Poor dog Taku's ever faithful.
> Has anger driven him away?"

Jack's green eyes glittered as he nodded grimly toward her, then took a seat at a nearby table, one of the few that was empty. Jessie sang a couple more songs, then joined him.

"Is Taku all right?" she asked.

Jack looked tired. Even a little discouraged—did heroes get that way? Real ones did, she supposed, even if fictional song subjects didn't. She had an urge to take his hand to comfort him; he looked as though he needed it. But she knew what kinds of lightning bolts shot through her whenever she touched him. She

299

didn't need the distraction. Not now. She kept her fingers intertwined in her lap.

"I took Taku to the jail. Filby's keeping him company. I've never seen Taku so upset; he didn't want to leave but kept trying to tug me back, from the moment we went out the door."

"Do you think he did recognize whoever hurt us, or was it just the scent?"

Jack shrugged. "I wish I knew." His expression grew distracted, and he took a swig of his whiskey. "Did you learn anything interesting while I was gone?"

"Not really," Jessie said. "I got a list of who was here, but—"

He interrupted, glaring at her. "I knew it. I told you to stay out of this, didn't I—to let me ask the questions? But the first thing you do when my back is turned is to disobey."

She stood so fast that her chair slid back noisily. "You asked," she responded angrily. "I don't have to obey you, Jack O'Dair."

"You were hurt the last time you didn't. Didn't you learn anything?"

"Yes," Jessie hissed. "I learned that you are a hero, but that you don't know the first thing about women. Good night, Jack." She turned her back on him and hurriedly returned to the stage.

Jack stewed over Jessie's words all that night. He didn't want to be a hero; he just wanted to do his job. And her fool idea of singing about his good deeds was almost as ridiculous as her claims of having come from the future to learn the song.

He didn't care if she were right, that he didn't know the first thing about women. He realized, though, in the wee hours of the night, with the wind whistling coldly around his cabin, and Taku sleeping restlessly by the fire, that he did care a lot in regard to knowing about one particular woman: Jessie.

He realized yet another thing as he paced the creaking wood floor, his muscles aching from fatigue and tension: Giving her orders wasn't going to stop her from asking questions. From putting herself into further danger. So, he decided, he would have to work with her.

There were worse things than spending more time with Jessie Jerome. The worst of all would be spending the rest of his life without her.

He knew now that he was falling in love with the headstrong woman with the wild imagination.

That thought both scared and relaxed him. It allowed him to lie down in bed, but not to fall asleep for a very long time.

The next morning, he went straight to Calvina's with Taku back at his side. Renny answered the door. "Jessie's not here, Jack," he said, looking distracted.

"What's wrong?" Jack asked.

"Little Lazarus was sick last night. Calvina said he was fine earlier, when she showed him off to some company, but then he screamed his head off till the wee hours. Is it normal for a child to be so fussy?" Renny, who had always appeared to Jack to look young and almost pretty, seemed to have aged overnight. Renny ran his fingers through his hair and looked pleadingly toward Jack. "I was planning on leaving today but can't do that to Calvina."

"Sorry, Renny, I don't know anything about babies," Jack said. "But where's Jessie?" A chime of alarm pealed through him. The last time she had left the boardinghouse so early was the day before, when she was nearly killed as she checked on Taku.

Still, he had no reason to be worried for her—yet. Not until Renny answered his question.

"What do you mean," Jack exploded in reply, "that she told you to let me know she was going up Chilkoot Pass, but that I wasn't to follow?"

"Are you certain you two know what you're doing?" Jessie asked. "And that you really want to do this?"

She'd been sorely disappointed that Renny had delayed his trip up the Chilkoot, though she applauded his decision to stay to help Calvina with the baby. But Otis Oetting apparently had spread rumors around Helen's. Before Jessie had had an opportunity to seek out another companion for the trek, or to accept the fact that she would have to wait, Gilda the Gold had come for her.

Gilda and Skagway Sadie had heard from Otis that Jessie was interested in a hike up the Chilkoot. Gilda had taken Jessie to Frank Dungel's, where Sadie was assembling the materials for a cache. Sadie and Gilda were finally going for the gold.

Now, inside the warehouse where Jessie had last been knocked over the head, she was questioning the two women who had invited her along to the Chilkoot Pass.

"Otis said you'd be interested in coming along sometime," Sadie said in her soft, shy voice. "Why not now?" She touched her brunette pompadour as though assuring herself it was still in place.

"That's right," Gilda said more boisterously. "We women need to stick together."

She was right. And what better opportunity would Jessie have, particularly this quickly, to get to the top of the Pass to pursue her own goals?

An image of Jack passed through her mind, his handsome brow puckered in irritation, his shoulders raised in frustration. He wouldn't like this, not at all.

That made Jessie smile.

She wouldn't be gone long. He probably wouldn't even miss her.

That made Jessie frown.

"Let's go," she said to Sadie and Gilda.

Jack went to Otis's; Renny hadn't been certain who Jessie had intended to go with since he was unable, but she had mentioned something about the little outfitter.

"He's one of the theft suspects!" Jack had exploded, then sped off toward Otis's, Taku close behind.

But Otis wasn't there. One of his assistants said that Otis had left early that morning with the first of his cache on a sled behind him. "He said he was going alone," the assistant timidly informed a stewing Jack.

At least Jessie had had sense enough not to go with Otis, Jack thought as he left. Jack doubted that Otis had the guts enough to pull off the thefts, let alone injure Taku and harm Jessie. Besides, he had been flirting with Jessie since he'd met her. He was unlikely to have attacked her.

Unless the flirting was just a cover for his true, depraved character. He was one of the few outfitters who hadn't been robbed. Was that because he had been one of the thieves? And had he harmed Jessie for failing to respond to his advances?

He had, after all, acted suspiciously without explanation.

Damn! Jack thought as he hurried along the slush-covered street toward Helen's. That kind of thinking wasn't helping anything, not now.

He would ask around at the saloon, then head up the Pass. How else would he be able to find Jessie?

He would talk her into letting him come along. They would ask their questions together, so he could keep her safe.

So he could be with her.

She had left word for him not to follow her up the Pass. She had warned him before of pending avalanches, of all things. He'd heard of none recently, only of soft snow. Was there some other reason she wanted him up Chilkoot Pass? Was this all a scheme on her part to get him up there?

The air he breathed was dank, with an edge to it. The street was noisy and crowded. People got in his way. He wanted to shove them aside. He didn't.

Instead, he stepped into the middle of the street, willing to take his chances at being struck by a horse or a sled. He was able to go a little faster there.

Before he got to Helen's, though, Eldon Riggs rushed up. "I didn't mean for this to happen," the portly banker said, his arms shaking at his sides.

"For what to happen?" Jack's hands went icy in their gloves.

"Miss Jerome. Jessie. She's in danger."

Jessie had known she was a little out of condition for hiking, but this was ridiculous.

The rising trail, crowded with other stampeders, followed the Taiyu River. She and her companions had only gotten as far as Finnegans Point, a bend in the river where a road had been built over a bog.

Snow-covered mountains loomed above them. Jessie had seen several bald eagles soaring around the treetops, and tracks of animals that might have been wolves or even bears dotted the snow leading into the surrounding woods. She saw the icy surface of a glacier in the distance, up one of the rugged slopes.

Every muscle in Jessie's body already reminded her of its aching existence. The worst was yet to come; they were still more than ten miles from the Golden Steps, the stairway carved into the ice that was the final part of the journey up the Chilkoot into the Yukon.

Maybe she was crazy to attempt this. She was a balladeer, not a detective, amateur or otherwise. And if she were just trying to show Jack she could do things by herself, well, there were other, better ways to prove it than by hurting herself.

And if they didn't slow up, or go a lot faster, they might be caught by the avalanche.

Part of the reason she was so sore was that they were bringing goods with them. Many stampeders carried supplies on their backs. At least Sadie, Gilda and she had strapped stores onto sleds and towed the sleds behind them. Too bad they hadn't dogs or horses to pull their goods, like some of the others. Jessie even saw a poor elk hitched to one sled.

"Can we rest for awhile?" she finally asked Gilda as a man with a huge hunk of goods on his back nearly pushed her to get ahead of them on the trail. She'd have stuck out her tongue at him, but she was afraid it would freeze.

"Rest? Not likely." The woman's blond hair was hidden beneath a fur hat. Her pretty face was flushed from the effort of towing her heavily packed sled with the heavy rope looped over her shoulders. None of the men here was likely to be able to recognize that she had a voluptuous body, not with the layers of

Linda O. Johnston

clothes she wore, topped by a big fur coat. "We have to get to the Scales fast. That's at the base of the Golden Steps."

"Why do we have to hurry?" Jessie asked. "We'd feel a lot better if we took our time." *Plus*, she thought, *we'd be far below the Scales when the avalanche hits tomorrow*. She'd intended to warn her companions when the time seemed right, and she wouldn't sound like a nut case.

"The gold has waited long enough, and so have we." This came from Sadie, at Gilda's far side. Her face no longer evinced that sweet, longing look she always managed to train on Jack. Her dark hair was half hidden beneath a wide-brimmed masculine hat. She, too, tugged a sled full of goods behind her. But there was something else in her eyes that Jessie did not recognize. She appeared angry and as cold as the snow through which they trudged.

This trail certainly had the capability of changing people. It had aged Jessie years already. It may have turned warm little Sadie to ice. Too bad Jack couldn't see her now.

Jack. What was he doing now? Probably sitting in his warm jail, feet up, laughing with Filby about what a fool Jessie was—if he even knew where she was.

She loved his wonderful, deep, hearty off-duty laugh. When would she hear it again?

Would she hear it again?

She missed him. Maybe it had been a mistake to come up here.

Climbing up to the summit to ask questions no longer seemed like such an astute idea. What could she learn there? No one was likely to say, "I'm the guy who stole from the outfitters and slugged you twice, Ms. Jerome." The goods were fungible; she was too unskilled to identify the exact barrels of potatoes stolen from Horace's.

She had heard stories of recent thefts from the caches at the top of the Pass. Some outfitters had told of vigilance committees formed at the summit to catch thieves and punish them. But even if a committee member could point out some of the culprits, she was unlikely to be able to tie one or more of them to the crimes in Dyea.

And what if she were tossed back into her own time from here, when the avalanche began, without an opportunity even to say goodbye to Jack? How would she live with that for the rest of her life?

"Look," she said breathlessly to Gilda as they continued forward in snow tamped down by the feet of hundreds of earlier stampeders. "Let's take our time, shall we? Enjoy the scenery. Hang out here for a couple of days. Then I'll help you bring this load as far as the Scales and go back to Dyea. I'm not really after the gold, and I really don't think I'll find what I'm looking for at the top of the trail."

"You have to come with us right now." Gilda's harsh voice brooked no argument. She glanced toward Sadie, at her other side, as though for confirmation.

Sadie's shrug was slight beneath the straps over her back. "There's a deserted cabin I heard of a little while further along the trail," she panted. "We'll stop there and rest. Talk about what we're going to do next. All right?"

"Okay," Jessie agreed. She could make it that far, despite the chill and her aching muscles and head. She hoped. And maybe she could convince them there. Even mention the avalanche.

She did make it to the cabin, although it took nearly

another hour. It was way off the main trail. She wondered how Sadie had heard about it.

Sadie answered her question. "It belonged to a man who froze to death last year. Arnett, who's made the journey up the Chilkoot lots of times already, told me about it. He said the trip is treacherous even for men. Thought that we women would want someplace to rest and suggested this."

"He was right, bless him," Jessie said, sinking onto a bare mattress thrown over a rotting wooden bed frame. She watched as Gilda lit a fire in the hearth. She doubted she would ever feel warm again, but the heat from the blaze certainly helped.

Her face began to thaw, and with it, her nose. As she inhaled, she smelled again Helen's signature perfume, worn by both Gilda and Sadie, who had removed their warm fur coats. They wore heavy woolen trousers, held up by suspenders over their heavy sweaters, a masculine outfit that emphasized their substantial bustlines.

The odor cloyed in Jessie's nostrils, reminding her of what she had inhaled when she had found Taku, slashed and hurting. When she had been hit over the head.

She had assumed it had been one of the johns who'd been with Helen's girls that night. Otis Oetting, despite his small stature, had been one of her primary suspects after his suspicious behavior. That was now bolstered by his apparent envy of the other outfitters on his street.

But Jessie was the one who'd tried to convince Jack that women were capable of doing a man's job. Did that include robbing outfitters? What about slashing dogs and hitting other women over the head?

She had suspected Helen, but what would her motive have been? The saloon keeper seemed successful. If she chose to stay off her back to earn her bread, Jessie was sure she could do it.

Who else, then? Eldon Riggs? She didn't much like the portly banker. He was near the top of her list, but she'd seen no evidence against him.

Lester Jones? While he was inebriated, he made all sorts of threats, but weren't they idle ones?

Dab Daugherty? Whiskey Tom? Someone she hadn't spoken with much?

But she was afraid she now knew the answer.

She hadn't really suspected the Gilda and Sadie she had met down in Dyea, but the women who were with her here seemed somehow different.

She looked as nonchalantly as she could toward them. They were huddled together near the fire. Both women's eyes were on her, staring. Why did they suddenly appear so venomous? It had to be Jessie's imagination.

But just in case. . . . "I'm really not feeling well," she said weakly. "We're not too far from town yet. If you'd like, I can keep an eye on these goods while you take some of them to the Scales or even up the Golden Steps. Then, you can come back for the rest. But I don't think I can go on."

"Oh, poor Jessie," Sadie said. "I know this is hard work." She stood and rubbed her own lower back. "But just think of the reward at the top. Gilda and I have planned a long time for this. We won't have to work for Helen any more, or anyone else." Her smile was wistful, sweet once more. "And you won't have to sing for all those nasty men, or cook and clean at Calvina's. Really, it will be wonderful. You'll see."

As she'd spoken, she'd neared Jessie. So had Gilda.

Gilda added, "There's a lot of gold up there, Jessie. That's what everyone says. We'll find it."

"But I didn't really come after gold," Jessie began to protest. She, too, had stood and was slowly approaching the cabin door. "I just came up here to annoy Jack—"

"Oh, yes. Jack O'Dair." Jessie would never have expected such a vituperative tone from Sadie as she spoke of the man with whom she had flirted so avidly. "The lawman who knows it all. Only he never suspected that women could do anything worthwhile, did he, Jessie? It would have taken more money than we earned at Helen's for us to come up with our caches. A lot more. But we found a way to get it. And dear Jack never suspected that women could have robbed the outfitters, or hurt his dear dog—or his woman."

"But I'm not—" Jessie began to protest, just as she realized Gilda was right behind her. She tried to turn and duck at the same time, but it was too late.

Pain shot through her skull. Her last conscious thought was, *not again*! And then there was blackness.

Chapter Twenty-one

They stood on the warm Dyea street.

"I admit," Eldon Riggs told Jack, "that the plot intrigued me: Steal supplies from successful outfitters who made plenty of money anyway from poor stampeders. Sell it to the stampeders for a little less than they could buy it for legitimately. Most would ask no questions, be glad for the bargain. I was in on it from the beginning, though I didn't have to steal anything. The schemers deposited their money into my bank, gave me a little extra cash not to ask questions. I didn't care where they got it, as long as I had it to lend to outfitters in trouble between shipments of goods—and to save toward my own cache."

Jack kept his fists to his sides. He had to fight to keep himself still, fight the urge to run up into the Pass after Jessie. He needed the story first—all of it, right now—so he could help her.

He ignored the flow of people around them. He

ignored the warmth of the springtime sun. He concentrated on the sad-eyed banker's words.

"Who were the schemers?" He tried to sound nonchalant.

"The two thieves you jailed, of course. That Madden, he was a nasty one. Good thing Frank Dungel got him before he could hurt Frank."

"What happened to his friend?" Jack couldn't recall his real name, only the nickname Jessie had given him: Dismal.

"He went to Skagway and up White Pass. He promised never to come back down Dyea way." Eldon paused, looking down at the street as though its whirls of mud held fascination for him. "Of course, the others paid him off, just to be sure."

"Who were the others?" Jack asked.

But Eldon was telling the story his own way. The portly man looked pleadingly at Jack. "I appreciate your saving me from those drunks that night, Jack. And I didn't know we'd wind up starting riots. That was never my intent."

"What *was* your intent?"

"Just to get enough together so that, when I left after gold, I'd never have to return to this miserable place."

"But I thought Horace and Frank were your friends, and you stole from them."

Eldon looked over Jack's shoulder, to where the mountains to the Yukon rose. "Yes." His voice was hoarse.

"What about Otis? Was he one of the schemers?"

Eldon laughed. "Hardly. I know I tried to get you to mistrust him, but the fool was just sneaking around giving supplies to stampeders too poor to get together caches of their own. That was why he never seemed to have enough supplies to sell. He'd go to his own store in the middle of the night to gather items to give away. That's why he was so eager to go off to the Yukon himself to get rich."

Good old soft-hearted Otis, Jack thought. Partly thanks to Eldon's hints, they had wrongly suspected him.

"What about Jessie?" he asked. "I know you like her." His curious, impetuous Jessie, who kept poking into thefts that didn't concern her, and got hurt. "Taku, too. They got hurt."

"That's why I'm telling you now." Eldon's voice sounded frantic. His puffy cheeks were bright red even though their surroundings weren't cold. Jack couldn't even see the air Eldon blew out through his pursed lips. "It was time, you see, for them to make their move—Gilda and Sadie."

Jack drew in his breath. They were the other ones behind the thefts? The attacks on Jessie and Taku?

He didn't interrupt Eldon, though his mind filled with questions.

"One of them would distract people away from a warehouse they wanted to loot and the other would sneak inside with Madden and the rest," Eldon said. "That's how the thefts happened so easily. No man could resist their attention. And now, they told Helen that their families in the States had sent them money, so they were buying caches and going off to the Yukon. The thing was, they were afraid Jessie had seen them, one or another of the times she interrupted their thefts at the outfitters. They intended to invite her to come with them, maybe tell her they'd pay her off by giving her gold once they found it. They got Otis to ask her to come along first. He didn't know why, but they'd intended to meet up with Otis and Jessie if she did agree." Eldon sighed. "Of course, I'm not sure what they'd have done to Otis to get him out of the way."

Jack could guess, but he didn't say anything.

"In any event, Jessie didn't go with Otis. And it was good fortune that little Lazarus became so fussy last night that Renny Sanders could not leave for the summit this morning."

Or was it good fortune? Jack had heard that Calvina, the new mother, had entertained guests. Had they slipped her something that would make her milk sour for the baby?

"Once they had Jessie up in the Pass, what was their plan?" Jack asked through gritted teeth. He'd imagined for a while that the whole plot was an elaborate scheme on her part to get him into Chilkoot Pass on Palm Sunday, in case the avalanche she raved about actually occurred, though he'd no idea why it was so important to her.

He no longer thought so. He was frightened for her.

"They just wanted her out of the way," Eldon said hastily. Jack's foul mood must have been evident, the way the chubby, spineless man cowered before him. "They told me they intended to take her to the top of the Pass and distract her while they finished getting their caches assembled. Then, when they went on into the Yukon, they would let her return here. They promised they wouldn't hurt her."

"And you trusted them?" Jack said in a tone as menacing as the crack of breaking ice. "After they already hurt her twice and slashed Taku?"

Tears rose to Eldon's eyes. Good. Jack hoped he intimidated the greedy snake of a man before him. Maybe it would keep him honest from then on, and get him to tell the law if he heard of another such nefarious plot.

But it might do Jessie no good.

"And now they've taken her up into Chilkoot Pass with them?" He managed to make his voice a tad less threatening.

Eldon nodded briskly, causing his jowls to flop. "Yes. But she should be fine."

"She had better be," Jack growled. "That Gilda, I knew she was a wild one, but for her to drag Sadie into such a nasty, cunning plot, and then to plan to hurt Jessie—"

"It wasn't Gilda," interrupted Eldon.

Confusion rippled through Jack. And then it dawned on him. "Sadie? Sweet Skagway Sadie—she was in charge all along?"

Eldon nodded sadly.

Jack had not been up the Chilkoot for a long time.

He had hiked it before, at first just to see what it was like, the next several times to follow up on fist fights, track thieves, keep the peace.

Never before had he traveled it so fast.

His snowshoes, rounded in front and tapering to a long point behind, fit awkwardly on his feet, but his progress would have been even slower without them. Past the trailhead he went, Taku unwaveringly at his side. Jack asked questions of the crowds of stampeders as he progressed up the trail. He spotted the start of the logging road, then the sawmill. In a while, he reached Finnegans Point.

He stopped several slow-moving, supply-laden stampeders and their native packers, Chilkat Indians. "Have you seen Jessie Jerome, the singer from Helen's?" he asked the stampeders. Some had not heard of her, but her reputation had spread, and many knew who she was.

But none had seen her. Nor had they seen Gilda the Gold, Skagway Sadie, or any others of Helen's girls.

The packers seemed restless and angry. A couple threw down their burdens in the snow as Jack watched and ran off, leaving the men who'd hired them shouting after them.

"What's going on?" Jack asked.

"The damned fools are superstitious, that's all," grumbled a grizzled, older stampeder with a bright red wool scarf around his neck and fingers peeking through holes in his gloves.

A younger man picked up some of the supplies the packers had dropped and began cramming what he could into his own pack. "Never should have trusted them," he growled. "Not today, anyway. They told us the weather conditions weren't right, claimed there would be an avalanche up in the Pass soon." He looked up at Jack and laughed, a donkey-like bray. "Can you imagine? An avalanche?"

Could he imagine? He hadn't before—not when Jessie had made her wild claims.

As he'd hurried up here, he had wondered once again if Jessie had somehow put Eldon Riggs up to relating his strange tale, to lure Jack up the Chilkoot. Sadie and Gilda?

But even if Jessie had somehow gotten Eldon's co-operation, she surely couldn't have paid off all the Chilkat packers. And these weren't the only packers he had seen head back down toward town.

And so Jack pushed his way up the Pass.

He had found no sign of Jessie. It had been hours. It was beginning to grow dark. He would have to camp at Canyon City shelter, then go on to Sheep Camp and the Scales the next day.

He only hoped he would not find Jessie too late.

An avalanche?

A moan woke Jessie. It took her a moment to realize that it had come from her.

She opened her eyes and saw ... nothing. Rather, just a little light, filtered through cloth. There was something over her head—a sheet?

A heavy weight lay on her chest, as though she were being compressed from above. She was warm and felt as though she could hardly breathe.

She was moving. She seemed to be traveling upward, head first, tied to something flat and hard. A sled? She moaned again as she was jolted; the sled must have hit a hunk of ice.

She tried to cry out but realized there was a gag in her mouth. It tasted oily, and she nearly choked. She stopped herself, though. If she threw up, as she wanted to, she could suffocate on her own vomit and die.

And she intended to survive, if for no other reason than to defy Sadie and Gilda, the slimy, thieving saloon girls. One of them had hit her over her poor, throbbing head. Probably had been the one to do it before, too, drat their deceptively innocent hides.

She wiggled her hands, but they were securely tied. Her feet, too. Sadie and Gilda had probably trussed her good, not letting her move too much or make enough noise that someone along the crowded trail would realize that the big bag of supplies at the bottom of the sled was actually a warm, wriggling body.

She should feel grateful, she supposed; they could have killed her.

Couldn't one of the many dogs pulling loads up the trail tell that there was a person down here?

Where was Taku when she really needed him?

Or Jack.

Not Jack. Hadn't he laughed at her tale of the avalanche, assured her he would be far away from Chilkoot Pass on Palm Sunday? He would make good on that promise, too, if for no other reason than to prove that she was full of baloney.

No, Jessie could not count on the hero of her ballad to come to her rescue. She had wondered before if she had never found the ballad's end because there had not been one; Jack hadn't been anywhere near the Pass or the avalanche. Which was fine. At least he'd not been killed by it.

But she was on her own. And, come hell, high water or deep snow, she was going to survive.

Jack woke before dawn. As planned, he had stopped at Canyon City. He'd rented a bed in a crowded cabin for a few hours' sleep. Before settling in, he had purchased a large kerosene lantern from a stampeder.

Now, before daylight had broken, he started out once more. There were a few other hardy souls who followed the trail in the dark, too, and the men banded together, lights in their hands, as they continued upward.

Dawn started to break, and with it, a surprising sight. Along the steep trail, covered by slushy snow, a few stampeders were heading back down toward town, fear in their eyes.

"What's wrong?" Jack asked.

"Up by the Scales," gasped one old-timer who appeared ready to collapse. He wore no hat, and his hair was as white as the hillsides that surrounded them. "Snow's sliding downhill."

"An avalanche?" Jack tried to sound incredulous, but he wasn't. Not really. Hadn't Jessie told him so? Hadn't the Chilkat packers believed it would happen, too?

"Not yet," replied another stampeder in tattered woolen clothing. "Just a bunch of small slides—so far. But it's warm enough up there; a big one's coming. If you're smart, you'll stay down here. Better yet, head back for town."

Some of the others with whom Jack had been walking hesitated. A couple turned around and joined those leaving the trail.

Not Jack, though. He couldn't. He squinted into the glare cast by the sun onto the snow straight ahead. He thought he could just make out a few of the wires of the long motor-powered tramways that had been built to carry goods to the top of the Pass—for the few stampeders who could afford it.

Jessie was still up there. She had been right in her prediction. She definitely was in trouble.

Beside him, Taku whined. Jack looked down. His dog was watching his face, his own expression uneasy.

"Let's go, boy," Jack said. "Go find Jessie."

"What's happening?"

Her sled prison had stopped. Jessie heard the frightened question in a female voice she recognized as Gilda's.

"Not a damned thing," Sadie responded. "Let's go."

"But all those people are running away. We can't—"

"We can," interrupted Sadie in a furious tone that allowed for no contradiction. "We've come this far."

But Gilda repeated her question. This time, she shouted it, obviously to someone else. "What's happening?"

"There's an avalanche threatening," came the reply. "Right here at the Scales."

Jessie had been right about the time, at least. For whatever good that did her. It was Palm Sunday.

It had sounded to her as though whoever had responded to Gilda was nearby. Was this her opportunity to save herself?

She wasn't even sure why they had kidnapped her. The best she could figure was that these two didn't take kindly to someone determined to catch them.

Did that mean they would hurt Jack? He might not be in the Chilkoot Pass, but they could still return to town after this trek. She pulled at her bonds, to no avail.

She had been thinking for a long while that seemed like eons about what to do. She knew the trail was busy, had heard voices now and then, but had no perspective about how close anyone was. Without being able to see, she had had to wait till she was sure they weren't alone. In the meantime, she had pretended to be Taku, chewing through the cloth gag in her mouth.

She hadn't been able to release any of her bonds. Still . . .

She began rocking side to side, gently at first. She felt the load on top of her chest begin to shift, just a little. Then a little more.

She continued to rock, until—

"Stop that!" She heard the shout just as she felt the sled tip toward her right side. It fell over in a heap. She gasped as the breath was knocked out of her, but at least the press of supplies on her chest stopped.

"Damn you!" It was Sadie's voice Jessie heard. She still couldn't see anything with the cloth over her face. Her hands and feet were still bound.

She listened. Hadn't anyone noticed? If nothing else, someone nearby should stop to help two ladies in distress as their sled toppled, even if they didn't know there was a third lady buried beneath the supplies.

But Jessie heard nothing. She spit what she could of the gag out of her mouth and hollered, "Help!" but it was cut off short as she was punched in the mouth through the cloth.

"Quiet, bitch!" demanded Sadie.

Tears filled Jessie's eyes. At least it wasn't as cold as it had been recently, or the wetness might have frozen. But no one came to help. She didn't even hear anyone express curiosity.

Had she picked the wrong time after all?

She thought of Jack O'Dair, down in Dyea. She would never see him again.

As terrible as her predicament was, that thought made her the most miserable of all.

"Now what are we going to do?" she heard Gilda wail. "All this stuff scattered, and we can't just put Jessie back—"

"You be quiet, too," insisted Sadie. "No one knows she's here. They're not paying attention to us, just to those cowards coming back down the hill. A little snow won't hurt them or us. There'll just be all the more gold, once we get there."

"But how are we—"

"Let me think," Sadie interrupted.

Jessie had caught her breath again. The gag was

still partly in her mouth, but she thought she could talk.

"Sadie?" she called. The name came out muffled, but she thought it was intelligible. "Gilda? I'll help you get away, if you'll just let me out of here." A lot of the consonants she tried to pronounce didn't sound quite right, but she thought they could understand her.

"Of course you will." Sadie's voice was low, practically in her ear. "And the moment we let you go, you'll run off, tell everyone what happened, especially your dear Marshal O'Dair. He was close to catching us when you arrived, but we still had some time, till you kept pushing him harder. He wanted to look good for you by finding out who was stealing from the outfitters in his damned precious town. You know that's what he calls Dyea—*his* town? And he just hates to see anything go wrong there. I tried to distract him. If he'd only responded to me instead of . . . Well, never mind that now. No, Miss Jerome, we'll go ahead with our plan. And if there is an avalanche, and if you're found buried in snow later, who's going to know how you got there?"

This time, the compression Jessie felt in her chest was from panic. What was she going to do?

"Don't scream. If you do, I'll drown you out with screams of my own, then hit you so hard you'll lose consciousness. And if I happen to kill you now . . . well, so what?"

"But Sadie—" she heard Gilda protest.

"Shut up!" Sadie snapped.

Jessie felt hands at her back and her feet. The sled was righted, and she was still upon it, though the supplies weren't on top of her.

She had to do something quickly.

As far as she could tell, the sled was sideways on the slope. Could she . . .

With a mighty effort, she twisted and rocked.

"Hey!" she heard Sadie cry.

She felt the sled begin to slide down the hill with her on it. Feet first, at least, but still. . . .

Oh, lord! Had she done the right thing? What if she were stopped abruptly by a tree?

She heard a crack that seemed to shake the very ground on which the sled slid. An abominably loud roaring noise rent her ears. Men and women alike began to scream. "Avalanche!" The cry was taken up by dozens of voices. Some were nearby. Would anyone stop the careening of this sled on its downhill plunge? Would Jessie be buried in the snow?

"Help!" she cried in terror. And still she continued her relentless slide.

Until . . . "Ouch!" she shouted as her feet ran into something. Fortunately, it wasn't too hard. In a moment, she realized her legs were wet beneath her canvas covering.

She must have hit a slushy snowbank. Thank heavens. Now, all she had to do was find a way to get loose, then—

The rumbling noise around her grew louder, so loud that it sounded like thunder no more than a few feet away.

The avalanche! Frantically, Jessie began to writhe on the sled, trying once more to unfasten the ropes that kept her prisoner. "Sadie! Gilda! Please . . . anyone!"

And then she was struck by a wall of rushing snow.

Chapter Twenty-two

Jack heard thunder in the distance.

Thunder? No—it had to be the roar of an avalanche.

Jessie had been right.

"Jessie!" As he called out, his voice was as weak and hoarse as if he had been buried in the snow. He stared up into Chilkoot Pass, far into the distance, and saw what appeared to be a wall of white smoke. But he knew better; it was snow. A lot of it. Hurtling downward.

He plunged forward, hurrying as well as he could in his snowshoes. He felt warm in his thick winter clothing. Too warm. Was there danger that the snow would fall this far down the mountainside? No matter; he had to go on.

Taku was already far ahead, barking at the unfamiliar noise accompanied by an even more chilling sound: the far-off screams of those caught by the tumbling snow.

It might have been Jack's imagination, but as he squinted again into the blinding glare, he thought he saw tiny black forms resembling ants being rolled and shoved and buried before the mass of snow. Stampeders? Maybe.

"Jessie, where are you?" he cried aloud.

In a short while, the noise stopped. It was quiet. Too quiet. The avalanche had ended ahead of him. He was safe.

He didn't care.

As he continued forward, feeling as though he were going no faster than an infant's crawl, he reached a group of bedraggled, warmly dressed men atop a pristine, white heap of snow. They were digging frantically. "Are there any other survivors?" he demanded. He thought he heard shouts in the distance, then realized the cries came from beneath him—under the snow.

"Help us," pleaded one somber man whose boots and black woolen coat were salted with snow. He wore a wide brimmed hat. "We were up above working on the Chilkoot Tramway. Soon as we knew what was coming, we ran." He hesitated. "Others didn't."

There were no shovels, so Jack began digging with his gloved hands. Could Jessie be here? Where was she?

But he had to help the people he knew were buried here. She was safe . . . somewhere. She had to be.

Even Taku seemed to know just what to do, for he used his forepaws to toss snow out of the way.

Their progress was slow. Too slow. And they could not tell for certain where people were buried.

325

Linda O. Johnston

"Let's try this," Jack said. He organized the construction workers into a line that dug one long, deep pit in the snow.

They found one man almost immediately and pulled him out. "Thank you," he said weakly as his rescuers lay him on the ground and gave him a sip of whiskey. His lips beneath his dark brown whiskers were nearly blue. "I couldn't breathe. I was dying down there." He began to shudder.

Jack asked, "Before you were buried, did you see any women around here—probably three women alone."

"Not here," the man said, "but I'd heard tell of the possible avalanche. I was way up the Pass, had started down when it hit." He pointed ahead. "I only saw two women—that Gilda the Gold and Skagway Sadie from Helen's, down in Dyea. Them the ones you're looking for?"

"Yes," Jack called over his shoulder as he sprinted up the Pass, his movements still awkward in his snowshoes.

"Thanks, mister," called the man he had helped to rescue.

Gilda and Sadie—but not Jessie? What had they done with her?

"Find Jessie, Taku," he demanded once more as his dog passed him along the path.

Ahead were more stampeders helping others from the snow. A couple of bodies were laid out side by side—men who hadn't survived. But fortunately a lot of people were being pulled out alive.

"Have you seen Jessie Jerome?" Jack asked everyone he met. None had. "Skagway Sadie? Gilda the Gold?" He gathered from the answers that the saloon girls had been in this vicinity when the avalanche hit, but no one knew where they were now.

Each time Jack saw someone needing help, he stopped. Time was precious if Jessie were one of the unfortunates who had been buried, but he could no more have ignored people in trouble than he could have prevented his heart from beating.

With each group of rescuers, he suggested the method that had worked before: organizing men into lines to dig pits straight down toward where voices still cried weakly beneath the snow. Below the surface, they could branch out and search for survivors.

Then he went on.

The whiteness around him was broken only by the dark, eerily groping branches of trees that had resisted the onslaught. Above, she sky was calm and blue. He inhaled crisp, fresh air as he hurried. It was an ironically beautiful day.

He reached an area where no survivors were digging—and then he heard a voice. A muffled female voice calling for help.

"Jessie?" he yelled. It didn't sound like her: too shrill. But fear could have sharpened her voice.

He heard a response—weak, somewhere near him. Somewhere below him.

He turned around. Taku was digging frantically in the snow.

There was no one nearby to help. Jack had no tools to assist him, either, but he knelt on the ground beside his dog. Using his gloved hands as scoops, he threw snow out of his way, digging downward, farther downward, until he reached a piece of cloth. It was a scarf. He pulled at it gently, not wanting to choke its wearer. "Oh, thank God," came the weak response. "Help me."

In a few moments, he had freed the snow's prisoner. A woman.

Not Jessie. He nearly shouted in frustration—and yet he still felt proud; he had saved a life.

It was Gilda the Gold.

He finished digging her out, then found someone else had been buried beneath her. Jessie?

Oh, lord, Jack prayed silently as he continued to dig. The woman he was releasing now did not move. Did not cry out. He touched her cold, cold skin and felt no pulse.

No. Not Jessie. This couldn't be Jessie.

It wasn't. He brushed snow off the blue flesh of Skagway Sadie's face.

Though he despised what these two women had done, Jack couldn't let them die, if he could help it. Neither of them. Steeling himself to get so close to a person he now despised, Jack began giving her mouth-to-mouth resuscitation.

Behind him, Gilda gagged, inhaled rapidly to catch her breath, then began to cry.

"Where's Jessie?" Jack demanded, pausing for breath from his attempt to revive Sadie.

"No one was supposed to get hurt," Gilda wailed.

Jack's blood nearly froze inside him. "What did you do to her?" he demanded.

"Is Sadie going to be all right?"

Jack thought he detected a small movement from the woman beneath him. "Maybe. We'll see." He breathed for Sadie once more, then felt satisfied as she moaned and coughed.

"Oh, thank you!" cried Gilda.

Jack turned back to her. "Now tell me, where's Jessie?" Gilda trembled beneath his scowl, but he had no intention of coddling the woman. Not now.

Not when every second might count.

Gilda pointed down the slope—toward snow. Only snow. Except for a couple of surviving, denuded trees, nothing else was visible.

"She . . . we had her tied on a sled. It went downhill just before . . . before . . ."

"Before the avalanche? What the hell was she doing tied on a sled?"

Gilda was crying now. She only shrugged shoulders that seemed slumped within her heavy wool coat still speckled with snow. "I . . . we . . ."

"Never mind!" Jack cried. "Just show me where she was."

Sadie moaned again, and Gilda knelt beside her.

"Leave her for now," Jack commanded, hauling Gilda up by her arm. "She'll be fine. I have to find Jessie. Taku, come."

But the dog was already far ahead, running down the hill of slippery white. Part of the mountainside rose beside the path, and Taku stopped, whining, looking around as though confused.

Jack caught up with him. "Find Jessie," he ordered.

Taku didn't move. He stood there with his pointed, wolf-like ears held high in the air, then turned his head.

And then he barked and ran a hundred feet back down the mountain. There he stopped and, whining, began to dig.

"Is Jessie there, boy?" Jack asked, his hammering heart pummeling the inside of his chest.

As if in answer, Jack thought he heard a sound. A very faint sound, one that seemed to come from far, far away.

But it was the most wonderful sound he had ever

329

heard. For if he weren't mistaken, it was Jessie's sweet, mellow voice.

"Jack," it called.

Jessie blinked at the sudden brightness. She inhaled deeply, letting her lungs fill with the clean mountain air.

She was still strapped to the dratted sled that had helped to save her, for it had created an air pocket beneath the snow. Jessie looked up at her rescuer: Jack O'Dair. She smiled—or would have, had the gag been fully out of her mouth.

"What took you so long?" she demanded.

He had the audacity to laugh, damn the man. And then he was on his knees beside her in the pit, unfettering her mouth, throwing off the rest of the snow that pinned her down, loosening the ropes that held her prisoner.

In moments, she was free.

She tried to sit up, but her muscles wouldn't hold her. She was too cold. Too stiff. "Ow," she moaned.

"Sssh," Jack said soothingly. He gathered her into his arms and lifted her from the hole, then climbed out.

At the top of the pit, Taku licked Jessie's face. Jessie hugged the large wolf-dog.

"I'd just learned you were around here," Jack said, "but Taku's the one who found you."

"Of course he is," Jessie crooned, hugging Taku around his silvery neck. His warm fur felt wonderful against her chilled, wet face.

"Let me see your hands." Jack took her fingers in his thick gloves, holding them up to his face. His brow furrowed as he studied her. She reached forward just a little bit to caress his craggy cheek. He startled, then smiled at her. "I take it you're not too badly hurt."

"Nope," she said, though her fingers smarted. So did her toes. Her cheeks . . . "But what does frostbite feel like?"

Quickly, he pulled off his jacket and put it around her. He chafed at the exposed skin of her hands and face. "You'll be fine, Jessie," he said. "I promise." The caring tone of his voice was enough to ignite the furnace within her. She wanted to throw herself into his arms. She was about to do just that when—

"So, Jessie, you think you've won."

Startled, Jessie looked over Jack's shoulder to see Skagway Sadie. She looked horrible, all wet and bedraggled, probably no better than Jessie herself looked.

Jack pivoted toward Sadie.

"I don't think anything at all, Sadie," Jessie replied carefully, "except that I'm cold."

"And I'm going up into the Yukon," Sadie said. "You, Jessie, are coming with me."

Jessie laughed. "Right. Just exactly how I want to spend my next few days here."

"If you don't, I'll shoot your lover. I'll need you to keep him from following me."

Only then did Jessie realize that Jack hadn't moved because he was protecting her. Sadie must be holding a gun on him.

"On the other hand," Jessie said, "I've always wanted to see the Yukon in the gold rush days. Maybe even dig up a nugget or two of my own."

She tried to move around Jack, but he put out his arm. "Stay back, Jessie."

"Oh, sure, Jack."

He glanced down at her, eyes wide. They narrowed

331

sharply. "You don't have any intention of listening to me, do you?"

"Of course not," she said sweetly. She grinned at his scowl. As she moved out from behind him, she shook her head. Sadie was pointing a gun at her. "Aren't men strange creatures?" Jessie asked. "They think they own us. It's dear of them to try to protect us, but that makes them feel superior."

Sadie frowned, then glanced at Taku, who was behind her, growling. Jessie noticed that her gun hand trembled. In fact, the woman looked ready to collapse at any moment.

"I have an idea, Sadie," Jessie said. She took Jack's arm and tried to tug him behind the skimpy trunk of a denuded tree that had somehow survived the onslaught of the avalanche. Jack, of course, didn't budge, darn the stubborn man. Jessie nevertheless continued talking. "You need to rest, Sadie. I need to rest. You want to be rich, don't you? Well, I have some pretty far-out ideas about how to earn money around here. You see, I can predict the future. Just ask Jack. I told him about the avalanche weeks ago. And I can tell you how to get rich without going into the Yukon."

"I'll just bet," Sadie said sourly.

"There's one thing I can predict. You can be sure of it."

The skepticism on Sadie's face didn't waiver. "What's that?"

"You're going to put down your gun in about three seconds."

"What?" She sounded confused, but the gun stayed where it was.

"You heard her, Sadie," said Gilda the Gold, who had come up behind her friend. "No one was supposed to get hurt. We nearly killed Jessie. I just want to go back to Helen's—if I don't have to go to jail first."

"Jack will work something out, won't you?" Jessie asked him.

He didn't deny it. How could he, when Gilda, too, had a gun?

"No!" cried Sadie—and she fired.

Jack fell into the pit from which he had just pulled Jessie. He'd been hit! Jessie screamed. The snow was still unstable. In moments, it buried him.

Sadie was sucked into the frothing mass of moving snow as well. So was Gilda.

Jessie continued to yell as she, too, felt herself moving as the ground beneath her turned to mush. She reached out and caught that silly, lone tree trunk.

It saved her.

In moments, the snow stopped shifting. Jessie didn't remain still, not for a moment.

"Taku, help!" she cried. She hadn't regained all of her own strength from being buried. She ached all over.

But that didn't stop her.

Down she dug, right where she'd seen Jack fall. It seemed to take forever to reach him.

But reach him, she did. She uncovered first his face, then the rest of him. She stared at his beloved body. Was he breathing?

"Oh, Jack," she cried, brushing more snow off him. She bent down to start CPR—and then he grabbed her. He gave her a thorough, unyielding kiss, then said, "So what kept you?"

Jack helped Jessie to unbury Gilda and Sadie once more. Both still were alive, though he doubted he would have grieved much over Sadie. He left her in the capable control of a Mountie, who had finally come down the Chilkoot to see if he could help anyone caught by the avalanche.

At least she was a poor shot. But he had slipped when he tried to duck.

Gilda was cold, but she was contrite. She apologized over and over. Jack left her to Jessie to handle.

Then Jack, with Taku at his side, sped from point to point in the Pass, digging out as many trapped stampeders as he could, breathing life back into some who appeared nearly dead.

After sending Gilda on her way, Jessie assisted, too. She knew other life-saving techniques similar to mouth-to-mouth resuscitation—that thing she called CPR, which she had mentioned along with the "high maneuver" a few days earlier.

And keeping close track of them all was that dratted photographer, Dab Daugherty. He seemed in his glory, taking one picture after another of the disaster that had occurred up here in the Chilkoot.

They ran into Otis Oetting, too. He had been at Sheep Camp when the avalanche hit and was now also trying to help save those caught in it. He seemed devastated, and Jack now understood why: The guy was soft inside; he lived to help people.

Time passed much too quickly. After a while, the people they located no longer had any life in them to save. After the twelfth dead body, Jack fell to his knees in the snow. He would have cried, if he hadn't been a man. "I've failed them," he whispered.

"You saved so many," Jessie said, putting her arms around him and drawing him back to his feet. "You're a real hero, Jack O'Dair. And now I know how your ballad will end."

That ballad. That damned ballad she was always talking about. But he hadn't time to think of it now. He heard a shout in the distance. Had someone else been found alive?

It was dark by the time Jack reached Canyon City again, the very cabin where he had taken refuge the night before. This time, though, he had achieved his objective.

Jessie was with him. She was all right.

He had pulled her along on that damned sled that had been her prison, for she had grown exhausted. No wonder.

She had nearly died that day.

But that hadn't stopped her from helping him. From saving a good many people who had been buried in the snow.

But they had lost a lot, too.

"Jack?" Jessie's voice was little more than a whisper. "Where are we?"

"We've borrowed a cabin for the night," he told her gently. Fortunately, he'd had no trouble kicking out all others who would have sheltered there as well; for some reason, everyone he'd met that day seemed to be mighty friendly and accommodating. "We'll get some sleep, then head back to Dyea in the morning."

"Okay." He hardly heard her soft reply.

He stoked the fire in the hearth, then lifted Jessie from where she lay on the sled up onto the mattress of the bed nearest the warmth.

She was a slender woman, and she felt like paradise in his arms.

She was alive.

As he tucked her beneath the thick wool blankets that had blessedly been left behind by some kind stampeder, she stirred. Her arms, still clad in a heavy knit sweater, reached up and drew his face slowly down toward hers.

He didn't resist. Hardly. Instead, he kissed her gently on her sweet lips. "Good night, Jessie," he whispered hoarsely. Damn, but that woman could stir him up just by breathing. And when he kissed her, even so modestly.

"Good night, Jack." There was a laugh in her voice. She seemed not quite as sleepy as before. In fact, when he attempted to walk away so she could rest, she said, "Now, where are you going?"

"To find myself someplace to sleep."

"I can think of a perfectly good place. One that'll help me keep warm, too. I was buried in snow today, Jack. I'm still cold. I may never feel warm again."

"I can help you with that, Jessie."

"I know you can."

He slid in beside her. The roaring in his ears this time had nothing at all to do with an avalanche, and everything to do with the blood that whooshed heatedly through his body at Jessie's nearness. He pressed himself tightly against her. "Does this help?" he asked.

"It sure does," she replied.

"How about this?" He began to stroke her sleek body through its clothes.

"Definitely." She turned to face him, and he could see a smile lifting the edges of her lips. "But I'd feel a lot warmer if we were skin to skin."

Jack laughed aloud as he hurried to accommodate her.

Jessie stretched like a sated cat when she awoke the next morning. Or maybe it was afternoon; light shone through the windows of the small cabin, displaying in the daytime the dirty decrepitness that the night's darkness had hidden.

No matter. The place felt like the most sumptuous of castles to Jessie, after the wonderful night she had spent with Jack.

Jack! Where was he? Lifting the blanket beneath her chin, she sat up and looked around.

Oh, lord—this cabin was so shabby. . . . Now that she knew how the ballad had to end, had she been thrust back into her own time overnight?

No, please no! she thought. She had to at least have time to say goodbye.

The cabin door opened. "Jack!" Jessie shrieked, and ran to him, ignoring the coldness of the bare wooden floor against her feet and the fact that her only covering was the blanket.

"What's wrong?" He grabbed her by the shoulders and looked quizzically into her eyes.

"Not a thing," she replied with a relieved sigh, hugging him tightly. Not now. But now that she'd accomplished what she needed here, how long would she stay?

They soon left for town. Everyone from the Chilkoot seemed eager to return to Dyea after the avalanche. The trail this day appeared like the uphill trek in reverse.

And wherever Jack went, stampeders came up to him, clapping him on the back, exclaiming over the way they'd heard he had pulled one buried soul after another from a bleak white grave. Taku, too.

"It wasn't really like that," Jack said, looking highly uncomfortable. "I just did what I had to."

"He saved people's lives!" That came from Dab Daugherty, who toted his camera equipment back down the mountain. "I've got a lot of it in pictures."

"But I don't want—"

"You're a hero, Jack, whether or not you like it." Jessie smiled at him, holding tightly onto his arm. He had give her his snowshoes, but still she felt as though she might slide down the pass on her rump without his support.

Or maybe she just wanted to touch him, now. While she still could. Fortunately, he did not seem to mind. In fact, he held her close the entire way down.

He related to her the plot to rob outfitters as told to him by Eldon Riggs. One main suspect, Otis Oetting, had been completely innocent.

So much for TV-learned investigative techniques, Jessie thought with a shake of her head. Sadie and Gilda had been on her list, though not at the top.

In the meantime, the tune to "The Ballad of Jack O'Dair" raced through her thoughts, tumbled by a tumult of words describing his heroic acts in the avalanche. She knew now how the ballad should end. Perhaps how it would end.

And she kept trying—hard—to push out of her mind what knowing the ending might mean about her ability to remain with Jack.

By the time they reached Dyea, night already had fallen. Jessie stopped at Calvina's to make sure Renny, the baby and she were all well. They fussed over Jessie; word had reached town of her harrowing experience with the thieving saloon girls. In fact, Gilda was already back at Helen's, telling the whole sordid story to all who would listen.

And Sadie? Well, she was sulking in jail, supervised by Filby. The Mountie had made good time getting her down here.

"Now, we're supposed to make sure you get to Helen's tonight," Calvina told Jessie, sitting in the cozy Sanders' parlor. "Renny, Lazarus and I are going, too. There will be some special goings on, we're told."

"Good," said Jack, hand on the doorknob. "You go to see Jessie there. I'll come when I can."

"Oh, no," Calvina contradicted. "You're to be the guest of honor, Jack."

In the end, Jessie convinced him to come. Standing beside him near the door, she said, "If they are going to make a fuss over you, don't you think you might as well get it over with?" She smiled at his obvious unease, then stood on her tiptoes to kiss him on that scowling mouth. "Whether or not you appreciate it, Jack, you've done some mighty spectacular things these last couple of days. Just think of the number of lives you've saved."

His frown lifted, just a little. He didn't say anything, but she suspected he was thinking of those dear to him whom he once thought he had let down by failing to protect them. This might not make up for it, but maybe it would let him believe that he was, after all, someone people could rely on.

So they all trooped to Helen's, even Taku. The saloon was crowded, and the smell of readily flowing liquor permeated the entire place, not to mention Helen's signature perfume.

In one of her corsets—bright green, this time, and decorated with golden feathers, Helen came up to them. She congratulated Jack and apologized to Jessie. "Gilda told me everything. She feels awful about it, I hope you know. And that lowdown Sadie—who would have thought? I'm sorry, Jessie."

"It wasn't your fault," Jessie said.

"Will you sing for us tonight?" Helen asked. "The crowd's been asking for you, especially after Gilda told about how you'd nearly died up there in the avalanche."

Yes, Jessie would sing. She wanted to. For she now had the ending of the ballad firmly engraved in her mind.

If she had been certain that not putting an end to the song would keep her here, she wouldn't have wanted to sing it.

But what she had sought for so long was not only the words, but what had happened. She knew that now, no matter what.

And if that fact sent her back to her own time, she wanted, at least, to leave Jack with her own small tribute to him.

She grabbed Jack's hand first, then whispered to him, "Please don't be mad at me, but this is something I have to do." And then she let go of him and took her guitar up on stage.

She wouldn't sing the very beginning of the ballad. She still didn't know who had written it, and it wasn't up to her to belt it out perhaps before it had even been created.

But the ending: If it had been written, not all had survived till her time. And she now knew exactly how it should go.

Some of what she'd already known had to be sung for her ending to make sense. She wouldn't write it down, though, or sing it here ever again. And the way folksongs changed through the years anyway, she could hope that no one would recall she had once sung words that hadn't been written yet.

She picked out a few chords to the ballad, then hummed its tune, one verse through. Then she sang to the silent crowd:

"The Dyea trails drew the greediest of males
Who would give up their grandmas for gold.
But none was too low too rate less than full
   show,
As Jack O'Dair defended his fold.

"Up passes, up trails, in the mightiest gales,
Stampeders all did go,
Stores of goods in their packs, strapped on their
   backs
And their boots all buried in snow.

"The Mounties who wait at the Klondike's gate
Let stampeders enter there
Only with batches of wares in huge caches—
Many saved by Jack O'Dair.

"For woe to those slobs who tried to rob
And woe to those who stole.
Daring Jack O'Dair was always there
To protect a stampeder's soul.

"Supplies for a year were required up there,
And captured pilferers fell
At the hands of the man who protected all
   bands—
Jack O'Dair shielded stampeders well.

"But even Jack could not attack
The Klondike's inevitable courses.
For when nature outlays its fiercest forays
Men can only respond to the forces.

" 'Avalanche!' came the gasp from the top of
   the Pass.
The snow's roar soon covered the screams.
"Do not despair!" shouted Jack O'Dair,
As he leapt in to salvage their dreams.

"The sea of snow hurtled toward below
Where stampeders stood still on the trail.
And with all his flair, brave Jack O'Dair
Was imperiled as all. Would he fail?"

Those verses were ones Jessie had previously learned, the ones that had piqued her curiosity for so long. What, she had always wondered, had happened to Jack O'Dair in the avalanche?

And now she knew.

She looked down at the crowd at the base of the stage. Hardly anyone stirred. All eyes were on her in the packed room.

Including the bright green eyes that she loved.

She dared a small smile at Jack. Was he angry with her for singing this much for everyone to hear?

No. He smiled back. In fact, he laughed, right out loud. Others around him, including Calvina and Renny, stared at him, and then they laughed, too.

"Don't leave us in suspense, Jessie," Jack called. "I want to hear how the song turns out."

She also laughed, then began again to sing, her eyes steadily on Jack's. She stumbled over the first line, for she was making assumptions, but what the heck? If he called her on it, she could say she was taking poetic license. She took a deep breath and went on.

"And way above was a lady, Jack's love,
In danger she cried out in despair.
Would the woman he craved die unsaved
By endangered Jack O'Dair?
"To and fro Jack scratched through the snow
Though buried like all of the rest.
For ne'er would he founder until he had found her
The woman so fair and so blessed.
"He dug and he labored until he had saved her
Exhausted he let himself fall.

But the woman, unshy, would not let Jack die—
And together they trod down the trail.
"And on the way, in the midst of the fray,
Jack managed to save even more.
Stampeders and others, their fathers and brothers
Owed their lives to Jack O'Dair's lore.
"Now the hero of Dyea has had his day
The whole town did him fair,
For none could deny that the gold town survived
Thanks to legendary Jack O'Dair."

She was still watching his reaction when the entire crowd exploded into cheers and applause. Both Jack and Jessie were lifted onto men's shoulders and acclaimed even more.

But the cheers were loudest of all when, in the middle of Helen's stage, with Dab Daugherty's camera trained right on them, Jack lifted Jessie into his arms and kissed her soundly.

Chapter Twenty-three

The evening at Helen's had ended. Jack had left for the jail to check on how Filby was getting along with Sadie. Jessie was exhausted, but her day was not yet over.

She had said goodbye to Jack, although he had probably thought it was just for that night. But Jessie had something she needed to do. And if it worked as she believed, she would leave his town Dyea, and his time, forever.

The moon above the ramshackle town was a blurred blot of white behind clouds skittering high above. The air was still warmer than it had been lately, but there was nevertheless a crisp Alaskan edge to it.

Holding a borrowed lantern in one hand, her guitar in the other, Jessie slogged through the slush on the darkened, near-deserted streets, exchanging an occasional greeting with a stampeder hurrying to wherever he called home during his stay in Dyea. Her boots tapped a muffled rhythm on the damp boardwalk.

She sighed heavily, thinking of what was to come. But then she straightened her spine. After glancing around to make certain no one was nearby, she said aloud in a soft but determined voice, "Okay, Curtis Fitzgerald. I'm coming back to salvage my career. Woe to you if you stand in my way."

That sounded good, she thought as she inhaled the fresh, moist air. The problem was, she cared a lot less now about her career as a folksinger than she had a few weeks earlier.

She didn't really want to stay here, in this miserable outpost of a town, where the weather was totally predictable—always bad—and the people, though friendly, were mostly crazed by the thought of finding gold . . . did she?

Absolutely!

No, she contradicted herself immediately. For by staying here, she would only become more miserable.

Jack O'Dair was every bit as heroic as his ballad had led her to believe. But if she had read between the lines, all those years she was yearning to learn its ending, she would have realized long before that he was a loner.

Maybe now he would realize that he hadn't failed those who once depended on him. He certainly hadn't failed his town. The crooks were caught. Nor had he failed those who'd needed his assistance in the last few days. Nevertheless, he had given no indication that he'd any intent of letting himself get close to any human being, not even Jessie. At least no closer to her than occasional, though admittedly, extraordinary, lovemaking.

That was too bad, for if anyone could have convinced Jessie that not all men were unreliable creeps like Curtis and her mother's lovers, it would have been Jack.

She passed the town's last-chance saloon on her way to her destination. A little tin-toned piano music rolled through the air, causing her to sigh again.

There were things she would miss here. Calvina, Renny and little Lazarus. Helen's, and her enjoyable singing career there.

Jack.

And that was the crux of it all. For even though she might be the biggest fool ever in this time and her own, she had fallen deeply, irrevocably, impossibly in love not only with the hero of the ballad, but with *him*.

Well, so what? She sang ballads every day of people who lost their loves, lamented, then went on. Why should she be any different?

She left the looming buildings of the small town and stepped onto the familiar path through the trees. Rather than appearing threatening, the forest welcomed her.

No, not the forest. The small house at the end of her journey. Jack's cabin.

She knew the door would be open. She went inside, put the things she carried onto the floor and lit one of the kerosene lamps on the wall.

She looked around, smiling sorrowfully at the small, homey room. It still had no bathroom, of course. It was tiny, sparsely furnished—and she adored it.

She would miss it.

She hung up the thick fur jacket she had borrowed on its peg on the wall, knowing she would miss its snug warmth, especially since Jack had finally revealed that he'd shot its former owner, a grizzly, in self defense.

She sighed yet again as she pulled a chair from beneath the small wooden table and sat it in the center of the room. She didn't bother to light a fire in the cast iron stove.

She didn't expect to be here long.

Jessie removed her guitar from its case, which she sat, open, on the floor beside her. She strummed a few chords, and then began to sing. Her voice was hoarse, choked with moisture.

"He kept the peace without surcease,
Did mighty Jack O'Dair.
Through Dyea-town fights, and dread Klondike
    nights,
None other could compare."

She had to stop for a moment to keep herself from sobbing aloud. "Goodbye, Jack," she whispered brokenly.

And then she continued,

"A brawny bear was Jack O'Dair,
His voice deep, mellow brass,
Bright red hair had Jack O'Dair
And eyes green as Ireland grass."

"Jessie, wait!" The door of the cabin was thrust open. Taku bounded into the room, followed by his owner.

They both were out of breath. Jack plunged forward, pulling Jessie up and into his arms. "What are you doing, damn it?" Though he sounded furious, his

347

lips were suddenly on her, kissing her temples, her cheeks, her neck, and finally finding her lips.

She should pull away, she knew. She would only feel worse, the longer she stayed here, fooling herself that Jack really wanted her. Wanted her to remain.

But his mouth didn't let her protest. His kiss demanded her response. It was easier to give in, to revel in the feel of his insistent lips and his inquisitive tongue. To feel his large, hard body pressed so sensually against hers, turning her insides to flowing lava. To drink in the sound of his low moans and whispered, if untrue, endearments.

Untrue? But . . . but . . .

She pulled back. "What did you just say?" she demanded of the red-headed bear of a man who did not let her go.

"I said I love you." Though she opened her mouth, whether to respond or because her jaw had simply dropped, she wasn't sure. But, sounding impatient, he didn't let her say a word. "Jessie, what were you just doing?"

"Singing your ballad." She eyed him warily. She knew he didn't like the song, even though he had laughed more heartily than anyone in the room when she'd sung the ending she'd written at Helen's that night.

"Why?"

"Because . . ." She inhaled deeply. "Jack, I know you don't believe me, but I really do come from the future. And—"

"What makes you think that?"

"That I come from the future?"

"That I don't believe you." His thick coppery brows knitted sternly at her.

She blinked. "Because you said so."

"That was before that damned avalanche. The only

way you could have predicted it was if you knew the future. And if you knew the future, it had to be because you were *from* the future, since that's what you'd told me."

There was logic there somewhere. Jessie was certain of it. But she didn't dwell on it. Instead, she felt herself grin. "Then you do believe me."

He nodded. "I believe you. I love you. Jessie—" The big handsome hulk of a man was suddenly on his knees on the floor before her. She was looking down at the top of his soft red hair, and she ran her fingers through it.

"Jack, I—"

"Wait." He grasped her hand. His eyes, as they bored into hers, contained a world of sincerity, a universe of emotion. "Jessie, will you marry me? I don't know the world you came from, but I do know that this Alaskan wilderness is a lot more primitive than the world even *I* came from. Dyea doesn't have to be my town any longer. If you want, we'll move somewhere else. But, please, Jessie. Stay with me. I won't fail you; I'll take care of you. We'll take care of each other. I know what the real ending of your ballad must be. I'm not a singer like you, but I was thinking all night about how it should go, after I heard your ending."

In a deep, melodic baritone, Jack O'Dair began to sing—the first time ever that Jessie had heard his wonderful singing voice:

"Now hand in hand, across Dyea land
Beneath silver skies above
Strolls Jack O'Dair and his lady so rare:
The sweet-throated woman Jack loves.

"He braved winter's woes and the deepest of
  snows,
Dark villains and a thievery ring,
But Jack met destiny in the person of Jessie
The balladeer who made his heart sing."

Before Jessie could comment, Jack said again,
"Marry me, Jessie."

Jessie could feel the incredulous joy that must have
been reflected on her face as it was dampened by her
tears. "Oh, Jack, I—" But then she stopped. She
pulled her hands abruptly away from his warm, strong
grip. "I'm not sure how the ballad will end, Jack.
Whether I can just stay here, or whether I'll be sent
back to my time, even if I don't want to be there."

A look of horror and pain washed over his features.
He stood and took Jessie into his arms once more. "I
don't want you to leave, Jessie. How can we be certain you'll stay?"

"Lizard Songthroat knew, damn his sorry ancient
hide. He sent me back here. I'm not sure if he actually
knew the end of the ballad, but I'll bet he knew just
what happened to Jack O'Dair. And if so, if I was
supposed to be here even for a short time, he had to
know if I returned to my time."

"I don't suppose there's any way to contact him,"
Jack said hopefully.

Jessie's sigh was long and deep. "No. But there's
one thing I have to do, Jack. Singing your ballad
brought me here. It didn't send me home when I tried
before, but that was before I knew how it should
end—what would happen in the avalanche. I have to
sing it, all the way through, right now. If . . . if I'm
still here at the end, then just maybe I'll be able to
stay."

"And you want to stay?" There was a harshness to his tone, as though he feared her answer would be in the negative.

She insinuated herself back into his arms and laid her cheek against his hard chest. "Oh, yes, Jack. I want to stay."

"Won't you miss anything in your time?" His voice, reverberating through his chest, rumbled against her ear.

Jessie thought of her career. What career? Curtis had probably dismantled it by now.

She thought of long, hot baths in real bathrooms. Well, bubblebaths weren't everything.

She thought of computers and airplanes, televisions, loud music . . . ugh!

She pulled back and looked up into his face. "Maybe a little," she said, trying to be honest. "But not enough that I would purposely give up the chance to stay forever with you."

"Then sing your ballad, Jessie." She saw his Adam's apple move as though he swallowed hard. "I'll be here with you."

She nodded, then took her place on the chair once more. Jack sat on the floor beside her. She wanted his comforting touch on her arm, her leg—anywhere— but she knew that the contact might prevent her from leaving now. And if she were going to go, it had to be right away, before things got any more serious.

This time, her voice quavered so much that she wasn't sure she could carry the tune.

She still hadn't learned who had written the ballad. It no longer mattered to her. She managed somehow to sing it all the way through to the description of the thefts from stampeders, and then she choked.

"Finish it now, Jessie," Jack said softly. "We have to know what happens."

She inhaled so deeply that she thought she could feel both her lungs refilling. And then she continued, all the way through the part she had known when she arrived.

When she was finished, she waited. She looked at Jack, who looked up at her from his spot on the floor beside her, his gaze unwaveringly supportive, unwaveringly hopeful.

Nothing happened.

"I fell asleep the last time," Jessie said. "I can't be sure I'll remain unless I'm still here tomorrow morning."

For good measure, she sang the last verses, the ones she had made up, and the ones Jack had created about her as he helped her with the words. By the time she had finished, she was crying so hard she couldn't speak any more, let alone sing.

Jack insisted that she take the bed. "Sleep beside me," she said.

"I can't. Not without wanting you. I'd have to touch you, to hold you and make love with you, and then, if you were still here tomorrow, we might not be able to trust your staying. The conditions would not be the same as the night you arrived here. We couldn't be certain whether, if everything became the same sometime in the future, you would be sent back."

She had to agree. When he blew out the lamp, she remained conscious of his form on the floor on top of a moose hide, rolled up in blankets before the low fire. This was just as it had been the first night they had stayed together in his cabin. It had only been a week or two earlier, but it felt as if she had been here forever . . . because she belonged.

I belong here, Lizard, her mind shouted. Did he hear her somehow? Did he care? *Let me stay!*

She watched Jack breathe, long into the night. Was he sleeping? She wasn't sure.

As for her, she couldn't sleep. She was certain of it. She closed her eyes nevertheless, for to know the truth, she had to try.

But sleep . . . never. . . .

Her eyes popped open. A little light shone through the cabin's windows. It was morning.

She was still here!

She glanced down toward the floor, where Jack had been. He was still there, facing her, with Taku rolled up at his side. Jack's eyes were open, and he was watching her.

"Jessie?" His voice was an uneven whisper. "I listened, heard your breathing grow deep, but . . . did you sleep?"

She considered for a moment, then said, "Yes, I'm sure I did."

"And you're still here."

"Yes," she agreed. And then, "Yes! Oh, Jack, I *am* still here!"

In mere moments, she was in his arms.

"Marry me, Jessie," he demanded as he covered her in kisses once more.

"But we don't know for sure if I'll stay. I could disappear at any time, and—"

"I'll take my chances. Will you?" The look he gave her was so full of love—and lust—that she laughed aloud.

"Absolutely," she said as he tumbled her backwards into bed.

353

Epilogue

"Mama!" little Augustus O'Dair cried as he dashed across Calvina's parlor and into Jessie's arms.

"What, sweetheart?" Jessie pulled her son into her lap and hugged him. Gus was just over a year old. He was the spitting image of his father, with his bright red hair and green eyes, and Jessie thought him the most wonderful child in this time or any other.

"We want 'nother story," said Lazarus Sanders, a handsome, intense child who had turned three years old a few weeks earlier.

Three years. Jessie could hardly believe that so much time had passed since she had come here.

And she was still here, thank heavens, married to Jack O'Dair, the man she had fallen in love with by reputation, then by actuality, so long ago.

She smiled at Lazarus, then at Gus. "You both want another story?" she asked as though she could not believe it.

"Yes," said Gus, with a decisive nod of his head.

Jessie laughed, pulled up her son's drooping cotton trousers, then launched into one of their favorites: the daring exploits of Jack O'Dair.

She never sang the ballad, of course. She didn't want to chance it sending her back somehow. Plus, she had never learned who had written its beginning. She could hardly continue to sing a song that might not yet have been created.

But she still wished that somehow she'd solved the mystery of who'd written it, and when.

After a while, Calvina came into the parlor, followed by Renny. They sat on chairs side by side. Renny was in town for good now. He hadn't made his fortune in the gold fields, which hadn't surprised Jessie. Now, he was in the process of building a small hotel—not in Dyea, but, at Jessie's suggestion, in Skagway. He held his wife's hand. Calvina was expecting their second child any day.

Jessie finished the story, "And then Jack O'Dair squeezed and squeezed the poor man who was choking on his supper until the man popped! After that, the man was fine, thanks to the hero of the day, Jack."

"Jack," Gus repeated with a smile that revealed his two front teeth, and he clapped his hands.

"That's Daddy to you, sport," Jessie said with a laugh.

"Daddy," said Gus, just as that very man walked into the parlor, followed by Taku. Jessie felt like running into her husband's arms just the way their son did, but she just sat there smiling as Jack picked Gus up and came over to give her a kiss.

He had just come from the jail, where he had checked on Filby and his new assistant. Though it was summer and the sky wouldn't grow completely dark,

355

it was still getting late—time soon for the O'Dair family to return home.

Jack had built them a house in Skagway after Jessie had convinced him that Dyea, a ghost town in her time, wasn't the place to start a family. They had rented his cabin to Filby, and the new deputy slept in the jailhouse. But Jack still made sure that his town remained a safe place to be.

They had made a deal with Dab Daugherty so that they owned all his photographs of Jack and Jessie, in exchange for Jack's letting him hang around to take pictures of arrests and bad guys and other interesting events to document the time. One day Jessie would destroy the pictures, difficult as that might be. After all, Jessie had seen no photos of Jack in the future . . . or of herself. The latter could be a particular problem, and she didn't want to contemplate the ramifications to the cosmos—or her own ability to remain in the past.

Not that they'd explained the situation to Dab.

Now, Jack put his son down on the floor. Jessie watched the baby toddle out of the parlor after Lazarus. She'd follow soon, but she had helped Calvina baby-proof this house, so there wasn't much mischief they could get into.

The adults all spoke of the dwindling numbers of stampeders; the gold strike in the Yukon had been a bust for most people. Still, Jessie had come to love it here. Though she knew people eventually would move on from Dyea, Skagway would survive. She and Calvina were talking of opening a small restaurant there. Soapy Smith was long gone, and the town at the base of White Pass, with its railway into the Yukon, had become quite charming.

As Jack pulled a chair beside her and took her hand

in his firm grip, Jessie smiled at him. She had never regretted a day that she was still here with him.

As the adults finished discussing the health of Dyea and of Calvina, Gus toddled back into the room.

" 'Tar," he said with a big grin.

"What does that mean?" asked Renny.

"That's my son's way of saying 'guitar,' " said Jack proudly. "Jessie taught him to say it."

" 'Tar," Gus said again, this time more insistently. He turned back toward the door to the hallway.

Only then did Jessie here the twang of her guitar strings. She still sang some evenings at Helen's, but she left her beloved instrument here at Calvina's to keep it out of the hands of the rowdy stampeders at the saloon.

"Where is my guitar?" she asked, standing quickly. She might be overly protective of it, but she loved that old instrument.

"Under the stairs, where you always leave it," Calvina said.

A melodic chord resounded through the parlor as Jessie reached the door. "Do you have a new boarder who plays it?" she asked, not too pleased that someone else was touching it.

"No." Calvina looked quizzical. Renny and she followed Jessie into the hallway. So did Jack.

Jessie hurried down the hall after Gus, toward the hiding place beneath the stairs—and stopped abruptly as a few other chords filled the air.

Lazarus Sanders, Calvina's and Renny's young son, was holding it. His fingering appeared excellent, particularly considering his size.

As they watched and listened, he played another perfect chord, then smiled at them gleefully.

Jessie recalled a day shortly after she had first arrived in which Calvina had demonstrated her musical talent by making up a wonderful lullaby on the spot. Her son came by his talent naturally, as would Gus someday, Jessie hoped.

" 'Tar!" chortled Gus. And then he said, "Lizard, 'tar."

"Lizard?" Jessie stared at him in puzzlement. She knew Gus loved all the wildlife he saw here: the eagles in the trees, the salmon in the streams, even mice. And lizards. But she didn't see any lizards in the house.

"When you've left him here with me," Calvina said, "I've tried to teach him to say 'Lazarus,' but he calls him 'Lizard' instead."

Jessie gasped as a wild notion came into her head. Wild? No—it fit. It tied together everything!

She sagged against the wall. "Oh, my heavens!" she cried.

"Jessie, are you all right?" demanded Jack.

"Absolutely," she said, giving her husband a huge smile. "But I think it's time for us to head home."

She wanted to tell him. She *had* to tell him, but only when they were in private, for no one else knew her secret. All Calvina and Renny knew was that Jessie had come here looking for whoever wrote the beginning of a ballad about Jack but had given up her quest.

They headed back for Skagway, over the road through the woods. Gus lay in Jack's arms. Taku was ahead of them, sniffing the ground. Though they now had horses, and Jack rode between Skagway and Dyea, Jessie preferred to walk when they had time and the weather was good. She still savored the fragrant, clean air here, the delight of the vast outdoors.

"What happened?" Jack demanded as soon as they were out of the Sanders' earshot.

Jessie laughed. "I finally received my answers. Or at least, I think I did. I told you that the strange old man who sent me back here was a musician, a balladeer, named Lizard Songthroat, didn't I?"

Jack nodded, then gave her a startled look. "Lazarus?"

"Lazarus Sanders; Lizard Songthroat. What if Lazarus takes the stories I've told him about you and puts them to music someday? What if he remembers the story that I knew the beginning, but not the end, of the ballad? Someday, maybe he'll put the beginning to music, but realize that if he writes the ending, too, maybe I won't come back here, and the past won't unfold the way it's designed to. So, someday far in the future, I find this Lizard Songthroat, who's more than a hundred years old in my time. He knows what he's supposed to do. He takes me to the decrepit old cabin that you once lived in, he owns it, not any of *our* descendants. He lets me sing the part of the ballad that he's made famous in order to lure me to him. Voilà! The rest is history. My history and yours, and little Lazarus's. Lizard mentioned to me the importance of paying old debts. Maybe he thought he owed you for helping little Lazarus—him—to be born."

"That's quite a story, Jessie O'Dair." He shifted Gus, who had fallen asleep in his arms, and gave Jessie a kiss.

"No more of a story than the legend of the star of 'The Ballad of Jack O'Dair,' " she said.

Jack smiled. "I love you, Jessie," he said. "And I bless whoever led you here to me. In fact, maybe I'll spend a little more time with little Lazarus Sanders, make sure he gets that darned legend right."

Linda O. Johnston

Jessie laughed. "I love you, too, Jack. And I think I'll spend more time with Lazarus, too, to encourage his skills in music." She took his arm, ever so gently so as not to disturb their sleeping son, and rested her head on her husband's shoulder as they headed home together.

THE BALLAD OF JACK O'DAIR

He kept the peace without surcease
Did mighty Jack O'Dair.
Through Dyea-town fights, and dread Klondike nights,
None other could compare.

A brawny bear was Jack O'Dair,
His voice deep, mellow brass,
Bright red hair had Jack O'Dair
And eyes green as Ireland grass.

Lawman Jack was bold in the Northland's cold.
Jack struck the scoundrels down.
With his wolf-dog Taku and his ulu, too,
Jack tended Dyea town.

Jack bested the length of ten men's strength
Said the ladies in Sweet Helen's nest,
In noble fist fights, and through hard-drinking nights,
And Jack's kisses were clearly the best.

What's more, it was said, that in ladies' beds
Jack O'Dair had no equal, 'twas true.
And in card games most fair always played Jack O'Dair
And he won nearly all of them, too.

On a Dyea night when the half-moon was bright,
A stampeder staggered to bed,
When a mob of wild urchins craving gold with no searching
Menaced the drunkard with lead.

"Help," the man importuned, clutching his fortune
And who was patrolling there?
The lawman extraordinaire with the bright red hair,
The dauntless Jack O'Dair.

The fight was finished in minutes,
The stampeder's gold was saved.
And Jack O'Dair, with untousled red hair,
Set the wild young rogues on their ways.

On a windswept night, the moon again bright,
The snow was crimson with blood.
A man lay near dead, a deep wound in his head.
Dyea's citizens quaked—as they should.

"Where's our Jack?" they did shout from every house.
"Who else can protect us from dying?"
Brilliant Jack O'Dair, with his dog Taku's flair
Readily solved the crime.

Upon the floor lying was a man who was dying
Jack was moved by the tears of his wife.
Jack stood, 'twas a fact, and then our Jack
Squeezed the dying man back to life.

Jack was rough and Jack was tough
But the gentlest of gentlemen, too.
From saving the ladies to birthing babies
There was nought our Jack couldn't do.

The Dyea trails drew the greediest of males
Who would give up their grandmas for gold.
But none was too low to rate less than full show,
As Jack defended his fold.

Up passes, up trails, in the mightiest gales,
Stampeders all did go,
Stores of goods in their packs, strapped on their backs
And their boots all buried in snow.

The Mounties who wait at the Klondike's gate
Let stampeders enter there
Only with batches of wares in huge caches—
Many saved by Jack O'Dair.

For woe to those slobs who tried to rob
And woe to those who stole.
Daring Jack O'Dair was always there
To protect a stampeder's soul.

Supplies for a year were required up there,
And captured pilferers fell
At the hands of the man who protected all bands—
Jack O'Dair shielded stampeders as well.

But even Jack could not attack
The Klondike's inevitable courses.
For when nature outlays its fiercest forays
Men can only respond to the forces.

"Avalanche!" came the gasp from the top of the pass.
The snow's roar soon covered the screams.
"Do not despair!" shouted Jack O'Dair,
As he leapt in to salvage their dreams.

The sea of snow hurtled toward below
Where stampeders stood still on the trail.
And with all his flair, brave Jack O'Dair
Was imperiled as all. Would he fail?

The missing ending:

And way above was a lady, Jack's love,
In danger she cried out in despair.
Would the woman he craved die unsaved
By endangered Jack O'Dair?

To and fro Jack scratched through the snow
Though buried like all of the rest.
For ne'er would he founder until he had found her
The woman so fair and so blessed.

He dug and he labored until he had saved her
Exhausted he let himself fall.
But the woman, unshy, would not let Jack die—
And together they trod down the trail.

And on the way, in the midst of the fray,
Jack managed to save even more.
Stampeders and others, their fathers and brothers
Owed their lives to Jack O'Dair's lore.

Now the hero of Dyea has had his day
The whole town did him fair,
For none could deny that the gold town survived
Thanks to legendary Jack O'Dair.

And the very last verses:

Now hand in hand, across Dyea land
Beneath silver skies above
Strolls Jack O'Dair and lady so rare:
The sweet-throated woman Jack loves.

He braved winter's woes and the deepest of snows,
Dark villains and thievery rings,
But Jack met destiny in the person of Jessie
The balladeer who made his heart sing.

STRANGER ON THE MOUNTAIN

Linda O. Johnston

The mountain lion disappeared from Eskaway Mountain over a hundred years ago; according to legend, the cat disappeared when an Indian princess lost her only love to cruel fate. According to myth, love will not come to her descendants until the mountain lion returns. Dawn Perry has lived all her life at the foot of Eskaway Mountain, and although she has not been lucky in love, she refuses to believe in myths and legends—or in the mountain lion that lately the townsfolk claim to have seen. So when she finds herself drawn to newcomer Jonah Campion, she takes to the mountain trails to clear her head and close her heart. Only she isn't alone, for watching her with gold-green eyes is the stranger on the mountain.

__52301-9 $4.99 US/$5.99 CAN

Dorchester Publishing Co., Inc.
P.O. Box 6640
Wayne, PA 19087-8640

Please add $1.75 for shipping and handling for the first book and $.50 for each book thereafter. NY, NYC, and PA residents, please add appropriate sales tax. No cash, stamps, or C.O.D.s. All orders shipped within 6 weeks via postal service book rate. Canadian orders require $2.00 extra postage and must be paid in U.S. dollars through a U.S. banking facility.

Name_____

Address_____

City_____ State_____ Zip_____

I have enclosed $_____ in payment for the checked book(s).

Payment _must_ accompany all orders. ❑ Please send a free catalog.

CHECK OUT OUR WEBSITE! www.dorchesterpub.com

Virtual Heaven
Ann Lawrence

The warrior looms over her. His leather jerkin, open to his waist, reveals a bounty of chest muscles and a corrugation of abdominals. Maggie O'Brien's gaze jumps from his belt buckle to his jewel-encrusted boot knife, avoiding the obvious indications of a man well-endowed. Too bad he is just a poster advertising a virtual reality game. Maggie has always thought such male perfection can exist only in fantasies like *Tolemac Wars*. But then the game takes on a life of its own, and she finds herself face-to-face with her perfect hero. Now it will be up to her to save his life when danger threatens, to gentle his warrior's heart, to forge a new reality they both can share.

___52307-8 $5.99 US/$6.99 CAN

Dorchester Publishing Co., Inc.
P.O. Box 6640
Wayne, PA 19087-8640

Please add $1.75 for shipping and handling for the first book and $.50 for each book thereafter. NY, NYC, and PA residents, please add appropriate sales tax. No cash, stamps, or C.O.D.s. All orders shipped within 6 weeks via postal service book rate. Canadian orders require $2.00 extra postage and must be paid in U.S. dollars through a U.S. banking facility.

Name_____
Address_____
City_____State_____Zip_____
I have enclosed $_____ in payment for the checked book(s).
Payment <u>must</u> accompany all orders. ❏ Please send a free catalog.
    CHECK OUT OUR WEBSITE! www.dorchesterpub.com

A Case Of Nerves
Angie Kay

Standing on the moors of Scotland, Alec Lachlan could have stepped right off of the battlefield of 1746 Culloden. Decked out in full Scottish regalia, Alec looks like every woman's dream, but is one woman's fantasy. Kate MacGillvray doesn't expect to be swept off her feet by the strangely familiar green-eyed Scot. But she is a sucker for a man in a kilt; after all, her heroes have always been Highlanders. Wrapped in Alec's strong arms, Kate knows she has met him before—centuries before. And she isn't about to argue if Fate decides to give them a second chance at a love that Bonnie Prince Charlie and a civil war interrupted over two centuries earlier.

___52312-4 $5.50 US/$6.50 CAN

Dorchester Publishing Co., Inc.
P.O. Box 6640
Wayne, PA 19087-8640

Please add $1.75 for shipping and handling for the first book and $.50 for each book thereafter. NY, NYC, and PA residents, please add appropriate sales tax. No cash, stamps, or C.O.D.s. All orders shipped within 6 weeks via postal service book rate. Canadian orders require $2.00 extra postage and must be paid in U.S. dollars through a U.S. banking facility.

Name_____
Address_____
City_____State_____Zip_____
I have enclosed $_____ in payment for the checked book(s).
Payment <u>must</u> accompany all orders. ❑ Please send a free catalog.
       CHECK OUT OUR WEBSITE! www.dorchesterpub.com

BELOVED WARRIOR
JUDY DiCANIO

Jennifer Giordano isn't looking for a hero, just a boarder to help make ends meet. But Dar is larger-than-life in every respect, and as her gaze travels from his broad chest to his muscular arms, time stops, literally. Jennifer knows this hulking hunk with a magic mantle, crystal dagger, and pet dragon will never be the ideal housemate. But as the Norseman with the disarming smile turns her house into a battlefield, Jennifer feels a more fiery struggle begin. Gazing into his twinkling blue eyes, she knows she can surrender to whatever the powerful warrior wishes, for she's already won the greatest prize of all: his love.

___52325-6 $5.50 US/$6.50 CAN

Dorchester Publishing Co., Inc.
P.O. Box 6640
Wayne, PA 19087-8640

The Seduction of Roxanne
Linda Jones

Roxanne Robinette has decided to marry, and Calvin Newberry—the sheriff's new deputy—has a face to die for. True, he isn't the sheriff: It was Cyrus Bergeron whose nose for justice and lightning-fast draw earned the tin star after he returned from the War Between the States, a conflict that scarred more than just the country. Still, with his quick wit and his smoldering eyes, Cyrus seems an unfair comparison. And it is Calvin who writes the letters she receives, isn't it? Those passion-filled missives leave her aching with desire long into the torrid Texas nights. Whoever penned those notes seduces her as thoroughly as with a kiss, and it is to that man she'll give her heart.

___52357-4 $5.99 US/$6.99 CAN

Dorchester Publishing Co., Inc.
P.O. Box 6640
Wayne, PA 19087-8640

Please add $1.75 for shipping and handling for the first book and $.50 for each book thereafter. NY, NYC, and PA residents, please add appropriate sales tax. No cash, stamps, or C.O.D.s. All orders shipped within 6 weeks via postal service book rate. Canadian orders require $2.00 extra postage and must be paid in U.S. dollars through a U.S. banking facility.

Name_____
Address_____
City_____State_____Zip_____
I have enclosed $_____ in payment for the checked book(s).
Payment <u>must</u> accompany all orders. ❏ Please send a free catalog.
     CHECK OUT OUR WEBSITE! www.dorchesterpub.com